"It will be forever beyond your power to take anything from me again, for you will either stay here and lose your starship and your captain—without which you are nothing—or you will go into exile with him, and your father and mother will become exiles as well, and I shall be well avenged indeed."

It was almost a minute before he could speak. Then all he could say was what he had said before:

"Flawlessly logical."

"I thank you," she said. "Is there anything else I can tell you?"

Spock shook his head.

"Then I will ask you to leave," she said. "I have some calls to make. I think perhaps you will see me once more, before the end; I shall come to the Hall of Voices to watch you and your captain plead for leniency for Terra. I shall find it most amusing."

"I dare say you shall," Spock said, and got up.

She saw him to the door.

"Farewell, Spock," she said.

DIANE DUANE

STAR TREK®
SPOCK'S WORLD

PAN BOOKS
London, Sydney and Auckland

First published 1988 in the USA by Simon & Schuster Inc.
This edition published 1990 by Pan Books Ltd,
Cavaye Place, London SW10 9PG
9 8 7 6 5 4 3 2 1
© Paramount Pictures Corporation

ISBN 0 330 31247 2

Printed and bound in Great Britain by Richard Clay Ltd, Bungay, Suffolk

For Kim and Nic Farey,
remembering U.F.P. Con 1986:

with thanks for the Klingon noisemaker
that made me late for all those panels.

Acknowledgments

──────── ☆ ────────

Many thanks to the Sysops of the SF Forum on CompuServe—Jim Schneider, Rita McConville, and the Chief Sysop, Wilma Meier, for their help in getting this book in on time.

Thanks also to Susie and Mike, who helped in the pinch . . .

and to Dave Stern, who could teach a Vulcan a few things about calm.

And lastly, thanks to Mr. James Hunter Blair and the people of Blairquhan Castle, Scotland, where much of this novel was conceived. Their hospitality and understanding made it all possible . . . and is much appreciated.

STAR TREK®
SPOCK'S WORLD

PROLOGUE

――――――――― ☆ ―――――――――

The joke in Starfleet is that the only thing that can travel faster than warp 10 is news.

Of the many jokes told in Starfleet, this one at least seems true. For a Federation of hundreds of planets, spread sparse as comet-tail dust over thousands of light-years, news is lifeblood: without it, every world is as alone as if there was no other life, no other thought but its own. Few planets, these days, are so reclusive or paranoid as to want to be all alone in the dark, and thus the passage of news has covert priority even over the waging of wars and the making of fortunes. By subspace transmission (faster than warpspeeds, but not fleet enough), by pumped-phaser tachyon packet and shunt squirt, by compressed-continuum "sidestep" technology and sine avoidance, and (within solar systems) by broadcast carrier of all the kinds from radio through holotrans, the news of the many planets of the Federation and of planets outside it slides its way through and around and under and past the billions of miles and thousands of light-years.

The terrible distances take their toll of the passed-on word. Signals are corrupted by subspace noise, data is dropped out, translations are dubious or ambivalent: distance makes some pieces of news seem less urgent than they should, proximity makes other happenings seem more dire than they are. But no

1

news passes unchanged, either by the silent spaces, or the noisy minds that cannot seem to live without it: and no news affects any two of those minds the same way.

This piece of news was no exception.

The door vanished, and the man walked into his rooms and stood still for a moment, then said the word that brought the door back behind him and shut all other sounds outside. His terminal was chiming softly, a sound that most people on the planet where he now lived could not have heard: it was pitched too high.

The man paused long enough to slip his dark cloak off and hang it on the hook beside where the door had been. Beneath it his tabard and trousers were dark too, somewhere between brown and black, his family's sigil bound into the fabric in gold at the tabard's throat. It was diplomatic uniform, made more impressive by his stature, tall but not slender anymore—late maturity had left its mark on his frame. His looks somewhat matched his dress; a man dark-haired, dark-eyed, deep-eyed, a hawk-faced man with no expression . . . at least none that most people here were competent to read. There was energy in the way he held himself, some of those people would have said . . . perhaps too much energy, bound in check by a frightening control. They never knew how tight a control; they never knew how it slipped, sometimes, and left their thoughts open to him. He would have been embarrassed, except that he considered himself neither a child, a brute beast, or an alien, to be so possessed by an emotion.

He turned and paused again, gazing out the window at the brass-and-gold afternoon lying over the browned lawns outside. It was approaching sunset of what the people who lived in this part of the world considered a ferociously hot day, much too hot for spring. Several times today, various of them had said apologetically to him, "At least it's *dry* heat." They need not have been apologetic. To him this was a fair day in early spring indeed, cool, bracing, with a hundred kinds of plant in exuberant leaf; it reminded him of hunting mornings in his youth.

Eidetic memory has its prices. For a moment, whether he wished it or not, he found himself out on the plain again under the burning sky, smelling the air, terrified and out of control of the emotion, knowing that at the day's end he would either be a man or be dead. Then the fragment of memory, like a still holograph refiled, fell back into its indexed place in his mind. He lifted an eyebrow at his self-indulgence, made a note to himself to spend a little extra time in the Disciplines that evening, and moved to the terminal.

Its chiming stopped as he touched it: another second and the terminal had read his EEG through his skin, recognizing the pattern. The screen filled with column on column of blue symbology, a list of calls to the flat since he left. Most of them were unimportant compared to the one name and commcode at the far right-hand side of the list, the most recent, the one message that had caused the "urgent" chime. He had rather been hoping that the embassy would not need him further today: but hope was illogical. Life was about dealing with what *was*. He touched the screen, and the computer dialed the code.

He waited a moment or so before speaking. The link was scrambled, and before communications began, the computer had to agree with the one on the other end as to the eighty-digit "satchel" crypton they would use to keep the link secure. He had the utmost confidence in the ciphering process. Ninety-six standard years before, he had invented it.

He paused two point three seconds to let the process finish.

"Sarek," he said.

The voice that answered him did so, by the good offices of the computer, well above the frequencies that most people on this planet were capable of hearing. The slightest high-pitched hissing or squeaking on the air was all any listener would perceive. That tiny speech whispering into the air went on for a moment, and then Sarek said, "By what majority?"

The air spoke softly to itself again. "Very well," he said. "Whose was the request?"

Another tiny answer. "Tell her I will come," he said. "If all the transportation connections work correctly, we will be there in four point nine six days. Out."

He touched another code on the screen, not bothering to scramble the communication this time. "Sarek," he said again. "I am being recalled, informally. Make the arrangements with the usual carriers, and begin distributing my appointments between Svaid and T'Aimnu."

"Affirmative," said his attaché. "Being handled now. What reason shall we give the Federation Council and the immigration authorities?"

"Personal political business," he said. And, hearing T'Lie's unspoken curiosity, he added, "The Referendum has been called. I must speak for the proposal."

There was a pause. "There was nothing about that in the packet this morning. Perhaps there has been an oversight."

"No, no oversight. I was just notified. There will be a full *précis* in the next packet out from the Executive. Call a press conference and issue the statement as soon as you have a context-positive translation."

"Yes, sir."

"Out."

The Ambassador Extraordinary of Vulcan to the United Federation of Planets, and incidentally to Earth, turned away from the screen and sat down very slowly in a chair that faced the windows. The light and heat came streaming into the room, into the silence. Sarek leaned back and closed his eyes, and became still, tried to become the stillness, the warmth. But he failed: the stillness was an illusion. His mind was in disorderly turmoil. He would have been embarrassed at *that*, except that it would have made the turmoil worse.

If I fail in this, he thought, *then my honor is in shreds and my family will bear the stigma of it forever. We will be ostracized. If I succeed . . . then my honor is intact and my conscience will remain whole. But my House will be broken . . . or if not, I will become an exile and outcast. And Earth . . .*

He opened his eyes. Out the window of the towerblock, a redtailed hawk was balancing on the hot wind, as if on an unresolved thought, hovering. In the hazy blue sky far behind it, past hills like cut-out cardboard, cream-white clouds piled along the horizon, basking and building in the heat, forging their thunders.

Earth will be dead to us, Sarek thought, and got up to make the call he had been avoiding.

Looking down from space, the miles-deep sea of atmosphere

that breeds thunders and winds takes on another perspective. The endless star-pierced blackness presses down against a thin delicate wrapping of air, a bubble of glass swirled with white, glittering where the Sun touches it, the blue of oceans showing through the faintly misted shell. A fragile thing, brittle-looking, an *objet d'art,* round and perfect: but for how long? From far enough out in orbit, one has no doubt that one could drop the Earth on the floor of night and break it. An urge arises to step softly, to speak quietly, so as to keep whoever might be carrying the pretty toy from being startled and fumbling it.

That view, the wide curve of the planet, blue and brown and green streaked with white, was the one that Spock kept on the viewscreen by preference when he was alone on the bridge. He was alone now: indeed he had been alone now for nearly sixteen days, except for the briefest interruptions by maintenance crew and the occasional visiting bridge-crew member. It was curious how, even though they were on liberty, they could not seem to stay away.

But then Jim would surely say that it was curious that Spock couldn't stay away, either. And he would have laughed at Spock's grave attempts to rationalize away the analysis, for in logic there was no reason for him to be there: after a month's peaceful work on the bridge instrumentation, every piece of equipment was tuned and honed to even Spock's relentless standards. Jim would have teased him most assiduously. That was of course the captain's privilege, to refuse to take Spock seriously: as it was Spock's to raise (outwardly) his eyebrows over the amusing and irrational conduct of his human friend, and (inwardly) to rest satisfied that someone knew him well enough *not* to take him seriously, Vulcan or not.

Spock sat quiet in the helm, watching the Earth and idly going through lists in his head. When the heavier and more involved of their repairs were finished—warp-drive adjustments, the replacement of the inside of one warp nacelle's antimatter containment system, installation of a new set of dilithium crystals—Fleet had moved *Enterprise* out of the major repair and spacedock facility at San Francisco High to a parking "spot" over the North Atlantic, where Starfleet Gander could handle the ship's reprovisioning. These were more mundane and simple businesses, like the complete replacement of the *Enterprise*'s forty million cubic feet of air: even with a starship's extraordinarily advanced air-conditioning and processing systems, a ship's air could become rather stale-smelling after a couple of years. Not even Spock had stayed aboard for that—he found breathing vacuum for any length of time to be aesthetically unpleasant. He had spent the day near Reykjavik, examining the volcanoes.

Then there was the matter of other reprovisioning to be supervised . . . stored food, hydroponics, dry stores, textiles, machine parts, data tapes and solids, cleaning and maintenance supplies, the hundred thousand things that a crew in space for long periods needs. Spock did not have to occupy himself with this—he was, after all, on liberty as much as the rest of the crew—but it suited his whim (and his commitment to his agreements as executive officer) to make certain for himself that the ship was perfectly ready for space in all respects, not just to take someone else's word for it.

It became sort of a game, after a time, to anticipate the quartermasters' department in things that they should have thought of first: it engendered in them what Spock considered a very healthy attitude of friendly competition. Who would be first to remember and requisition the right grade of granite (and some slab marble, as a treat) for the ship's single Horta crewmember, who sometimes complained in a good-natured way that man was not meant to live on nickel-iron alone? Who would know where to find "pinhead" oatmeal for the chief engineer's occasionally— and loudly—demanded porridge? Where could one obtain the best price for hundred-ton lots of Arabica coffee? (Spock's simple but admittedly elegant storage method for coffee—beaming it aboard in small lots, each time purposely aborting the upload in mid-transport, but holding the coffee's completely analyzed pattern in the transporter's data solids until wanted—had become standard Fleet practice for "extraneous" cargo in starships on tour, and had changed coffee from a rarely enjoyed and much-longed-for luxury into something that the whole crew could have when they pleased. But after all, McCoy and Kirk were both very fond of coffee . . . and this kept it fresh.)

And there were even more pleasant forms of maintenance to handle: most specifically, the refreshing of the ship's data libraries. Spock had himself spent nearly a hundred hours scanning the refresh lists sent him by the British Museum on behalf of the Smithsonian, the Library of Congress, the Ryeshva Moskva, der Schweizerisches Landesmuseum, la Bibliothèque Nationale, reh Xiao-Mih. Then had come the uploading, the checking, the indexing, and just as important, the exchange of information—for after debriefing, *Enterprise* declassified all but the most sensitive material on returning to her registry port. At the end of it all, some seventy-two hours without a stop, he had slept, as McCoy would probably have observed, like a log. Though how a log slept was beyond him, and certainly past McCoy.

Now, approaching the end of the reprovisioning process, Spock let the lists go momentarily and gazed at the North Atlantic for a while, watching the tiny, precise patterns of weather flow by in curls and curves of white and gray, while in the background the stars seemed to turn around a fixed globe. The view was familiar. Spock had taken to predicting the Earth's weather lately, as a pastime and an exercise of his logic. There was a fascinatingly large number of variables—seasonal tendencies, solar storms, the fluctuations of the Earth's ionosphere and ionopause, the occasionally successful attempts to control weather on a local scale, and in the midst of it all, the endless fluxions, perturbations, and movements of jet stream and a hundred lesser winds. He had spent a week mastering North America's weather; and after writing the master algorithm with all the necessary seasonal variations and sending it off to the Western Hemisphere Weather Service, he turned away to something more challenging. Greater Britain and Ireland seemed sure to keep him busy for a long while: the algorithms promised to be exceptionally complex. Perhaps ten days this time. He wondered idly if the people living there would be happy to have their weather solved at last.

Spock considered the three small, patchy lows presently sitting over the British Isles, while the lists in his head slipped back for attention. Almost everything was complete now: the last few deliveries would be cargo and mail for parts of the Federation that no normal carrier serviced . . . or at least, no carrier quite so well armed. There were twelve tons of container cargo, mostly heavy machinery or electronics, and the equivalent of fifty tons

of mail, some as data storage, more in the same kind of "abeyance" as the coffee. It cost too much to ship most paper over
interstellar distances, but executable documents, currency, and
personal mail still needed to be paper (or plastic or metal) at both
ends of the process, for varying reasons. And the coffee solution
was a good one for paper, since energy was cheaper to ship than
matter, even with the "overhead" energy that the transporter
spent keeping the solid goods in flux. Nor was security a problem:
Spock had himself devised the ciphers that would make sure no
mail was tampered with while in transit. They were satchel codes
of extreme complexity, their basic structure derived from a most
reliable source—

The comm console went off.

Spock punched a button on the arm of the helm.

"*Enterprise;* Spock here."

"*Sarek,*" said the voice, and Spock's eyebrow went up.

"Father," he said. "Are you and Mother well?"

The dry voice, far away, got an ironic tone to it. "*I had not
thought you gone so far into human behavior, my son, as to
begin indulging in 'small talk' with me.*"

Spock held himself quite still for a moment, then said,
"Father, I rarely hear from you by voice transmission unless
either you or Mother is *not* well. Therefore my logic is intact for
the moment."

There was a moment of stillness on the other end as well.
"*That line of reasoning is justifiable,*" Sarek said. "*However,
your mother and I are both in good health.*"

"Then I would assume that your call has something to do
with the vote that took place on Vulcan this morning."

"*You have had the news?*"

"No. But it seems a reasonable assumption. What was the
result?"

"*In favor of considering secession, four thousand three
hundred fifty-one to fifteen hundred twelve.*"

Spock sat for a moment and let one level of his attention
flicker back to the British Isles, contemplating a low pressure
area moving slowly toward the Midlands. There was another
small low hovering over the Borders that made it difficult to tell

whether the first would head north or south. At any rate, it was surely raining in the Cotswolds—

"Then they have certainly called for you to return home and speak for the secessionists," Spock said.

Another pause. *"They have. More: T'Pau did."*

"And will you?"

A much longer pause. *"My son, you know my reasons."*

Spock was silent too, for a moment, regarding a band of cloud over Ayrshire. "Too well, my father," he said. "But you must do your conscience's work."

"So must you. The Council has called for your testimony as well."

Spock considered what this was going to mean to the *Enterprise*'s liberty schedule and experienced a moment of regret, which he swiftly put aside. "I should have expected that," he said. "Noted. I will make the necessary notifications here and advise Starfleet . . . though I think I know what they will do."

"Agreed. I will see you at home, my son. I estimate that you will be there before me."

"As do I," said Spock. He paused, then said, "Tell Mother that I think of her."

The silent sound of an eyebrow going up somewhere in Los Angeles. *"It would be illogical of you not to,"* said Sarek, with an edge of humor on the dryness. *"Out."*

Spock touched the button on the arm of the helm and eyed the south of Britain, toward Wales. That little cloud, reaching back eastward from Gwynedd and across the Irish Sea: that was perhaps the symptom of the solution. That persistent backwash, leading into the major northeastern flow—Spock examined its path, calculated probabilities, and then reluctantly put the half-born algorithm aside. A wonderfully complex problem: but life had handed him a thornier one. The weather would have to wait.

He got up, leaving the empty helm behind him, went to his Science station, and began making calls.

It was blowing up a gale outside the pub. Wind whipped rain against windows gone glassy black with night, and rattled the damper in the fireplace. Once he heard a skitter and crash as a roof slate blew loose and smashed against the chimney, then clattered down into the rain-gutter in an arpeggio of chunks and splinters. But on the whole, James T. Kirk was beyond caring. He was sitting in a chimney-corner seat with his feet out in front of a coal fire, and an Irish whiskey in one hand: he was warm and snug, and he didn't have to go anywhere, and there was nothing to do but relax and listen to the wind mutter and moan in the flue.

"There's the Jim, then," said a familiar voice behind him.

"Ronan," Jim said, looking up. "They keeping you busy?"

"Not tonight." Ronan Boyne sat down next to Jim in the twin to the chair he was sitting in, an old overstuffed horsehair business, heaven only knew how old. Ronan ran the place, which everyone called the Willow Grove even though "Deveraux's" was painted over the front door. He put down his ever-present oranges-and-lemons drink and ran his hands through his hair: black hair, for Ronan was about as black Irish as they came, with a big bland face and big strong hands. "It's only the fools and the desperate cases out tonight," he said. "Even the ferries from Wales have all been canceled."

"Doesn't surprise me. I wouldn't want to be out on that water. Eight-foot swells, at least."

"If *you* wouldn't, then the rest of us had better stay home! Chess later?"

"Sounds good."

"You're on, then." And Ronan got up and went off to see to one of the desperate cases, who was bringing a brace of empty pint glasses back to the bar.

Jim sighed and put his head back against the padded wall behind him. That was the way it had been for a couple of weeks now. A friendly inquiry or two, then he was left alone if he wanted to be . . . but there was always the promise of companionship if he wanted it. He couldn't have found a better place for a vacation.

He had certainly needed one. That business with the Romulans, and right after it the interminable famine runs for gamma Muscae V, and after *that,* the intervention at 1210 Circini, with the *Enterprise* caught in the middle and everybody on the four planets in the neighborhood shooting at her: it was enough to turn your hair gray. When it was their turn in the Fleet heavy-cruisers' rotation to come back to Earth, Jim had been cranky enough to pull a little rank on his crew's and his own behalf. Within an hour of their arrival in Earth orbit, he had informed Fleet (as was his right) that he was taking his last two years' accumulated leave all at once. Then he had mentally braced himself for a fight. But Fleet had responded blandly that the *Enterprise* was badly overdue for retrofit, which would involve at least a month's worth of equipment testing and resupply. So for now, they told him, he and his crew were on indefinite paid liberty unless they specifically requested reassignment to other ships. Jim smiled, knowing about how likely that was. He packed a couple of bags, said goodbye-for-now to his crew, and set about getting himself lost.

Technology had made Earth smaller than it had ever been, but you could still get pretty lost if you worked at it. It had been a matter of only three hours' travel, and Jim did it the tourist's way, on purpose—after all, there was no point in simply beaming down to where you were going on Earth, as if it was any other world you had business with on your tour of duty. He caught a shuttlecraft from the *Enterprise* to the Fleet orbital facility, then took the transporter to San Francisco Interplanetary, and the BA hyperbolic shuttle from SFO to London; after that, the Spas Lingus ionjumper from Luton Spaceport to Dublin, and finally a rental dual-mode flit for the run south down the coast road. In fact, the travel was really only two hours' worth: most of that last hour of the three had been spent sitting caught between annoyance and bemusement on an abeyance apron at Luton, waiting for launch clearance. Jim had been a little careless about his timing, and got caught in the commuter rush hour, all the businessmen heading home to Europe and Asia from the City.

But it had been more than worth it for the view on the drive down, as ahead and to the right the Wicklow mountains rose up before him, all slate- and emerald-shadowed in a long fierce sunset that piled up in purple and gold behind them; and on the left hand, the sea, a blue gray like quiet eyes, breaking silent with distance at the stony feet of Bray Head. There were not too many houses to mar the bleak loveliness of hill and water and sky; the towns themselves seemed to crouch down to one or two stories, and make themselves small. And Dublin's fair city, where the girls were so pretty, had grown in many directions, but not this one. Only its spires could be seen away across the tidal flats of Dublin Bay—civilization kept properly at a distance, where it would not frighten the horses. The Irish had their priorities.

Using the road for the delight of getting down between the hedgerows, Jim had driven past the Willow Grove, only half noticing the bed-and-breakfast sign, and half a mile down the road had stopped and turned and come back. It had looked promising, in a quiet way: an ancient Georgian house, big for this part of the world, with two huge bay windows at the front, full of cheerful drinkers. He had walked in, inquired about prices and credit systems, and half an hour later he was sitting where he was sitting now, eating clear lamb stew and drinking Guinness, and being checked out by the locals.

"Jimmy boy, how are you tonight?"

"Fine," he said, automatically, because no matter who was asking, it was definitely true. Looking up, he caught the tail end of a wave from Riona and Erevan Fitzharris, passing by on their way to the bar for their nightly pint: a tall blond man, a tall redheaded lady, computer consultants who commuted home to Wicklow from Hamburg every day. They had been the first ones to realize who Jim was.

Ronan hadn't even thought about it, he claimed, till he was told. "It's not my fault," he said later: "Kirks are common as cowpats around here, for pity's sake. Also I don't watch that damn box," that being how he referred to the holovision, except of course when it was showing soccer. But Jim had his suspicions—Ronan had taken an image of his direct-credit plate, after all. It was not until Riona and Erevan accused him in public, one night, of being in Starfleet, of being, in fact, *the* James T. Kirk, that he admitted it to anyone. And to his astonishment, after the laughing, hollering group in the pub that night had been told the secret, and howled with merriment to see Jim blush (it had to have been the whiskey they kept feeding him), they all pretended it hadn't happened. Only once in a while, if out of habit he had activated his universal-translator implant that morning, he would hear one of the Irish-speaking regulars murmur to someone new about *ar captaen an t-arthaigh an rhealtai* Eachtra: *our* starship captain, the one with the *Enterprise*. And he would turn away, so as not to let them see him smiling.

Jim sipped at the whiskey, and stretched a bit in the chair. The people here were mostly interested in who he *was*, and only occasionally in what he did—that was what made the place so marvelous. They had been piqued by not being *told* what he did, but once that was settled and he had been properly ragged for being a galactic hero, there were other more important things to talk about: weather, farming, sport, and especially local gossip, which most everyone took covert or overt delight in sharing with him. The regulars seemed to think it a point of honor that he should know their neighbors, and themselves, as well as they did. Jim, not to put too fine a point on it, ate it up. There was, after all, a resemblance to part of his job as a starship captain. It was his business to be very familiar indeed with the gossip of what amounted to a small spacefaring village—to know where to share it, and when to spread it, and how to keep quiet and smile.

And if of an evening someone *did* tempt him to talk shop, it was in the gentlest sort of way. One night someone happened to mention Grainne, the pirate queen who raged up and down the Irish Sea in the first Elizabeth's day, and it had seemed natural enough to talk a little about Orion pirates and their depredations, and the deplorable trade in green slave girls. Or another time someone else might admit how his five-times' great-grandfather had been one of "the Gentlemen"—for smuggling had been more or less the national sport, some generations back—and if Jim could put on an innocent face and tell them a little about how one might get Romulan ale across the Neutral Zone without attracting the attention of Customs and Excise, well, it was the least he could do. . . .

"He pulls the slowest pint in the county, and that's a fact," Riona said from just behind Jim, as she picked her way around the chair and flopped in the other chimney-corner seat.

"It's a virtue," Erevan said, coming around the other side and sitting in the chair next to Jim. He was carrying a perfectly full pint glass of Guinness, which he put down with exaggerated care on the table between them. "Agree with me, Jimmy boy."

"I agree with you," Jim said immediately. "What am I agreeing with?"

"You cannot pull a pint of this stuff fast," Erevan said. "All those little air bubbles, *phah,* they get into it and ruin the flavor."

"When you're dying of thirst, the flavor doesn't enter into it if it's half an hour before you can drink it," Riona said, and drank, and got herself a beige moustache from the luxuriant head. She wiped it off surreptitiously. "Ronan ought to do what they do in town, and pull pints ahead of time, and leave them on the shelf to settle down."

"Slops," Erevan said. "That is slops. Jimmy, ignore this woman."

"You'd hit me if I didn't," Jim said. Then added, "Come to think of it, you'd hit me if I *did.*"

"You be still, then; I'm discoursin'. Slops. Say you have a barman on the bad, and closing time comes, and he hasn't sold those pints: what then? What's to keep him from pouring them back into the tank for the next day, eh? Slops." Erevan said the word with great satisfaction. "Each drinker to his own pint, and if you have to wait, that's the price of quality, and besides, it's worth waiting for."

Jim smiled and said nothing, just sipped his whiskey. Much to his annoyance, the thick, brown black brew called stout had been one Irish taste he had been unable to acquire: to him, it tasted like roofing tar. He had heard this particular argument before; and the worse arguments about brands of stout sometimes progressed almost to physical violence before Ronan made it plain that such was not permitted, and besides, it would spill the drinks.

"And what's that you're drinking?" Erevan said.

"Whiskey," said Jim.

"Oh, now, what are you drinking *that* down here for?"

Jim was opening his mouth to laugh when in the pocket of his jacket, slung over the back of his chair, his communicator went off. It had been so long since he'd heard it that the sound startled him almost as much as it did Riona and Erevan. "Phone," he said, as casually as he could, and dug around behind him in the pocket among the car's code plate and the loose change, till he came up with the communicator and flipped it open.

"Kirk here," he said.

"*Spock here, Captain*," and out of the corner of his eye Jim noted with mild amusement that Riona and Erevan were eyeing one another, for here was another name they knew from the newscasts. "*Are you busy?*"

"Chatting with friends. Do you want to call me back?"

"*No need: this news will be quite public shortly, if indeed it is not public now. I would suggest to you, Captain, that all liberties are about to be canceled. I thought you might appreciate an advance warning.*"

"Noted. What's going on?"

"*A vote was taken this morning, and Vulcan has decided to call the Referendum. My presence will be required there, and I would strongly suspect that the* Enterprise *will be sent there as well, to . . . reinforce the planet's memory of favors done it in the past by the Federation.*"

Jim was still for a moment. This particular problem had been a long time brewing . . . and he had thought something might happen to make it come to a head fairly soon. *At times like this,* he thought, *I really hate being right.* "We have no orders yet?"

"*No, sir. But I judge the probability of the imminent arrival of such orders to be ninety-third percentile or higher.*"

He means he's sure, but he's leaving me the option of one more day's holiday, Jim thought, entertaining the idea . . . then reluctantly rejecting it. *Better get it over with.* He put down his whiskey. "All right," he said. "Give me half an hour to check out of here, and I'll be ready to beam up."

"*Acknowledged. Enterprise out.*"

He snapped the communicator shut, looked at Erevan and Riona regretfully, and shrugged. "There goes the vacation."

"It's a wicked waste, that's what it is," Riona said.

He agreed with her, but there was nothing to be done about it except get up from the pleasant fireside and take care of business. He spent ten minutes in the comm booth, getting someone from the rental company to come out and fetch the flitter; another five minutes settling his bill with Ronan; the rest of the time getting things out of the flit and packing them. And then there was nothing to do but wait for the communicator to go off again, and say his good-byes.

He was shaking hands with Ronan at the door when his

pocket whistled. "That's me," he said sadly. "The chess game will have to wait. You take care of yourself."

"I'll do that." Various people in the bar were shouting goodbyes, waving: even Renny, Ronan's daughter and assistant behind the bar, was calling something to him. He missed it, but was curious: she was very shy and had rarely said more than a word or so to him before. "Pardon?" he called back.

"Go maire tú i bhfad agus rath!"

He hadn't turned the translator on that morning. Jim looked at Ronan, bemused. Ronan raised eyebrows at him and said, "Old Irish wayfarer's blessing. It translates as 'Live long and prosper.' "

Very slowly, Jim smiled. "I'll be back," he said, and since only a galactic hero would have made a spectacle of himself by beaming up from the middle of the pub, he stepped out into the black, blowing night and shut the door behind him, holding on to it carefully so that it shouldn't slam in the wind.

Several seconds later, the rain was blowing through the place where he had been.

The spear in the Other's heart
is the spear in your own:
you are he.

There is no other wisdom,
and no other hope for us
but that we grow wise.

—attributed to Surak

ENTERPRISE: ONE

───────────── ☆ ─────────────

Position yourself in the right place—on the surface of the moon, say, somewhere near the slow-moving dayline, or in one of the L5 habitats swinging in peaceful captivity around the world—and you can see it without any trouble: the old Earth in the new Earth's arms. Some people prefer her that way to any other. Not for them the broad blue cloud-swirled disk, all bright and safe and easily seen. They want mystery; they want the Earth's nightly half-bath in the old dark. She always emerges, but (to these people's relief) she always dips in again—the blue fire fading away down through the spectrum, the rainbow of atmosphere's edge, down through the last flash of crimson, to black.

And when she does, the stars come out. Faithful as the other, farther stars, in steady constellations, they turn as the night that holds them turns—the splatters of spilled-gem light that are BosWash, Ellay, Greater Peking, Bolshe-Moskva, Plu'Paris. The great roadways across continents are bright threads, delicate as if spiders of fire had spun them: here and there the light is gentled by coming from far underwater, as in the Shelf cities off the Pacific coasts of Japan and old North America. At the edge, a limb of brightness shows, the sunrise inexorably sliding around the curved edge of things: but the limb is narrow, the merest shaving of pearl and turquoise curving against the breadth of night. And for the time being, night reigns.

In places light shows without man having made it. When the moon is in the right phase, the polar icecaps are one wide sheen of palely burning white; the Rockies and the Himalayas and the Alps and Andes glow with a firefly fire, faint but persistent. Sometimes even the Great Wall will show: a silver hair, twisting, among the silver glint of rivers . . . and afterward the Moon will slide away and around in her long dance with the Earth to gaze at the great diffuse bloom of her own disk's light in Atlantic or Pacific. Half a month from now the Moon will swing around at the new, and all these places, under the sun again, will give their light back to her, ashen, a breath of silver against the dark side of the satellite's phase. But for now the Earth keeps the moonlight and the romance to herself, slowly turning, shimmering faint and lovely like a promise made and kept a long time ago. Darkness scattered with diamonds, and the darkness never whole: there she lies, and turns in her sleep. . . .

. . . and over her comes climbing other light, passing out of the fire of the far side's day: a golden light like a star, dimmed from a blaze to a spark as it passes the terminator, twenty-five thousand miles high. Moonlight silvers her now as she approaches, not hurrying, a shade more than eleven thousand miles per hour, not quite geosynchronous, gaining on the Earth. She seems a delicate thing at first, while distant—a toy, all slender pale light and razory shadows—then bigger, not a toy anymore, the paired nacelles growing, spearing upward, reaching as high as thirty-story buildings, the main dish blocking the sky away from zenith to "horizon" as it passes by, passes over. Silent she passes, massive, burning silver, gemmed in ruby and emerald with her running lights, black only where shadows fall and where the letters spell her number and name in one language of her planet of registry, the planet she's about to leave. NCC 1701, the Starship *Enterprise*, slips past in moonlight, splashed faint on her undersides with the light of Earth's cities, ready to give all the light up for the deep cold dark that is her proper home. . . .

* * *

It takes time to walk right around a starship. Eleven decks in the primary hull, twelve in the secondary, from an eighth of a mile of corridors per deck to maybe two or three—the old simile comparing a starship to a small town becomes more obviously true than ever to someone determined to do the hike. Jim, though, didn't mind how long it took, and he did as much of it as time allowed, every time he came aboard after a refit.

This time he altered his usual routine a little. *After all day stuck down at Fleet,* he thought, *I'm entitled to a change of pace. Bloody desk pilots. . . .* But a second later he put away the annoyance: he had what he had gone for. Jim laughed to himself, and shortly thereafter beamed up via the cargo transporters, along with a shipment of computer media, toiletries, and medical supplies.

Cargo Transport was a more pleasant place, in some ways, than the usual crew transporters. The huge room was in the space next to the shuttlecraft hangars, and needed to be, since anything too big to ship up any other way, from warp-engine parts to container cargo, wound up here. The place tended to be noisy and busy any time the ship was near a planet: at the moment, it was a vast happy racket, boxed and crated and force-shielded matériel being carried in all directions on gravflats of varying sizes. Jim got down off the pads in a hurry to avoid being run over by a couple of G-flats the size of shuttlecraft, and then paused on the loading floor, seeing who was maneuvering the flats by him—two Earth-human crewmen, a small wiry auburn-haired man and a tall dark-haired woman with a Valkyrie's figure under a cargoloader's coverall.

"Mr. Matejas," he said, "Mz. Tei," and as they heard his greeting and realized with surprise who he was, they started to come to attention. He waved them off it. "As you were. How was the engagement party?"

The two of them looked at each other, and Jorg Matejas blushed, and Lala Tei chuckled. "It was terrific," she said, shaking her red hair back. "Everybody had a great time, especially the Sulamids . . . Rahere and Athene got into the sugar, and you know how Sulamids are about sugar, it was a riot, their tentacles got all knotted, and it took us about an hour to get them undone. Sir, thank you so much for the 'gram! Jorg's mom nearly went to pieces when Fleet called and read it in the middle of the party, she was so excited. . . ."

Jim smiled, for that had been his intention. One of his more reliable sources of gossip had let him know that Mr. Matejas's mother was very uncomfortable about her son marrying someone holding higher rank than his. Jim had responded by studying Jorg's record very carefully, noting that he was somewhat over-due for promotion, and then correcting the matter . . . making sure that the news of his promotion hit him during the party, via the addressing of the congratulatory telegram. The source-of-gossip, also present at the party, had let Jim know later that the name signed at the bottom of the 'gram had counted for almost as much as Jorg's jump in grade to quartermaster's mate. Jim had been gratified—there were apparently times when being a galactic hero could be turned to some use. "You're very welcome."

"Sir," Jorg said, "I'm glad we had the chance to see you. I wanted to thank you, very much indeed."

"You earned it," Jim said. "Don't think otherwise. If I helped with the timing a little, consider it my pleasure. Mean-while, how's the loading going?"

Jorg heard the *when* under the "how." "Half an hour, Captain," he said. "Less if possible."

Jim smiled more widely, for reasons that had nothing to do with the timetable. "Good enough. Carry on," he said, and went away feeling unusually pleased inside.

He strode across the loading floor, and all the way across it was "Good morning, Captain," "Good evening, Captain," and Jim's smile got broader and broader: not at the inconsistency among greetings, for the ship was back on cruise shift schedules again, three shifts relieving one another, and some people were working overtime. Out into the corridor, and it was the same thing, when he said hello to his people or they said hello to him: no "Admiral," nothing fancy, just "Captain" again, as God intended. It was a great relief. As he walked the halls, Jim acquired a grin that would not go away.

The long afternoon in Fleet Admiral Nogura's office had been trying, but the results had been worth it. Twenty hours after beaming up from the Willow Grove, eight hours after beaming over to Fleet to handle the inevitable paperwork involved with a new set of missions, he was happily demoted to captain, effective immediately, revocable at Fleet's discretion. Some people would not have understood it, this desire to be de-admiraled. But most of those people weren't naval, or had lost touch with the naval tradition that was so much a part of Starfleet. And Nogura, in love (Jim told himself tolerantly) with the power of the Fleet Admiral's position, couldn't understand it either. *It's not his fault*, Jim thought. *He's been one too long, that's all.*

Admirals, from time immemorial, didn't command anything but fleets: they managed strategy and tactics on a grand scale . . . but Jim wasn't interested in a scale quite that grand. Captains might be obliged to give admirals rides to where they were going, and to obey their orders: but for all that, the captains were more in command than ever an admiral was. There might be more than one admiral on a ship . . . but never more than one captain. Even as a passenger, another captain would be "bumped" a grade up to commodore—partly out of courtesy, partly to avoid discourtesy to the ship's true master. It was *real* sovereignty, the only kind Jim cared for, and he was glad to get rid of the extra braid on his arms and settle into the happy business of interacting, not with fleets, but with people.

Jim did that for the hour it took him to cover the manned parts of the engineering hull, stopping last at Engineering. He strolled in, and almost immediately began to wish he hadn't. Pieces of the backup warpdrive were all over the floor, or hovering on placeholders, and Scotty was thundering around among his engineering ensigns, shouting at them. Fortunately, he was doing so in the tone of voice that Jim had eventually learned meant everything was going all right, and so he relaxed and stood there for a bit, enjoying the spectacle.

"Ye can't put a drive together as if it was a bitty babbie's picture puzzle, for pity's sake," Scotty was telling the air with genial scorn, as junior crewmen scuttled around him with calibrating instruments and tools and engine parts, looking panic-stricken. "There's got to be some system to't. You can't bring up the multistate equivocators until the magnetic bottle's on-line, and where's the bottle then? Ye've had ten whole minutes!—Afternoon, Captain," he added.

Jim smiled again. "Problems, Scotty?" he said, not because

he perceived any, but because he knew Scotty expected that he would ask.

"Ah no, just a drill. What if these poor children have to reassemble a warp engine by themselves some one of these days, with only impulse running and a pack of Klingons howling along behind 'em? They've got the brains for it: would they be on the *Enterprise* if they didn't? Best they learn how now. We'll be tidy again in twenty minutes. Or I'll know the reason why!" Scotty added, at the top of his voice. The scuttling got much more frantic. Apparently Scotty's crew considered the chief engineer in what Jim had heard them describe as "one of his moods" to be slightly more dangerous to deal with than mere Klingons.

Jim nodded. *I might as well get out,* he thought; *they look nervous enough without me watching as well.* "Officers' briefing at point seven, Scotty," he said.

"Aye, I checked my terminal for the schedule a while back." Scotty looked around him with satisfaction. "Just before I crashed the Engineering computers."

Jim was astonished, and looked around him . . . then felt mildly sheepish, for he'd never even noticed that every screen in the place was blank. "They're putting this thing together *without* the computer prompts? Not even the emergency systems?"

Scotty shrugged. "Who's to say we could guarantee them that the backup systems would be working in an emergency?" he said. "Even backups fail. But their little brains won't . . . if we train them properly. FIVE MINUTES!!" he told the world at large. Then looking around the floor, he said, "By rights I should evacuate the place and make them do it in pressure gear. If her side was blown this far open that they'd have to reassemble from scratch, they'd need that practice."

Jim shook his head, feeling sorry for this Engineering crew, all doomed to be turned into mechanical "geniuses" like their mad teacher. "Talk to Spock about scheduling, if you feel the need."

Scotty nodded, and together he and Jim stood and watched the matter-antimatter mix column being put together from the field generators up. "By the bye, Captain, have you scheduled the crew briefing yet?"

"Point four, tomorrow morning."

"Right."

Jim patted Scotty on the back. "I'm off, then," he said.

Scotty eyed him suspiciously for a moment. "You've picked up a bit of an Irish accent," he said.

"Might not be strange," Jim said. "The people I was with were claiming that my family wasn't Scots. Sorry," he said, as Scotty looked at him with an expression of shock that was only partly faked. "Really. They claim the name Kirk was an Anglicization of O'Cuire. It would explain why my family was in the east of Ireland to begin with. . . ."

"Those people will say anything," Scotty said, and grinned a little. "Get on with ye. Sir."

Jim headed out. "THREE MINUTES!" the voice roared behind him, as he got to the turbolift and stepped in.

"Where to, Captain?" the lift said to him.

He smiled again. "Bridge."

The place looked a little strange when the lift doors opened on it, as home often does when one's been away from it for a while. Jim stepped out, nodded greeting at Uhura and Sulu, who gestured or smiled hello at him. He waved them back to what they were doing and glanced around to the Science station. Spock was bent over it, making some adjustment. "Readout now," he said, straightening and looking over his shoulder at the large, shaggy-fringed rock that was sitting in the center seat.

Some of those glittering fringes stroked the open circuitry of the communicator controls in the seat's arm. "Point nine nine three," said a scratchy voice from the voder box mounted on the rock's back. "A nice triple sine."

" 'Nice'?" said Spock. Jim raised an eyebrow: you could have used Spock's tone of voice to dry out a martini.

"Within high-nominal limits," said the rock, and there was a definite smile in the voice, despite the fact that the voder should not have been able to convey emotion. "A third-order curve, sir. Skew no more than e minus zero point two two four six. No crystal infrequency, no parasitic vibrations, signal loss within accepted IEEE and CCITT parameters, layback less than point zero two percent, hyperbolic—"

"That should be sufficient, Mr. Naraht," Spock said, looking over at the captain with a slight wry expression.

"Mr. Naraht," Jim said, stepping down beside the helm. Lieutenant Naraht was a Horta, a hatchling of the original Horta on Janus VI: one of an intensely curious species that could no more have stayed out of space, once they came to understand it, than they could have stopped eating rock. Jim had watched Naraht's career since he was transferred to the *Enterprise* with both interest and pleasure: the Horta had gone from eager, avid "space cadet" to seasoned officer in a very short time . . . no surprise, considering some of the things he had been through, with the rest of the crew, since he came aboard. Now Jim patted the back of the center seat and said, "Trying her out for fit, mister?"

There would have been a time when the remark would have made Naraht wriggle all over, embarrassed—and the sight of a quarter-ton of living stone, the shape and color of a giant fringed asbestos pan pizza, being embarrassed, had occasionally been memorable. But now Naraht merely looked up—at least Jim felt he was being looked at, though he was unsure as to how—and said, "Respectfully, sir, I think I would need something a little bigger. There was some distortion showing up in the commcircuits, that was all, and Mr. Spock asked me to assist him in isolating it."

Jim nodded, seeing the point: there were certain advantages in having a crewman who could make direct "neural" connections with solid circuitry and *feel* what was wrong with it as an itch or a tic, rather than as a string of numbers. But one who could feel the problem and then translate it into the numbers as well—*that* was someone invaluable. As usual, half the departments in the ship were fighting over Naraht's services. Biochemistry, geology, xenoarchaeology, they all wanted him—Naraht could do detailed chemical analysis, or even carbon- or selenium-dating, by merely eating a piece of the object in question and reporting on the "flavor." As far as Jim knew, Naraht's only complaint about being on the *Enterprise* was that he was gaining weight at a shocking rate and didn't know what his mother would think when she saw him. . . .

Jim glanced over at Spock. "I could have sworn that Mr. Naraht had almost given you more data than you needed."

"There is no such thing as too much data," Spock said calmly, "but there *is* such a thing as unnecessary detail. Nonetheless, the job is adequately completed. Thank you, Mr. Naraht."

"My pleasure, sir," said the Horta, and slipped down out of the helm onto the floor with his usual speed and silence, always surprising in someone so massive. "Captain? Your conn?"

"Thank you, Mr. Naraht," Jim said, and sat down. The seat was very warm—not surprising: McCoy usually referred to the liquid-mineral complex that Naraht used for blood as "fluorocarbonated lava with asbestos hemocytes."

"Sir," Naraht said, and shuffled off into the lift to be about his business. Jim sat back in the command chair, and Spock stepped down beside him, holding out a padscreen.

Jim glanced down it, tilted the pad slightly to scroll through it. It was a very condensed, compressed version of the ship's schedule for that day, parts of it flowcharted where an activity of one ship's department was dependent on some data or action by another. Most of it he had already seen, at Fleet, when signing for his orders and *Enterprise*'s "sailing papers" and authorizing the usual too-numerous vouchers, invoices and inventories.

"We're ready to go," he said.

"Of course," said Spock. "All transfer personnel are aboard and all assigned personnel are at post or accounted for. Our two scheduled rendezvous, with *Swiftsure* and *Coromandel,* are estimated on-time in one-point-one-three and one-point-six days respectively."

"Fine." Now Jim's eye lighted again on the listing that scheduled the senior officers' briefing, and he glanced up at Spock.

Spock bowed his head slightly. "I will be doing the mission situation analysis," he said.

"Thank you. You do seem better qualified than anyone else. . . ."

Spock got an expression that would hardly have seemed like anything on a human face, but on a Vulcan was a most astonishing look of irony. "I am certainly considered by some to be part of the problem," he said. "It seems only appropriate to attempt to be part of the solution."

Kirk nodded, scanned farther down the list. "Crew mixer's starting a little late."

"I would suspect this is so that the senior officers can attend," Spock said.

"Right." On *Enterprise,* as on many another ship, there was a tradition of a first-night-out "mixer" party for the crew, so that people could get together and debrief about what they had done on leave and catch up on personal business before getting down to the serious business of working on a starship. Some civilians had considered this frivolous, when they found out about it— until surveys done by the Fleet Surgeons General proved that if the debriefing didn't happen formally, first night out, it tended to stretch out across the next month of travel time, impairing the crew's efficiency as it did so. With the release of that data, the complaining stopped. And the *Enterprise* always threw a very good party. "It had better be good," McCoy would say, only half joking, since Recreation was considered a part of Medicine, and the chief of Recreation reported directly to him.

"Captain," Uhura broke in, looking over her shoulder at Jim, "a private message has just come in for you—the computer just finished decoding it. Shall I hold it?"

"No need," Jim said. "Put it here." He held up the pad-screen.

Uhura touched a couple of controls to dump the material to the commlink in the pad. Jim hit the combination of shorthand-keys for "newest," and the message came up. Spock politely looked the other way.

"No," Jim said. "Take a look at this, Spock. . . ."

TO: Cpt. J. T. Kirk, cmdg NCC 1701 USS *Enterprise*
From: T'Pau, ac. affil. Vulcan Science Academy/shi'Kahr/
      a'Shav/Vulcan

Captain:

You will have noted that your First Officer has been requested to give testimony in the proceedings regarding the Referendum on repeal of the Vulcan Articles of Federation. Logic dictates that due to previous close association with Vulcan and Vulcans, you should be asked to speak as well. This matter is left entirely to your discretion, and no onus will rest specifically or generally on the Federation or Starfleet if you elect to refuse. Please notify us as to your intention. T'Pau

"Well, Captain?" Spock said.

Jim stared at the pad. *Lord, how I hate public speaking. . . . Still, this is something worth speaking about.* "Uhura," he said, "send a reply. My great respects to T'Pau, and I will be delighted to speak—no, make that honored. Respectfully yours, signed, etcetera etcetera. Copies of the message and the reply to Starfleet, as well."

"Aye aye, sir." Uhura said.

Jim brought the ship's schedule back up on the screen of the pad and looked up at Spock.

"Anything further here that needs my attention?"

Spock reached over Jim's shoulder and tapped the pad: it cycled ahead to one entry. "A discretionary. Ship's BBS has asked for the release of more core memory."

Jim looked at the already substantial figure in gigabytes that the ship's bulletin board system was using already, and the fat increase being requested—almost double the present memory storage. "What does Dr. McCoy say?"

Spock glanced momentarily at the ceiling, as if it might assist him in his phrasing. "He says that the Rec chief thinks it would be a good idea, and in general he agrees, especially as regards the message net—but himself he thinks Mr. Sulu has already blown up more of Starfleet than is good for him on the 'damn bloodthirsty war games machine.' " Spock glanced mildly at Sulu's back: the helmsman was chatting with Chekov about a restaurant somewhere. "Apparently he has been experimenting with Klingon ship design in the BBS's ship exercise simulator. Improving both their design and their performance, if the comments of the people from Engineering are any indication. The Klingon ships in the simulation are apparently doing much better after 'Sulu refits.' "

"How have Mr. Sulu's efficiency ratings been?" said Jim, very softly.

"All above point eight and rising steadily," Spock said, just as quietly.

"And Bones hasn't scheduled him for a psych profile of any kind."

"No, sir."

"So basically, Bones is just grouching off."

Spock looked at the captain as if he had announced that space was a vacuum: his look said both that the statement was obvious, and one about which a great deal more could be said. "In other regards," Spock said after a moment, "message traffic on the BBS has been up significantly in recent days."

"Are you recommending the augmentation?" Jim said.

"Logically," Spock said, "it would be a reasonable assumption to expect crew stress levels, and therefore volubility, to increase over the mission ahead of us. And it would be illogical to withhold what will be a valuable 'safety valve.' "

Jim cocked an eye at the pad, then tapped in an authorization code on the shorthand keys at the bottom. "Give them half again what they asked for." He let the pad scroll to the bottom. "I want a look at those refits, though. People elsewhere may be having the same ideas, if you get my drift."

"Affirmative. Mr. Tanzer has installed one of the optimum refits in the small simulation tank in Rec One."

"Tonight, then, at the party." Jim got up, handed Spock back the pad. "I'm going to get something to eat. I'll see you at the briefing."

The communicator whistled. *"Sickbay to Bridge—"*

Jim nodded at Uhura. "Bridge," he said. "What is it, Bones?"

"I just got the most interesting piece of mail—"

"From T'Pau?" Jim said. He glanced at Spock. Spock put an eyebrow up.

"You too, huh?" There was a moment's silence, and then McCoy said in an aggrieved tone, *"Dammit, I'm a doctor, not a—"*

"Belay it, Bones. What's your answer?"

There was another pause, then a sigh. *"Dammit,"* McCoy said, *"when did I last turn down an argument with a Vulcan? I can hardly pass up one with the whole planet."*

"Noted and logged," Jim said. "We'll talk about it later. Bridge out."

He turned toward the helm. "Mr. Chekov!"

"Sir?" said the navigator, turning in his seat.

"Plot us a course for Vulcan, warp two. Mr. Sulu, take us out of the system on impulse, one-tenth c, then warp us out."

"Sir!"

"And if you see any Klingons," Jim added as he paused at the bridge entry, waiting for the lift doors to open, "for pity's sake, don't stop to sell them new warp engines! No need to make your job harder than it is. . . ."

Sulu's chuckle was the last thing Jim heard as the lift doors shut on him.

The officers' mess was one of the more enjoyable parts of the ship, and not merely because it was for the officers. One could make a case that numerous parts of recreation and the arboretum were much nicer. But there was no faulting the view from the officers' mess. It was on the leading edge of the disk, with real windows, not viewscreens: floor-to-ceiling windows that gave the illusion of sitting at the twenty-third century equivalent of a ship's prow. At sublight, the stars naturally didn't seem to move, but Sulu was apparently opting for the scenic route out through Sol system, the so-called "Grand tour," which more than made up for it. Jupiter swam slowly into view, a huge striped-candy crescent, then grew gibbous, then full, as Sulu slipped the *Enterprise* around the planet's curvature, slowly enough to pick up a little slingshotting from gravity, swiftly enough not to let the impulse drivers disturb or be disturbed by Jupiter's radiopause. Various moons whipped or lazed around the planet like thrown ball bearings as *Enterprise* passed her. Saturn was a yellow white star in the distance, growing in the darkness as Sulu made for her.

Jim pushed his plate aside, having finished with his steak, and pulled the table screen close again on its swinging arm. Holding on it, amber on black, was a page of data.

Msg: 2003469
Date: 7416.664
Sec: WANTED/BUY/SELL/EXCHANGE
From: Cally Sherrin/spec4:sci
Subj: USED B'HIVA

Origin: XenoBiology Lab IV/term:1154/606

```
*********************** FOR SALE ***************************
            Best Quality Andorian B'hiva
                 One Careful Owner
           No Dropouts! No lost meaning!
               Warranty still in force
               180 cr or best offer
      Leave msg in BUYSELL or email area 6
**************************************************************
```

Now what the devil is a b'hiva? Jim thought, and kept reading.

```
Msg:    2003470
Date:   7417.903
Sec:    WANTED/BUY/SELL/EXCHANGE
From:   Nyota Uhura/Cmdr:comms
Subj:   Taped Dictionaries
Origin: Communications/term:181/53
```

While on leave planetside (Terra or Luna), did anyone happen to pick up one of the taped or solid "tourist dictionaries" of local languages sometimes sold in souvenir shops, etc? Want to dump the thing? I'll trade you classical music, third-stream jazz, exotica, drama (BBC, RSC, Bolshoi a specialty). Looking particularly for Romanian, Kampuche, t!Low, Eurish (Dalton recension if possible), and other artificials (Anglish, Neolangue, Sino-Francaise, Cynthetic). Thanks! N.U.

Still working on her doctoral thesis, Jim thought. Uhura was busy working on improving universal translator theory, mostly by taking the old theory to pieces and putting it back together in shapes that were causing a terrible furor in academic circles on various planets. Jim vividly remembered one night quite a long time ago when he had asked Uhura exactly how she was going about this. She had told him, for almost an hour without stopping, and in delighted and exuberant detail, until his head was spinning with phoneme approximations and six-sigma evaluations and the syntactic fade and genderbend and recontextualization and linguistic structural design and the physics of the human dextrocerebral bridge. The session had left Jim shaking his head, thoroughly disabused of the idea (and ashamed of how long he had held it) that Uhura was simply a sort of highly trained switchboard operator. . . . And as regarded her doctoral thesis, he could have found out simply enough that she was still working on the Earth-based algorithms, just by asking her: but this was a more interesting way of finding out. *Cynthetic?* he wondered, and made a mental note to ask her about it at the party.

He scrolled down through various replies to Uhura's message—apparently quite a few people had picked up dictionaries that were now (or had immediately turned out to be) useless— and finally determined to leave these messages for later. "Change area," he said to the screen. "Common room."

The screen flickered and gave him another page.

COMMON ROOM
OPINION, INFORMED AND NON-

RANTING AND RAVING PERMITTED
NAMES NOT NECESSARY

It was one of the places he came to find out what his crew was thinking. Messages did not have to be attributed to a name or terminal, but they could not be private. The office of common room system operator rotated through the crew, offered to various members on the strength of their psych profiles in areas like calm reaction to stress and anger. The common room sysop tended to be closemouthed and dependable, the kind of person that others refer to as "a rock." (Once it had actually *been* Naraht, to the amusement of just about everyone.) Here tempers could flare, awful jokes be told safely, suspicions be aired, rumors be shot down. The common room was sometimes a peaceful place, sometimes a powderkeg. Jim never ignored it.

He scanned through the most recent messages, and one caught his eye:

From: BUGS
Date: 7412.1100

VULCANS: WHO NEEDS 'EM?

They can't take care of themselves anymore. They can't even take care of a starship if you give it to them—and now they claim that they're not good enough for us? Well, **** 'em and the sehlat they rode in on.

Just fooling.

Jim breathed out. *Serious? Or not?* The statement mirrored some that he had heard on Earth, as this crisis had built and brewed. He scanned down the page.

Farther down, other people came in and maligned Bugs, whoever he or she or it was. Remarks appeared along the lines of "Maybe they've got a point: maybe we *aren't* good enough for them. Or good *for* them, anyway—." Other people said, "We need them. Someone has to tell them so. Let's hope that someone here can get it through those thick Vulcan skulls of theirs. . . ." —and Jim would heat up slightly under the collar: he was sure they were thinking of him. The problem was, so did Starfleet. Somehow they expected him to pull this rabbit out of the hat.

The problem was, the rabbit was a sehlat . . . and he didn't fully understand the shape of the hat. He thought he might never fully understand it, even if he lived to be as old as, well, as a Vulcan. And if he didn't come to understand it, pretty damn fast . . . then there would no longer be Vulcans in the Federation to be as old as.

Not to mention that he would suddenly be bereft of one of his two best friends. And Starfleet would come down very, very hard, right on his neck. He refused to try to choose which of those options bothered him more.

Jim scrolled down through the messages. They were not all about Vulcans: some of them were about investing your pay, or relationships that were going well, or going sour, or the nature of God, or the awful way the meatloaf from Commissary Five tasted lately, was the computer there having a crash or something? But Jim read right through them, the complaints, the hello's, the nattering, until he came to the one message that made him simply stop and stare at the screen.

From: LLARIAN
Date: 7412.301

REPLY: to BUGS, 7412.1100

You're not thinking any more clearly than they are. It's not a question of whether we're good enough for them. Or not. They don't even know who we *are* . . . and they're going to judge us.

But *we've* been judging us for thousands of years . . . and *we* don't know who we are, either.

So why all the noise? It won't matter. Until it's too late.

Jim looked up. Uranus slid into sight, slid past on the port side, glowing dim jade, its moons caught climbing topsy-turvy up one side of it as *Enterprise* passed. In a little while the ship would go into warp: in little more than two days, they would be in orbit around Vulcan.

It won't matter.

"Log off," Jim said after a pause, and spent some time gazing out into the darkness.

"Secession," Spock said, "is not the most accurate term for the act which the Vulcan planetary government is being asked to consider; but for the moment, it will serve."

The main briefing room was empty except for the department heads of the *Enterprise,* sitting around the table in the places that tended to become traditional over long periods of time. Spock, as department head of Science, sat at the "corner" that held the main table reference computer, the one that sent images and data to the subsidiary screens set around the table in its surface, at each place, unless the people sitting in front of them chose to override. Next to him sat Scotty, for the Engineering department: behind him was one of his sub-heads, Lasja Ihirian, who managed most routine maintenance and repair aboard ship. Lasja looked bored, but then he always looked bored in meetings—fixing badly broken things was his metier and chief joy. A big, dark-skinned man in a Sikh's white turban, he sat and toyed with the hilt of his knife and looked just a hair from yawning.

Next down the table was Uhura, as head of communications: next to her, Lt. Meshav, who handled Data Management for the ship. What with routinely overseeing and programming the ship's computers, regularly rewriting or debugging their software, and making sure that the many complex interlocking computer systems didn't interfere with one another, it was the kind of job that almost required eight hands and four brains: and since Meshav effectively had both, s/he was very good at what s/he did. Meshav was a Sulamid, who looked like nothing more than a seven-foot-tall pillar of pink violet tentacles, with a waving rosette of stalked eyes on top . . . at least, when s/he was feeling like being pink, or feeling expansive enough to wave the eyes around. S/he had an octocameral brain, which meant s/he might manifest up to eight personalities. S/he tried to restrain herself from doing this too often, citing (as Jim had heard it put it) "pity for the poor single-mindeds." All the same, a poker game with Meshav was an interesting experience, especially considering that one personality was completely capable of hiding the contents of one's hand from all the others . . . not to mention from any opponent.

Next to Meshav sat the head of Security, Ingrit Tomson, a six-and-a-half-foot-tall, icy-looking woman with close-cropped blond hair and a deceptively gentle look about her; and down at the end of the table, next to Tomson, was Dr. McCoy for Medicine, and behind him, his sub-head, big silver-haired Harb Tanzer, for Recreation. Round the far corner of the table, the quartermaster, Seppu Visti, a small slender dark man with Finnish blood in his background and a computer in his head—literally: he was testing the new Second Thought accounting implant for Starfleet, and could tell you the *Enterprise*'s tonnage at any moment of the day or night, down to the last gram, depending on where and when you were in a voyage. Jim found it unnerving: one Spock should be enough for a ship. *At least his ears are the right shape.* . . . And then came Defense, with Sulu sitting in as department head—the headship shifted back and forth between the chiefs of Navigation and Weapons Control. And at last, at the head of the table, sat the captain.

He sat a little uneasily today, concerned by Spock's unusually somber look and tone. Jim glanced down the table and saw McCoy twitching slightly; he seemed to have caught the mood too. "I take it," Jim said, "that there have been no major new developments in the past few hours."

"Nothing major," Spock said, "but the situation is such that even very small changes in the equation, as it were, may have widespread effects."

He keyed up a string of commands on his console as he spoke. "One could say," Spock said, "that this situation had its roots in the first meeting of our peoples, when the UNSS *Amity* found a disabled Vulcan spacecraft adrift in Sol system in the year 2065 old Earth dating." He glanced up at Jim, a casual look, except that Jim knew Spock's differing memories of that first encounter, and shared them. McCoy's eyes were hooded: he too had a different experience of that early history than the one offered by the history books, but he gave no sign of that at the moment—he merely sat listening in the head-bowed position that so often caused Spock to ask drily if would care to interrupt his nap and comment on something.

"That first encounter was lively enough, but peaceful, by human standards," Spock said. "The inhabitants of Terra had had a chance to lose their xenophobia somewhat, by meeting the Andorians peacefully, earlier on in that century: so the existence of Vulcans, and Vulcan, came as less of a shock to them than it might have. Diplomatic relations were opened within several years, and the trade and data exchange agreements followed very shortly thereafter. They have continued, and grown, over the past hundred and fifty-six years. Doubtless from this side of the Terran-Vulcan relationship, matters have seemed settled enough."

The screens came alive with the annotated time line that Spock had called up. "However, this easy relationship has largely been an illusion, the nature of which is little understood except by those who have some knowledge of Vulcan's history. The time line before you matches Vulcan's and Earth's developmental history, scale for scale, over the last six thousand years. Please direct your attention to the marked period starting around Vulcan old-date 139000. This corresponds approximately to Earth old-date 900 B.C.—"

"Approximately?" McCoy muttered.

"I would not like to disturb your rest with unnecessary pedanticisms," Spock said gently, "but if you insist—"

McCoy opened one eye, cocked it at Spock, then closed it again, as if deciding against another verbal passage of arms. A soft chuckle ran around the table: Meshav rustled its tentacles in amusement. "You go right on, there, Spock," McCoy murmured, "I'll wake up if you say anything interesting, believe me."

Jim restrained a smile. Spock flickered an eyebrow. "At any rate," Spock said, "if you look at the evaluation of technological advancement, you will see that the first landing on the Vulcan neighbor-planet Charis took place late in that millennium, approximately three hundred years before the birth of Surak. Exploration and exploitation of the 40 Eri star system by Vulcan industrial and scientific interests continued through those three centuries without major incident. But here—'' a marker flickered into existence on the screens, tagged with a date, 139954—''an incident occurred indeed. Vulcan had *its* first contact with another species, and the encounter was more than enough to set the planet into a xenophobic reaction that not even the influence of Surak, then alive, would be able to stop.''

The time line went away, replaced by a map of part of the Sagittarius Arm of the Galaxy—the arm that Vulcan and Earth shared. But on the scale of this map, both of them were tucked away far down in a corner, and mapped-out zones of contrasting colors, one large, one small, tangled through one another like amoebas having an argument. ''You will recognize from your history,'' Spock said, ''the area of influence once controlled by the interstellar empire our historians call the Inshai Compact. The compact was an association of thirty-six hominid- and nonhominid-settled starsystems in the Galactic-northward part of the arm: a very old association, quite stable, quite resistant to the economic and military pressures of the only other major force in those spaces, the 'nonaligned' planets of the southern Orion Congeries. At least, the compact was resistant to the Congeries until someone put a sunkiller bomb into sigma-1014 Orionis, and thereby destroyed the hearthworld of the compact, the planet Inshai itself.''

''I thought they had never proved that it was a bomb,'' said Tomson, frowning.

''The odds are exceptionally high,'' Spock said. ''The star was not of a flare type, and the old records of its spectrographic history are quite complete and unremarkable. It should still be there now . . . but it is not. With it gone, and Inshai and all its subsidiary planets in that system—the heart of the Inshai bureaucracy—the power and restraining and protective influences of the compact fell apart in a very short period. The result was a reign of terror in those spaces, as the worlds of the Orion Congeries swept in and began the piracies they had long desired. Wars, and economic and societal collapse, destroyed planetary populations: starvation and plague finished most of those who managed to survive the invasions. And the great interstellar corporations of the compact, long decentralized but also held in check by Inshai's rule of law, now took the law into their own hands or became—the law, by fiat. The company ships went out armed with planet-cracker weapons to fight over the trade routes and raw materials they felt they had to have: they blackmailed whole planets and destroyed those that would not submit. In the power vacuum, even the more scattered compact worlds, formerly peaceful places like Etosha and Duthul, fell into this kind of piracy. They could not otherwise maintain their influence, or their technology, much of which derived from Inshai. They entered into deals with the corporations, or with other planets equally desperate, and made terror and rapine their industry.'' Spock's eyes were shadowed; Jim felt a slight chill, having his own suspicions of what a Vulcan thought of such behavior.

''Those worlds and corporations later degenerated into the guilds and companies that were the direct ancestors of the Orion pirates of today,'' Spock said. ''But the Vulcans of that time knew nothing of that—just yet. Suffice it to say that after the pirates had exhausted the richer and closer prizes and settled old scores with the remnants of Inshai, they turned their eyes farther afield. Estimates are that the first notice of electromagnetic signals from Vulcan was taken around the time of the birth of Surak. It was about the same time,'' Spock said drily, ''that the light from the novaed sigma-1014 Orionis reached Vulcan. Some later claimed that it was a sign in the heavens acknowledging Surak's birth. It came as something of a shock to discover differently, some forty-five years later.''

Spock turned away from the computer, folding his hands reflectively. ''There had been discussion since spaceflight began of what the first contacts with alien life would be like,'' he said. ''Generally, it was anticipated with pleasure, or at least great interest. The earlier Vulcan tradition lacks 'the fear of the stranger.' On old Vulcan, there was no need to fear the stranger who came out of nowhere: to him, one offered hospitality without stinting. The one to be feared was the one who habitually competed with you for water and food and shelter. Your enemy was your neighbor, and vice versa. So other life was by and large perceived as a marvel, and possibly economically exploitable. By Surak's time, research had already been in hand for a century or so on the physics and psi-technologies that would be needed to take generation ships out to the nearest stars."

Spock let out a long breath. "However," he said, "the Duthulhiv pirates who were the first to arrive had no intent to be satisfied merely with the Vulcans' hospitality. They had spent some time developing their technique for first-contact of a planet they wished to loot, and it worked perfectly on Vulcan. They surveyed the planet covertly, from well out of sensor range, and then made properly stumbling first radio contacts from several light-weeks outside the system. To reduce the story to its shortest form, they were invited into the system as the planet's guests, and a party of dignitaries agreed to meet with them regarding diplomatic relations. But the Duthulhiv arrived with an invasion force, and the treaty group was taken hostage or killed. From such a point of perceived advantage, the pirates usually went on to subdue the planet in question by extortionate ransom and outright destruction."

Spock got a wry look. "However, they had made the mistake of assuming that the unity of their reception, by all the planet's nations, meant that the planet was unified and at peace, and therefore mostly disarmed. Their observation of the Vulcan merchant fleet, which from agreement in earliest times has never carried arms, seemed to confirm this. What the Duthulhiv pirates did *not* clearly perceive was that the planet was in probably its most violent period of many—and that in fact several wars had been postponed so that the Duthulhiv 'negotiations' could be handled. The pirates were driven out, most bloodily, but with dispatch." Spock paused. "There were many terrible aftereffects of that episode, but the rift that the first arrival of aliens drove into the Vulcan people was one that almost tore the planet apart. Many said that the only way to handle a universe that held such species was to go out in power and subdue them—to become a terror ourselves. Others said that such vileness did not need to contaminate us—we should shut ourselves up in our planet, with our own wars, which we understood, and let no one ever come near us again, whether potentially friend or foe. Only Surak was able to bring the planet through that time." Spock bowed his head. "And he died of it."

"I dare say the aliens are blamed for that as well," Meshav said in its soft fluting voice.

"By some, yes," Spock said. "Insofar as a Vulcan of today will admit to an emotion as crass and debasing as blame. That is the context in which the rest of this information must be viewed."

He brought up the time line again. "This kind of time scale seems very remote to Terrans, I suspect," Spock said. "Rather as if an Earth person of our time were insisting on reacting adversely to something that happened while the pyramids were being built. But the racial memory of the peoples of Earth is a mercifully vague and sporadic thing compared to the precision, and intimate nature, of racial memory as a Vulcan experiences it. Those old memories are closer to us than any dream: they are more accessible than the Terran subconscious. They are not archetype. They are experience, passed down via direct and indirect engram implant, through a psi talent of which, by tradition, I may say little. But every Vulcan experiences Surak's time, and its events, to some extent, as if he or she was there—and rarely with any guarantee of homogeneity of reaction."

"But with logic," Harb Tanzer said.

"You hope," McCoy muttered.

Spock nodded. "The doctor is, unfortunately, correct. Logic is not a disease that all Vulcans have somehow managed to catch, though sometimes Terrans like to pretend it is so. It is a taught way of life, one that affects some Vulcans more profoundly than others; just as one religion or another, or one philosophy or another, will affect a given Earth person more or less profoundly than another. We are not of a piece, any more than the people of Earth are. Some of us will regard the Terrans, and the Federation, with logic in place . . . and others will not."

"I suspect," Jim said, "that it's mostly those others that we have to fear."

"Not necessarily," Spock said. "It is some of the most logical who appear to be spearheading this move to have Vulcan leave the Federation."

He tapped at the keyboard again. "Here is the English-language text of the official communiqué that was sent to the

Federation High Council,'' said Spock. "You will note the wording. This is a statement of intent to consider withdrawing a prior legislation . . . that legislation being Vulcan's Articles of Association with the Federation. The document comes from hr'Khash'te, only one of the three legislative bodies which handle Vulcan's planetary legislation. The other two bodies—their names translate as the 'Proposal Group' and the 'Rectification Group'—put forward and pass or amend legislation. But the hr'Khash'te, the 'Expunging Group,' exists only to veto or remove laws. And it is the easiest to drive a change through. The other two bodies require a large majority to pass legislation. Expunction requires only one-fourth of the body's two thousand six members to remove a law . . . the idea being that a good law should require a fairly large consensus—avoiding the proposal of frivolous or unnecessary statutes—and a bad law should be made easy to stop or change.''

"Very logical,'' said Scotty.

"Also exploitable,'' said Spock. "There has been a considerable dependence on the rule of logic to keep good laws from being illogically removed, or bad ones from being illogically passed. It happens sometimes. Vulcan is not quite Heaven, I am afraid.''

"News to *me*,'' McCoy said under his breath.

Spock flicked him a glance, no more. "At any rate, the system can be subverted, and has been. There are numerous parties and groups on Vulcan who find the planet's association with the Federation, and Terrans in particular, distasteful or unethical for a number of reasons. Some—many—hold the view that there should be no association with a species that goes through the Galaxy armed: such association, they say, is inevitably a corrupting influence on the rule of peace and logic. These groups point at the increasing number of Vulcans affiliated with Starfleet—and at the fact that they are sometimes required by their oaths to handle weapons or perhaps to act violently in the line of duty—and they claim that this is the beginning of the corruption of the species and a potential return to the old warlike ways that almost doomed the planet.'' Spock looked, for eyes that could see, just mildly embarrassed. "For a long time my father was one of the staunchest adherents to this theory, and I understand from him that he has been called back to the planet to give evidence on its behalf. He will be a powerful proponent.''

"Wait a minute there, Spock," McCoy said, and this time he looked wide awake, though there was no telling from his face just what he was thinking. "You aren't tryin' to tell me that anyone can tell your father what to say if he doesn't want to say it. Even I know Sarek *that* well."

"There are forces moving that it would take a long time to explain, Doctor," Spock said. "I doubt even I understand them all: I have been away from home too long. But if T'Pau calls a Vulcan in to testify, she has considerable power to exert to see that just that happens. Not that she would stoop to mere power, when doubtless she considers that she has marshaled reasons in logic sufficient to produce the result she desires. Unless my father can produce a logic more compelling than hers, and reasons that cause her to change her mind, he will do exactly as she bids him. And of his own free will.''

That caused a brief silence. *All of Vulcan in one package,* Jim had once called her, and correctly. The only being ever to turn down a seat on the Federation High Council when called to it, T'Pau was immensely old and immensely powerful, in ways that humans found difficult to understand. He still didn't understand her, not really. His one brief encounter with her, on the sands of the mating-place of Spock's family, had been quite enough. He still could feel it on him like hot scorching sun, that fierce, old, dry regard—eyes that looked on him as impersonally as on a stone, but with intent and calculation eternally and sedately going on behind them . . . calculation that would make a computer ask for shore leave. "Is she behind this movement to get Vulcan out of the Federation?" Jim said.

"I do not know," Spock said. "It is one of many things we must discover. But this much I know: the matter as it stands now could not have gotten so far without her approval . . . at least her tacit approval.''

Jim nodded at Spock to continue. "As I mentioned, these groups have been in existence on Vulcan for, in some cases, hundreds of years. The groups who want us out for fear of Vulcan being contaminated are in the ascendant in numbers and popularity, but there are also groups who believe that *we* are infringing *your* rights—your human rights, you might say—to be Terran; that our life-style should not be allowed to influence yours to the detriment of your own." McCoy's eyebrows went up. "Before you approve, Doctor," Spock said, "I should perhaps mention that these groups also consider logic and reason to be out of the grasp of humans. Some of the more extreme of them suggest that humans would be better off swinging in trees, as they did long ago, before they learned about walking upright, and fire, and genocide." McCoy opened his mouth, then shut it again. "What they suggest for Vulcans," Spock said, "you may imagine. Or perhaps you had better not. But the one piece of this situation that I find most interesting is the fact that never have all these groups, large and small, come together to coordinate their efforts. They always seemed to have too many points of disagreement. But many differences seem to have been resolved . . . and the number of resolutions, and the speed of them, has made me suspicious."

"T'Pau?" McCoy said. "And why?"

"Unknown," Spock said. "But unlikely, by my reckoning. She is indeed in many ways the embodiment of our planet—both ancient and modern—but for the past two centuries she has been content to let matters take their course, through much worse times than these. It seems illogical that T'Pau would take so extreme a course against the Federation, and so traumatic a course for the planet, at so late a date: it argues a most shocking series of flaws in her logic not to have seen the status quo coming and prevented it sooner." Spock steepled his fingers, gazed into space for a moment. "I think we must look elsewhere for the architect of the secessionists' unity. I hope to have time to reason out exactly where. But time is going to be short."

"How fast is whatever happens going to happen?" Scotty said.

Spock tilted his head to one side. "Essentially, as long as the planetary population finds it interesting or edifying to listen to the arguments. It is safest to reckon no more than a week for this proceeding. The Expunging Group has agreed that the law making Vulcan part of the Federation should be removed from the statute rolls. Normally the law would already be void. But T'Pau prevailed on the Vulcan High Council, the senior legislators who put final approval on statutes that have passed the "lower" legislature, to offer this expunction to the planet for approval by plurality. She told them, I believe correctly, that the issue was too large a one to leave in the hands of mere legislators."

Jim's eyebrow went up at that. "So we have a week to debate this issue, on the public comm channels, I take it."

"It may be a week. It may be more. A prior plurality of the Vulcan electorate will be necessary to *stop* debate before the voting on the Referendum itself begins."

"Are any of them really going to pay attention to all this filibustering?" McCoy said.

"Doctor," Spock said, "in the modern Vulcan language, the word for 'idiot' is derived directly from an older compound word that means 'one who fails to participate in civil affairs.' Ninety-eight percent of all Vulcans have held some sort of public office by the time they are two hundred. They will be paying attention, and participating."

McCoy looked slightly stunned. "Debate will go on until a threshold number of viewers have indicated they want it stopped," Spock said. "Some two billion, I believe. The exact number is being determined at the moment. Then the electorate will vote. Many votes will be swayed by what is said in the debates, and who says it—though I suspect many minds of being made up already. Illogical though that may be."

"What are *you* going to be saying?" Harb Tanzer said quietly. "Whose side are you coming down on?"

Spock looked at him, a steady gaze. "I have not yet decided," he said. "Logic must dictate my stance—most especially in my case, for I will be most carefully watched . . . as carefully as my father, or T'Pau. Or you, Captain."

"Noted," Jim said.

"If my credibility suffers," Spock said, "so will the Federation's cause. I must take great care. But the issues are complex . . . and it might be that the best way to support the Federation would be to argue against it."

There was a long silence at this. "So after the debates," McCoy said, "come the votes. And if the vote is to stay in the Federation?"

"Then we go back on patrol," Jim said.

"And if the Vulcans vote to secede?"

"Then all public trade and defense agreements lapse. Private ones are subject to renegotiation if all involved parties desire. But all Vulcan civilians must either return permanently to Vulcan—or emigrate permanently, if they desire to reside elsewhere. All Vulcan bases and vessels in Federation service will be withdrawn; all Vulcan diplomatic personnel, starships, and starship personnel will be recalled," Spock said. "Those who disobey the order will be stripped of their Vulcan citizen status and exiled. The Federation will cease to exist for Vulcan." Spock looked up. "You will be dead to us."

The silence that followed was considerable. "Any further questions?" Jim said.

There were none.

"Very well," Jim said. "A somewhat abbreviated version of this briefing will be given to the crew at large tomorrow: please note it in your scheduling. Dismissed, and I'll see you all at the mixer later. Mr. Spock, Doctor, will you stay a moment?"

The room cleared out. Jim stretched a little, trying to get rid of the crick that his back always acquired during a long briefing. When the door hissed shut for the last time, he said to Spock, "What are the odds?"

"Of Vulcan seceding?" Spock said. "They are high. I have been running syntheses of the most pertinent data through the computer, on and off, for some months now. The odds are presently on the close order of seventy percent."

McCoy whistled softly to himself. "Not the best odds for a gamblin' man," he said.

"Time to change the odds, then," Jim said.

McCoy looked at him. "How?"

"I haven't the faintest idea. But this ship's encounters with Vulcan never go quite according to the rules . . . you notice that?"

Bones smiled. "You want me to slip the whole planet a mickey," he said, "I'd better get cooking. What are you thinking of, Jim?"

"I truly don't know. Just both of you . . . keep your eyes and ears open and tell me anything you think I need to know.

Spock, is there a chance of my having a quiet talk with your father when we get to Vulcan?"

"Almost certainly. I believe he will have had the same idea."

"Good." Jim stretched again in the chair, put his hands up behind his head. "We're not going to let the best first officer in the Fleet go that easily . . . or the rest of the planet, either." He brooded for a moment, then said, "Go on, you two. I'll see you at the mixer."

They went. After a while Jim leaned forward to flick at the controls of the screen in front of him. The graphic view on it gave way to the darkness of space, and stars rushing past in it, a silent stream of threads of light. He put his head down on his arms and gazed into the darkness, thinking. . . .

VULCAN: ONE

★

One of the mistakes people tend to make about their own planets, or others', is that a world's location is a fairly permanent thing. It's true that we speak of planetary coordinates as if you could point at them on a map and find the planet there again in the same spot the next day. (You will, but only because the computer has obligingly updated the starmap to take into account the million and a half miles your planet has moved in its orbit since yesterday and the million miles sideways your star has pulled it in the same time, as the whole starsystem cruises off toward some other star whose company your primary has been covertly seeking for the past eight thousand years. . . .)

These same people may tell you about the Big Bang a sentence later—making it plain that they've never considered the phenomenon past the fact itself; never thought about the kinds of changes that that picture of the Universe implies . . . the vast silent journeys, the terrible speeds. Star travel gives us back a sense of scale in terms of the Galaxy's size, but (most especially since the discovery of warpdrive and its sidestepping of relativistic effects) it can do nothing about our perception of its scale of time. This is no surprise, considering. When a single rotation of ten million years will see all but a very few of our civilizations destroyed by the mere attrition of time, the galaxies seem to move with ponderous dignity, with awful grandeur. And this perception, for living creatures, is a true one. But just as true, and harder for us to see, is the way (in its own terms) in which a galaxy roars through the universe, hurling itself along, seething, churning, changing itself with every whirlpool rotation, changing all its stars and all its worlds: star systems caroming in and out of one another's influence, clusters shifting shape, stars flaring, dying, being reborn from exploded remnants: a cosmic billiards game, run marvelously amok. Our Galaxy has hauled us, all unprotesting, along with all the myriad planets of the billion humanities, across untold and untellable light-years, at speeds that starships easily surpass but could never maintain . . . not for a trillion years at a time.

With all this in mind, it is pointless to try to locate one bit of space and say, "Vulcan was born *there*." The birth took three billion years, and was dragged across half that many light-years— a storm track, a cloudy set of possible loci, like an electron's shell, rather than anything that could be pinpointed. Indeed computers could trace that track, but to what purpose? Many stars have streaked through that area: many more will plunge through it before the Universe goes cold and starts to implode. Right now there is an X-ray star there, used by the Federation as a beacon for navigation purposes. But by tomorrow the beacon will be three million miles somewhere else, and that space will be "empty" again. Everything moves: therein, in paradox, lies our only stability.

We can postulate, though, a moving point of view—one that tracks along with that foggy stripe of probability loci, the long, broad, spiraling shape traced through those parts of space for three billion years. Not that a point of view would have had much to see but what seemed empty space for the first seventy percent of the stripe.

The space was of course not empty at all. Unseen forces and pathways crammed it full—the shallow curvatures of gravity, the occasional immaterial Klein-bottle nozzle of a wormhole, the little-understood "strings" of nonmatter/nonenergy that define the structure of space itself. Matter and energy passing through those pathways responded to them, ran down them, converged in places, like raindrops running down a cobweb. This was indeed how the Galaxy's first generation of stars had congealed out of the hurtling dark ghost-cloud of dust and gas in its earliest life, as the dust gathered at countless gravitational nexi, compressed itself, kindled slowly or swiftly to starhood.

Few of those most ancient stars had any planets. Free energy in that early, formative galaxy was at a terrible premium, and very few stars "did anything" with what energy was available except kindle themselves. Even fewer of the ones that did have planets, as far as we can tell, ever played host to life. Time and the normal life cycle of the oldest stars have long destroyed almost all traces of the earliest sentience. Many stars vaporized their planets by nova-blast or wiped out all life and artifacts on them by starflare, and their humanities' histories are silence to us. A handful of other worlds, more fortunate, still have histories nearly as oblique. Among them must be counted the worlds that were first homes to species like the Organians and the Metrons, who eventually became pilgrims among planets, outliving their worlds over millions of years—finally giving up bodies for existence, and becoming for being. How many of these creatures move still about the Galaxy, by our definition immortal, untroubled by space and time and physicality, no one can say they know.

However, our concern lies not with the oldest stars, mostly now dwarfed or yellow-white with age, but with the second generation of stellar formation, what astronomers call Population II. The broad flat starry oval of the young Galaxy, traveling through patches and tangles of "strings," began to stretch itself (or to be pulled out by the resisting tangles) against the old night. Helped by the oval's own rotation, arms reached out of it: first as blunt bars from the ends of the oval, then curving back into the familiar long graceful glowing arcs of spiral arms, inexpressible tonnages of interstellar hydrogen and dust, all lit by the first-generation stars that had been swept into the arms by immense gravitational-tidal forces. The arms multiplied; the Galaxy became a pinwheel, a whirlpool of dust and light. The dust once again gathered and compressed itself in a billion nexi of strings and gravitation, a network even more complex this time because of the added tidal forces and gravitation of the spiral structure—gathered, and kindled, and burned with blue fusion-fire. Billions of these second-generation stars were born of the forces intermingling in the arms; and with the new stars, planets, almost everywhere that stellar formation took place. Here again, time-scale confuses us. We can choose which we see: a slow glow into burning, like the coals of a fire burning hotter as they're blown on—or (from the Galaxy's own viewpoint) a burst of celestial firecrackers, life leaping into being, light born and blazing in the time it takes to speak a word. . . .

Considered in large, the process was continual: but there were bursts of more rapid stellar creation within the larger steady progression. The same "creation cluster" produced many of the Federation stars, and both Sol and 40 Eridani, about eight billion years ago. Earth came later in the process. 40 Eri, as the astronomers call Vulcan's starsystem in shorthand, came earlier by sixty million years, a difference barely significant on the planetary scale.

But at the time we are considering, there was no sight of either world yet, much less either world's star. Interstellar dust is as nearly invisible as anything that exists, especially without a nearby sun to excite it to a glow, or at least to silhouette it from one side, coal-sack style. Nonetheless, there were untold trillions of tons of dust, more than enough to make up five "hard" planets, three gas giants, and a star . . . and thereby hangs a tale.

In most ways the formation of Vulcan's solar system was typical, the so-called "planetary formation" that every schoolchild knows. Dust and gas gather together in the dark, swirling about in tiny mimicry of the Galactic spiral structure. In the small mimic spiral arms, matter clots, gathers itself to itself in little hurricane swirls, hardens down to a core, begins to attract more. Slowly gravity becomes a force to be reckoned with, at least on the local scale, rather than (as it more usually is) one of the puniest forces known to science.

You would have to bring your own light to see all this by, of course, for at the time we deal with, there would be nothing to break the old dark but the cool faint glow of the distant, dust-blocked galactic core. The Milky Way Galaxy was at this point just three billion years old. It had barely begun to develop the earliest stages of its present spiral structure, and from a distance (if anyone had been there to look) would have seemed a fairly tightly packed oval, all ablaze with that first crop of stars, the then blue white giants of Population I. But the tight-packed look was an illusion. Emptiness was almost everywhere, except in such vicinities as the one we're considering—a track along which three stars were being born.

They started out as huge, vague, quietly glowing orbs, warming slowly, shrinking as gravity compressed them through red heat, to yellow and white, and finally past mere moltenness to the point at which gravity overcomes atomic forces, stripping the atoms bare, reducing them to plasma, and atomic fusion starts. One, the biggest, flared white; the other two, much smaller, burned orange yellow and golden, respectively. They were a true triple star, or more exactly, a pair-and-a-half, all formed from distant segments of the same cloud and all influencing one another gravitationally, to differing degrees. The two smaller stars quickly came to orbit one another quite closely. This may have had something to do with their rapid aging, so that both rather prematurely collapsed into dwarf stars, one hyperdense and white, its companion rather light and diffuse, very red, and unusually small.

The dwarf pair and the white giant were distant neighbors at best. They each would be a very bright star or pair of stars in the other's sky by night, and perhaps occasionally by day, but none would ever be so close as to show a disc to the other's worlds. They would spend the rest of their lives tumbling about one another, around their major and minor centers of gravity, if nothing catastrophic happened to them. Certainly such things had often happened before, to other multiple stars. One of a close pair might be too big, might burn blue white awhile, then go unstable, explode through its Schwartzchild radius and collapse into a black hole—and afterward spend millennia sucking the plasma out of its neighbor in a long deadly spiral, leaving one primary a lightless gravitational tombstone, the other a husk. Or other stars might break up a happy couple or threesome, pulling one or another off by tidal forces. But in the case we're considering, this didn't happen. The tidal effects of the red dwarf and white dwarf on the white giant were minimal, and the member stars of 40 Eridani passed a long and uneventful partnership while their planets condensed.

This process had started while the three stars themselves were barely beginning to collapse. Now it swiftly gained impetus from the solar winds generated by the increased magnetic fields in the stars' early stages of fusion and from the intensified gravity of the collapsed bodies. The spiral-arm clouds of dust around them had already sorted themselves into wide bands; now they became narrower ones, then clumps. Some of the clumps, those farthest out from 40 Eri A, the white giant, tended toward the lighter elements and became gas giants. Four of the planets—three close to the big star, one farther away—had acquired sufficient heavy and metallic elements to develop the standard iron-nickel core and silicon-dominant crust of a "hard" planet. On none of these did life ever arise. The nearest three were too close and hot, the farthest too cold. But in the fourth orbit out from 40 Eri A, odd things were happening.

Usually when clumps occur, one is sufficiently large to draw other clumps to it by gravity and consolidate all the matter in one spot, eventually sweeping the band of dust clean and incorporating it all in a single planetary mass. There can be variations to this process. Two clumps of a fairly balanced size may start orbiting one another within the band: or a cloud of dust within the band may begin to eddy around itself, developing two foci within an elliptical boundary, and matter will accrete to both foci. The actual mechanics of the formation are still obscure. But the final result of this sort of variation is the same—two bodies orbiting one another, sharing a common center of gravity, both achieving planetary or at least near-planetary mass. This is a double planet system.

Such systems are commoner than one might suspect. The Earth and Moon are one such system, though even in this day and age, few people seem to realize it. The popular assumption is that the Moon is Terra's satellite. But the Moon fails the most basic test to find out whether a body is a satellite or not: namely, as it orbits, it falls only *toward* the star it and the Earth jointly circle, and never away. A true satellite or "moon," completely in the gravitational grip of its primary body, would occasionally fall away from the star at the heart of the system. The poor misnamed Moon never does . . . leaving us with the astronomer's laconic statement that while a satellite may sometimes be a moon, the Moon is not a satellite.

And the Earth and Moon give a good indication of how delicate the balance can be while such a system is forming. If one partner gets too much of the heavier elements, "cheating" the other, the other body of the pair may never develop an atmosphere—or may lose it, as some astronomers think the Moon did, long long ago. There are pairs in which the balance abruptly changes in mid-formation due to the influences of other passing bodies, causing *both* planets to lose their gaseous elements. And without an atmosphere, at least on planets suitable for carbon-based life, there is no chance of that life arising. When a double-planet system is forming, the balance can be turned by a hair.

The pair that formed in the fourth orbit out from 40 Eri A was luckier than some. One planet, the larger one, kept its atmosphere: though what it kept was thin and hot, even then. It also kept almost all of the water . . . which was as well, since if the division had happened more fairly, life might never have sprung up on the larger planet at all. The larger world kept a significant fraction of the nickel-iron available from the primordial cloud, though almost all of it was buried in the seething heat and pressure of the core: the tiny fraction that remained was erratically scattered as iron oxides in the planet's crust.

The other planet, shortchanged on the denser elements, was able to settle into an orbit with its partner that would seem, to those unfamiliar with the physics and densities involved, to bring it dangerously close to Vulcan. It rarely fails to *look* dangerous, especially when a Terran used to a small, cool, distant, silvery Moon, looks up at dusk to see a ruddy, bloated, burning bulk a third of the Vulcan horizon wide come lounging up over the edge of the world, practically leaning over it, the active volcanoes on its surface clearly visible, especially in dark phase. "Vulcan has no moon," various Vulcans have been heard to remark: accurate as always, when speaking scientifically. "Damn right it doesn't," at least one Terran has responded: "it has a nightmare." T'Khut is this lesser planet's name in the Vulcan—the female-name form of the noun "watcher"; the eye that opens and closes, but that

(legend later said) always sees, and sees most and best in the
dark. "Charis," the Terran astronomers later caller her, after the
ruddy, cheerful goddess, one of the three Graces, who married
the forge-god Vulcan after Love jilted him for War. No one really
knows what the Vulcans think of the name—any more than we
know what they think of the name "Vulcan" itself. They were
polite enough about accepting it as standard Federation nomen-
clature. But they have other names for their world, and at least
one name that they tell to no one.

But all this is long before names, or those who give them.
Both planets swung around one another and around their blazing
white primary for many, many centuries, and their star and its
tiny companions dragged them away through the new Galactic
arm, while orbits settled down, continental plates ground against
one another, and quakes and volcanoes tore everything. For this
while, the planet looked like the popular images of Vulcan, a red
brown desolation, full of lava and scorching stone and fire. But a
change was (quite literally) in the air, as Vulcan's atmosphere
slowly filled with smoke and vapor, and eventually with cloud
and rain. Standing on Vulcan at present, it is hard to imagine the
rain streaming down in its first condensation from water vapor—
years-long, cataclysmic falls of water, relentlessly washing away
the slow-weathering volcanic stone, mingling unexpected combinations of minerals in the first sea beds. But the fossil record is
clear: Vulcan, now ninety-six percent dry land, was once ninety
percent water—a few islands, and nothing else anywhere but the
new hot sea. T'Khut would rise for thousands of centuries to be
paced by the reflection of her sullen, fiery face in the wild waters.
It was a period that, on the cosmic scale, would not last long: but
it lasted long enough for the miracle to happen.

The exact nature of the miracle, as usual, is as obscure as
the manner of the formation of the double-planet system itself.
By conjecture, of course, we can seem to see what the laboratory
tests have proved possible: the right elements present in the
water, the right nucleic acids ready to come together to form one
more complex: the long seething incubation, the waters hissing
with near-boiling warm rain, shuddering under the thunder—and
then the lightning-strikes, one or many. That would have been all
that was necessary. Remnants of those earliest sea-bed strata

indicate that Vulcan's was more a primordial stew than a soup: sludgier, but far richer in nucleic acids, than the initial mixture present on most carbon-life-form worlds. Great variety existed there in terms of available molecules, and there are theories that the present Vulcan analogues to DNA and RNA show signs of having been the result of arguments, or agreements, among several rival strains that sorted out among themselves, by attempted and successful recombinations, which one was the most likely to survive in the murky waters. Some have since found it ironic that even here, at the earliest point in life's history on Vulcan, warfare of sorts seemed to be going on.

But after the initial combination of DNA settled down, and the face of the waters grew still, peace seemed to reign for a long time. It was illusory, of course: the analogues of algae and plants, and many life forms which have no analogues on other worlds, were jostling one another with innocent and primitive ferocity under the water's surface. But the illusion held for a long time. Many thousands of centuries went by, and the climate shifted radically, before any creature had need to crawl up out of the shrinking, blood-colored waters to burrow into the red-brown sand, or take its chances under the naked eye of day. Until that happened, the world that would be Vulcan dreamed huge and silent under its seas, with T'Khut gazing down on it. Together the two of them tumbled around their burning white shield of a sun, and the sun around its tiny white red and white jewel-partners, as all danced through the expanding arm of the Galaxy: life going to meet life . . . with who knew what consequences.

ENTERPRISE: TWO

———————————— ☆ ————————————

The style of crew mixer that a ship threw to "debrief" after refit or extended leave was always very specifically its own. Some of the ships in Starfleet were known for classy meetings, heavy on protocol and fine food; some of them had formal dances; some of them (especially on ships running more decorous variants of command, like the Vulcan or Andorian patterns) had what amounted to panel discussions. And then there were ships that threw unashamed wingdings. *Enterprise* was definitely one of these. It put something of a strain on the chief of Recreation, but he didn't mind the occasional strain.

Harb Tanzer was of Diasporan stock. That is to say, he came of a planet which one of the first waves of colonists from Earth had settled in the early twenty-second century. They tended to be tough people, and handed down that toughness, of both looks and constitution, to their children. There had also been some minor mutations, since some of the earliest generation ships had not been as well shielded against radiation as they needed to be, and the children of the Diaspora tended to lose their hair early, or if they kept it, to be startlingly silver-haired. Harb was one of the latter, and that thick, slightly unruly silver mane was the first way a new crewman would come to recognize him at a distance—that, and his stocky, solid build, a function of age, for Harb was (as he put it) "pushing three figures." Later they would get to know the broad, friendly face, mostly unlined (that was another of the mutations) except for smile lines, and laugh lines around the eyes.

Harb stood in Rec One, the *Enterprise*'s main recreation room, and surveyed the crowded, noisy place with immense satisfaction. This was his "stomping ground," the place where the chief of Recreation did most of his work. It wasn't all easy, helping people play: there was a lot of setup to be done, but the results were worth it . . . always. Getting the place ready for this party, for example: working out the best arrangement for the furniture, and which kinds of furniture would be needed, in what amounts—it was a job. After all, a Denebian, half a ton of supple invertebrate, used to sitting in something that resembled a salad bowl, would find an Eames chair fairly useless. And what about the Mizarthu crewmen, half dragon and half python, and twenty feet long?—or the Irdesh, silicon-based and so delicate and crystalline in their structure that a hasty move could shatter one like a pane of glass? Their usual Starfleet-issue gravity neutralizers were all right for everyday duty, but in a crowd an accident might happen. For the Mizarthu Harb had stolen (well, temporarily appropriated) several sets of parallel bars from the ship's gyms: they could coil up on those to their hearts' content and discuss philosophy with all comers while they got tiddly on ammonia–and–water. For the Irdesh, Harb had laid hands on enough inertial neutralizers from the people in the Physics labs that all the Irdeshi crewpeople could float around like the big animate snowflakes they were, and never fear a brush from an elbow or a stumble by a dancer, since the neutralizers would sop up the inertia of any blow without transmitting it to the Irdeshi in question.

With questions of comfort handled, there was nothing to do but worry about the catering.

No one *else* was worrying about it, that was certain, since the tables where food was laid out were completely surrounded by crewpeople eating, drinking, and talking at a great rate. Some functions, like this one, were still handled in the old-fashioned buffet style: it was a nuisance to have to call up a plate of hors d'oeuvres on a terminal and wait for the thing to be beamed in. Besides, the orders tended to come in so thick and fast that the computers sometimes got a little confused . . . and a transporter accident involving both people and food was something that didn't bear considering. So Harb did it the old-fashioned way and put low-grade stasis fields over the cold cuts and the starch-based snacks to keep them from curling up. The drinks situation, fortunately, needed little supervision; the liquids synthesizer had only a little local transporter to worry about, which it used to produce glasses from stores, as well as cherries and paper umbrellas, things like that. It hadn't malfunctioned since the last time someone tried to get it to synthesize buttermilk. Harb smiled slightly to himself and hoped seriously that no one would try it tonight.

Elsewhere around the room people were doing what they usually did in Rec One—playing hard—with the exception that there were a lot more of them than usual. On the night of the mixer, the usual three-shift crew rotation was laid aside to make it possible for as many people as wanted to take part. Crewpeople not scheduled for duty went out of their way to relieve other crewpeople who were on post, even if just for a little while, so that they could make it to the party; schedules were juggled until the personnel computers (those with sufficient personality) muttered about it. Now, the place was crammed. There was a big crowd around each of the games tanks, pointing and laughing and making helpful (or not so helpful) suggestions; and everywhere else, it seemed, knots of people, big and little, were talking and shouting and laughing and squeaking and hollering and singing in as many voices as the Federation seemed to possess. The language seemed the same whoever spoke, of course, due to the good offices of the universal translators; but the sound of the three-hundred-odd mingled voices made a cheerful cacophony that Harb wouldn't have traded for any peace and quiet in the world.

The singing group was one of the largest: forty or fifty people had taken over one of the biggest conversation pits and were making some very peculiar but satisfying harmonies. Quite a few of them had brought instruments. There were guitars, both acoustical and synthetic, and velodicas, and a squeezebox, and Uhura had Spock's Vulcan harp, as usual; but most noticeably, one corner of the pit was taken up entirely by the members of the Starship *Enterprise* String, Reed, and Banjo Band. The group played once or twice a week, for fun or for scheduled parties. It was comprised of three people on banjo—one of whom, an Alarshin, attracted a great deal of notice because of his three-handed strumming technique—a portable pianist, one tenor and one soprano sax, and a synthesized percussionist (the musician, not the instrument: Dethwe was a clone).

Harb watched them with some mild concern. They seemed cheerful enough—but perhaps a bit too cheerful, for people who had just come back from vacation. Their energy level seemed a bit *too* high, and had a nervous quality to it. Harb recognized that twitchiness. He had seen it before, when the crew knew itself to be going into a dangerous situation that the ship might not be able to do anything about. And there was nothing to do with such a mood but keep an eye on it, and let it run its course, while being there to lend support if needed.

Harb began to stroll over toward the group, brushing through several different conversations as he did so, saying his hellos, eyeing the various tables as he passed them to make sure the food was holding up all right. "Harb," someone said in his ear.

It was a rather sultry voice, the synthesized voice of the Games and Holography computer. Because of its complexity, it was able to have a personality, and Harb had had one installed as soon as he could . . . to his occasional regret. His computer had a bit of a temper, and occasionally refused to acknowledge that she was "his" computer. This sometimes made his job interesting. "What's the scoop, Moira?"

"We're out of onion dip."

He rolled his eyes a little as the voice, focused for only him to hear, followed him slowly across the room. "So make some more."

"Can't. Stores say they're out of the culture for the sour cream. It doesn't seem to have been reordered."

Harb muttered something rude under his breath in Yiddish.

"I'll tell Seppu you said so," Moira said. "It should be fun to watch him grow upside down on his head in Hydroponics."

"Snitch. Look, just use what we use for yogurt, but do it with cream rather than milk, and accelerate the batch. You know the recipe."

"It won't work," Moira said. "The yogurt uses *Lactobacillus acidophilus,* and the sour cream calls for *Lactobacillus bulgaricus.*"

Harb stood still and thought a moment. Behind him, several people in happy conversation drifted by. One of them said admiringly to another, "I love your new skin color, where did you get it?" Harb chuckled, and then the idea hit him, and he missed the reply.

"Moira, where's Harry?"

"Your yeoman," Moira said sweetly, "is watching Mr. Sulu rebuild another Klingon cruiser."

"Why shouldn't he be? It's his party too. Do this for me. Whisper in his ear and tell him to run down to Biology with one of the empty bowls. My compliments to Mr. Cilisci, and tell him if he'll clone me about half a pound of the organism in the bowl and get it back up here in an hour or less, I'll get Commander Wen to put aside a cubic meter of greenhouse space in Hydro for his basil. He'll have enough pesto to keep him going for the whole mission."

Moira snickered. "No sooner said than done, boss."

Harb nodded, satisfied, and resumed his course across the room. As he went, someone said in his ear. "We're out of dip."

"Keep your pants on," he said, turning, and then laughed a great laugh and added, "—Captain!"

"I do try," Jim said, rather drily. Then he smiled. "Nice party, Mr. Tanzer."

Harb smiled back as they began to stroll together through the crowds of people. "Their doing, as usual," he said, glancing around. "I just clean up afterward."

Jim made another small wry smile. Recreation was viewed by Starfleet as being an extremely important part of the ship, especially for the captain: a commander who could not play—and could not relax—was a liability. So was a crew that could not unbend, and in any starship going into a battle situation, the Rec officer was consulted for his opinion of the crew's readiness and morale. Therefore, a Rec officer who described himself as just part of the cleaning crew could be assumed to be indulging in humor. "Mr. Tanzer," Jim said, "I need to talk to you about something."

The "Mr." alerted Harb to this being something official. "Certainly, sir. We'll find a quiet corner."

"In *here?*" Jim said, glancing around with an amused look. The musical group had begun clapping and stomping along with an instrumental in almost *too* spirited a manner.

The captain noticed this and glanced at Harb as they turned away. "They're a bit loud, aren't they?"

Harb nodded. "Best they express it now," he said, as he and the captain headed off toward one side of Rec, toward the big blank walls behind which the holography area lay, and past that, Harb's office.

"No," Jim said, "there's no need to be private really: just out of the crush. Have you been in the ship's BBS lately?"

They came to the wall by the door next to the holo area, and Harb leaned against it, folding his arms. "I have."

"Do you find anything unusual about the level of discussion going on in the 'common room' lately?"

Harb tilted his head a bit and thought. "I've been running the standard semantic checks," he said. "The computer doesn't find a threshold number of loaded words."

"That's not what I meant. The computer doesn't have hunches."

"My hunches are sometimes wrong."

"That's better than not having any at all. . . ."

Harb looked at the captain. "You're worried about some of the anti-Vulcan feeling you've been seeing."

Jim nodded.

Harb shook his head. "It's always been there," he said quietly. "But when an opportunity like this comes along, it tends to come out more strongly."

Jim looked uncomfortable. "I just find it hard to believe," he said, "that in this day and age, bigotry is still with us. . . ."

"I seriously wonder if it's anything as complex as bigotry," Harb said. "Simple envy, more likely. Consider the Vulcans from the point of view of someone who is unsure about his or her own position in the Universe, someone who's looking to see whether a Vulcan is a threat. All kinds of obvious reasons not to like the species come up. They're peaceful, they're extremely strong, both physically and in terms of personality; they're mysterious, they have powers that 'normal' people don't understand; they have a great deal of political status and influence. But at the same time they keep to themselves; their stand on the requirement for personal privacy sounds suspiciously like ego, like being stuck up, to people looking for a grievance. Why *wouldn't* human beings dislike them every now and then?''

Jim nodded. "I'm not seriously worried," Harb said. "Sometimes, in the BBS especially, sentiments like those get aired so that the people airing them can get them out of the way and move on to something else."

"But not always."

Harb nodded too. "I'll keep my eye on it, for what it's worth. It's not as if we're going into a battle situation where someone's stance on the subject is likely to affect the mission's effectiveness. But at the same time a starship is a microcosm . . . and usually accurately represents in small the things going on in the Federation at large—"

Sirens began whooping, and all around the room people looked up suddenly and put their drinks down. The singing stopped as if someone had thrown a switch. But before anything else happened, Chekov's voice, echoing very large, said on the allcall, *"All hands, yellow alert for Engineering and Nav staff only. Rendezvous with USS* Coromandel *in thirty seconds. Going sublight."*

This caused a stir of pleased excitement, and a lot of people made a rush for the observation windows on the upper level of the Rec deck. No one paid much attention to the view out the windows while a ship was in warp. The otherspace in which *Enterprise* traveled at such times had a speed-of-light much faster than that of Earth's universe: even the slowest-moving particles moved faster than tachyons there. Most of the humanities found the effect of this strange light an unnerving one, and while in warp, ports were usually closed, or the views through them filtered and processed by the ship's computers. But starlight in normal deepspace was another matter; most of the *Enterprise* crew, like the crews of most other starships, were addicted to it.

"Up?" Harb said.

"Why not?" said Jim, and together they went up one of the catwalk-stairs to the upper level to join the many crewmen leaning on the railings and looking out the great glasteel windows. So they saw what not too many people have an opportunity to see—a starship decelerating hard from warp, the point of a silver spear piercing through from the far side of the darkness in a trailing storm-cone of rainbows, as *Coromandel* came out of warp in a splendor of Cherenkov radiation from the superrelativistic particles she dragged into realspace with her. She streaked toward *Enterprise*, braking hard, and the rainbow lights burned low and faded and went out as she matched her sister starship's course and speed.

"I've always had this feeling that there should be some loud noise when that happens," Jim said to Harb. "A bang, or a thunderclap or something."

"Romantic," Harb said. "What was the reason for the rendezvous, sir? Staff transfer?"

Jim nodded. "We have some people destined for Vulcan who've come in from some of the more remote starbases and systems. Fleet detoured *Coromandel* in to drop them off. *Swiftsure* is coming in for the same reason later. Then it's the straight run for Vulcan for us."

They leaned there and watched the smaller ship ease closer—not that she needed to: her transporters would have been effective fourteen thousand miles away—but doubtless her own crew were as interested to get a glimpse of *Enterprise* as vice versa. After a little while, a nearby wall comm whistled. *"Bridge to Keptin Kirk."*

Kirk stepped to it. "Kirk here, Mr. Chekov."

"Our transfers are all aboard, Keptin. Keptin Warburg wants to know if there's anything you need out Vashath way."

Jim smiled. "Tell her if she sends me another package of that blue stuff they eat for breakfast there, I'm going to get McCoy to send her grits by way of revenge."

"Aye, sir," Chekov said, chuckling a little. *"Bridge out."*

"Blue stuff?" Harb said.

"Don't ask," said Jim. "Vashath is a beautiful planet, but if I were you, and you go there on vacation, I wouldn't get up till lunch. . . ."

Coromandel accelerated away on impulse, then flung a cloak of spectrum-colored fire about herself, leaped away, and was gone from sight on the instant. Jim and Harb turned away from the window and headed down the stairs again. "Well," Jim said, "keep your eye on the BBS, as you say. I'm going to be a little busy pretty soon. . . ."

"Aye aye." Harb's practiced eye glanced over the room as they came down the stairs, and he paused. "Look, here comes Mr. Spock."

Jim was surprised at that. "So he does. Unusual to see him come back to a mixer once he's made his appearance at the start. Hope there's nothing wrong on the bridge—"

"He would have called. We'll find out soon enough."

They got down to the floor level, where their path was crossed by a group of crewmen bursting out of the holography area, all rather out of breath. "What have you got in there this time?" Jim asked, a touch suspiciously. "I was hoping for something pastoral to stroll around in. . . ."

Harb smiled a little. "Not that, I'm afraid. But come take a look."

They went over to the wall, and Harb waved the door open. A blast of music blew out past them, something with a hard, driving beat and almost no identifiable melodic line. Together Jim and Harb stepped a little way through the doorway to let their eyes adjust.

They were standing somewhere high up, in darkness, over a great city. At least it might have been great once, but the high glassy buildings had a grimy look about them; there were shattered panes, stone stained and acid-etched, an aura of old decay. A soft bloom of rain was falling out of the starless sky, and through it blazing signs in odd languages, and strange symbols, burned with a fierce light that the misting rain fogged into slight unreality. Some kind of small shuttle craft, iondrivers perhaps, swooped past through the wet dark night on their business. In the middle of all this, seemingly in the middle of the air—for the view from where they stood was very high—numerous crewpeople were dancing on platforms, sheets of softly glowing, translucent force. Some of them were dancing cheek-to-cheek, however incongruous the effect was with the ferocious music, and some of them were doing dances that had possibly been current on the planets where the people had taken their leave . . . but were otherwise unidentifiable.

"What is it?" Jim said.

Harb shrugged. "A synthesis. It could be Earth, or Andor, or the Cetians, or a hundred other places where humanoids have lived."

Jim shook his head. "Looks old. I prefer the present. . . ."

"Mmm," Harb said. "That's doubtless why you keep pulling out that 18th-century naval scenario. It soaks the rugs. . . ."

Jim smiled and said nothing about that. "Funny, though," he said. "This music sounds fairly dissonant. Twelve-tone, isn't it?"

"I think so."

"Well, putting wind chimes in it seems a little strange—"

"I *said*," the wind chimes repeated, more loudly this time, from behind them, "you look marvelous, Jim; have you misplaced some weight?"

Jim and Harb both looked around, and down, in astonishment. Behind them stood a twelve-legged glass spider about a meter tall, with delicate glassy spines on her domed body, and fiery blue eyes, twelve of them gazing up at them with what looked distinctly like amusement.

"K't'lk!"

"I've added a syllable," she said, putting out a slim glassy claw as Jim dropped to one knee and stretched out a hand to her. "I'm K's't'lk now." There was a wind-chime chuckle. "After all, you're entitled to another syllable when you've been dead. . . . It's good to see you, J'm."

"Dead" was probably not the most accurate way to put it, for K's't'lk's species, the Hamalki of alpha Arietis IV, did not deal with death in quite the same way that other species did. K's't'lk—or K't'lk as she had been then—was a physicist, a 'creative physicist,' who had done some work on the *Enterprise*'s warp engines and helped to take her most emphatically where none had gone before. She had died of what happened to the ship, there beyond space and time, but she had left an egg case behind her with Jim, a forgotten piece of spun-glass bric-a-brac in his cabin. On her death the egg had hatched, with her new life in it, and her old memories; and with the *Enterprise*'s return to normal spaces, her daughter-self had gone back to her work in physics.

"But what brings you here?" Jim said with surprise and pleasure. "Not that we're not glad to see you. Scotty'll be delighted." It was a slight understatement: the chief engineer had become first disturbed by, then very fond of, this sprightly creature who found nothing wrong with the idea of rewriting the laws of physics if they didn't do what you wanted them to. There were certainly going to be people on the ship who would not wonder twice, in the light of this, why the syllable K't'lk had added to her name was "s".

K's't'lk shook herself all over, a slightly dissonant chiming more in touch with the blast of background music still coming from the holodeck. "The Vulcan thing; what else? I did most of my basic research with the people at the Vulcan Science Academy, after all; so when this mess came to the boil, Starfleet reactivated my commission again and recalled me to give testimony."

"Well, how long are you going to be with us?"

"Till Vulcan, no longer. I have one evening to spend talking the kinesics of galactic cores with Mr. Spock . . . then it's to business, I'm afraid. And likely to be dreadfully difficult; the Universe is easier to reshape than a Vulcan's mind if it's made up." She cocked a cheerful eye at Kirk. "However . . . would you particularly mind if I had a quick look at your warp engines while I was here? There are some minor adjustments I've come across in my research that, if you made them—"

"NO," Jim said, and then burst out in completely delighted laughter. "Don't you dare! You so much as *touch* my engines and I'll toss you in the brig, madam, and keep you there on—" He paused. "I don't know what you eat. Except graphite."

K's't'lk glittered and sang with an arpeggio's worth of laughter. "You might as well lock Sc'tty up with a case of Scotch, Captain. But your orders are heard and understood. . . . Pity," she added.

"It's just that we have somewhere to be," Harb said. "Somewhere *nearby*."

She chimed cheerfully. "Well enough. Where *is* the graphite, by the way?"

"Over there by the green salad," Harb said, and indicated the table.

"Right you are then, gentlemen. Until later," K's't'lk said, and spidered off through the crowd, exchanging greetings with the crewpeople as she went. Harb chuckled a little and waved the holodeck door shut. Everything suddenly seemed very quiet.

Jim and Harb headed casually in K's't'lk's wake. Harb was shaking his head. "Who else came in on that transfer?" he said.

"The manifests are in the computer," Jim said, pausing by one of the drinks dispensers. "Angostura and soda," he said to it, and watched bemused as the machine beamed in first the liquid, then the glass—just in time—and finally a drinks stirrer with a tiny model of the *Enterprise* on the end of it. "I'm not sure I believe this," he said, and got rid of the drinks stirrer. His eye lit on something else on one of the nearby tables. "And what in space is *that*?"

Jim was pointing at a bowl that at first sight seemed to be black bean soup . . . except that black bean soup usually does not have an oil slick. From the other side of the table, one of Naraht's fringes came up holding what looked like a piece of singed metal, or plastic, or both. Naraht dunked the singed thing into the bowl, and his fringe then whispered back out of sight again, to be followed by slight hissing and munching noises.

"Dip," Harb said. "The silicon-physiology people like it. It's crude oil and iron filings, flavored with sodium oxides and a few rare metals. At least," he added, "most of the sillies eat it, but the Andalusian crewmen won't, even though they like it. Religious reasons."

Jim shook his head again, bemused. "That looked like a piece of a used data solid he was dunking in it."

"It was. We used to incinerate them when their effective lives expired, but then someone found out that Naraht likes them as a snack."

They walked on and paused by the spot where one of the games tanks was situated in the middle of the floor. It was simply a large three-dimensional video tank—a bare platform six feet by six that projected synthesized holographic images upward into empty air. The tank was hooked into the master games computer, and could run any one of a number of games: "board" games like 3D and 4D chess, or role-playing games with animated characters, or action games in which a player handled controls, rather than simply talking to the computer. It was in the latter mode now, and Sulu was sitting in the "hot seat," tapping or stroking at the touchpads that curved around him. In the tank was the image of a Klingon D7D battle cruiser, diving toward a star, or appearing to. Sulu seemed to be trying a slingshot maneuver at extreme warp speed—not exactly the safest move in the world, since going into warp too close to a star usually made the star in question go nova. The crewmen gathered around were offering encouragement or cheerfully predicting disaster, or sometimes simply passing credit chits back and forth. Harb and Jim watched long enough to see that the money changing hands seemed to be slightly in Sulu's favor. "Want to make a small side bet?" Harb said in Jim's ear.

Jim smiled. "I already made one. Come on. I have to see someone."

"Oh? May I ask who?"

Jim shrugged. "It's just a suspicion. But Spock *is* here, and we've just had a rendezvous."

They walked over toward the main doors, where Spock was standing gravely talking to some of the crew, people from Sciences. "Mr. Spock," Jim said, "have you seen K's't'lk?"

"Indeed yes," Spock said. "I anticipate a most stimulating conversation with her: her latest paper on the applications of string theory to matter-antimatter reaction is likely to revolutionize warp technology—"

"Oh no," Jim said.

"—that is, if the Federation's scientists can be convinced that the intermix formulas she suggests are anything less than insane." Spock looked resigned.

"And what do you think of them?" Harb said.

"I do not understand them in the slightest," Spock said, "and they appear to make no sense by normal parameters. But with K's't'lk's brand of physics, appearances are usually misleading. I will reserve any final evaluations until the trial runs. Meanwhile—"

"Yes," Jim said, as the main Rec room doors hissed open.

Darkness walked in: Sarek, in his usual diplomatic dress. He was not alone. He was holding out two paired fingers, and touching them with her own as she stepped through the door was Sarek's wife, Spock's mother, Amanda. She had always been a handsome woman, from the first time Jim had met her, years back: now she was gorgeous. She was smaller and lighter than she had been once, but the effect this produced was to make her look like one in whom time had burned away nonessentials, leaving pure essence: and her hair was so perfect a shade of silver that it was enough to make one want to run out and see a professional hair colorist, or a ghost. She wore a Vulcan lady's standard traveling clothes—long overtunic, soft breeches, and soft boots—all quite logical, but when done in the heavy silks of Earth, luxurious and exotic-looking as well.

Jim bowed over her free hand. "It's been too long," he said.

"It's good to be back," Amanda said. "And in the middle of a party as well." She looked a little wry. "A little entertainment will be pleasant before the deluge."

Sarek's eyes flicked to Kirk, a considering look. "My wife speaks figuratively," he said, "in the tradition of her people. Deluges are not common on Vulcan."

"My husband speaks circumspectly," Amanda said, just as drily, "in the tradition of his."

Sarek bowed his head just a fraction in acknowledgement, then said to Jim, "Captain, my son met us immediately upon our transport over from *Coromandel*. I would welcome a chance to discuss matters with you before we reach Vulcan."

"Choose your time, Ambassador," Jim said. "I will be delighted to accommodate you."

"I believe your people have a saying," Sarek said; " 'there is no time like the present'?"

"My quarters are perhaps a little confining," Jim said. "The officers' lounge?"

"As you wish."

"And if I may, I would like Dr. McCoy to attend."

"The doctor met me in the transporter room as well," Sarek

said, " 'to check his handiwork,' as he put it. I had already taken
the liberty of asking him."

"Then let's go."

"I had thought we weren't going to see you until Vulcan,"
Jim said, when they were all settled in the lounge. McCoy was
off by the wet bar, making a great show of mixing himself a mint
julep while he listened.

Sarek allowed himself a slight smile. Jim was at first surprised to see it, but then realized that what he was seeing was
another diplomatic tool, as consciously used a tool as the diplomatic uniform Sarek wore, or the studied elegance of the way he
spoke English. Somewhere along the line there had been a
decision when on Earth, use the tools that will make you effective
there . . . but remain Vulcan.

"I had planned to take the usual commercial carriers," Sarek
said, "but someone at Starfleet got the idea that it might be wiser
for me to see certain personnel here before setting foot on
Vulcan." His eyes were amused, even though the smile had
faded. "My suspicion is that various persons highly placed in the
Federation were concerned that there should be no obvious
evidence of collusion among us."

"But you're here," McCoy said, sitting down beside Spock,
"and some people are going to notice that we all arrive together,
and suspect collusion anyway."

"True enough," Sarek said. "But at least here our meetings
take place under our own eyes, no one else's: and this is much to
be desired. It may in some small way assist the Federation's case
if you are seen to arrive at Vulcan without needing coaching in
the proprieties of the coming debates. The fact will impress those
of our people who believe that Terrans cannot act like civilized
people without extensive coaching."

"We're going to need that coaching, though," Jim said.
"Spock has told us about the format of the debates in a general
sort of way. I was pretty effective on the debating team at
Academy, some time back. But debating Terrans is one thing.
Debating Vulcans—" Jim blicked an amused glance at Spock. "I
have occasionally lost."

"Half-Vulcans," Sarek said, without any tone of reproach.

"Forgive me, Captain, but I must be certain that you understand the distinction. My son—" He paused here, looking just slightly embarrassed, even for so "pure" a Vulcan as Jim felt sure he was about to claim to be. "My son, though a most excellent officer, and innovative and flexible in his use of logic, is a child of two worlds, two environments, and though he understands how it must be to be of only one of them, he has no direct experience of it. The 'pure' Vulcan heritage is less flexible than you might think from Spock's example; far less willing to give up what it perceives as its own prerogatives and rights; far less willing to give up any of its perceptions at all. I am afraid that the Vulcan 'cultural image' of Terrans, and of the Federation, is quite set in some areas—and the vast majority of Vulcans have never taken the opportunity to go out among the people of the Federation, or among Earth-humans, to acquire data and experiences that would change their minds."

"It's rather shocking, Captain—" Amanda said.

"Jim, please."

Amanda smiled. "Jim, of course. It really is shocking, though. Earth people have this picture of Vulcans as being a great force in space, because of the influence they wield in the Federation's counsels. But at the same time, judging them against other planetary populations, a smaller percentage of Vulcans go to space for holiday or business than go off-planet in any other species. Something like less than five percent, where on other planets as many as thirty or forty percent have been off the planet at least once in their lives."

Jim nodded. "I had heard that," he said, "and it sounded so odd that I wasn't sure that I trusted the figures."

"Nonetheless they are accurate," Sarek said. "Captain, I submit to you that, as open-minded as you have proved yourself, you have difficulty believing such a fact when it is presented you. Imagine how much less likely Vulcans are to have their minds changed by data about humans . . . especially when so few of them have direct experience of them. We have a great reputation for intelligence among the humanities, but I fear that our major weak point in that regard is our rigidity."

"Stubbornness," McCoy said, sipping his drink.

"A word with unfortunate emotional connotations," Sarek

said, "but possibly accurate. Doctor, this may come as a shock to you, but not all Vulcans are free of emotion."

McCoy lifted one eyebrow in an extremely Vulcan mannerism, and said nothing.

"It's actually a linguistic problem, at its root," Amanda said. "There are Vulcan concepts that the universal translator system has been mishandling for many years. *'Arie'mnu'* in particular." She blushed for some reason, but went on smoothly enough. "The concept keeps getting translated as 'lack of emotion,' or 'suppression of emotion,' which is a little better . . . but not much. A more accurate translation would be 'passion's mastery.' The word itself acknowledges that Vulcans do *too* have emotions, but are managing them rather than being managed by them."

"You'd think a mistranslation like that would be easy enough to correct," McCoy said. "There's a Federation committee that handles this kind of thing, isn't there? Approves the changes, and updates the computer programs regularly?"

Amanda sighed. "Doctor," she said, "I used to be *on* that committee. The problem is, now I'm resident on Vulcan—and the committee suspects that my viewpoint is no longer unbiased. Not that they shouldn't have suspected as much when I still lived on Earth. What human being *isn't* unbiased about some things? The illogic of it!" She threw her hands in the air, disgusted.

Sarek looked at her with an expression that Kirk suspected was very restrained affection. "So the problem perpetuates itself," he said, "and resists solutions. Well, it is our business to impose a solution on it, of one sort or another."

Jim nodded. "Sir," he said, "I need to ask this, and if I offend, I'm sorry. Spock tells me that T'Pau is attempting to prevail upon you to take the position that Vulcan *should* secede. Are you in fact going to do that? And if so, am I correct in believing now that you are trying to assist our side of the argument nonetheless?"

Sarek was silent for a moment. "T'Pau does not make attempts," he said at last. "What she sets out to do, that she does, by one means or another. Captain, you understand, I think, that T'Pau could easily have me dismissed as ambassador to Earth if I defied her."

"Yes," Jim said.

"Not that that fact by itself would necessarily stop me from doing my own will," Sarek said. "I accepted my embassage to Earth as much for ethical reasons as for any others, and though it is my business to voice my government's views, if they became intolerable to me, or I felt improper pressure was being put upon me, I would immediately resign."

"But you haven't done so."

"One must not act with unnecessary haste," Sarek said. "I have not yet had a chance to talk with T'Pau, for one thing: I have only a rather brief written communication from her, stating what she desires me to do. Until I have more data, I cannot make final decisions. This I will say to you, Captain: I find being forced to speak against the planet of my embassage immensely distasteful, for reasons that have nothing to do with my history there, my marriage, or my relationships with my son and Starfleet. My whole business for many years has been to understand your peoples and to come closer to them; to understand their diversities. Now I find that business being turned on its ear, and all the knowledge and experience I have amassed being called on to drive away that other diversity, to isolate my people from it. It is almost a perversion of what my career has stood for."

"But if you feel you have to do it," McCoy said, "you'll do it anyway."

"Of course I will, Doctor. Here, as at many other times, the needs of the many outweigh the needs of the few. What if, as the next few days progress, I become certain that my own people would be more damaged by remaining within the Federation than by leaving it? Must I not then preserve the species of which I am part? But the important thing is that this matter be managed with logic." He blinked then, and spoke again, so that a word came out that did not translate. "No. *Cthia*. I must not be misunderstood. *Cthia* must rule this, or we are all lost."

Jim looked puzzled. "I think I need a translation. It's obviously a Vulcan word, but I'm not familiar with it."

Amanda looked sad. "That is possibly the worst aspect of this whole mess," she said. "It's the modern Vulcan word which we translate as 'logic.' But what it more correctly means is 'reality-truth.' The truth about the universe, the way things really *are,* rather than the way we would like them to be. It embraces the physical and the inner realities both at once, in all their changes. The concept says that if we do not tell the universe the truth about itself, if we don't treat it and the people in it as what they are—real, and precious—it will turn against us, and none of our affairs will prosper.'' She sighed. ''That's a child's explanation of the word, I'm afraid. Whole books have been written attempting to define it completely. What Sarek is saying is that if we don't handle this matter with the utmost respect for the truth, for what is really needed by everyone involved, it will end in disaster.''

''And the problem,'' McCoy said softly, ''is that the truth about what's needed looks different to everybody who faces this situation. . . .''

Sarek nodded once, a grave gesture. ''If I find that I must defend the planet of my birth by turning against my many years on Earth, then I will do so. Alternately,'' he said, ''if I find I can in good conscience defend the Federation in my testimony, I will do that. But what matters is that *cthia* be observed, without fail, without flaw. Otherwise all this is useless.''

''And if you find you have to take the case against us,'' Jim said, ''and it means you can never see your son again, or your wife—or that you have to go into exile with them—''

Now an expression appeared, just for a flicker of a moment: anguish. Jim was instantly sorry he had seen it. McCoy had already turned his head away. ''Then that is what will be,'' Sarek said, his voice calm and cool, though his face had betrayed it. ''You must understand, Captain, that from acts such as will happen over the next couple of weeks, ripples spread. They spread from *all* acts, but especially from such as these, when people knowingly take their worlds' fate in their hands. The short-term effects of a withdrawal from the Federation—our little personal loss and pain, the small matter of exile or estrangement—do not weigh significantly against the loss of the diversity, the well-being, the *selfness,* of a whole species. Ours, or yours. Here, at least as far as I am concerned, the needs of the many *do* indeed outweigh mine. My son and my wife will make their own decisions, and make them well, I am sure.'' Sarek looked from Amanda to Spock with almost palpable pride. ''But for myself, I dare not count the cost. I have served my world for longer than you have been alive; I swore such oaths to serve it as Vulcans do not normally discuss with outsiders. I will serve it still, and serve it as well as I can choose how, regardless of the consequences.''

Then Sarek took a deep breath. "But I do not have to like it.''

"Liking is an emotion," McCoy said quietly.

"Yes," Sarek said, looking him in the eye; "it is. It would be a relief if you could declare me incompetent to testify on such grounds. Unfortunately, I doubt the Vulcan Medical Association would admit your diagnosis as valid.''

McCoy shrugged, resigned. "It was worth a try. . . ." He shifted a bit in his seat, folded his arms. "Why were *we* asked to testify, Sarek? Jim and myself, I mean.''

"It is a fair question," Sarek said. "Most of the choices have been made by the High Council, or by delegates they selected, to represent a fair cross-section of the arenas and types of interactions which Vulcan and the Federation have shared over our association. There are logicians, historians, scientists of various types—you will have noticed K's't'lk: she has done more work with our people, for longer, than almost any other scientist in the Federation, and is known for the results she produces . . . if not necessarily for any brand of logic *we* use. But results are as valuable to our people as theory. —And there are a few representatives of Starfleet: but I would imagine your testimony will carry more weight than theirs will. T'Pau, being on the High Council for many years now, has the right to make choices that no one would dare gainsay: and the fact that she chose *you* will have been noticed.''

"That's what I'm having trouble with," Bones said, "because frankly, Sarek, the last time we came visiting, we didn't exactly obey the rules. By Vulcan standards, of course. When we beamed down for Spock's bonding, and found out that what's-her-name, T'Pring, didn't want him—''

"It is widely acknowledged," Sarek said, "when Vulcans discuss it at all, that T'Pring's behavior in selecting your Captain to enter mortal combat with Spock was improper in the extreme. Nothing in the briefing Spock gave you could have prepared you for the rather distasteful sequelae.''

"Distasteful is the word," Jim said, rubbing his throat reflectively. "Being strangled with an *ahn woon* can ruin your day."

"My point," McCoy said, looking embarrassed, "is that if I hadn't slipped Jim a mickey while 'treating' him, he'd be dead . . . but by so doing, I violated the letter, if not the intent, of the whole Marriage-and-Challenge ceremony. —Dammit, Sarek, I *cheated!*"

Sarek nodded gravely. "I find myself wondering," he said, "whether that might not be exactly why T'Pau chose you. . . ."

McCoy looked astonished. "Your Captain conducted himself with the utmost propriety for his part," Sarek said, glancing approvingly at Jim, "and for your part, you obeyed your oaths to Starfleet and to the Other, and preserved life, as best you knew how. No Vulcan is going to blame you much, or long, for that. . . . If, of course, we stoop to such an ugly emotion as blame in the first place."

"Uh, yes, well," McCoy said, and trailed off.

"I estimate one point six days to Vulcan once the *Enterprise* returns to warp, assuming she maintains her earlier speed," Sarek said. "Captain, Spock is already familiar with the format and style of the debates and questioning that will take place. If you have some time early in the ship's day tomorrow, I will go through some library material with you and give you some pointers. The Doctor will doubtless want to look on."

"Certainly, Ambassador. Around point three five, if you like."

"Excellent. I will then retire. My wife will attend me." Sarek stood up: all the rest rose as Amanda did. "Good night, Captain. My son."

They left, and the door closed behind them. "Your mother gets more special as times goes on," McCoy said to Spock.

Spock nodded.

"She blushes pretty well, too," McCoy said. "Was that something you can explain?"

Spock quirked an eyebrow, thought about it for a moment. Before she went into teaching, Mother worked on the early versions of the universal translator, as you will have surmised," he said. "One of her contributions to the original Translation Committee was the mistranslation of '*arie'mnu*' which she mentioned. It occurred some time after she met my father, while she was still mastering the language. I am afraid he teases her about it somewhat."

McCoy smiled a little. "I wondered if it was something like that. Well, to err is human."

"That is precisely what the Vulcans will say," said Spock. "Captain, Doctor, good night."

"'Night, Spock," Jim said. The door closed after Spock, leaving Jim with McCoy and the end of the mint julep. "Well, Bones?"

He was shaking his head. "Sarek," he said. "Who was it said, 'The only thing worse than a scoundrel is a man of principle'?"

"Sounds like Twain, or Averith."

"Mmf." McCoy put his glass down. "Vulcans. . . ."

Jim looked at him. "For so strong a species," Mccoy said, with pity in his voice, "they sure are afraid. I wonder what of. . . ."

"What Spock told us about this morning," Jim said, "should be quite enough, for starters."

"No," McCoy said. "There's something else. . . ."

VULCAN:
TWO

---------------- ☆ ----------------

There were no words, yet. Thought was enough.

He had no name: at least, none that he was able to tell others. Certainly the others had ways they thought of him; the big one, the one with the black hair, the one who caught the beast, the one who knew where the firestones were. But he did not see that these thoughts about him were really him, or even accurate descriptions of him, not the *him* inside. Sometimes he wished he could think of his own name for himself, but it never seemed to matter, not for long. He was himself. The Other knew.

He spent most of his time in the daytimes doing as did the rest of the ones he lived with—wandering among the trees, eating when he was hungry, drinking when he was thirsty, lying down to rest when he was tired. There were other urges, but they came less frequently. It had been years since the Rapture came upon him, and others of the ones he traveled with had pursued him, or been pursued, through the shadows of the greatest trees, there to do strange deeds upon one another. They had no idea where these urges came from and would not have thought to question them, any more than they would have thought to wonder why one got hungry or thirsty. What did it matter? There was always food and drink and ground cushioned with green things to sleep on. Sometimes, after the Raptures, others came, after strange pains and pleasures; but there was always food for them as well. No one understood the sources of this nourishment, why it suddenly came from bodies, why it went away. It did not matter. The Other knew.

While they stayed among the trees, food never failed them. The fruits came and went—sometimes one fruit being in season, sometimes another one. During the cooler weather there were the great sweet gourds, and the flat flowers that grew on the stones and were good to eat, and the long pods that hung from vines, and the hard fruit like stones that had to be cracked, but were full of small tender fruits and sweet juice. There was almost nothing that was *not* good to eat, except the rocks. Some growing things simply tasted better than others, had a different savor or a more interesting fragrance. The group often experimented, one of them calling others to see some new plant or fruit that the group had never seen before, passing it around to taste. There was admiration for the ones who did this the best; they were touched, surrounded by others who wanted to learn to do as well. They slept warm and woke again to wander the endless forests, and eat, and look around them in wonder. There was nothing else for them to do. Sometimes they died, without understanding what was happening, without knowing what death was at all. It did not matter. The Other knew.

They were hominids, of a kind that would have been familiar to any modern xenopaleontologist; perhaps "seeded" on Vulcan by that strange peripatetic species called the Preservers, perhaps not. They looked enough like paleolithic Earth-humans, at that point, to have been easily mistaken for them; a young species that had come to be stocky, strong-armed and strong-limbed, the braincase rapidly expanding to handle an environment rich with stimuli. It would have taken close examination to determine that these were in fact not human. The cast of skin, under the shaggy hair and the unconsciously—and cheerfully worn coat of grime, would have given away the most obvious indication—would have led an examiner eventually to the blood that was green, not red, and to the molecule that betrays so many species' kinship to the plant life of their worlds. On Earth there is only one atom's difference between the molecules of chlorophyll and hemoglobin: manganese at the heart of the compound for the chloroplasts of plants, iron for the blood cells of beasts and men. On Vulcan there was not even that much difference: vulcanoheme and cuproplast alike each had a copper atom at the center of the compound. Few planets have been as verdant as Vulcan was in its lush and beautiful youth—whole continents covered with mighty forests of trees, some a thousand feet high; oceans in which weed as high as trees reached up and bent against the sky-ceiling of the surface, from rootstalks hundreds of feet deep. The lesser animals were more like plants than anything else: the greater ones broke away from being plants only with difficulty. It was a kindly world, in the evolutionary sense, and there was far less reason to struggle than on Earth or many another world—less reason to push an organism into becoming. Being was easier.

There were places where it was not so easy. The wanderers tended to avoid them without specifically naming them or thinking about them. There were places where the trees grew sparser, where fruit was not so easy to find, where water was scarce and did not flow down from every high rock, or sometimes even from the trees themselves. They came upon these places, did the wanderers, and felt vaguely uncomfortable and unsatisfied with them, and drifted back to where the fruit was sweet and the water poured down without having to seek for it.

At least, most of them did.

He was an exception. If he had not been so good at finding the sweetest fruit, the coldest water, they might have drifted away from him and left him on his own long since. But he had that gift of finding, because he looked harder and better than the others; and so they tolerated (without knowing it) the other gift that was part of the first, the tendency to look further ahead, to wonder whether a fruit a little further along might be sweeter, or stranger, than the last. Sometimes he did indeed leave his group alone, though it tore his heart to do so—even then, even though he could hear their minds somewhat, still aloneness hurt—and he would spend long weeks wandering under the great leafy canopy, listening for new sounds, tasting, touching, wondering at what he saw. Sometimes he found nothing. Sometimes he came back

weary with the burden he carried from great distances, strange
new fruits and leaves. Sometimes he came back with nothing but
tales he could not tell, except in the halting picture-speech of the
mind—and the pictures were incomplete, fragmentary, from the
undiscipline of a mind that leapt from one image to another,
delighted past control. Images were all he could share, and
increasingly this upset him. There had to be a way to make the
others understand, understand *everything*. He would hunt for it.

And so he did. More and more he was away from the grounds
where his group habitually wandered. Odd it was how he defined
himself in terms of them, but the group, when he was gone,
tended not to wander too far, so that "their" strange one would
find his way back to them. Their thoughts went after him, but
being as untrained as his imagery, they reached him only rarely:
so that sometimes in the middle of a wet dark night, or a day's
climbing and scrambling, he would feel a brush against his mind,
like a wing—the concern of one of them. He would go about his
business, or back to sleep, feeling curiously reassured. They
knew him, as the Other did.

It was a world for wandering, if ever there was one; a warm
summery world, moist and twilit under its trees even by day, the
endless sea of treetops and the wide waters sheened with coppery
light by night as T'Khut slipped up over the edge of the planet.
Vulcan's year was a touch shorter than the year of Earth would
come to be, but it lacked the severe axial tilt that caused cold
winters and fierce summers on other worlds, and the eccentricity
of its orbit was so slight as to make it nearly a perfect circle.
Summer was forever, and mild. The warm oceans, now long
calmed from their boiling, and green as old bronze, watered the
landmasses liberally with long soft rains all year round; the
atmosphere, richer in oxygen than the norm because of the
abundant plant life on land and in the sea, held the heat of the
white sun close. There was ice in two tiny circles, at the poles,
and hardly anywhere else, ever. Even there at the farthest north
and south the surface of the ice melted and grew warm, sometimes, and turned green for a season with the tiny temperature-
tolerant algae that had first colonized the planet on behalf of
everything else.

Through this quiet world the wanderer made his way, without a direction, without a set purpose. He only knew that he was looking for something. The life of the forests went on around him as he passed through, and the wanderer paid it as much heed as he usually did, no more. There were many other forms of life in those forests, some of which preyed on one another, rather than on the fruits of the trees. The wanderer did not fear them, any more than any other of his people did. One sometimes died of them, but no particular notice was taken of that. That strange stopping, that change, always happened sooner or later, and it was no great sorrow. The stopped ones could still be heard in the others' minds, and there was something indefinably *more* about the ones who had been stopped, so that though they spoke rarely, hearing them was a joy. No one knew the whys of the Change: no one gave it much thought. The Other knew.

The wanderer made his way under the great trees, eating and drinking and sleeping, for a long time. Time itself did not matter to him, or would not have, if he had had a concept of it. It would have seemed folly to make a business of counting one's breaths when the days were so full of wonder, and there were other things to do. What the wanderer finally began to notice was that food was becoming a little harder to find. He rejoiced in the knowledge, the way one might rejoice to see an unusually large fruit hanging on the branch. He knew that he was coming close to what he sought: the places where things were different. He kept going.

Soon there were fewer kinds of tree, and then, eventually, only one kind of fruit: and the other trees around were not the sort that gave water when you broke their branches. The streams that came from the stone were becoming fewer. The wanderer stopped for a while and considered this, sitting by one of the streams, munching a gourd and dabbling his hands in the water. He knew enough to know that if one went without water long enough, one stopped: and he had no desire to become a voice in anyone else's ears, no matter how well and glad the voices sounded. It occurred to him that he was going to have to go back to his group again, if he could not find more water on the way that he was going. He decided to drink deep and make one long walk, and if there was no water at the end of it, to turn again for the place where his people were.

The wanderer drank until he thought he would burst, and then walked. As probably the most experienced traveler that his little group had ever known, he had learned to read certain signs about the land that he was hardly aware of reading. One of them was that going downhill was likely to take you to somewhere strange faster than going uphill; indeed, all along this long journey, he had been aware of going slowly downhill. Now he purposely chose that path: chose, too, the way in which the great trees seemed thinnest. He walked.

He walked for nearly a week, without another drink, without more food. Then as now, Vulcans were tough, and perhaps, in that distant morning of their world, tougher than they are now. The trees grew few: the white sunlight came through them in great patches. The wanderer looked up at the sky, a rich blue green in those days, and wondered at it. Only rarely had he seen it, and at those times he had suspected it was somehow part of the trees. Now he began to wonder whether it might in fact be the other way around, and the trees actually some darker, closer part of this overarching brilliance that hurt his eyes. Doubtless the Other knew: perhaps one day he would ask. In the meantime, he walked on.

Around the time he first began to be thirsty, the trees very suddenly disappeared entirely. The wanderer saw this sudden end of greenness ahead of him, saw the belt of brightness, the horizon, for the first time, and had to stop and hold onto a tree for the terrible vertigo it gave him. The world was not walled with the trees' shadowy greenness everywhere, after all: it was flat. The flatness of it stretched out before him in a shorter, tougher greenness than that of the trees, all starred with bright color like the flowers that grew from some of the trees of home, but brighter, frailer. And past the long flat stretches of green was another flatness stranger still, a bright pale color that threw the hot white sunlight back into his eyes until they squinted. The wanderer was the first Vulcan to look upon a desert.

There was certainly no fruit there, certainly no water. But he had to know what *was* there. He walked.

The thirst came to be with him constantly now. Only once did he manage to break it, when a rainstorm caught him by surprise, far out of its normal purlieus; he lay with his mouth

open to the torrent of it, no matter how astonished he was by the
vast racketing of the thunder out in the open, and afterward he
supped up every drop of water from every blade of greenery he
could reach before the warmth of the day sucked the precious
droplets back up into the brazen sky. Then he began to walk
again.

The greenery gave way to stones, and hills without dense
groundcover—nothing but dirt and barren scree and gravel. All
his life he had scarcely walked on anything harder than moss or
soft herbage. His feet left green footprints behind them now, but
he did not notice. He only had eyes for the eye-defeating white-
ness ahead. He walked into it, to the edge of it, where even the
gravel stopped, and there was nothing but sand. And there he
stopped.

The dunes went on forever. White, white, burning white,
they rolled away into impossible distances in perfectly sculptured
knife edges of sand, and over them the wind rode in toward him
and flung the sand off the crests of them into his face in occasional
gusts. He stood there, his eyes tearing in the almost unbearable
light, and stared at a world that had edges instead of walls: edges
too far away for him ever to reach.

And beyond the edges . . . something reached up to the sky,
and he saw it, and fell to his knees.

It was a mountain. It was alone: it rose out of the distance
unchallenged by other peaks, impossibly high, forested almost to
its summit. And its summit was a pure white that glanced the
light back at him clear and sharp as pain. So it seemed in its
youth, Mount Seleya, rearing up tallest of the mountains of
Vulcan, in those ancient times when its lone crest still speared up
virgin-sharp and uneroded, and still knew snow. Numinous
enough it seems to Vulcans in the present day, that ancient and
inviolate mountain at the edge of Vulcan's Forge, the unmoving
point around which so much of their history has stormed. But to
the wanderer, there at the lost beginnings of things, it was the
tallest thing in the world, the thing that must surely reach up to
heaven as even the trees did not: the center of the universe. And
the wanderer fell down on the sand and yearned for it as no
Vulcan on the planet ever had yearned for anything. There had

never been *need,* on Vulcan; not until now. Now one Vulcan
needed, and that need would change almost everything.

The wanderer rose up, at last, and sat down on the hot sand,
and looked across at the mountain with something other than the
eyes of longing. There was no accurately judging its distance,
even for as expert a traveler as he. He was used to worlds that
had walls, and pillars of trees near at hand, rather than this
pellucid visibility that went on seemingly forever into an infinity
of clear blue-green air. It would take a long, long time to walk
there, he was sure. And if that thing was as far off as he thought
it was, and the height it seemed to have would change the same
way that the seeming height of a tree changed when one came
close to it or went away from it, then the great wide stone tree—
so he thought of it—must be very tall. He might climb it, as he
had climbed some trees before: and if he got to the top of it, he
would touch the heavens. And then— But there his thought failed
him.

A long, long way away: that was the problem. But there was
no food here, and no water, and probably no food or water there,
either. To climb to heaven, he would have to solve that problem.
And he was already desperately hungry and thirsty; and another
hunger had been added, the hunger for the mountain, which no
one else had ever suffered, and which was thus doubly terrible.

At last the sun went down, and with its setting, as was proper
for that time of month, T'Khut leaned up slowly over the edge of
the world and looked at the wanderer. He had no doubt he was
being looked at. Until he saw the mountain, nothing but the
others with whom he wandered had seemed to have that ability—
to look, to see. Now the great shape stretched itself up past the
horizon, its shape shifting and changing through strange oblate-
nesses, warped by the lens of atmosphere, and the wanderer
gazed at this apparition and was no longer so sure about the
inanimate nature of the world. He and his people had caught the
occasional glimpse of T'Khut through the leaves of the highest
tree canopies. But they had only seen her in fragments, flickers
through the parting veil of leaves; and most often as a vast perfect
roundness, serene, unchanged, seemingly unchangeable. Now
the horizon and the heat-wavering atmosphere carved her into a
new shape every moment, and she seemed a live thing, slipping

up over the edge of existence, breathing, changing, growing like the shes' bellies after the Rapture. T'Khut's outlines trembled, she swelled, she grew round, though still flattened—a gravid-looking shape, swollen with promise. Fire flickered in the dark sliver of crescent she still carried on her new limb.

The wanderer trembled and hid his eyes. If the Other knew about this enormous beauty, this strangeness, it had never given the fact to be understood.

But the trembling went away after a while as T'Khut resumed her wonted shape, and the darkness fell, and the Eyes came out, first the white, then the red. The wanderer realized that he had to go back before he could go any further forward.

The return journey was much longer than the journey outward, for the wanderer had pushed himself to his limits to reach the edge of the desert, and several times on the way back he had to simply lie down for a day or so in the shade of some fruit-bearing tree, moving nothing, merely breathing. Shade at first was a precious thing; when the trees were many again, he wallowed in shadow as if in some forest pool . . . then, astonishingly, began to sicken for the sight of clear turquoise sky. When he refound the first (or last) stream springing clear from its rock, he drank from it and rolled under it and lay in it and fell asleep in it; and the next morning he sat eating the sweet gourds that hung about, and then drinking, drinking, as if there were to be no water left in the wide world the next morning. He stayed for several days by that spring, eating the gourds, regaining his strength, thinking of the long way back, the long way to the mountain, and how there was no water. . . .

Then one morning he decided he would stay by the spring no longer: that day he would start once again for the glades where his people roamed. His heart grew light in his side at the thought, and he cracked several gourds at once and ate the sweet meat out of them, then playfully tossed half the shell of the last of them into the little pool that the spring made at the bottom of its rock.

It did not sink like a stone. It floated, and spun in the downflow of water, and water splashed into the hollow of it, and stayed there.

The wanderer stared at this for a long time.

He got up, went to the nearby tree, plucked down another

gourd—though he was not hungry—and took it back to the spring and sat down. He cracked it open on a handy stone and tossed half the gourd into the pool.

It floated. Water splashed into it, and rolled about in bright beads, and did not float away.

The wanderer picked up the gourd carefully from the surface of the water. The beads and drops of water rolled about in the curve of the gourd, but did not spill.

He tipped the gourd clumsily up to his lips, and the water ran out, and he drank it. His face was wet by the water running out.

He dipped the gourd again in the pool, and this time stood up, and took a few steps with the gourd half full. The water sloshed a little, but stayed in the gourd. He drank again, more sloppily this time.

He dipped the gourd, and rose, and walked, and drank again, and was refreshed.

Then he dipped the gourd one more time, in jubilation, and tipped it over his head. Even then, Vulcans did not laugh . . . but it was as close as they were to come for some millennia.

The wanderer did not leave that spring for some days, and when he did, with a gourd cracked only slightly at the top, he did so nervously. What if the water should not stay? What if there was something special about the gourds in this part of the world, or the springs? But the next morning he found that the next spring along worked just as well; water was water. And as he made his way back into the parts of the world he knew, he found that some gourds worked better for carrying water than others: they were lighter, or bigger. He went his way in delight, heading home, well pleased with himself and the Other, whose doing this surely must be.

The people he was looking for, as usual, had not wandered far. They saw him coming with gladness but without much surprise: he always came back. And they saw him carrying fruit, but, rather to their surprise, it was a fruit they all knew well. They were much more surprised when they found that its insides were not the same as they usually were. They thought it was some new kind of fruit after all.

He tried to explain it to them. The images in his mind failed him again. He tried to show them the great tree of stone, how far away it was, how high; he tried to show them the desert of gravel and stone, the flat greenness, the torrents of rain and the thunder, so unlike their placid rainstorms: he tried to show them T'Khut in her soundless splendor, looming over the world. Only now and then did he succeed. Or the image came across, but not the wonder he had felt at the sight, the awe, the terror. He could not make them understand. Particularly about the mountain, he could not make them understand, and this wounded him deep in a way he could not have explained to any of them. There had to be a way to make them understand. There *had* to be.

The gourd they understood well enough, though not the need for it. Why should anyone want to store water? There was always enough. Why should anyone want to carry water? It was heavy, and besides, when there was plenty to be had from the streams or springs, or from the very trees, what was the point? They played with the gourd like a toy, and this wounded the wanderer too. Finally he stopped trying to tell them things, or explain things to them, and began preparing for his greater journey.

He gathered together many gourds and cracked them in the way he had discovered, and then tried carrying them. This worked, but he could not carry many, and when even the empty gourds tired him, he thought what they would be like when they were full. No, there had to be another way. He sat down as he had sat down by the pool and looked at himself. Two arms, two legs. The legs were no good for carrying anything. He looked around him for anything that looked like more arms; and then it occurred to him that one of the thin vines had leaves lobed like hands. He pulled down every vine he could find, until his people wondered whether he had lost his senses. Perhaps he had, but six days later he had invented the net bag, and woven it big enough to carry five or six of the biggest gourds.

He practiced with them full of water, and discovered that it made a great deal of difference how he packed them: they leaked exuberantly. He thought then that it would be even better if he could get the gourds to be whole and uncracked after he had cracked them and filled them with water, so he sat and thought about that for a few days, but not even a Vulcan could do anything about *that* problem. Some days later he invented the stopper—a thick chunk of moss and earth from one of the streams, forced into each gourd's opening.

And then there was nothing to do but go back to the desert, and cross it.

His people watched him go, again, without surprise. He knew they were thinking that sooner or later, he would be back; or not. He had an odd, hollow feeling inside him, as he left, that even now, after he had spent so much hard work getting ready for his great journey, that not one of them would come with him. He did not know what to do with the feeling. Then as now, emotion was an ambivalent matter for Vulcans. He set off, and put thoughts of his people behind him.

The wanderer had little trouble retracing his steps. It took him a long time—especially as he did the later parts of his journey burdened down with water and the lightest of the fruits that could be eaten as food—but finally he stood again at the edge of the world, looking at the great height of stone and snow that reared up against the sky, far away. There had been some additions to his gear while he traveled. The light, for example, that hurt his eyes so: he had found a solution of sorts to that problem. He had tried covering his eyes, first, but that interfered with his ability to carry one or more of the net bags. He invented a shoulder sling for the bags, out of some spare vine, but covering his eyes still did little good against the merciless glare of Vulcan's white primary. Then he thought of how the leaves of the trees shaded the ground, in the forested parts of the world, and so he went back to the sparse edge of the forest and plucked leaves to make shade for himself. With leaves bound about his eyes, and others tied tight about his head and wetted—for he had learned about sunstroke, now—he went on again, much more at his ease. He came to the border with the desert and looked upon Mount Seleya in great awe and desire: and this time he did not stop. He went on.

The sand took its toll of him. The brief encounter with it on his last journey had not prepared him for the ferocity with which it took the sun's heat and radiated it back, and after a very short time he was staggering, half-blinded despite his cobbled-together eyeshades. One day he walked, and another, and another, and the mountain grew no closer. He refused to drink for almost a week, determined to reach the mountain no matter what happened. After another day he realized that it was wiser to walk by night and to try to hide and rest by day; and so he did, with T'Khut's coppery light glinting on the snows of Seleya for his only guide. His walking, with no other thought touching his own, and no other sight of anything, Vulcan or beast, slowly became an exercise in sensory deprivation. He heard strange sounds and saw movements on the sand which proved to have been no movements at all when he came where he judged them to have been. He felt lightheaded and detached from himself; not knowing exhaustion when he felt it, he kept going, and when he fell in his walking, he lay there, at the bottom of dune or sheltered hollow, until he felt like getting up again. He responded affably enough to the sounds he heard, though none of them responded to him. And in the evenings, he got up and walked again: a lonely, dirt-caked, mat-haired, sand-scraped creature, with leaves tied about its head, parched, confused, but determined.

And then he heard the voice.

It was like enough to things he had been imagining lately that at first he paid it no heed. The wanderer had over the past days learned the difference between hallucination and the mind-touch of his people; he was surprised, for he had not thought at first that it was possible to experience anything that was not real. Now he had found that some realities seemed to be more persistent than others—than this new kind, which fled away before he had a chance to touch them. He had become practically resigned about it. When the voice spoke to him, therefore, he stopped, listened, and waited a little to see if it would repeat itself. When it did not, he went on, toward the faint glimmer of the mountain in the night.

Then the sand moved under his feet, and the wanderer sat down, rather suddenly, and wondered whether something real was going to happen after all.

It was not precisely a movement in the sand, but a vibration, very deep: it felt as if the sand, and the stone beneath it, and the solid world itself, were breathing. The wanderer considered this for a moment. People like himself breathed: might not the world be a person, simply made very large and strange? Might it not have trees for hair, and stones for bones, and sand for skin? If these things were true, then there would be nothing particularly strange about it having a voice. Perhaps it did. The Other knew.

The voice spoke again, and the wanderer spoke to it in turn. Not in words, of course; there were no words yet. But he made a sort of sound that he meant to mean "I am here." The sound was not entirely without emotion. The wanderer had never made it a habit to talk to the world itself, and he was interested, but nervous.

And the sand began to stir, and sing, and rumble, and slide away from itself; and in a tremendous hissing and rush of sand, a hissing like the parting of waters by wind, the owner of the voice came up from the depths and looked on the wanderer.

Even now, when Vulcan has been mapped millimeter by millimeter, and satellites can see any grain of sand on the planet that they wish to, very little is known about the movements and nature of the intelligences of the deep sand. *A'kweth*, is one of the names for them: "the hidden"; and *tcha-besheh*, "the under-liers." There is much speculation about their physiology, even about their evolution, for their way of life is strange in a carbon-based world: they seem not to respire, not to need oxygen, or to feed. Some scientists think they were seeded on Vulcan by the Preservers as an experiment, the only silicon-based species (until the Hortas) to coexist on the same planet with a carbon-based one. Some point out that this stance is unsubstantiated by any data: that there is no telling what kind of feeding and respiration takes place in a creature that habitually lives under hundreds or thousands of feet of sand. No more than glimpses have ever been seen of them, through all the many centuries: a huge, broad, glittering back—but is it a back?—crusted with sand, the size of a great house; or a tentacle or two, playing with a bright stone, vanishing when surprised. Scan has proved of little use, considering the weight of natural elements usually between the creatures and the scanning equipment. Sensors turn up vast life-sign readings, a level of vitality and power that would normally belong to a thousand creatures: but movement readings rarely pinpoint more than one source of motion, sliding leisurely through the deep sand of the greater deserts, skirting the outcroppings of mountains as a cruising whale might skirt islands or shoals.

Sometimes a tracked vital sign disappears completely, without explanation, without trace.

There is little agreement about the Underliers. Some have likened them to the Vulcan equivalent of dinosaurs . . . but dinosaurs that never became extinct, content to live their long, strange lives in remoteness and silence, only occasionally having anything to do with the busy, hungry hominid species that came to spread across their planet. In silence they go their own ways, and what thoughts they think about the planet above them, in our day, they do not share.

What the wanderer saw was literally too large for him to comprehend. He had desired mountains: now one had come to him. Glittering under T'Khut, it reared up, and he was regarded. He sat there on the sand and endured the regard. He was not afraid, but again that slightly nervous feeling came over him, that there were some things that the Other had somehow neglected to make known. This one in particular the wanderer would have been glad to know about in advance.

The *a'kweth* spoke again. The sound was not one that the wanderer could repeat, and barely one he could hear. If the world spoke, from stone rumbling against stone, it would sound so. And again it spoke, and the wanderer sat astonished, not knowing what to do.

Then it was in his mind, and it spoke again, the same word, stone on stone: and he saw an image, a picture of a poor bedraggled creature, all sweat and dust, sitting on the sand with a bundle of gourds in a net. It spoke again, and gave him the image again, with terrible clarity and ease.

And he understood. The sound it made, *meant the picture.*

The wanderer would have sat down hard, had he not already been sitting. This was it: this was what he had been looking for; the answer, the way to tell people about the mountain. If everyone was using the same sound for a given picture, then everyone would understand. All that needed to be done was to make the sounds, the words.

He did it, right then. He did his best to make a picture of the creature inside him; difficult enough it was, for the thing filled the whole world. And he made a sound, the first sound he could think of, a sort of clicking grunt; and then the picture again, and the sound to follow it.

The *a'kweth* reared up higher yet, higher than the mountain, till it leaned over the wanderer and filled the sky; and it roared a long singing roar like the wind in the trees during a hard rain. The flood of images that blasted through the wanderer made him clutch his head, so strange they were; lives and deaths were in them, and terrible heat and pressure, and odd desires and triumphs, but above all darkness, a sweet, enclosing, down-pressing darkness that made this mere night look like white day by comparison—a barren, exposed, inhospitable thing. The roar dwindled to a mutter, to a breath, to a hiss; the sand slipped aside, booming underneath the wanderer; and smoothed itself over, and was silent again, and still. The *a'kweth* had gone.

For a long time the wanderer sat there, gazing across the cooling sand at the Mountain. Ruddy and warm the light of T'Khut shone on the snows of the peak, and it actually looked a little closer, for the first time. He wished it had not, for now the choice was before him. To go back to his people and give them this gift? To go ahead to the mountain and bring them the news of it first?

But he might not come back from the mountain. And the gift would be lost. For who but he had ever come here, or ever would?

Two days he sat there, ignoring the sun: two nights, ignoring the stars and the silence, his eyes on the mountain.

On the third day he rose and turned back toward the forests.

The word spread slowly, but there was no stopping it, as usual: the word once spoken always finds its way where it is going.

The Wanderer was his name, now. He had made a word, and taught it to them. His group drifted still about the forests, eating, needing nothing, but now they spoke to one another. They had all taken names, and hard on the heels of their own names had come names for other things; and then words for ways of doing and going; and then some of them started stringing the words together and making sentences out of them. Shortly after that, someone else invented song. The forests became full of music,

and words rang out. More people came into his group: and some
went away and came back bringing others; there were visits, and
meetings and partings, and many people not of the Wanderer's
group now knew about words, and used some of his, and made
some of their own.

The Wanderer made new words for everything. He had
brought the first one: his people seemed to think he should make
all the rest, and so he did. But he kept coming back to the first
word he had made for them, which he thought was his best.
Heya, it was: an outward breath of surprise, a cry of delight, on
seeing something wonderful—and to go with the word, the image
of the mountain as he had first seen it, all green forest and white
fire, immensely distant, wonderfully great and tall. The image
seemed easier to make and clearer, since the huge thing had been
in his head. Indeed all the Wanderer's images did. But that was
the one he kept thinking of, while they brought him fruits and
beasts and tools to name. He thought often of the sand out in the
desert, and the great voice; and often he wished he had paid no
attention to it, and kept on walking. But then he would remember
the size of the creature that had owned the voice in the sand, and
he would sigh. It is hard to make the world go away when it has
decided to notice you.

It was a fine day in the shade of the trees, one that seemed
brighter than usual, so that it reminded the Wanderer of the
lessened shade beneath the trees nearer the desert. He put aside
the fruit he was trying to think of a name for and began instead
to make a song, which was an invention of another of his group,
a she too young for Rapture yet. To make a song, you said the
words you liked, one after another, and made a noise with them
too; and the Wanderer was pleased by this art, since he had been
good at making noises since before his own first Rapture, long
long ago.

So now he sat and leaned his back against the great tree
which was his favorite and made his song; and it was this, that
the world was good, and the light was bright, and there were
good things to eat, and the Other knew all this and had intended
it so. A couple of others of his group, hearing the song, thought
it was good too, and took it up themselves: and it spread from
one person to another, to those eating, and those lying still under

trees, and those wrestling and playing, and those drinking: and those asleep stirred in that sleep, and some of them muttered words, though what they were could not be heard. All this seemed good to the Wanderer, and he sang, under his tree, for a long time.

He paused, after a while, because he smelled something strange. It was an odd smell; he had never smelled its like except near places in the forest where something had happened to a tree to leave it blackened and broken and shriveled. The Wanderer looked up into the bright day—indeed it was much brighter than usual: were the trees bending apart to let in more light, as they did when the wind blew? But there was no wind. Well, no matter. The Wanderer thought he ought to make a name for that smell. He breathed deeper.

And the tops of the trees flashed into flame, and everywhere the song stopped, and people stared upward in dumb astonishment—while the heat grew and grew, and the tops of the trees burned away and let in the light, the terrible light, and the trees themselves caught fire. Screaming, the people fled, and the Wanderer looked up betrayed, betrayed by his song, and by the Other, for certainly no one had been given to understand anything about *this*. Shocked, uncertain what to do, he turned toward the edge of the forest, toward the mountain—

Not many stars are prone to solar flares, and they tend to happen quickly, when they happen. This is probably a mercy: better the sudden incineration of a planet's surface than a slow scorching like the expansion of a red giant. The fossil record on Vulcan shows plainly enough how quickly the star flared, and how violently, growing ten percent in size as something went radically wrong with the fusion reaction that had gone on so steadily inside 40 Eri A for so many millions of years. It took no more than ten or twenty minutes to burn almost all the forests: a day to boil the oceans again, leaving seventy percent of the ocean beds turned into bare, scorched sand and mud. The deserts were charred, melted to glass in some places. Metal, where it lay close to the surface, ran molten. Trace gases in the atmosphere ignited: a great deal of oxygen and nitrogen was ionized and whirled off the planet in the terrible heat. Mountains slumped. The polar caps vanished. Seleya's snows flashed into steam, and her wooded slopes into slag studded with the burning sticks of trees. When T'Khut rose, she came up like a demon, reflected flarefire turning her a burning, blinding, violent red like the fires that had burnt everything. She was scorched herself, and volcanoes spoke with bright and silent rage on her dark side.

Most of the living creatures on Vulcan died.

There were some fortunate ones. Creatures that were on the far side of the planet when the first flare hit were usually able to hide; and those that did, lived. Those early Vulcans who lived near caves, and took refuge in them, lived to emerge days later into a world terribly changed. Many of them died in the terrible storms that followed the flare, or else they died of lack of food and water, or because they could not stand the change in the atmosphere. Some simply died of the shock of the change of the world.

Only the very toughest survived that time. Vulcan was done with being kind. Some of those who survived were ones who used words; but after the flare, they began to make words that were about anger, and pain, and betrayal; and for a long time, there were no songs. The world had betrayed them—that was the word passed from mouth to mouth and mind to mind: and the word got into the words, into the cast of the language itself. The world is alive: the world is angry. Beware trusting in the world, beware when its face smiles, for then it will reach out and make you and Death familiar. Flee, rather; beware the strange and new; beware any light in the sky that you do not know; drive it away, and live. Fight the world, fight what it does, strike the world while you may. Sooner or later it will strike you.

The Other became silent; or perhaps, in anger, was no longer listened to. Many words, too, were lost, as the language worked and reworked itself over the ensuing centuries; the words for fruit, for rain, for peace and leisure to do nothing. Now there were words for blown sand, for blasted stone, for whole forests found charred, for hot dry winds and a sun that had become quiet again but could not quite be trusted; words for despair and loss and being alone, and for the desperate union of minds that seemed the only way to survive in the hell the world had become.

But the word for "mountain" remained *heya* . . .

ENTERPRISE: THREE

————————— ☆ —————————

"You know," McCoy said from behind the helm, "this place gets a lot of bad press about its climate, but it's a lot prettier than you might think. Kind of grows on you."

"Wait'll you get down there to say that," Jim said, stretching in the center seat. "You're the one who's always going on about how much better dry heat is. Until you get down into it. Then it's 'Where's the damn air-conditioning?' for hours at a time, until we get you back up to the ship and toss you in the pool."

McCoy folded his arms and looked blasé while the chuckle ran around the bridge. "Status, Mr. Sulu," Jim said.

"Approach control has us, Captain. Standard orbit in about three minutes."

"Very good. All hands," Jim said, hitting the button on the arm of his chair. "We have planetfall at Vulcan in three minutes. Normal standdown procedures. Shore leave is approved for all departments: check your heads for the rotation."

"I envy them," McCoy muttered under his breath, leaning on the helm. "A nice vacation in the sun."

"While you're going to have to spend all your time in a

conference room somewhere. Poor Bones." Jim leaned back and watched the image of Vulcan swell in the viewscreen.

Bones was right, of course: there was something lovely about the place, though to the eye trained in looking at things from space, it was one of the more forbidding landscapes imaginable. Still, Vulcan was not quite the intolerable aridity that the popular press painted it. There was some surface water—not a great deal, but a couple of respectable small seas, each about the size of the Mediterranean on Earth. And one never tended to think of Vulcan having much in the way of weather—at a distance. Jim tended to think of it as southern California with less rain. But swirls of weather patterned the planet as completely as they usually patterned the Earth. The clouds simply released very little moisture to the surface, and they were usually too thin to provide much but a thin, hot haze over the area they covered. White clouds above, and below, the dun and red and golden surface: here and there a meteor crater or a great dry sea bed, and in many places, chains of ancient mountains, worn by millions of years of wind and sand. It was a beautiful place, and a desolate beauty. The last times he had been here, he had had little time to admire the planet for itself. Maybe this time there would be some leisure to do that.

And you'd better do it now, he thought, *because if things don't go well, this is going to be the last chance you get. . . .*

"Standard orbit," Sulu announced. "Fourteen thousand miles, hephaistosynchronous."

"Maintenance impulse, then, for station-keeping. Helm and Nav on automatic. Thank you, gentlemen."

He turned to Spock. "I take it that from here we go through the immigration formalities as usual, and then—?" He made a questioning look.

"Various of the Vulcan authorities will be expecting us," Spock said. "They will doubtless want to discuss scheduling of the debates with you. Then we are free until tonight, when there will be a reception for many of the attending dignitaries at the Vulcan Science Academy. Tomorrow is unscheduled time for us. The day after, the debates begin."

"Good enough," Jim said. "Let's get on with it. Uhura, please have the transporter room stand ready, and see if Sarek and Amanda are ready to accompany us. No rush: we'll meet them later if they're not.''

"Aye, sir."

But they were already in the transporter room when Kirk and Spock and McCoy got down there, standing by the pads with their luggage in place. Sarek looked placid as always—or almost always; Jim could not quite get rid of the image of the pain that flickered across that fierce face last night. But Amanda looked openly excited, and she flashed a lovely smile at Jim as he nodded to her.

"We've been away so long," she said quietly, as Jim got up on the pads next to her. "Two Earth years this time, almost. I'm looking forward to seeing our house again."

"One point nine three years, my wife," Sarek murmured, as the transporter effect took them.

The transporter room sparkled out of existence, and another room came into being around them, as Amanda said something to Sarek that the translator refused to handle except as a stream of fricatives. Sarek blinked, then said calmly, "You may have a point."

One side of Amanda's mouth quirked in a smile, and Jim glanced away, suddenly convinced that he had just seen a Vulcan be successfully teased in public. *He may have a point too*, Jim thought. *He doesn't seem to find it odd to respond to illogical behavior every now and then. It's true what he says: I've spent very little time with Vulcans other than Spock. We may be a lot more alike than we think we are. And that may be good . . . or bad. . . .*

The room where they materialized was not as bleak as one might have expected an immigration facility to be. Apparently Vulcans felt that efficiency in performance didn't necessarily require clinical barrenness. The room was sparsely furnished with computer terminals and seating, and nothing was there that didn't need to be; but the seating was comfortable and pleasing to the eye, and in one corner a graceful plant that looked like a cross between a prickly pear cactus and a weeping willow was perfectly silhouetted in graceful curves against a window. Outside was a garden of sand and stones so perfectly smooth and subtly symmetrical that no monk in a Zen monastery could have improved it.

Behind one of the computer podiums was a grave-faced young man in Vulcan civil-service livery who took their ID chips and slipped them into the computer, then handed them back with a slight bow. When Jim handed his over, the young man looked up from the chip—apparently having read Jim's identity directly from the interference patterns encoded in the chip's surface, no mean feat—and looked at Jim with a cool, steady expression. "You are very welcome to Vulcan," he said.

Jim was good at trusting his feelings, but he had no idea whether to believe this or not. "Thank you," he said. "I have looked forward to returning here, though I would have preferred not to do so on business."

The young man put the chip through the computer, handed it back without another word, and bowed to the group. "That concludes all necessary formalities," he said. "Please proceed through that door to the staging areas." And he vanished through another door, without any further ado.

The group headed for the door, and Jim turned to Sarek as they walked. "Sir," he said, "one thing I discover: my instincts for reading people seem to fail more often than not down here. Did that young man mean what he was saying, just then?"

"Well," Sarek said, "it is said that a Vulcan cannot lie."

"But they can exaggerate," Jim said, "or leave the truth unspoken—or sometimes even prevaricate."

Sarek got a wry look as they headed out into the staging area, where the various local and long-haul immigration transporters were arranged around the curve of the big circular room. "This is true enough. Captain, here again our people are not of a piece. Those of us who practice *cthia* find lying offensive because it perverts the purpose of speech, to accurately describe the world; and there are other reasons less logical, more founded in the emotions. But some practice *cthia* more assiduously than others, and some hardly at all. And even those who practice parts of it most vigorously are prone, on occasion, to ignore other parts of the philosophy." They paused for a moment in front of the transporters for the regional capital, tu'Khrev. "I remember a time some years ago, on Earth," Sarek said, "when I was invited to attend a religious gathering as part of a cultural exchange program. The people at the gathering were professing their belief in one of your people's holy books, and stating that the only way to be saved—I am still unclear as to what they felt they needed saving from: we never got as far as an explanation— the only way to be 'saved' was to follow the book's directions implicitly, to the letter. Now that book is a notable one, in my opinion, and filled with wise advices for those who will read them and act on them wisely. But some of the advices have less bearing on the present times than others; at least, so it seemed to me. I asked these people whether they felt that *all* the book must be obeyed, and they said yes. Then I asked them whether each of them then did indeed, as the book said they must, take a wooden paddle, when they needed to evacuate their bowels, and go out the prescribed distance from the city where they lived and dig a hole with the paddle, and relieve themselves into the hole and cover it over again? They were rather annoyed with me. And I said to them that it seemed to me that one had no right to insist that others keep all of a law unless one keeps it all himself. I am afraid," Sarek said, mildly, "that they became more annoyed yet."

"The 'rag' infoservices ate it up," Amanda said, with a mischievous smile. " 'Demon Alien Pursued By Lynch Mob.' "

Spock looked at his father with something like astonishment and then subdued the expression quickly. McCoy's expression was of someone delighted and trying to keep the fact to himself. Sarek shrugged. "They were not behaving logically."

"It was the ears," Amanda said.

Sarek looked at her curiously. "You have said that before. Now tell me, my wife, what it is about my ears that made those people so angry."

Amanda began to choke with laughter. "Let me," McCoy said, and he started to explain about demonography and iconography and pitchforks and pointed tails until Sarek was shaking his head in wonder. "They thought, then," he said, "that I was a personification of entropy. Or resembled one."

"That's one way you could put it," Jim said. "Are there any such in Vulcan legend?"

"Yes," Sarek said, "and they *all* have pointed ears. We

know ourselves well enough to know that entropy needs no image but our own to do its will. All the same—" He looked at McCoy with an expression of mild concern. "All the same, Doctor, I would recommend that you not mention this peculiarity of some of your species to any of mine. There could be . . . misunderstandings."

"Could there ever," McCoy said. "No problem, sir."

The transporter cleared, and they stepped up onto the big pads, while Sarek slipped his diplomatic credential chip into the accounting slot on the terminal and began tapping out settings. "This will take you to the consular and embassy complex," he said, "where I will leave you gentlemen in the care of the people you need to see. Amanda and I will stop at home first: then I will proceed to the meetings I have scheduled. Too many of them, I fear. And we will see you at the reception tonight. The officials at the consulates will give your ship the coordinates for the Academy, Captain, or will be glad to handle transport themselves, if you desire."

"I'll have them call the ship," Jim said. "Ambassador, thanks again for your kindness."

"Courtesy to a guest is no kindness," Sarek said calmly. "Energizing now."

The world dissolved in sparkle again, leaving Jim and Spock and McCoy standing in front of a building designed by an architect whose family Jim suspected of owning a glass factory. It was an astonishing piece of craftsmanship, a group of delicate-looking towers seemingly welded together by bridges and buttresses of glass; and the surface of the glass was everywhere iridescent, golds and greens and hot blues all melding into one another up and down the shimmering surfaces.

"That's gorgeous," Jim said.

"And I bet the coating is a sunblock," McCoy said.

"It is our way," Spock said; "art and science combined. There is no reason that function should not be beautiful—in fact, beauty usually makes it more effective. It does come as a surprise to those who think everything on Vulcan is either utilitarian or made of stone and sand, or both."

They headed toward the building. "Your father," Jim said, "is a little unusual sometimes. An ambassador doesn't usually go out on a limb, the way he did that time, in the place where he's assigned. 'Softly, softly' is usually the rule."

"My father is not the normal sort of ambassador," Spock said, as they came to the building and its doors dilated for them. "A fact for which we may yet have reason to give thanks."

The afternoon would have been something of a bore, except that Jim found himself in the company of someone whom he immediately and wholeheartedly disliked.

The man's name was Shath, and he was one of the senior officials in charge of the debates. He was small for a Vulcan, barely five foot nine, and he was blond, which caused Jim to look at him with great interest when he and McCoy were first introduced to the man in the offices at the consulate. The fair hair was a surprise, since blond Vulcans were rather rare: also a surprise were the blue eyes, a vivid dark blue like Vulcan's daytime sky in clear weather. Nearly as much of a surprise was the coldness in those eyes. Not the cool reserve that Jim had grown used to on an everyday basis in Spock, in the old days, or in Sarek now: but a genuine shutting out, an assumed coldness, purposeful and uncaring of the response.

Spock had been escorted off by another consular official, a slender older woman; Shath had led Jim and McCoy into a side office and left them sitting there alone, with nothing but a table and a computer console to keep them company, for almost twenty minutes. At first they simply chatted and assumed there was some kind of bureaucratic tangle going on outside: but then Shath came in at last and made no excuses whatever for the delay. He simply began interviewing them as to their schedules and their intended itineraries, with an air about him as if he were being forced by his job to be polite to monkeys.

Jim answered Shath's questions politely enough, but next to him McCoy stirred several times, as if about to say something and stopping himself. Jim suspected what was going through his mind. *What am I going to make a fuss about? I'm a starship captain and not being treated with the proper respect?—Well, yes. But Sarek hit it. Not all these people are of a piece, and not all of them like us. If I allow myself to be nettled by that, I'm*

*giving them the satisfaction of letting them see me prove myself
to be what they think I am. I won't do it—*

"Very well," said Shath, breaking Jim's train of thought in a
sharp tone of voice that no one, *no* one, used on a starship
captain, as far as Jim was concerned. "You will be at the Halls
of the Voice at point three, two days from today, for your
declarations. You may bring reference materials with you if you
need them." The look in his eyes made it clear what Shath
thought of anyone who needed to use notes for anything whatever. "That is all."

Jim opened his mouth to give the insolent creature a piece of
his mind, but McCoy beat him to it. "Shath," he said, "do you
practice *cthia?*"

The look on Shath's face was that of someone asked an
embarrassing question by a parrot: annoyance, and scorn. "I
do."

"But not the part about courtesy to guests, I suspect,"
Bones said, very calm.

Shath's eyes blazed. *"Cthia* does not apply to *tviokh,"* he
said. "Nor, soon, to any creatures of your sort. That will be all."

"That's not all by a long sight," McCoy said, drawling a bit,
but still quite calm. *"Tviokh,* huh? You are a *rude* little son, and
you not past fifty yet. But you're still old enough to have some
manners. Good thing I have too much to do this afternoon to be
bothered tanning your hide." He stood up. "Come on, Jim, let's
leave this spoiled brat to his paper-pushing."

There was something so outrageously provocative about
Bones's tone of voice that Jim held in his initial reaction to it.
"Shath," he said, and lifted his hand, parted, "long life and
prosperity. Doctor," he said, and they went out together into the
outer office.

Bones did not stop but went straight out of the office into the
corridor that led down to the 'tween-floors transporters. "Now
what was *that?*" Jim said under his breath.

"Wait till we get outside," McCoy said, and would say
nothing until they were out in the plaza in front of the building.

They found a simple stone bench under several of the prickly
willows and sat down. McCoy blew out a breath, looked at Jim.
"That lad up there," he said. "You recognize him?"

"No."

"Well, you were busy at the time, as I recall. He was at Spock's 'wedding.' "

Jim digested this. "He was?"

"Sure enough. Just one of the crowd, but nonetheless, I recognized him. It was the blond hair: it caught me by surprise, that first time."

"He certainly was rude, though." Jim shook his head. "He hated us. No, it wasn't hate. Contempt. We were dirt to him."

"Correct. Hatred requires some personal knowledge of the hated. He had none. And I didn't want him to realize that I recognized him," Bones said, "so I made something of a point of acting the way he was expecting me to act, and hoped you wouldn't do the same and attract attention to yourself. Which you picked up very neatly on and acted like a Vulcan, which probably made him even madder than he was and distracted him more." McCoy leaned back against the tree, then said "Ooch!" and bent forward again, rubbing his back: the tree had its own ideas about people leaning on it, and the ideas took the form of spines about an inch and a half long. "Anyway," he said, "no question, but *he* meant what he said."

"That much even I got," Jim said. After a moment he asked, "What's a *tviokh?*"

"*Tvee'okh*," McCoy corrected him. "More of an 'e' sound. It's a pejorative. 'Auslander.' 'Gringo.' 'White-eyes.' " He looked a little resigned. "Actually, it means 'neighbor.' Which tells you something. It's not a nice word. It implies that the person may live over on the next piece of land, but you would prefer them to be under it rather than on it."

"Charming. But you think that it was just Terrans he felt contemptuous of, rather than us in particular?"

"I'm pretty sure." McCoy leaned back again, more cautiously this time. "Remember, Jim, I've had a long time to study Spock's kinesics. Even though he's half Earth-human, and his mother's body language has influenced his somewhat, the influence of his father's side is still quite strong, since everyone else in Spock's life while young was exhibiting Vulcan kinesics. They tend to wash out the Earth influence somewhat, in fact; which is why you'll notice that when new crew join us on mission, their own body language will be stiff around Spock's for a few weeks. It takes them that long to realize that just because he's not making the proper kinesic responses to their own body-language cues, he's not snubbing them. He's just different. Once they realize that, their own language smooths out."

Jim nodded. "So you read Shath as just generally angry about humans."

"Angry is exactly correct. Angry enough not to show the proper courtesies even when he knows we could complain and possibly get him fired for it . . . or at least reprimanded. He apparently is very sure of the vote going for secession, in which case nothing we've done will or can matter."

Jim sighed. "How many more of them are like that, out of all the Vulcans who'll vote? Bones, this is beginning to scare me."

"Just now? I've been scared bloodless since I realized that my testimony might actually *affect* this outcome somehow."

They sat quiet on the bench for a few moments. "Well," Jim said at last, "I guess we've just got to pull ourselves together and do this the best we can. Still—" He shook his head. "I'm not used to running into that kind of thing from a Vulcan. They're always so controlled and polite. The thought of what a whole bunch of angry Vulcans would be like if they let go—"

"That thought scared them too, some time back," said McCoy, "and it looks like that's the only thing that's kept them here this long."

"Which reminds me," Jim said, "my translator didn't do anything with that word. Do you suppose the thing's on the blink again? You just replaced my intradermal transponder a couple of weeks ago."

"No," McCoy said, and looked a little guilty. "I took a second-level RNA language series while I was on leave. I must confess I was worried about exactly this situation coming to pass—I was watching the news—and so I stayed at home and did the course."

"Instead of going to Bali?"

Bones shrugged. Jim looked at him in astonishment. Not many people chose to learn languages by chemical means any more: though a course of messenger RNA gave a very complete knowledge of a language, it tended to wear off with time, and made the person who took it extremely sick for days. Most people preferred simply to use the universal translator in one of its portable forms, and update its data when necessary. The RNA series did have advantages, though. Fluency was immediate and conscious—you could choose words for effect, and make puns, in those languages that had them—and there was no fear of a complete breakdown in communications if your translator should break down, or if you found yourself in a place not served by a translator transmission with the right protocol for your receiver. Jim was impressed. "Was it a listening course, or speaking-and-listening?"

"*Hwath ta-jevehih tak rehelh kutukk'sheih nei ya 'ch'euvh,*" McCoy said, and then coughed and rubbed his throat. "Damn fricatives," he said, "they're worse than Gaelic. My accent isn't worth much. I asked for a native north-continent accent, but instead I got RNA from some Vulcan who'd been first to Cambridge and then to UCLA." He rolled his eyes. "The native clones are more expensive, though. . . ."

"Didn't you charge this to Fleet?"

Bones looked wry. "You kidding? You know how long it would have taken to process the requisition order, and the voucher, and the departmental approval, and the authorization draft? Vulcan would have seceded by the time the paperwork sorted itself out. I did it on my own nickel."

Jim made an amused face. Shortly Spock came across the plaza to them and paused in front of them. "Was there some problem, Captain?" he said. "You seemed to spend very little time in the consulate."

"We did the business we had to do," Jim said. "No problem. . . . You missed McCoy tanning one of your people's hides, though."

McCoy stretched lazily while Spock looked at him in total noncomprehension. "Vulcans do not tan," Spock said.

"Depends on what you soak the pelt in after you get it off," McCoy said, and grinned.

Spock shook his head. "I must confess that I do not understand you."

"He' elef ka hij," McCoy said, and Jim's translator rendered it clearly as, "Oh yes you do."

Spock blinked.

"Come on," Bones said, getting up, "I want to do some shopping, and we'll tell you the whole thing as we go."

"Fascinating," was the only thing Spock found to say as they headed off into the hot, bright afternoon.

They spent a cheerful while walking around the city, looking in shop windows, admiring architecture, and sitting down late to a dinner of what McCoy described happily as "better lasagna than they make at the Vatican." The day was cool and pleasant by Vulcan standards, no more than about a hundred and ten degrees Fahrenheit. All the same, Jim was glad he had had the stores computer supply him with some hot-weather pattern uniforms, the ones interwoven with the heat-sink fiber that radiated heat away from the wearer as fast as it developed. Even in the shade, at their table in the courtyard of the little restaurant, the breath of the failing day was hot, and Jim was drinking a lot of the cold, clear water that came bubbling up from the restaurant's own spring, in the middle of the courtyard.

McCoy was gazing at the spring reflectively as he sipped at his wine. "You know," he said, "for such a dry place, you people have a lot of fountains."

"We conserve our water very carefully," Spock said, "but there are places and times in which conservation comes close to meanness of soul. The spirit must be refreshed, as well as the body."

McCoy pushed his wineglass away. "There was a time," he said, "when I would have been astonished to hear you say something like that."

"It would have been a time when you did not know me as well as you do now," said Spock. He turned his glass idly around on the table. "But times change. Let us hope they change for Vulcan as well."

McCoy nodded, then said, "I have to ask you something. There's something I don't understand about the language—"

"The accent, for one thing," Spock said, sounding drily amused.

"You leave that out of it. You know how RNA transfers work: you get the context behind the word as well as the definition and the usage."

"Yes."

"Well, there are a couple words whose contexts seem to have gone missing, though they translate well enough. *a'Tha*, for example."

Spock said nothing, merely tilted his head and looked at McCoy.

"If it's something I shouldn't be asking about," McCoy said hastily, "just forget it. I understand about the Rule of Silences, but I'm not always sure where the privacy taboo starts, if you know what I mean."

Spock shook his head. "No, Doctor, this is not a taboo subject. It would be taboo to ask about particulars—the way it affected a particular person. But you are asking in the abstract."

He folded his hands, steepled the fingers. "There is no context in your translation because it is probably the one concept in the language that must be continually reexperienced to be valid. You cannot freeze it into one form, any more than you would want to repeat the same breath over and over all your life. One must experience *a'Tha* differently every second. But that is not a tradition or a stricture imposed by people—merely a function of the structure of the universe. Your position in spacetime constantly changes: *a'Tha* must change as well."

Jim shook his head. "I'm missing something."

"I think not," Spock said. "I think most human languages would render the concept as 'immanence,' or something similar. *a'Tha* is the direct experience of the being or force responsible for the creation and maintenance of the Universe."

"God," Jim said, incredulous.

"Are you using the word in the exclamatory mode, or the descriptive?" Spock said. "In either case, 'God' is as good a name for it as any. Vulcans experience that presence directly and constantly. They always have, to varying degrees. The word is one of the oldest known, one of the first ever found written, and is the same in almost all of the ancient languages."

McCoy looked at Spock curiously. "You're telling me," he said, "that the piece of information that most species spend most of their time searching for and complaining about and having wars over—and can never achieve certainty about—is the one piece of information you just happen to have. *All* of you.''

"Yes," Spock said, "that is an accurate summation."

Jim sat quiet for a moment, absorbing it. It would certainly explain the uncanny—un-Earthly—calm and serenity of many of the Vulcans he had met: they all seemed to carry some certainty around with them that everything was all right. If this was the root of it, he understood at least some of that serenity, at last. But there were problems still. "Spock," he said, "in the light of this, how do you explain someone like Shath?"

Spock looked a little somber. "Captain," he said, "I think I can understand your viewpoint. Humans have no innate certainty on this subject and therefore must think it would solve a great deal. In some ways it does. But there are many, many questions that this certainty still leaves unresolved, and more that it raises. Granted that God exists: why then does evil do so? Why is there entropy? Is the force that made the Universe one that we would term good? What is good? And if it is, why is pain permitted? You see," he said, for McCoy was nodding, "they are all the same questions that humans ask, and no more answered by a sense of the existence of God than of His nonexistence. Some of the answers become frightening. If God exists, and pain and evil exist, while God still seems to care for creation—for that sense is also part of the experience—then are we effectively 'on our own' in a universe run out of the control of its creator? Such a view of the world leaves much room for anger and aggression. We spent millennia at war, Captain, Doctor, despite the fact that almost every Vulcan born knew that a Force then extant had created the Universe, and now maintained it, from second to second. It takes more than the mere sense of God to create peace. One must decide what to do with the information."

McCoy nodded. "And I suspect you're going to add that not all Vulcans experience *a'Tha* to the same extent."

"Indeed they do not, for the simple reason that they occupy different positions in spacetime," Spock said, "but there are doubtless many other influencing factors as well."

He fell silent. McCoy's eyes were on him, but the doctor

said nothing, only reached out to his glass and had another drink of wine.

"You would like to ask how I perceive *a'Tha*, or whether I do at all," Spock said. His glance was dry, but humorous. "I think I may safely break the privacy taboo from my side and tell you that I do. But whether the degree in which I experience it is greater or lesser than normal, I could not tell you. It is indeed one of the matters involved in the Silences, the code of privacy which is part of Surak's guidelines regarding *cthia*. However, in my life as in most of my people's, *a'Tha* raises more questions than it answers. . . . I will admit," he added, "that I have wondered how it feels to be a human, and *not* to know that certainty, that presence. At any rate, Doctor, have I answered your question?"

"Mostly."

"That's good," Jim said, glancing at his chrono, "because we're running late. We have to get back to the ship and change for the reception. Where did Sarek say it was? The Academy?"

"Yes," Spock said as they got up.

"Great," Bones said, picking up his purchases from beside the table. "Another cocktail party in the school auditorium."

Spock put up one eyebrow and said nothing.

Later, in the transporter room, they spent no more than a few moments inspecting one another's dress uniforms before they got up onto the pads. Jim was mildly surprised to see that to his other rank tags and decorations, McCoy had added a small, understated IDIC. "If I didn't know you better," he said, "I'd think you were going native. When did you get that?"

"Today in the gift shop, when you were looking at the snowball paperweights with Mount Seleya in them. Tackiest things I ever saw."

"Yes," Spock said; "they were imported from Earth."

"You be quiet. We can't let these people leave the Federation, Jim. At least not until they teach us how to make tasteful souvenirs."

Jim groaned. "Energize," he said to the transporter technician.

The world dissolved and reformed itself into a dusky landscape, all sand and stone, over which stretched a tawny darkness filled with stars. The sunset was now almost completely faded down from an earlier splendor that must have been enough to blind the eyes of anyone not Vulcan. They were standing in a great open space outside the walls of the Academy itself. The expanse of silvery sand ran featureless from where the three of them stood nearly to the horizon, where a range of low hills lay silhouetted against the crimson and golden glory of the sky. The air was hot but still, and from far over the sand came the cry of something alien but sweet-voiced and distant and sad.

"The place really does grow on you," Jim said.

McCoy nudged Jim to get him to turn around. "You don't know the half of it."

Jim turned away from the horizon and the sunset and actually took a step back from the massive pile of stone that stood, limned sharply as a cutout, against the rising bulk of T'Khut. It was a castle, or looked like one: but no castle so large had ever been even thought of on Earth. It looked to have been carved out of a whole mountain.

"It was a fortress once," Spock said, "when this was the only place for thousands of miles where water sprang from the stone. Wars were fought for possession of Pelasht, even when the winner might only possess it for a day. Then Surak came . . . and when the fighting stopped, and the Academy grew up here, Pelasht became its ceremonial house and banqueting hall. Shall we go in?"

They did. Jim half expected a brassy cry of trumpets as they went up the switchback stair that led to the main gates. He would have welcomed a fanfare or two, to milk for the delay: a steep climb in this atmosphere was not exactly what he had in mind. But he had had McCoy give him a time-release TriOx before they left the ship, and a couple of treatments to increase his lungs' ability to extract oxygen from the air. He would be all right. *Just so long as no one challenges me to any duels,* he thought ruefully.

They went in through the massive gates, and McCoy looked mistrustfully at the huge holes in the ceiling of the vast passageway between the outer gates and the inner ones. The holes were perfect to dump large rocks down on the heads of a trapped enemy. And certainly enemies had been trapped here once or twice: the scars on the floor, where boulders had been dropped long ago, were many and deep.

"Those gates are solid rock," he muttered. "What are the hinges made of to support that weight?"

"Titanium-steel alloys," Spock said. "Our people discovered them some five thousand years ago, during weapons research."

"When else?" McCoy said softly, and walked on. There was a light ahead of them down the passage, and the echoing sound of conversation.

They paused in the doorway, and not for effect, but because of it. The Hall of Pelasht is one of the largest rooms in the known worlds—nearly half a mile long, a quarter mile across, five hundred feet up to the roof, and all carved out of the living stone, an ancient volcanic basalt. The hundreds of lamps driven into the walls were tiny and distant as stars. It was rare to feel so oppressed, so dwarfed, by an empty space, but Jim did. He simply held still until his feelings calmed down somewhat, until he got over the feeling that that great roof, lost up there in the shadows, might take it into its mind to come down on him without warning. This was earthquake country, after all. . . .

Over some kind of annunciator system, a calm voice said, "Captain James T. Kirk. Doctor Leonard E. McCoy. Commander Spock."

They headed in, Jim doing his best to stroll and look unconcerned. It was a long walk. That hall was the sort that could have swallowed the largest party alive, and people were tending to congregate in small groups near the tables which had been set out in the center with food and drink.

They made their way to the nearest of the tables, and there they found Sarek and Amanda and a great many Vulcans to which they were all introduced one by one. Jim swore quietly at himself one more time for not taking the time to get the Name-Filer memory enhancement done to his translator . . . but things kept coming up, and he was forced simply to say the names as they were said to him and try to keep them all in order that way.

There was this to be said, though: these Vulcans treated him with all the courtesy that Shath had not, and they talked to him as if he were an intelligent being. It was a pleasant relief, after

that afternoon, when Jim had begun to wonder whether or not
the whole planet might be in the mood to consider him a pariah.
Paranoia, he thought, and got happily involved in small talk.

As he chatted with them he was once again rather delighted
that Vulcans were in fact different from one another. A lot of
people had the idea that Vulcans were all tall, dark, and slender,
men and women alike: but though a large percentage of them did
indeed fit into those parameters, there were also short Vulcans,
blond Vulcans, even a redhead over by one of the tables, talking
earnestly to K's't'lk: there were delicate, light-boned men and
ladies, and stocky ones, and Vulcans who had rather pleasantly
ordinary faces, rather than the chiseled good looks that seemed
to be the rule. *They look like people,* Jim thought, and then had
to laugh a little at the idea.

Jim got himself a drink—more of that pure water, which was
highly prized hereabouts for its sweet taste—and went back to
chatting with the group of Vulcans who had gathered around him.
There was Sreil, the burly, brown-haired biologist from the Academy, and T'Madh, a little bright-eyed woman of great age and
curiosity, a computer programmer; and her son Savesh, who
when asked what he did, said, "I am a farmer," with a sort of
secret satisfaction that hinted he thought his job better than any
of the more technical ones that the people around him held down.
Jim had to smile; the thought of a Vulcan farmer was slightly
funny, even though there naturally had to *be* some. But the image
of a Vulcan in coveralls, chewing on a stalk of hay, kept coming
up and having to be repressed.

Savesh turned out to be rather more than a someone who
drove a tractor, "though I do that on occasion as well," he said,
as if that too was a matter of great pride. Savesh was involved in
research on improving the yield of several of the breeds of *tikh,* a
native grain-bearing grass that was a Vulcan staple, and one of
the few things that would grow in plain sand without much added
nutrient. The problem, it seemed, was that the plant's biology
would not stand much tinkering, in the way of genetic engineering
or hormonal treatments; and if you added more nutrient to the
soil in an attempt to get the *tikh* to grow faster, it would simply
ignore the stuff. So some other solution had to be found.

"It is rather important," Savesh said. "Over the past three

hundred years, the planet's population has increased far beyond the self-sufficiency point. Perhaps an illogical outcome, but it must be handled soon. Already we import too much food, and there is no telling what will happen to our imports after the debates. . . ."

"Savesh," Jim said, "may I ask you your opinion of something?" It was the standard courtesy, so Sarek had explained to him; the Vulcan to whom one spoke might then safely refuse if he thought his privacy might be breached by the answer.

"Ask, please," Savesh said.

"What do you think about the secession? Is it something you personally would want?"

Savesh frowned, and for a moment Jim wondered whether he should have asked at all. *But I have to ask: I have to get a better feeling of these people . . . I can't just stop at Shath.* "If I've offended—" Jim started to say.

"Offended? Indeed not," Savesh said. "It is just that, Captain, you must forgive me, but I have never met an Earth person before this evening, and I begin to wonder now whether much of the data I have about your kind is hearsay evidence and no more." He frowned again. "I am not sure how to explain this so that it will make sense for a person from a different cultural context, so you must bear with me. There is a word in our language, *nehau*—there are many translations, but usually they come out as 'feeling,' and the translation is inadequate—"

"Araigh 'tha takh-ruuh ne nehauu vesh mekhezh't-rrhew," McCoy said quietly from behind Jim, and then coughed.

Savesh and Sreil and T'Madh all looked at McCoy with astonishment. "Yes," Savesh said, "that would be more like it. Doctor, where did you study Vulcan?"

"Flat on my back," McCoy said ruefully, "and then spent a week regretting it, usually in the bathroom." Even the Vulcans smiled slightly at that. "Jim," he said, "the best translation of *nehau* would be an old word: 'vibes.' The feeling-in-your-bones that something gives you. It's highly subjective."

"Right. Go on, Savesh."

"Well, Captain, I have heard numerous Vulcans say that losing the Federation and the Earth people would be no particular loss, because they had bad *nehau*, and that could not fail to affect us sooner or later. But I must tell you that I find your *nehau* not objectionable at all; pleasant, even. And this being so, it makes me wonder whether many of the other things I have heard about Earth people are similarly inaccurate. I wonder where the other Vulcans have been getting their data; whether they have even met an Earth person, to make the decision."

Jim smiled a little. "They might not have. But for my own part, it might just be that I'm a nice Earth person; there have to be a *few*. Or perhaps I have good *nehau,* but I'm not really as good as I feel."

"That might be," Sreil said. "But usually *nehau* is not that easy to deceive; it accurately reflects a being's inner status. In any case, some of us perhaps will desire to revise our thinking. But whether those revisions will make a difference to the vote that will be taking place . . . that is impossible to predict, and the odds do not look promising."

Jim nodded. "Well, " he said, "I hope it may."

T'Madh looked at him out of her little bright eyes. "Hope is not usually logical," she said, "but in your case, I would wish that matters go well for you, and for all of us. I for one would not care to lose the Federation; our differences are so great that we will never find such an opportunity to celebrate them on so grand a scale. But I wonder sometimes whether there are many of us who think ourselves unequal to the task . . . and so naturally become unequal to it." She shook her head. "It is saddening. Nevertheless, let us see what can be made of tomorrow."

The conversation drifted to other things, and eventually Jim drifted along to other conversations. After an hour or so, he noticed that he was feeling curiously tired. It was probably the heavier gravity . . . it caught you behind the knees after a while, made you feel wobbly.

"Running down a bit?" McCoy said in his ear.

"A little, yes," he said.

McCoy gestured at one of the side doors. "Go have a bit of a walk in the fresh air. It's actually cooling down out there; it helps a little."

"All right."

It was another long walk to the door. Jim paused in the doorway, looked around. He was standing on a sort of long balcony or gallery carved out of the stone of the side of the mountain; the cliff fell away sheer a hundred feet or so below him, and the Science Academy was laid out before him, all its graceful buildings glimmering in T'Khut's coppery light. To left and right, the gallery stretched away, and railed stairs reached up from it, leading to other balconies on the mountain's side.

Jim picked a direction and began to stroll. The air was indeed getting cool, cooler than he had ever felt it; but this was a desert climate after all, probably the archetypal one. *They should have called it Sahara or something,* he thought to himself, amused, as he walked. *Vulcan: why did they name it that? Unless it was a return to that habit the astronomers used to have, of naming the planets after the old gods. . . . Not a bad name, I suppose. The god of the forge—and if ever a planet has been thrust in the fire and hammered, this one was, to hear the paleontologists tell it. . . .*

He went up one of the sets of stairs to better his view. The sky had become a most marvelous shade of purple blue, some light of the sun still lingering as twilight, and the desert glowed red beneath T'Khut. Jim leaned on his elbows on the railing and wondered how many balconies there were carved into this sheer wall, how many rooms inside the bulk of the fortress itself. To hear Spock tell it, the place was tunneled through and through like a Swiss cheese with strongrooms, living quarters, lesser halls, stores to hold food against siege. . . . Jim wondered what it would have been like to withstand a siege here, to look down and see those sands full of people shouting for your blood. . . .

History: he could never resist history. He hoped there would be time to see this place properly later.

If there was a later. His own actions would help to determine that.

Oh, please let it work out all right, he said to Someone Who might or might not be listening. Unlike Spock, he had no certainties on the subject.

". . . resist this," a voice said, faintly, some distance away. "I resist this most strenuously. Why will you force me to this action?"

"You know my reasons," said a second voice: a little, thin, frail voice, but Jim thought he knew it from somewhere . . . and the hair rose on the back of his neck. "You know the work that other has done, to what purpose. Our people must vote *rightly,* not because their prejudices are exploited. And indeed they have them."

"I would not argue that with you. But I resist this course nonetheless."

"I will tell thee again," and Jim's hackles rose once more at the suddenly formal turn of phrase. The voice was a little louder, as if its owner had come nearer. *"Our people must vote rightly.* It is disaster, it is the breaking of *cthia,* if they do not. They must not be moved by their prejudices, or by the advertising campaign—" the words were almost spat out—"that those others conduct to sway the electorate. They must vote for secession because they think it is logical and necessary. And to do this, they must hear the truth. And no one is better qualified to tell them the truth than you are. They know it: the whole planet knows it. You are the keystone—or one of them."

There was a long silence. "I cannot help but think," said the other voice, Sarek's voice, low and rough, "that the matter of thine own honor is involved in this, madam."

"When has it not been?" The voice was cool. "I am the Eldest. I rule the Family; in some ways I rule the planet, and well I know it, and feel the weight of what I rule. Too long now I have felt it. I think I weary of it. But for the time being, I will not put down the burden, and neither will the Family. *Cthia* must be observed. The truth must be told. There is no one better to tell it. Eighty-six of their years, you have been ambassador to Earth; you have married a woman of Earth; you have sired a son of mixed parentage; you know the Terrans better than any other. And Terra is at the heart of the Federation, as well you know. We do not hear complaints about the Andorians, or Tellar, or the other worlds. The species that troubles us, the species whose policies determine those of the Federation, are the humans of Earth. Your course is laid out for you. You may resist it as you like. It will not avail you."

There was another silence. "And you, James?" the voice said, quite close. Jim turned around, shocked.

There T'Pau stood, looking at him: and in the background, in the shadows, Sarek, looking somewhat diminished. But Jim had eyes only for T'Pau, frail and small, leaning on her carved stick, robed in plain dark robes now instead of the ceremonial splendor she had worn at the Place of Marriage and Challenge. Again Jim remembered the hot sand, and that regard, more scorching than the white sun, pinning him, examining him. It did so now, and the darkness did not blunt the edge of it. "You did not mean to overhear, I am sure," T'Pau said. "We shall assume that this was intended." Jim blinked: *what does that mean?* "But no matter. You know what Sarek will do?"

"He will give testimony, and the intent of it will be that Vulcan should secede from the Federation," Jim said.

"Do you know why he will do this?"

"Because you have told him to," Jim said.

T'Pau drew herself up a little taller, took a step forward. "Many will think that," she said. "Certainly most folk of your people would think so. They look at me and see the powerful matriarch—" She snorted. The sound was so unexpected that Jim almost laughed at it. "They have no idea of the strictures that bind my power," T'Pau said. *"Cthia, cthia* above all. But they do not understand it. If they did, secession would not be necessary."

"And perhaps if they did, their diversity from us would be diminished," Sarek said. "What is the point of celebrating diversity if one tries to make all the elements of it the same?"

T'Pau glanced at him, and then back at Jim. "James," she said in that oddly accented voice, "there are forces working on this planet who desire this secession mightily. It is not in my right to stop them: they are a symptom of larger forces, they have a right to arise, and they must be allowed to work out the fate of the planet in the open air, under the sky and the regard of the One, without interference."

"But you *are* interfering. Or so it seems to me."

"I am," she said, "but not in the way you think. The forces of which I speak are many, but some of them have been carrying on—the Earth phrase for it is 'a hate-mongering campaign.' They are inflaming Vulcans' prejudices against Earth people, by inflaming their pride, their sense of superiority." Jim looked surprised, and T'Pau said, "Oh, indeed, many of them would say that those are emotions, to be eschewed. And many of them have them, nonetheless. To combat such lies, the only weapon is the truth. Sarek has that truth. And he must tell it in full, no matter what the consequences.''

Jim stood still a moment, and then nodded. "It had been my intention as well," he said, "to tell the truth. Whatever the consequences."

"That itself," T'Pau said, "is more powerful a weapon in your hands than any other. I counsel you, bear it as well as you can." She looked a touch rueful at the martial metaphor. "For again we go to war, though all our philosophy counsels us otherwise. No physical weapons may be raised, but war it is nonetheless." She cocked her head at Jim. "I am relieved by what you say, however. I had thought perhaps you would desire to keep Vulcan in the Federation at any cost."

"I am not sure," Jim said slowly, "that I would want to be in such a Federation, or to have on my head the Vulcan that would be in it, afterward."

T'Pau nodded. "Then we understand one another," she said. Jim put an eyebrow up: he was far from understanding *her,* except in the most roundabout sort of way, and he was resigned to that.

"And what will you do," T'Pau said, "should the vote go for secession?"

Jim gazed at her a moment, then shook his head and turned away. "Leave Vulcan," he said; and it was all he could say. He had been refusing as much as possible to think about those consequences, except in the abstract.

"Enough," T'Pau said from behind him. "It is illogical to suffer consequences before they befall. Do what you must, James, and know that you are doing right. It is all any of us can do, I fear."

The silence grew long. When Jim turned around again, they were gone.

He stood on the balcony until he got his composure back; and then he went back to the party.

T'Khut set, dyeing the sands below with the tinct of alien blood.

VULCAN: THREE

———————— ☆ ————————

Kesh was her name. She had the Eye, but in all other things she was the least of them, and the rest of the clan brought her to remember this often. She swore, quite young, that they would regret this: but more came of her oaths, in the end, than regret.

She was born among the stones around the pool, of a woman who had been called Tekav, but now had no name, being dead. No petty-house had yet housebound Tekav; their mothers were waiting to see if she would bear her child alive, and would thereafter be worth the binding. But the birthing killed her, and not even the Oldest Mother could save her when the womb-mooring tore loose untimely, and the blood burst forth.

They cut her body open to bring out the child, and Kesh took breath and cried out lustily as the stove-heat of the day struck her. This the Oldest thought was good. She lifted the babe and took her straightway out of the shelter of the stones, and held her up to the high sun and shook her until she opened her eyes. The babe screamed, as all newborns did in that ferocious light. But when the Oldest turned her back to the sun and looked narrowly in the babe's eyes, she saw the flicker of reflected sunlight inside the constricted pupil, the shining like a wild beast's eye in the firelight. Then she knew that the child had the Eye.

They raised the cry, then, and gave the babe to another mother who had been nursing and still had a little milk. Some of the young warriors walked away muttering that it was unfair for the mother to have died, when she brought forth children with the Eye: she should have been given to one of them. But the only ones Tekav was fit to be given to now were the sehlats, and that was done. The snarling went on well through the day, until the bones were clean and had been cracked for marrow. Then some-one came from the camp and buried them, to keep the scavengers from being attracted to the place. The clan had enough problems without *cheveh* and such like raiding the place. They had taken newborn babes before, and there was no use losing this last one when it had just caused so much trouble.

The clan knew itself as the clan of the Eye, but this name was secret, especially from the other clans of the great sand: false names were invented to tell any clan their paths crossed. This happened rarely. Too little water there was in the sandy world, too little shelter: it took a great deal of land to support a few people, and once you had found such a place, you did not stray from it by choice. Wanderers were usually suspect—they were usually spies, come from another tribe to find out whether your source of water was better than theirs. The clan of the Eye knew well enough about spies, for many of them had died spying on the accursed Phelsh't, who had the high ground. It was, of course, no particular distinction to die spying on the Phelsh't. Many people of other tribes had done the same.

There was, at least, no need to do it at the moment. The pool had not failed for a long time. It was courtesy to call it a pool; it was actually a small brackish puddle, from which the water had to be sieved to get the worst of the mud out, or the beast fur—for there was no use trying to keep the sehlats out of it. They had to drink, and they did enjoy their roll in the mud—no matter that everyone else had to spend the rest of the day pulling sehlat hairs out of their drink. No one complained too much. The sehlats were protection of a sort, and besides, at least there *was* drink for them to get their hairs in. There were enough other things worth complaining about.

Hunting was one of them. There was never enough food, and no one in the clan of the Eye had a spare bit of flesh on them. Children grew expert from their very young days at grabbing a passing lizard, grubbing up a bit of sweet root (if one managed to escape the sharp eyes of their elders); and nothing went to waste, not the stringiest tuber, not a drop of blood. As they grew older, even the smallest and weakest children sharpened sticks for themselves, wove nets from the dried strings of the *chakh'* plant, and went hunting among the rocks for the unwarier small beasts that crept close to men's dwellings for a bite to eat or a drop to drink. It was only wisdom, for a child that was considered too weak to prosper would not be given anything to eat—the adult members of the clan considered this throwing good food after bad. A child who hunted effectively was given more food, by way of encouragement.

Kesh was one of the good ones. From the time she could toddle, she seemed able to hear movements that the others never did. She began putting things in her mouth to see whether they were good to eat long before she was weaned, and at this the Oldest Mother and some of the other mothers nodded sagely. She made her first twig-spear young, and the lizards shortly learned that their lives had become more difficult than before—or, at least, potentially much shorter. Her ears grew sharper still as time went on and better feeding improved her health. They were sharper than the others' anyway; mutation had set in on two counts—because of the increased solar radiation that Vulcan's atmosphere no longer properly filtered, and the thinner air, less able to carry sound. Kesh's ears were like those of several others of the clan's children, with the larger, slightly pointed, more delicate pinnae that caught soundwaves better than their parents' ears did. The ears were the cause of occasional trouble; Kesh had more than once taken vicious buffets from one or another of the adults, when she caught a lizard or one of the *yie,* the little burrowers, that the adult had been hunting but had heard too late. However, the Oldest Mother scowled when such things happened, and cursed the adult, more likely than not: she knew that the children with these ears would do better than those without, and the clan needed their blood to sire more of the same.

It had been so with the Eye. It had been the Oldest Mother's mother's mother, some lives or so ago, who had first found one of her children staring at the sun, seemingly untroubled by it. At first they had thought that the child was lackwitted, and had now gone blind. But the blindness passed, and the child could walk for hours out in the sands and come back walking, not feeling his way. For many a year people had had to bind skins about their heads, or over their eyes, when they went hunting in the sand; and the *lematyas* tended to make short work of them. Now, looking at this child, the Oldest Mother thought there might be a way to bring such poor makeshifts to an end. She coddled the child as if he were the last in the world, and bound him to one of her outdaughters; and three of the children born before his death had the Eye as well, and two of them were girls.

Then the Oldest Mother became mighty in the clan, and elders and young alike fought for her favor, that she might allow them to be bound with one of the children of the Eye, and take the blood into their own lines. All thought of growing up and having children who could hunt better than all others, who would bring them food when other adults had long lain down to die because there was no more. And the Oldest Mother chose as she willed, and every lightest word of hers was heeded as if the sandstorm would strike if she was displeased.

Now, though—so Kesh thought—the Eye was becoming common: half the tribe had it. And to what purpose? They would not do anything useful with it. Not the kind of use she had in mind. Not that they paid any attention to her in council. "Hunt," they said, "since you are so good at it." And they mocked her— orphaned and unbound as she was, with none but her milkmother to speak for her. If she might be got with child, they said, and pass on the Eye, she might be worth listening to. But Kesh had other things in mind than children.

When she was not hunting—and often, when she was—her eyes turned northward. The clan's present camp was nothing more than a great pile of boulders around a little mucky spring, and Kesh hated the place—the sprawl of bodies huddling for cover, the stink of the sehlat-hides stuck on poles that were the only shade, except for cracks in the rock. Shadows crawled, people fought for place under the shades, pushed out people they disliked into the pitiless sun. Even the water stank. Much better, by Kesh's way of thinking, to go out onto the sand, which at least smelt clean, and feel the fresh hot wind blowing. One could think out there. And one could see for miles: and miles north of them, there was something to see. It rose up all alone, a dark huge shape reared up against the sky: Phelsh't.

She had heard the stories that they told about it, around the fires at night, after the last few scraps of meat had been toasted on sticks and eaten, and the sticks hardened in the ash and given to the smallest children for their spears. Phelsh't, they said, was an image of the Distant One, S'l'heya the Great, chief of mountains. It had been raised up by one of the gods of the sand, and given to a mortal, to whom he bound himself, and then gave a great gift, the gift of a well of water. It was no mere muddy puddle. It was a spring, that rose up from deep in the stone of the mountain, cold clear water, sweet to the taste, without muck or weed; and there was so much of it that it ran down the side of the mountain into the sand, and plants grew there, despite the scorching sun, and grew great—grew almost as tall as a man.

It did not seem fair that one clan should have this great gift, and not another: and all the clans that wandered in that empty waste had at one time or another thought of taking Phelsh't for their own. Some had tried. But the clan that lived there had grown very strong and numerous—how not, with all the water they desired?—and they easily beat off any clan that tried to take their high ground with its sweet water. Finally the Oldest Mother of the clans—and the clan of the Eye was no exception—had declared that there were to be no more attempts on Phelsh't. But Kesh sat on the sand for hours, after having made a kill, and looked north at the dark shape against the burning blue horizon, and dreamed: dreamed of limitless water, and shade, and having as much food as ever she wanted. . . .

"Here," said a voice in her ear. She did not bother turning: she knew the voice, knew the shadow that fell over her. He sat down beside her, offered her something. It was a *yie*, one of the black-furred ones, fat and sweet-looking.

Kesh took the bowl that a hunter always carried, slit the *yie* open with the flake of stone that she carried in her belt, and drained out the blood: then offered it to him. It was a poor mouthful, but she smiled as she handed Tes the bowl, and he smiled as he took it from her and bowed from the waist until his hair brushed the sand, as he would have done for the Oldest Mother. Then, quickly, he drank. There was no use letting the gift clot up.

Halfway down his drink, he stopped and offered her the bowl again. "Are you mad?" she said. "Drink it." But she was warmed, as she always was warmed by Tes; as she had been since they became friends while toddling on the rocks.

"There's plenty of juice left in this one, anyway," she said, and set to work on the *yie*. Quite soon there was nothing left of it but the bones, and between the two of them they disposed of the marrow in those as well, and buried them.

"Why did you come away in the heat?" she said. "There's a hunt tonight: aren't you going to sleep?"

"When was the last time I caught anything in a great hunt?" he said, stretching his legs out in front of him. "With all of them scrambling about and making more noise than a sehlat in heat, all these little grunts and hoots and prayers? It's a wonder they catch anything, and as for me, I do better on my own."

She laughed a little as she scrubbed her hands in the sand. Tes was right enough about the noise and fuss when the clan went on a great hunt; all the bustle of preparation, tying-up of clothes, making of small sacrifices to the gods that cared for the hunt, prayers to the spirit of the *lematya* or the *tshin;* and then the crowd of them slipping out into the dark, trying to be quiet, failing. Somehow the game always managed to find the hunting party, rather than the other way around. It was as if a great group of people had something about them that a *lematya* could sense. On days as hot as today, Kesh rather thought it was the smell. But anyway, either they would kill the prey, or it would kill some of them: sometimes it killed some of them and then got away, which sent the survivors home in a foul mood, for the Oldest Mother had a dim view of such goings-on, and her tongue would strip the hide off you as she demanded to know why she cared for the clan's blood so, when fools like you threw it away? Kesh had heard those reprimands and had thanked whichever god was hers that she had never had one directed at her in her young life.

"You've done well today," Tes said, glancing back at the lump in the sand near where Kesh sat. She had killed early, a tshin, a fairly big one—almost half her size; the Oldest Mother would be pleased when she came back, for tshin had a lot of blood in them, and the meat kept well when dried. "How did you manage to get close to it without it knowing you were there?"

"It's a secret," she said.

He made the sign to turn away foolery, and Kesh smiled. "Ah, come on, tell me. I can use the help."

She wrinkled her brow for a moment, thinking. "It's something about the sand," she said. "If you hunt them in the morning, they always know: but when the sun is high and the day is hot, they get confused—they turn around and around on the sand as if they can't find you. If you keep still in some rocks, and then wait till they're confused—" She shrugged. "It seems to work. At least, no *tshin* has killed me yet."

"Try not to let them kill you," Tes said.

She smiled at him. He was always saying things like that. He turned his face away.

"How did you know where I was today?" Kesh said.

He tilted his head a little. "You're always around here somewhere," he said. "Away from the clan—and somewhere where you can see *that*." He pointed at the tall dark shape reaching up against the edge of the sky.

She nodded. "Tes," she said slowly, "they're fools."

"Yes, but why?"

"We should take that. It should be ours. Or ours as *well* as theirs. Do you know how many people all that water could support?"

Tes shrugged. "The Oldest Mother forbade it."

"And it should just stop there?"

"What else can be done? It's forbidden. Go against the clan and you're cast out . . . and you die. Anyway," he said, trying to be reasonable, "there aren't enough of us to take Phelsh't from them."

"Someday," Kesh said, "there might be. . . ."

"It'll still be forbidden."

"There might be a new Oldest Mother."

He stared at her. "That would take years and years! And you would have to—"

She was silent.

"But you couldn't," Tes said, sounding sorrowful, and yet relieved. "None of her sons would bind with you."

"Not that I would want them," Kesh said scornfully. "Heavy-footed, empty-bellied, blind-eyed—" She stopped.

"*I* would bind with you," he said.

Kesh stared at him.

"I know how, now," he said. "I saw someone do the Touch. I heard what they said. It was easy."

Kesh held very still, then began to shake her head. "But there has to be something else—" She scrambled to her feet, looked around her as if looking for a place to flee to, then dropped to her knees beside her kill and began digging it out of the protecting sand. A few moments later she looked up again. Tes had not moved, other than to look over his shoulder at her.

"I have that," he said. "Do you?"

She breathed out, and in, and the pain hit her in the side so that she sat down hard. "Oh yes," she said. "Yes." And then she set to digging her kill out again, and wept hard, making sure to lick in the tears as they fell.

That was all they said about it. Years later, Kesh would remember the sight of Tes turning the bowl around and around in his hands as she dug: and the way he smiled. Years later it would seem that she had always known it was going to happen: that as little as a few hours later, that night around the fire, it would seem that he had been her bonded forever, since first they toddled in the rocks, and fell down, and bled on one another.

There was some comment when Kesh did not go on the great hunt that night: but the Oldest Mother looked at her and said that she had brought in her *tshin* that day, the biggest that had been seen for some time, and what other hunter of the clan could say the same? Kesh might have a night's rest if she pleased, and two bowls of blood from the kill, and first and last drink of the pool. The hunters went off grumbling, too angry to see the look with which the Oldest Mother favored Kesh, or her glance at Tes.

T'Khut rode high, the brightness shaped like a tilted-down

bowl, the darkness glittering with her fires. They went away into the sands, far from where the hunters were, and found a little place of stones, where there was some shelter, and a feeling of privacy. They were both of an age for the Rapture, and though it had not yet fallen on them, their bodies were ready. They fumbled out of their ragged belts and skins, laid them carefully aside, and looked on one another.

"Are you sure you know how to do this?" Kesh said, shaking a little. It was not the coolness.

"Yes," Tes said. "I think so." Very slowly, trembling too, he reached out and touched her face, and said the words. They would change many times in the thousands of years to follow, but the meaning always remained the same. *My mind to your mind: my thoughts to your thoughts: never touching, and always touched: apart, yet one—*

One they became: filled, both of them, with one another, as the bowl of the moon above was filled with light, always outpouring, always full; touching everywhere, till the cries broke out in delight; pierced, enclosing, the spear, the prey, willingly caught, willingly pierced, willingly sheathed. The last cry that rose up, the cry that slew them both, was one. And then silence.

Much later they got up, slipped into their clothes and gear again, and went back to the camp. The hunters never noticed their absence: they were much too busy hanging their heads before the Oldest Mother for losing Vach to the *lematya*. And few noticed in the days that followed that there seemed to be an invisible connection between Kesh and Tes, one rarely out of sight of the other. They were both of little importance, and so they had almost a sun's round of joy together.

And then the Dry came.

It seemed very sudden to some of the people of the Eye, but Kesh had been watching the pool for some time, and it seemed to her much muddier than usual, as if someone were stealing drink from it—which no one would dare: there was never enough to have all that you wanted, and stealing the water was punishable by beating or death. And the sehlats were not rolling in it any worse than usual. In fact, it was rather strange, but one by one the sehlats went missing, along with some of the smaller lizards.

There was a lot less easy food around the camp than there had used to be. Children died, and there were complaints that they were just not as strong as they had been in the old days.

To Tes, Kesh said, "We are going to have to move."

They were sitting up on an outcropping, flaking fresh stone for spearheads. He paused—he was knapping a flint—and looked down at the flat little puddle. "Yes," he said. "I think so."

And he was very quiet. Kesh went back to the piece of stone she was chipping, and said, "It will do the clan some good, I suppose. Shake out some of the useless ones, the ones who eat and don't hunt."

"Maybe." Tes looked around him. "But all the same, this is a bad time for it. The Winds are soon."

She had to agree. Vulcan's seasons were slight, but there were some weather patterns that tended to recur regularly, due to the influence of sunspots; and one of them was the Winds, a storm pattern even drier than usual that turned the great sands into a hell for weeks at a time. One became used to breathing through hides, and if you went out to hunt, the sand blasted you raw. And game was hard to find, for it fled when the Winds started. It was a time of grit and thirst and suffering even when you had a source of water at hand. The thought of traveling during it was highly unpleasant . . . but not as unpleasant as staying in one place and dying.

"When will the Oldest Mother make the choice, do you think?" Kesh said.

Tes shrugged. "I don't know her mind. But I don't think we'll have to wait long."

They did not. T'Khut was waxing when they spoke on top of the flint ridge. In her wane, the Oldest Mother sent the hunters out and told them not to come back until they had caught no less than three *tshin,* and if they ran across some of the wild sehlat, they were to bring those back too. There was muttering, but disobeying the Oldest Mother was unwise: the hunters filled their stomach-bag skins with as much water as they could coax out of the thickening pool, and went. Kesh went with them, not willingly; she wanted Tes with her, but the Oldest Mother kept him by her with another of the clan who along with Tes was the best at spearheads. For some reason she wanted a great many of them, enough to arm the whole tribe twice. There was much muttering about this as well, but no disobedience. Kesh looked reluctantly over her shoulder, trailing after the hunting party as they headed away from the camp; she gazed at the flint ridge, where a small figure sat bent, then paused to raise a hand to her.

Always touching, said the voice inside her. *Don't worry, my love.*

Kesh tried to put her concern behind her. She acquitted herself well on the hunt: the first *tshin* was hers, and the second: another hunter killed the third, and there was a fourth that took Kesh's spear through the flank and loped away at speed, so they had to chase it across the sand for hours until it dropped. One of the hunters died in that chase, of a burst heart, and the others buried him where he fell and put the beast's head in his grave, as revenge on its spirit. Then home they went, in very mixed mood, fearing the Oldest Mother's tongue but glad about all the food. No one minded carrying such a weight of meat back: their minds were all on the feat ahead of them.

So there was anger (though muted) when they brought their kills in, and the Oldest Mother ordered that all the meat, *all* of it, was to be cut thin and dried on the rocks, for keeping. The decision was unpopular—dried meat did not compare to sweet fresh meat with blood in it, or even better, meat that had been roasted—but there was nothing to be done, especially when the Oldest Mother then announced to them, "We are leaving soon."

There was consternation at that, far worse than over the meat, and argument, first polite, then heated: but her mind was set, and they dared not defy her. "What," she said. 'Will you lie here and roast yourselves, in your laziness, and dry out like the meat on the stones? We must have water, and there is shortly going to be none here. We will make for the little pool across the sands, where we went nineteen sun-rounds ago when the pool before that one dried. The little pool is a good one, and when we find our way to it we will not have to move again till after the Winds are done. Cease your complaining, and do as I bid you!"

They did. Five days later there were no further traces of resistance, for the pool had almost dried, and everyone was praising the Mother's wisdom for filling and hiding away many bags of water against the evil hour. Another day would see them set out on their journey.

"They are a docile lot, suddenly," Kesh said to Tes, as they sat scraping out two of the *tshin*'s stomachs to make a last pair of waterbags.

"This will need a lot more scraping," said Tes. And inwardly, *Yes,* he said down the bond between them. *They are afraid. And so am I.*

She looked at him in surprise, then turned back to her scraping. *Of what?*

How do we know we are ever going to find the other pool? he said. *How do we know that some other clan is not there already, armed, and waiting for us?*

She shrugged. *Even if they are, we cannot stay here.*

Tes looked down at the stomach. "This will need more curing, too," he said. "Someone is going to have to carry it on a pole while we walk, so the sun can get at it."

"Probably you," said Kesh. *Beloved—there is something else you are afraid of. . . .*

Tes looked up at the flint ridge and sighed. *It's stupid.*

Tell me.

He shook his head. *I am bound to these stones,* he said. *I was told so, in a dream. I think if we leave them, I will die.*

Kesh straightened up and looked at him. If true, this was a serious business. *When did you have this dream?*

Long ago. Before we were bound.

Kesh scoffed, then, relieved. *A child's dream. Children do not dream true.*

T'Khut was high, he said. *She saw. It was a true dream.*

Kesh began to feel desperate, for the higher T'Khut rode, the more she saw: she was the Eye, and it was unwise for one of the Clan of the Eye to scoff at her. *Perhaps it was only true then,* she said. *You are strong now, one of the strongest of us.* She leaned over and pinched one of his arm muscles, trying to be cheerful. *There is no reason for you to die.*

I know, he said, and fell silent again.

They were uneasy with one another until it came time for the clan to go: and then Tes seemed to relax a little, as if he had cast his worry away. The actual going took little time to organize:

once the meat was all dry, it was parceled out among the clan, a bit for everyone to carry, even the smallest child; and then everyone simply got up and left. All the clothes they had were what they wore—someone might keep a bright bit of stone for a plaything, or a binding of woven leather for an ornament, but that was all they had, except for food, and all of that they took with them. And everyone had a spear: Tes had been worked hard, the last few days, finding enough of the dead ironwood that grew in long straight tubes in the desert, and socketing the spears. The Oldest Mother stepped out in front of them and led the way into the sands. There were many backward looks, but Kesh particularly noticed that Tes did not look back once.

They went on for a day and a night that way, not stopping. They followed no path that anyone could see, but the Oldest Mother led them a straight run across the sand, south and west. Off to the left, far away, Phelsh't could be seen: or its head could. Its feet were hidden in a haze like blown dust.

The first place they stopped was nothing but sand, and the clansfolk threw themselves down on it gladly, and ate and drank: but the Oldest Mother seemed to be watching every sip of water, and every stomach-bag, and it quickly took some of the cheer out of the drinking, and slowed some people down. When she ordered them to get up and walk again, there were murmurs.

"Up, fools," she said. "The Winds are coming! Can you not see?" And she pointed at Phelsh't, whose base was hidden thicker than ever by the dust.

Then they realized what was happening, and people scrambled to their feet again, and slung bags over their shoulders, and hastened as she bade them. It did not help, of course. The wind had wings instead of feet and overtook them a day later, falling upon them with a scream like a thousand *lematyas*. The darkness descended in broad day, and the clan of the Eye staggered blind, for even the Eye could not help them now.

It went on for a hand of days and never stopped, that screaming, the blast of sand and dust against the body: to stop was almost impossible—the wind blew one along, urged you from behind, dispassionately cruel—and to keep going was endless, weary torment. The Oldest Mother told the clansmen to tie themselves to one another in a long line, with thongs of gut: and

this they did, and stumbled all in a long line through the screaming sand, not knowing where they went, though the Oldest
Mother led them straight as if the sky were clear and the stars
bright to show her the way. All sense of direction was lost: the
world was reduced to a dun-colored wall of stinging sand. Kesh
put out her hand often to feel for Tes behind her, and always his
touch was there, and always he would say to her, *Always touching, beloved.* . . . His thought sounded cheerful. She took
reassurance from it.

And then the last day came, the day of the worst wind. The
Oldest Mother cried that this was good, that it meant that the
wind was about to break: and the others did their best to believe
her. Tes did, and was delighted. He was singing, or shouting a
song against the wind, when the greatest gust came, that blew
half the clan off their feet, and snapped the gut, and rolled them
all about like dry weed.

"Tes!" Kesh screamed, but the wind swallowed her scream
as it tumbled her over and over too. There was nothing to see, no
way to tell where Tes was.

Always touching, loved— The sound of the thought was
rough, a little surprised, as might have been expected if the
sender was being rolled over and over on hard sand. *It's all
right*—

Relieved, she huddled into herself to make it harder for the
wind to blow her. Eventually she managed to find some purchase
by digging into the sand. Grimly she hung on. *Tes*—

We touch, my love. I'm all right—

She hung on. Gradually, so gradually, the wind began to
decline. It took it hours. The sky grew dark, with night this time,
and they could actually see it. The night progressed, and the
wind quieted. *Tes*—she said inside, for the thousandth time in
that weary while.

Don't worry. . . . The thousandth response sounded faint
and tired. Kesh sighed: she could understand why. She chafed
for morning to come again, and light, so that she could find out
where Tes had got to.

Around dawn, the wind gave a final shriek, faded to a sigh,
and then to nothing. The silence was incredible. Kesh stood up

from a few minutes' sleep—she could not hold it off any longer—and looked around her.

There was no sight of Tes. There was nothing but blank sand, as far as the eye could see: and several dunes, heaped high.

Tes!!

No reply came back. The bond was broken.

Kesh ran like a mad thing over the sand, calling, crying his name, digging at the sand. It was hopeless. The Oldest Mother called to her: Kesh would not come. The Mother sent other hunters after Kesh and had one of them strike her down, to keep her quiet for a while. When she sat up at last, rubbing her sore head and moaning, the Mother was sitting on the sand beside her.

"He is gone," she said. "Five others are gone as well. The sand has buried them. We all mourn with you."

Kesh sat mute.

"We must go on after we rest awhile," said the Mother. As she got heavily up to go away, she looked at Kesh with pity. It was not what Kesh wanted. The only thing she wanted, she could not have: could never have again.

She wept bitterly, and did not bother to lick the tears, and others were shocked by the waste.

They found the pool which the Mother had sought, and it was untenanted, and the water in it was good; much better than that in the old pool. The clan decided that this was a place where they should stay, at least for as long as this pool lasted. It was wide and open, and there were more rocks with which to make shelters. The clan was well content.

All but one.

Most now thought Kesh was mad. It happened sometimes, that one who was bonded went mad at the spouse's death. Kesh hunted still, but now she hunted alone, always: no one else cared to be about her when she had a spear in her hand—not with that odd cold look in her eyes. It came and went—no one understood why. It came more often when she had been looking at the emptiness outside the camp, and it came often indeed under T'Khut, when she was at the half, pouring out her light on the ground. And it was strong in her eyes the night she stood up at the fire, after the eating was done, and said to the Oldest Mother, "We must have Phelsh't."

The clan stirred and murmured at such rudeness. It sounded like a direct challenge. One did not suggest courses of action to the Oldest Mother, as a rule, unless one was asked to. But the Mother simply sat back against the stone that was her seat, near the fire, and said, "Why?"

"Water," said Kesh.

"We have water."

"But not like that," Kesh said. "If we had such a well as Phelsh't has, we would never have to move camp again. We would never need to go out in the Wind. And no more of us need die."

"Many of us would die," said the Mother, "if we tried to take Phelsh't. And if we did by the grace of some mad god manage to take it, more of us would die when other clans came hunting us. We will stay where we are."

"We need Phelsh't," Kesh said, and walked away.

The clan buzzed with gossip of Kesh's mad obstinancy and wondered that the Mother did not have her beaten. People started to watch her, now, and saw how she would look, night and morning, toward the shape of Phelsh't on the horizon, for it was visible from the new camp: and the hatred in her eyes was terrible to see. A double handful of days later, she came down to the fire from the stones above the camp, and she said, "We need Phelsh't."

"We will stay here, Kesh," said the Mother. "You know my reasons."

So it went for a long time: at certain times of the moon, Kesh would come to the fire and demand Phelsh't, and the Mother would turn her away. Her madness was deemed harmless, but folks' opinion of it increased when the Rapture came upon her and she took *none* of them, not one of the men, though many had sought her in their own times.

A sunround went by: two. And in the middle of the second sunround, the Mother went to sleep one morning and did not awaken again. There was wailing as they buried her: and at the burying, even Kesh wailed with the rest. But when she was done, she stood looking at Phelsh't far away, and a great unease came over the clansmen nearest, and they hurriedly left her alone.

There was a new Oldest Mother, but she was not as strong as the other, not as wise. It took her time to learn how to be mother to more than her own children. And while she was learning, Kesh spoke to the younger hunters, and the warriors who respected her spear: and what she whispered in their ears made them begin to finger their weapons. Kesh did not hurry: she made sure of the young ones. And then she moved.

The new Oldest Mother had been so for two months when Kesh came down to the fire, from the rocks, after the eating, and said, "We must have Phelsh't."

"We do not need it," the new Mother said: "we stay here." But she was merely repeating what the old Mother had said, not from her own conviction or strength, but because that reply had always worked before.

Kesh smiled, and it was a horrible look. "We could have Phelsh't," she said. "Phelsh't of the sweet water, and you prefer this mucky sandpit, this hole in the ground? We could have it easily. I can tell you how."

"No," said the Mother, but someone in the circle said, "Yes. Tell us." It was Sakht, who was another hunter, and who desired Kesh; she had refused him in her Rapture.

Kesh looked at him with scorn: she knew his motives. But she smiled and said, "Listen. Are we not the clan of the Eye? We see in the day, when few can: we move easily over the sand in the sun, those of us who have it. And we are many. What other clan dares fight when the sun is high? They must wait for the dark. But not we. Our spears strike home and do not miss, even when others are blinded."

There was a murmur of approval at this. The Oldest Mother sat looking faintly shocked. Kesh said, "This is my plan. Let a group of us arm ourselves and take good store of food and water, and go to Phelsh't and wait for day to be well risen: and then let us take it, and kill the hunters and warriors, and take their children for our own, those that do not resist. They will not be able to fight us by day, and when we are done we will have the sweet water, and the clan that held Phelsh't will be our slaves."

The reaction was compounded of shock and delight, but the

Mother cried, "No! The Eye is secret! It must remain so! If we did such a thing, the other clans would know that we had the Eye, and they would raid us for women and children to bring the blood into their lines as well! Soon they too would have the Eye, and our advantage would be gone!"

The Mother's anger and fright had a curious effect on the hunters: it made them side with Kesh, who though she might be mad, was still mad in a way they had long been familiar with. They murmured against the Mother, and Kesh said sweetly, "What use is an advantage we do not use? What use is the Eye except to win us a great place among clans? We eat better than other tribes, but what use is great plenty of food without water? Let us have the water, and more. Let us use the Eye for something besides seeing. Do we desire favors of other clans? Then let us offer them this great gift—that they may sire children of the Eye on our women, in return for food, or slaves, or what we think fit. We shall grow greater, not less, and rule all the clans of the sand!"

"No!" the Mother cried, but her voice was lost this time in the screaming and shouting, the argument, the sound of fear and desire. The argument sprang up again and again, many a night, around the fire. The Mother contested against it, but feebly, for over against her, on the other side of the fire, Kesh sat every night, saying nothing, smiling, and turned a spearhead over and over in her hands.

And finally the decision was made: the first in the history of the clan to be made without the active consent of the Mother. She let the warriors and the hunters go, at last, keeping enough behind to protect the rest of the clan; and she let them go with relief, for Kesh was at their head, and the Mother was glad to be rid of that terrible smiling regard. She felt sure Kesh would be dead in short order. Indeed, she had told two of the warriors to see to it.

They saw to nothing. They bled their lives out green on the sand as soon as Kesh judged they were far enough out of sight of the camp, for she had heard of the Mother's whispering while doing her own. And she and the warriors and hunters buried the bodies and shouldered their loads of food and water and headed off across the sand toward the upward-pointing finger of Phelsh't, from which had come the wind that had killed Tes. And as they walked, Kesh thought of the reckoning that would now be required of that mountain, and the smile never left her face.

It was a slaughter. The clan of Phelsh't lived like any other clan, out in the open, tented over with skins to protect them from the sun. That they lived on the knees of the mountain was only a slight complication. In the heat of the day, when it was well along, silently the hunters and warriors climbed the stones and looked down on the sleeping clan: and were astonished. They were few—they were barely more in number than the clan of the Eye.

Kesh looked down on this, and her heart was full of bitter thoughts, for if they had come this way in the Wind and taken this place, Tes might still be alive. She hefted her spear, and pointed down at the camp. It was the signal.

The closest hunters knocked the poles down, taking the shading skins with them. The slaughter thus began in confusion—bodies rolling under collapsed hides, voices raised to shout in surprise—and then turned to terror as the hunters of the Eye leapt down and wielded their spears to terrible purpose. Surprise did much of the work: the sun did the rest, beating down from a frightfully clear sky, making eyes not shielded from it wince and water, making the Phelsh't hunters stagger helplessly. The stones ran green, and more frightening to the Phelsh't people than the slaughter, almost, was the sound of a woman laughing, and laughing, and laughing, through the cries and the blood.

Three-quarters of the Phelsh't died, but not their Oldest Mother. Her Kesh took aside, and laid her sharp flake of knife-stone against her throat and let her see her people die—let her see the hunters bind the women and the children. And to her Kesh said, "Your clan is mine now. If you resist us, I will kill you all. But if you accept us, we will teach you our art by which we see in the day; your clan will become great as ours is great. And in return for this favor, you will serve us: and we will live among you and share your water: and we will be as brothers and sisters to you."

And Kesh smiled.

The Oldest Mother agreed to all she said. Kesh left her, then, and went up the mountainside, past the place where the ironwood grew in wild abundance, and the trees grew as tall as a man: but she had no eye for them. She climbed up among the rocks to the place where the cleft in the stone was deep, and the water ran down. And there she found it, the cold water, the sweet water, welling up in a hollow as deep as she was tall, as wide as her arms could span; spilling over, spilling out like light, running down the stone, whispering, singing softly as it ran. She reached down and plunged her face in, plunged in the whole upper half of her body, stood up cold and wet all over, shaking the wet hair out of her eyes. She went down so to her people, and none of them could tell, with the water running down her face, how much of it was tears.

They took Phelsh't for their own, did the clan of the Eye; they took the other Oldest Mother to be second Oldest to their own, but Kesh spoke for both for many years. Tribe after tribe heard of their gift, or of the well, and came to try to steal one or the other from them: but those that came were driven off with a ferocity they could hardly understand, or were taken captive and offered the same bargain that the Phelsh't had been offered. The Eye slowly began to spread itself through the Vulcan gene pool, and the clan made it plain that other gifts were welcome too: the long sight, the ability to dream true, the touch on the shoulder that sends a foe asleep, or kills—they traded the Eye for these and grew great. The effects of this amateur eugenics program were many, down the years, and sometimes strange. It became traditional for clans to marry out their sons and daughters in exchange for children of another clan who possessed some desirable trait. Many thousands of years later, a Starfleet officer's career was saved by the Eye; a little thing, in a long history of careful or savage changes that shifted the nature of the Vulcan species.

But Kesh would have cared nothing for it all. Her they feared and respected for many years, never daring to question her ways. She would go off on long journeys and come back pale and haggard from weeks in the sand, and none dared ask her where she had been. When they finally found her in the well, head first, drowned, they took her as far out in the sand as they could and buried her there; and then many of the clan of the Eye felt they had peace for the first time in many years. And indeed they were better off than they had ever been—there was no denying that.

But when T'Khut rode high, and her copper face gazed at itself in the well, some clansmen claimed they heard weeping, or terrible laughter. They were laughed at by others, of course. But nevertheless, at such times, the clan went thirsty till the moon went down. . . .

ENTERPRISE:
FOUR

———————— ☆ ————————

Jim sat in his cabin on the *Enterprise* the next morning, gazing at the small data screen in annoyance.

FROM: Bugs
DATE: 7611.01
SUBJECT: Our Friends in the Federation

From an editorial published on one of the major Vulcan information services:

. . . this bloody sword hanging in our skies, this machine of war, should be ordered away immediately by our government. Yet no action is taken. Creatures who solve their problems with bloodshed rather than reason now orbit our planet without hindrance. Why is it that, though they declare their missions to be peaceful, their ships nonetheless are equipped with weapons that could crack a planet open? Can they not perceive even this most massive evidence of illogic? There can be nothing but disaster in dealing with such creatures as if they were civilized. Indeed, we have been trying to civilize them for almost two hundred years, but the result of our efforts is apparent in the skies over ta'Valsh and Seleya. . . .

Hmm. Yellow journalism? Or green?

Jim fumed quietly. On one hand he was very glad to have seen the message—it certainly confirmed what T'Pau had been saying—but on the other hand, he wanted more and more to know who Bugs was.

Not that he could find out, of course. Here was one of the places where the crew's privacy had to be respected utterly: otherwise the whole system of the BBS lost its value. Speech here, at least, had to be free.

And pretty free it is, Jim thought, annoyed. He kept paging through the messages. There were many agreeing with Bugs, annoyed at being considered a "bloody sword." There were some who refused to take the quote seriously at all, and others who suspected it had been taken out of context, and one who pointed out that Bugs was probably in violation of copyright by transcribing the message from the Vulcan information service without obtaining permission. But the last reply to the message brought Jim up short:

FROM: Llarian
DATE: 7611.72
SUBJECT: Re: Our Friends in the Federation

A skillful leader does not use force.
A skillful fighter does not feel anger.
A skillful master does not engage the opponent.
A skillful employer remains low.

Even four thousand years ago they knew it:
don't believe everything you read.

How about that, Jim thought, and gazed at the screen with interest.

Llarian. Now who would that be? And what's the reference? It sounds familiar somehow. Jim chewed absently on the one knuckle of his folded hands. *But he or she or it has a point. 'A skillful employer remains low.' Who in Vulcan has enough power and influence to get something like that into the information services?*

He started to shut the screen down, then paused for a moment and reached out to touch the communicator toggle on his desk. "Bridge. Communications."

"Communications, Uhura," came her cheerful voice. *"Good morning, Captain!"*

Jim rubbed his head ruefully. He still had a touch of headache from the party last night: the high gravity seemed to have that effect on him. "More or less, Nyota," he said. "Screen dump coming in to your station. Have the computer run a check on it. I want to know which Vulcan news service it came from, the name of the author, the date, any other information you find pertinent."

"Aye aye, Captain. Ready."

Jim touched the key to instruct the desk screen to dump its contents to the Communications board. "Got it?"

"It's in. Will advise, Captain."

"Good. Kirk out."

He stood up, stretched, rubbed his head again. His knees still ached, too. *I could always have Environmental get me a grav neutralizer,* he thought . . . then rejected the thought immediately. Vulcans probably thought Earth people were weak and delicate enough as it was: why help the image along by showing up in a neutralizer? He would take their gravity with the best of them, and be damned to the whole lot of them.

Still, his head hurt. He reached down to the communicator toggle on his desk. "Sickbay."

"Sickbay," said a cheerful voice. *"Burke here."*

It was Lia Burke, McCoy's head nurse since Chapel had started working full-time on her doctorate. "Lia," Jim said, "where's the Doctor?"

"He's gone downplanet already, Captain. Said he was looking for something."

That made Jim blink: McCoy was not exactly an early riser by preference. "Did he say what?"

"He said if you called and asked, I was to tell you he was going to buy a gross of paperweights with snowflakes inside them. Sir." Lia sounded mildly bemused.

She's not alone, Jim thought. "All right. Listen, I need something for my head."

"High-grav syndrome," she said immediately. *"I can prescribe you a little something for that. Come on down."*

Jim put an eyebrow up. "Nurses can prescribe?"

There was a brief silence on the other end, and then a laugh. *"Are you living in the twentieth century? Sir. Of course we can."* There was a brief, wry pause. *"We can count, too."*

"Noted," Jim said. "I'll be right down."

When he got to sickbay, Lia was scribbling something with a lightpen on a computer pad. She was a little curly-haired woman, very slender, almost always smiling; it took something particularly grave to remove that smile. "Captain," she said, putting down the pad and picking up a hypospray. "Here you go."

"Am I allowed to ask you what it is?"

"Would you ask Dr. McCoy?" she said.

Jim considered. "Probably not."

She gave him a cheerful shame-on-you! sort of look. "Well, then. It's just hemocorticovilidine; it thins your blood out a little."

"Thins it out? When I'm going to Vulcan? Get away from me with that thing."

"Too late," she said, and it was: the spray hissed against his arm. "It simply changes the density of your blood plasma slightly, on demand from the air pressure on the outside, or lack of it. The problem on these high-grav planets is similar to high-altitude syndrome some ways." She put the hypo away. "But you should drink extra water while you're down there."

"Lieutenant," Jim said patiently, "there's a problem with drinking extra water on a heavy-gravity planet. . . ."

She raised her eyebrows at him. "Tell me about it. But unless you want your head to ache, you'd better do it."

"All right," he said, and thanked her, and headed back to his cabin. *Well, I should head down to Vulcan and stir around a little, see some people and things. Then go visit with Sarek and Amanda. They've only invited me to their house about ten times.*

. . . But paperweights? What's Bones up to?

Leonard Edward McCoy was a researcher at heart. The tendency had almost kept him out of active practice, when he first got his M.D.: the year of pure research he had done at Cornell had come close to spoiling him. But when it came down to the crunch, he liked people better than papers and test tubes and lectures: and he had dived into practice and never looked back.

But every now and then a nice juicy piece of research came his way, and when it did, by God he got his teeth into it and didn't let go until he was satisfied with the answers. And a nice one had fallen right in his lap yesterday. It had that perfect feeling about it, the kind of feeling he had when as a kid he would be out in the north forty and find a big flat rock that he *knew* had lots of bugs under it.

It was Shath that did it to him. Not that the son wasn't just the most irritating thing he had come across in a long time: but the man's body language was wrong, completely wrong. On seeing himself and Kirk, the guy had actually had to leave the room for many minutes to regain his composure. It would have been unusual in a human: it was positively shocking in a Vulcan. And the reaction was not to him, McCoy felt certain, but to Kirk.

He had considered going up to the consulate and demanding to see the man again, fabricating some story about a change in schedule or something, to talk to him a bit longer and make sure of that aversion reaction, or the lack of it. But then Bones considered that it would probably be wasted effort: likely enough Shath would be able to cover up the effect this time. No, McCoy would get his information in other ways.

He spent a little time in his cabin that morning calling up detailed maps of shi'Kahr, the little city nearest the Science Academy, and found what he wanted—the electronic equivalent of the public library. He could have gotten into it from the ship, via downlink from the main computers, but he had no desire to attract quite that much attention. Discreet inquiry was what he wanted, not an electronic snatch-and-run mission that might leave the librarians feeling annoyed.

He then indulged himself in a little bit of subterfuge and went rummaging in the packages he had brought home from his shopping trip yesterday. *A word or two in Spock's ear was a good idea,* he thought, as he took out the somber tunic and breeches and boots he had picked up. They were all in a soft tan beige color, very inconspicuous, and Spock had told him that the cut was such as a student or scientist might wear for either work or relaxation. McCoy slipped the clothes on, tapped one of his closet doors into reflectivity, and turned from side to side to admire himself. He really did look rather good: the slight cape hanging from the shoulders somehow made him look about ten pounds lighter, which he didn't mind at all. And this suit of clothes would definitely attract less attention than a Starfleet uniform. Most people knew his face best in conjunction with his uniform anyway. But in this getup he was just one more Terran on Vulcan, out for a day's research—there were quite a few Earth people working at the Science Academy.

He stopped in to check sickbay, found everything well, and then beamed down to the streets of shi'Kahr. It was just past dawn there, and the town was getting lovely: the very early hours, before things got too hot even for the Vulcans' liking, were when much business and marketing were done. Depending on the nature of one s work, one might start at dawn, work through till noonish, break till three for a siesta, and then start up again and not leave work till well after dark. *Or,* he thought as he strolled through the streets, *being Vulcans, they might just work for four days without stopping, and then take a day off, and then—back to it. The stamina of these people! You have to admire it—and wish you could have some yourself. . . .*

The town reminded him, in some ways, of some university towns he had been to in upstate New York: but there was also a strange resemblance to the roofed arcades of Berne in Switzerland—thick stone walls with wide arches cut in them, sheltering the windows and doorways of shops and houses. In places the arcades were two-tiered, and most of them were of a handsome golden stone with a wide grainy texture: McCoy suspected it was a very effective insulator. The pathways under the arcades were wide, and there was room to stroll comfortably, sheltered from the sun and wind, and look out through the arches at the little parks and plazas one passed. The Vulcans seemed to be great ones for tiny parks, each one always with its fountain; and never the same kind twice. Little whispering waterfalls, fine misty sprays, strange carved beasts with water pouring out of them, once even an ancient millstone with water bubbling up out of the hole in the middle, he saw them all on his way to the library.

This turned out to be a noble building of the same golden stone as most of the rest of the town, but this one had a portico borne up on tall smooth pillars, all of which had the slightest swelling at their centers. The effect was actually to make them look straighter than if they had been built perfectly straight. The trick was one with which McCoy was familiar from ancient Greek architecture, and he smiled at the familiarity as he passed into the shade of the portico and into the library.

Inside everything was utterly modern—computer carrels and voice accesses were everywhere. The floor looked like the same golden stone as the walls, but McCoy was fascinated to find that it appeared to have been treated with something that made it spongy-soft: sound fell dead in it. He nodded a greeting to the librarian at the front desk and headed on past him toward the carrels.

He did not trust his typing in Vulcan. He stopped by one of the keyboard carrels and peered at the keying area: it had more keys and levers and switches than he wanted to see, so he passed on to a voice-activated carrel and sat down. Softly he cleared his throat, praying that his accent wouldn't be too outrageous for the machine to understand.

"General query," he said in Vulcan.

"Acknowledged," said the machine. Bones winced. Its accent was the Vulcan equivalent of BBC Standard Received: pure, cultured, and somewhat intimidating.

"Public events," McCoy said. "Cross-index to registry. *Koon-ut-kalifi*. Familial name uncertain. One participant for cross-index: Spock cha'Sarek. Go."

The machine thought about this for a second, then brought up a picture of the Place of Marriage and Challenge: Spock, McCoy, and Kirk in the background, T'Pau on her litter, and an assortment of spear carriers and extras with bell-banners and various implements of destruction. McCoy shivered at the sight of the place, and was surprised at his own reaction. *What a horrendous day that was . . . and what a naughty thing I did*. He smiled a little. *And worth it*. "Confirmed," McCoy said. "Display list of participants."

Obediently it did so. And there it was: Shath cha'Stelen hei-Nekhlavah, age 43 standard years. *How about that*, McCoy thought: *I hit his age right on. Maybe Spock is teaching me something after all.* "Query," he said. "General information, Shath cha'Stelen."

Another page of information came up. Most of it was not very interesting: information about education, occupation, a commcode. *Not that I'd want to call him up and invite him on a night out: no indeed.* But at the bottom was a little list of Affiliated Organizations. McCoy had the carrel's printer note them all down, and then he began to go through the files and pull down some of the organizations' most recent publications. The names were mostly very innocent: the Institute for Interworld Studies, the Study Group on Nonvulcanoid Species, names like that. But what McCoy noticed, as he began reading their newsletters and papers, was that none of the organizations Shath belonged to liked humans very much. One of them was of the condescending let-them-swing-in-their-trees sort: the others were outright smear rags—there was no kinder word for them.

McCoy sat back after about half an hour of reading, very upset, actually shaking a little. *This is not something I wanted to find out about Vulcans,* he thought. *There are Vulcan bigots. Right here where Surak taught, and died.* He shook his head. "Damn."

"Null input," the computer said politely in Vulcan.

"Sorry. Cross-reference. Lists of membership of all the above organizations. Star or otherwise indicate members who are also members of other listed organizations."

"Working," said the machine. "Output?"

"Print."

"Acknowledged," said the machine, and began spitting out truly astonishing amounts of the fine thin plastic that Vulcans used for printout. McCoy watched with amazement as it piled up.

The printing did not stop for nearly twenty minutes. When it did, there was a stack of printout some three inches thick, all in very tiny print, and McCoy shook his head. "Solid duplication also," he said.

"Working," said the computer, and after about three seconds spat out a data solid at him.

"End."

"Credit authorization, please," the machine said sweetly.

McCoy rolled his eyes, felt around for his downplanet

"cash" solid, stuck it in the slot, let the machine click and whirr and deduct however much money from it. It spat the solid back at him almost with the air of a machine unsatisfied with the amount of money spent. "Hmf," McCoy said to it, pocketed the solid, picked up the printout, and headed out.

He made his way to the little restaurant where they had been before. It was open early, as most Vulcan restaurants and refectories were, for the daymeal. "Lasagna, please," he said to the waiter, and started going through the printout. It was going to be a long morning.

Or so he thought. Five minutes into his reading, he found a name that brought him bolt upright in his chair. Very soon thereafter he found it again, and again.

"Damn," he said. "Damn. *Damn.*"

After a long time he put the printout aside and ate his lasagna, even though he wasn't sure he had the appetite for it anymore.

The world dissolved from sparkle to solidity around Jim as he beamed down. He found himself in a little park, like many he and Spock and McCoy had seen the day before. This one Spock had described to him in detail: there were three paths that wound out of it, and Jim was to take the one that led off to the left, toward the old city wall.

He took that path, walking slowly. It was a pleasant park: the "grass" was some sort of tough dun-colored growth, broken with tiny, delicate trees with feathery maroon-colored leaves. They looked, in fact, almost exactly like giant featherdusters. Out of curiosity Jim went over to one and touched it . . . and was very surprised when the entire branch folded its leaves away and rolled itself into a tight spiral.

"Sorry," he said, and then laughed at himself. *Do Vulcans talk to trees, I wonder?*

Slowly the branch unrolled and unfurled its leaves once more. Jim restrained himself from touching it again—no reason to make a plant crazy—and headed down the path that led toward the old city wall. It curved broadly, to parallel the wall. Now he recognized where he was: he followed the curve of the path, and sheltered from view by an outcropping of rock, he saw the house.

It was fairly large by Vulcan standards, though not as large as one might expect the house of the Ambassador Extraordinary to Terra to be. It was built all on one level, as most of the houses here seemed to be: Vulcans seemed to have an aversion to blocking away others' view of the sky. The place, in fact, with its surrounding wall just higher than eye-height, looked rather like something one of the old "postmodern" architects might have built, with curves rather than sharp corners. But at the same time it had a look about it of the old Roman villas: a house that looked inward, rather than outward, and kept its secrets and its privacies to itself.

He went up to the gate in the wall and touched the annunciator plate. "James Kirk," he said when it glowed.

"Jim," came Amanda's voice, very cheerful, "come on in." The gate swung open for him.

A narrow path bordered with stones led to the front door of the house. It opened as he stepped toward it, and there was Amanda, wearing a coverall, rather stained around the knees, with a pair of pruning shears in her hand. "Welcome!" she said. "Come in and see the garden! I'll give you the two-credit tour later. Or Sarek can do it when he gets back from town. Would you like something cold to drink?"

"Yes, please," Jim said. Amanda guided him in through the front hall. It was large, and the rooms were built on the open plan: the living area and dining area and kitchen were all one clean, beautiful sprawl of rough or polished black stone, and the rear wall was one large window with dilating panels that gave on the garden.

"Here," Amanda said, stopping by the drinks dispenser in the kitchen. "Water? Something carbonated?"

"Soda water would be fine."

"I'll join you." Two glasses slid out from behind a panel. "Cheers," she said, lifting one of them in salute, handing him the other.

They both drank thirstily. "Oh, that's much better," Amanda said. "I worked up such a thirst. Come on this way." She led him out the dilation, into the garden. Most of it was raked sand and gravel, but one patch about thirty feet square was given over to rosebushes. Several were in profuse bloom: some had no bloom at all, having been cut back.

"That's amazing," Jim said. "I'm still astonished those things will even grow here."

"Oh, they do well enough," Amanda said. "It's no worse than, say, Arizona would be, as long as you keep them watered. And they seem to like the spectrum of a white sun a little better than a yellow one. You know what will really grow wonderfully here?" She pointed off to one side, where some small new plants had been set in. "Tomatoes. They're pigs for water in this climate; they need a soaker at their roots all day. But you should see how they look after a couple of months. I have to hand-pollinate them, but I don't mind that."

Jim shook his head. "You've been pruning the roses back pretty hard," he said.

Amanda nodded. "We haven't been here for two years, remember," she said. "We have a gardener who comes in and takes care of things, but he's best with the native Vulcan plants, the succulents over there, and the sandplants. I don't think Vulcans really understand about roses: they think they're delicate. But to bring out the best in them, you have to be mean to them." She clicked the shears meaningfully.

"I have trouble believing you could be mean to anything," Jim said.

Amanda looked at him kindly. "Flatterer," she said. "Come here and sit down in the shade."

They went over to a bench under a pergola smothered with some kind of leafy vine. Amanda settled herself on it and looked out at the garden. "You know," she said after a moment, "there were a lot of times when we were raising Spock that I felt I was being mean to him. At the same time I felt I had to: Sarek and I agreed that Spock needed to grow up as a normal Vulcan child, with the disciplines that Vulcan children have to deal with. If we had been on Earth, it might have been different. Earth people are a little more flexible about such things. But Vulcans expect . . ." She broke off, then looked a little bemused. "They expect you to be very conservative. Everything has to meet the status quo . . . everything has to be the same."

And Amanda smiled. "It doesn't make much sense in terms

of the IDIC, does it? Sometimes I think things have slipped a little.''

Jim nodded. "I can see your point.''

They sat there in silence for a few minutes, enjoying the wind, which was not too hot to be unpleasant as yet, and much softened by the wall around the garden. "May I ask you something?'' Jim said.

"Ask.''

He gestured at the garden. "You're pruning the roses as if everything was going to turn out all right, later this week. . . .''

She gazed at the roses and then let out a long breath. "Well,'' she said, "I'm a gardener. No matter what happens, the roses need pruning.''

Jim smiled.

"But you're right,'' she said. "I'm worried.'' She turned the shears over in her hand, studying the blades. "If the vote for secession goes through,'' she said, "the ban will certainly fall on me. The government will certainly not be in a mood to allow exceptions—certainly not at the highest levels: it would be seen in some quarters as nepotism, favoritism. I will have to leave Vulcan—or Sarek will.''

Jim shook his head. "It doesn't seem fair.''

"Oh, there's nothing fair about it,'' Amanda said, "but if the vote goes for secession—'' She sighed and looked around at the garden and the house. "I gave up one home, a long time ago,'' she said softly. "I suppose I can manage it again.''

"Giving up a home isn't the same as giving up a husband, though.''

She nodded. "We will find somewhere else, I suppose,'' she said. "The Federation would be glad to have Sarek. And Spock certainly is in no danger of losing his present job.''

"Lord, no.''

"But at the same time,'' Amanda said, "think of it from Sarek's point of view. To have to leave your homeworld forever: never again to see the rest of your family: to be an exile on cold damp worlds, never to feel a sun that's warm enough—or if you do, to have it shining on you in a strange sky—'' She shook her head.

"You must excuse my wife, Captain,'' said Sarek, coming

into the garden and slipping out of his overtunic: "she is obviously exercising the Scots part of her heritage, which she has described to me as 'predicting gloom an' doom.' " He laid the overtunic neatly over the back of another bench nearby and sat down.

"Did your business go well?" Amanda said.

Sarek nodded. "As well as could be expected. The town is becoming positively tense. At least, so I would describe the atmosphere, having seen it on Earth many times: I have never seen the like here before. But then, the like has never happened."

"Tomorrow we start debate?" Jim said.

"Tomorrow. Some of the less, shall we say, 'loaded' testimonies will come first. K's't'lk, various other scientists, economists, and so forth. Then the people arguing for ethical reasons. Then the professional liaisons—such as ambassadors and starship captains."

"Sarek," Jim said, "about last night—"

"It happened," Sarek said, "but I would not advise you to tell anyone else about it, save for Spock and the doctor. That one prefers to keep her doings quiet, and it is usually wise to respect her wishes."

There was a soft chime from inside the house, and an amplified voice said, "It's McCoy."

"Speak of the devil and you see his horns," Jim said.

"Let us not get into *that* again," Sarek said, rather emphatically.

"Doctor, come in!" Amanda said, and got up to greet him at the door.

"The doctor sounds winded," Sarek said. "I hope he is not unwell. The heat can take people by surprise here."

Amanda ushered McCoy in a few moments later. He was sweating and was wearing an expression that Jim had seen on him before—a combination of excitement and dread. "Bones, are you all right?" Jim said.

"No," McCoy said, and handed Jim a thick printout. "Look through that."

Jim did, mystified. McCoy turned to Sarek. "I was out following up a hunch I'd had," he said. "These anti-Federation, anti-Terran organizations that have been around the past century or so: I was doing some reading of their latest publications this morning."

"No wonder you look distressed," Sarek said, with an expression of distaste.

"It gets worse. I pulled their membership lists and did some correlation. Shath," McCoy said to Jim, "he's prominent. But you know who else is?"

Jim stared at the printout, looking at a circled name on one list. "T'Pring," he said. And turned several pages. "T'Pring. T'Pring."

He riffled through the rest of the printout, then folded it back up and laid it aside. They all looked at one another: Sarek looking nonplussed, Amanda amazed and angry, McCoy apprehensive, Jim simply astonished.

"I think we'd better call Spock and let him in on this," McCoy said.

Jim nodded while Bones got out his communicator.

Dear Lord, he thought. *T'Pring.*

Hell hath no fury . . .

VULCAN:
FOUR

———————— ☆ ————————

The old woman sat by her window, looking down on the spires of the city, and sighed, stirring uncomfortably on her bench covered with furs. The silences of the evening were falling: past the edge of the lands, her lands, T'Khut was sliding toward the edge of the sky, her bright crescent a rusty sickle holding darkness between its downpointing horns, and a sprinkling of wildfire sparks: so she looked, and for the time being, that was appropriate. Doings were toward that would release those fires at last, and the woman leaned on her windowsill and waited. There was no need to send her mind out on quest, to touch and pry. Soon enough, those she desired would come to her. There was nothing to do but wait, now.

Mind had made Vulcan different from the start. How many thousands of years, now, since the arts of mind had begun to spring up among men in earnest? They had made all the difference, for without them there would have been no taming the terrible place. It was one of their names for the world, *ah'Hrak*, the Forge. The name would have been an irony, nothing more, despite the melted mountaintops that one could still see in places, if it had not been for the arts of the mind, the inner magics that could draw things from the stubborn crust of the world that no tool could.

Vulcan was metal-poor. Or rather, most of its metals were trapped well below the crust, in the mantle that no one knew yet how to tap, and in the seething core. No tool that men could make, in those first days, could dig deep enough to find metal in any great amount. The smiths of ancient days, when they came to invent their craft, might have to spend years wandering the world, scratching at its surface, gathering enough ore to make one sword, one spear, and never another again. So matters remained for a long time. Stone was cut only with stone: a house might be a life's work: a plough was a precious commodity that a whole community would finance together and take turns using. And even then, frequently all they had to plough was sand.

But it all changed. Mind changed everything. To the first arts—the bonding of mind to mind, the touch that incapacitates, speech-without-words—others slowly began to be added. Sometimes they occurred naturally and spread themselves through the gene pool on their own, like the internal corneal nictitating membrane that protected the eye from excessive light. But some were sports, and the houses in which they sprang up cultivated them and made them a source of power or wealth. To one of the ancient houses, for example, was born a child who could feel where metal was. That house secretly hired every smith they could find, and after some small number of years—a hundred or so—had massed enough metal weapons to take thousands of acres for their own, while most houses had to be content with several hundred. Another house had produced a child with an even more precious gift—the ability to feel water. When this was discovered, the child was fought over, kidnapped back and forth, and finally died many years later, in misery, an old and broken man. But the trait bred true in the children he was forced to sire, and soon spread through the gene pool; now it was a poor sort of house that did not have a waterseer, and enough water for all its needs. One had to dig deep, but the water was there. It had opened the way for technology: for enough food and enough time to do something besides hunt and survive. Vulcan became civilized, began to pursue pleasure and exploration: began to practice war as an art form, rather than the rather sordid necessity it had always been until natural resources began to be more easily available. And of course there were forays, as one House decided another had something it needed or wanted. Rarely did patience last through much in the way of negotiation: that was not how Vulcan had become what it had become. The occasional war broke out over the theft of a well-drilling technique or the kidnapping of an adept of one of the more useful mindsciences; the rich and powerful raided one another's people as the tribal chiefs had raided one another's herdbeasts in the longago. These days, at best a stolen talent could make one's fortune. At worst, it was something to pass the time.

The woman stirred again on her couch, then stood up and began to walk to and fro. She had no eyes for the rich appointments of the room, the tapestries and carpets, the rare treasures of art in stone and carved bone and bright metal. Her reflection in the mirror—a sheet of polished bronze that would have been the price of a kingdom, once—she passed again and again, taking no heed of it. *The waiting is hard,* she thought. No matter that she had become expert at it, these many years past. This particular prize she had waited for for a long, long time, moving subtly toward it, never being seen to be too hungry, too eager. And now everything was ripe, and tonight, perhaps, or tomorrow, it would come to her of her own free will. She turned her eyes again to the sickle of T'Khut, and lust glittered in them. *Soon,* she thought. *Quite soon.*

A small gong chimed softly on the worktable she kept in the chamber. She went to it, touched the control attached to it. "Speak."

"Madam, the lord Evekh is here and desires to see you." The voice on the other end of the comm sounded frightened. "My apologies, lady, for troubling you so late, but he would not leave without seeing you."

"Bid him enter," the woman said. She sat down by the windowsill again, on her couch, and gazed out on the spires of the city, as if more concerned with that view than with the setting crescent easing itself toward the horizon, shimmering uncannily in the uprising heat.

The carved doors swung open, and Nesheh her maid let the

visitor in. The woman heard the soft rustle of stiff, rich robes behind her, ignored them till they stopped, then turned. There he stood, Evekh, all in a splendor of embroidery of violet brocade and silver wire, with *lasha* stones set in a great silvern collar at his neck: they caught the lamplight and a gleam or so from sinking T'Khut and gave it back in a shimmer of opalescent violet. Above all the finery, there was the plain, hard, blunt face, noble in its way; but the cruel eyes hinted that the nobility had fallen on hard times. That was all to her advantage. She made a graceful gesture of welcome. "A social call, I take it, my lord," she said.

"Lady Suvin," he said, and held his hands up to her in reverence. "Yes."

"At such an hour." Now that he was here, finally here, she could not resist baiting him a little. "Do sit, then. Will you take water with me?"

"Gladly."

She stepped over to the little singing fall in the corner, chose two cups from the sideboard. All were a message in themselves. The waterfall spoke of the wealth of someone who could afford to have such a thing directed seven floors up from the living stone; the cups were of perfect design, simple and clean in a time when more obvious ostentation would have had them covered with rare gems from the Hehei or gilded in platinum electroplate. Suvin despised gauds of that sort: or if she stooped to them, she made sure they far surpassed anything else a rival might find. The cups were of simple enough design, but each one was carved of a single nightfire, all black with glitters of gold in it, like T'Khut outside the window.

She filled the cups, gave one to her guest, and sat down on a bench opposite him. They drank, first, without speaking, as the guest had by the proper laws of hospitality to be refreshed before telling his tale. "Tell me, then," Suvin said when the cups were half drained, "since this is a social call, how fares your family? How does your lady wife?"

It was meant to be an arrow in his side, and the flicker of rage that went across his face told her that it had gone home. "She is as well as can be expected."

"Ah, I am glad to hear it. And the family prospers."

He said nothing.

"I am glad to hear it," she said again. "These are such busy times for all of us."

"For you, at least," Evekh said. "The lesser houses rally behind you, I see."

"They have seen the sense of what we mean to do," she said. She turned and gazed out the window. T'Khut was half set: through a gap in the towers one could see that the horns of the crescent were beneath the horizon now, and the crescent made a sort of bright bridge, with a few sparks of fire caught under it. "The latest researches have proved very compelling indeed. There is metal beyond our wildest dreams—iron, steel, rare metals, and rare earths—lying scattered about T'Khut like pebbles. No need to dig for it. Untold riches lie there, and untold rewards for our people and our industry. We must get there: it hangs so close. We can do it. And now we shall."

He sat silent. She knew what he was thinking. *It should have been us. Unfair, unfair*— Suvin felt like laughing out loud to mock him, saying, *Your house had its chances and let them slip: now reap what you have sown!* And it would have been true enough. Evekh's house was anciently involved with trade. Many centuries back, as the smaller city-states grew up and goods began to be traded between them, his house had come to run the caravans that went back and forth between the tiny outposts of the civilization that was then Vulcan. The great difficulty with handling many such caravans at a time had proved to be communications: without it, there was no way to predict when goods would arrive, where they were in transit, whether they would be late. Evekh's forefathers had solved the problem by hiring, buying, or kidnapping as many people as they could find who had the talent of clear mindspeech at a distance. Then they had begun a selective breeding program, and bred the talent true, and increased its power and honed the training of it until the talent was no longer an accidental thing that worked only in times of stress, but a predictable and manageable power that would operate over thousands of miles. It made them rich and powerful enough so that, after some centuries, Evekh's house let the caravan-trade-cum-overland-shipping-corporation go, and concentrated on psi-communications technologies alone. Their people were in demand all over the planet, except in one regard . . . and Suvin knew it.

"We are quite close," Suvin said, so casually that it could not possibly be regarded as a taunt. "The hulls of the first two ships are complete, now, and the instrumentation is being installed by the various lesser houses." She looked out the window as the last scrap of T'Khut slipped beneath the horizon. The sky grew dark, except for the red Eye and the white one, that gazed down brightly enough to cast faint shadows. Outside the window, somewhere in the middle air, a nightvoice spoke: a sweet, mournful sound, answered just as mournfully from somewhere close by. "We will launch for the first time at the end of the year."

"So soon," Evekh said.

Suvin nodded. Inside, she was shaking with mirth that she dare not show. It would lose her too much, just for the sake of a little entertainment. "I should like to speed things up somewhat," she said, "but there seems no way at this point; we are depending mostly on machines, except for the construction itself."

"And more speed would make that much difference?"

"The difference between eighteen million *nakh* next year," she said, "and four thousand million." She paused enough for the thought to sink in like water into sand. "It is a matter of the subsidiary voyages," she said, "out to the sister planets. The delay of normal ether-wave communications adds a certain unavoidable delay to the process of assessment and pickup of the raw materials. Delay is costly, as usual. . . ."

She trailed off. *And psi-communication is instantaneous. Come along, old fool. Make a fine show of pride for me, so that I can offer you what I have for you.*

Suvin waited. It was just as well for her that Evekh had no training in his family's gift and could not hear her. Otherwise this deal would be much more difficult to drive.

Evekh drank from his cup. After a little while he said, rather tightly, "I have often wished that my family had not let the transportation side of our House fall into decline."

I dare say—because if they had not, you would be sitting in my place now: the place of one about to be mistress of the richest and most powerful House on the planet, one that even kings bow to, knowing their betterment when they see it. "Evekh," she said, again so casually, "surely you could come into it again if you wanted to."

She watched him look at the meaning under her words, watched him shy away from it, with another flicker of anger in his face. Perhaps he was getting the feeling he was being toyed with. *Ah, softly: have a care.* "We would be glad to ally with you in this regard," she said. And added, "If you would have us."

The five words took the rage that had abruptly shown on his face and as abruptly erased it. He was silent for a minute or more, looking at the cup in his hands. "Our house is somewhat fallen from its early grandeur," he said, trying to make light of it.

"Ah, hardly," Suvin said.

He looked sharply at her. She looked back, a frank and dissembling look that was meant to say, *But I meant it.*

He swallowed his pride again. She watched with mild astonishment. It was worth all her waiting, this delicate debasement. She knew quite well that pride was at the root: that Evekh could not bear the sight of what he considered a young upstart house advanced far beyond his . . . and his own house reduced in wealth and status. Only that had made him refuse her first offer of alliance, some years ago. But now he was tasting the bitterness his pride had brought him to: his own house and his lady wife were not beyond reminding him of their opinion of this situation from time to time. *Pain, and pride: we will see which is stronger. I think I know. . . .*

Suvin put the look on her face of a woman who has a sudden thought. "If you would be willing," she said, "there would be a way to do this that could not invoke a question of loss of face, if that concerns you." *If!*

Evekh blinked. "Speak on, lady."

"A binding. I have a grandson of age. He is past the Raptures without ill effect, and we were looking him out a match among one of the nobler houses. Surely yours would be one of those."

Evekh looked slightly pale for a moment. "We have no one who would suit, I fear."

"Ah, but surely you do. That youngest right-line daughter of yours. T'Thelaih, that's her name, is it not?"

Evekh stared at Suvin in shock.

"And what is more," she said, "after the wedding, we would *keep* her."

Evekh was quite still for several minutes. "And the groom-price?" he said.

Suvin shrugged. "That would be negotiable. But the match is a noble one, and the alliance between our houses would be most profitable, both in the short and long terms. Your share—it would certainly be at least five percent of our takings. As for the groom-price—shall we say," and she paused for thought she had taken long ago, "all the extant adepts of the Last Thought long-range psi-communications technique, and their offspring? And all necessary chemical training and teaching materials. That should more than suffice our space program's needs for many years."

There was a long, long silence: and then Evekh began to curse her. He cursed her in the names of gods that had been removed from the official calendar, and gods that had not, and in the names of beasts and men, and in the name of the One Who Does Not Hear. She sat unmoved, and when she spoke again, it was as if nothing had happened.

"Does the offer please?"

"It pleases," Evekh said heavily. "I will have my bailiff see yours tomorrow to make the instrument of binding. May I call on you tomorrow evening?"

"It would be my pleasure."

Evekh got up, then, and bowed. Not hands up in reverence, but the bent-double bow, showing the back of the neck, of a new-bought slave. And he went from there with no other word.

Well-pleased, Suvin gazed out the window a few minutes longer . . . then called her maid to prepare her couch.

She slept soundly for the first time in many months and got up in the morning in a good temper, to the astonishment of the household staff. Then, her toilet and levee done, she sent for her grandson.

Their meeting was brief and to the point. It was nooning: the family was resting at such a time, but for Suvin that made little odds, and they knew better, by and large, to fly in her face about such little things. When she called them, they came.

Mahak stood before her and fidgeted, looking about him at all the rich and costly things, and obviously wondering why under the moon he, the least of the family, had suddenly been called up here. She let him stand there and worry for a moment, pretending to work as she did. *He is goodly enough to look at, I'll give him that,* she thought. He was dark-visaged but well favored, with great dark eyes and a long face, and well made in his body.

"You are to be bonded," she said, without any preliminaries, "to a daughter of Old House Yehenik, at the full of T'Khut. You may go to the merchants and arrange the festivities to your liking: so long as the binding is properly carried out, I do not care about the expense. See to it."

Astonished, he bowed and went out without a word. Soon this information would be all over the house and out into the streets, where the professional gossipmongers would get their hands on it and spread it all over the planet . . . some of them using Evekh's techniques. There was a choice irony to it. To Suvin, her grandson was a playing-piece, one of many: she cared little enough about him to hear what else the tongues would be wagging about—that he was unlikely to survive his binding night. Even if he did, she was unconcerned. *But it would be better far if he did not,* she thought, *for then my old enemies will have given me their most priceless asset, and they will get nothing in return. Nothing. While I will have everything they have . . .*

. . . and perhaps something more.

Smiling, she went to her work.

When T'Thelaih heard of it, her first response was to rage, and then to weep. But she dared do nothing else. Her father, who had made the match, she saw perhaps once a month, when his leisure allowed it, and then rarely for more than a few minutes. At such times she often wanted to cry out to him, *It's not my fault!* But there was no hope of his understanding, and no use in making trouble.

She was a murderess.

It wasn't her fault.

T'Thelaih had most of her family's traits: the fair or light brown hair, the light bones and short stature, good looks that tended to be blunt rather than finely drawn. There the obvious assets of the Old House ended in her, for she did not have the psi-communications gift: she was mindblind, like her father, and

that had been hard enough to bear in a house where almost no
one ever had to speak—the slightest intention to communicate
with another person was always heard.

One gift she did have, though, that the house had acquired
long before and striven hard to be rid of. They had never suc-
ceeded: every six or seven generations it would pop up again,
and there would be curses and fear. It was associated with the
communications gift, but independent of it. When angry, the
person with this pernicious gift could kill with the mind.

She had not known until she was betrothed for the first time.
She was frightened: she had not yet suffered the Rapture, and
though her body was ready, her mind was not. Her first husband,
a son of rich House Kehlevt, and one who thought well of himself,
had taken her to the room set aside for their binding and had
simply begun to rape her.

She killed him. Without touching him, without laying a hand
to a weapon—though she would have liked to—suddenly she was
inside his head: suddenly the connection that had never been
complete before was complete: and her rage and terror burst out
through it and froze his heart and stripped the receptor chemicals
out of his brain and deadened the life-fire in his nerves. He was
dead before he rolled off her. No healer had been able to do
anything.

There had been the expected uproar. But the bruises on her
body spoke clearly enough about what had been going on, and
the matter was hushed up, and money changed hands to keep the
quiet well in place. So much she had heard later. She had been
very afraid that that would be the end of her—that some evening,
someone would slip something deadly into her cup; or that some
day before dawn, someone would come in over the sweet white
flowers on her windowsill and put a knife in her. Such things had
been heard of. But no one troubled her. T'Thelaih went about the
house keeping small and still. It took her some time to realize
that other people were now keeping small and still around *her*.
No one had ever cared a *jah* before whether she was angry. But
now, the people of the house were not sure that *any* anger of hers
was something to cause, or to be near.

She tried to ignore the changed status of things and went
about her studies and work as usual. Everybody in the house

worked, whether they were marriage-fodder or not. T'Thelaih
was very clear that that was just what she was—a gaming piece.
She was not an own-child, but a "right-line child"—that was a
euphemism that said she had some relationship to the head of the
house, but not one confirmed by binding or other legal instrument. She was a by-blow, destined to be married off to some
other house in return for some political favor or potential alliance.
Now she went about her accounting work as usual and wondered
whether the business with her first husband would put her out of
the marriage market. That could be bad: she could wind up
disowned, or sold as a servant. But things quieted down after a
while, and another offer was made, this time from House Galsh.
It was a good enough match, and the young man was very nice,
and T'Thelaih wondered whether or not the first time might have
been a quirk or an accident. In any case, she looked forward to
the wedding. She felt the slow burn of the Rapture coming over
her as the days till the binding grew closer, and she welcomed it.
The binding fell in the middle of it: her blood fever kindled her
new husband's, and the night was wild and memorable.

But in the morning he was dead.

There were no more matches made. T'Thelaih had leisure to
work with the house's accounts, now: all the leisure she liked.
Everyone, the servants, her half sisters, her mothers, looked at
her with terror. Sometimes it relaxed a little, but never for long.
No one dared tease her or say something that might make her
laugh . . . because it might make her angry, too.

The time that followed was long and lonely.

But now she stood in front of her father, listening incredulously to the news that she was being bound again. To a young
man of House Velekh, of the "High House." She stared at her
father.

"But they are great," she said. "What do they want with
us?"

"Alliance," he said.

T'Thelaih had her own ideas about that. She handled the
accounts, after all. "Noble father," she said, "surely there are
other houses they might more profitably ally with."

He glared at her. Yes, he knew perfectly well that he was
being condescended to.

"Noble father," she said, "how can this match be made? Do they not know about the—the other bindings?"

"The Eldest of the House knows. Yes." Her father breathed out. "You have nothing to fear from them if there is an accident." He paused. "They will adopt you."

You are giving me away, she thought, *and relieved you are to do it. Foul, ah, foul!* "But noble father," she said, desperate, "the young man—"

"I care nothing for the young man," he said angrily. "No more do they. And I'll spare no tear if you make an end of him: it will rather please me if you kill something of theirs, than otherwise. So do your pleasure, girl. The match will be made when T'Khut is full. The young man comes to meet you tomorrow."

And that was that. She bowed her father reverence, and left, and sat long by her window that night, smelling the sweet white flowers, and contemplating the knife in her hand. It was very sharp.

The crescent set late: watching it, she thought that there was time yet. There was no harm in seeing the young man, at least. The knife would not be any less sharp for a couple days' delay.

Then she saw him.

They were left alone for the meeting, in the great hall of the house's lower level. It was all barren, there being no great dinner or festival there, no reason to adorn or garnish the place with the old banners and the riches garnered from long years of trade. And indeed many of the rich ornaments had been sold, over time, or were the worse for wear. Some kindly person among the servants had brought out two couches, of the antique style, and each of them sat on one and looked at the other.

T'Thelaih liked what she saw. The young man had a frank, calm look about him, and his eyes rested on her in a friendly way. "Well," he said, "they say we're going to be bound. I hope it's something you desired."

"It's not," she said.

He colored. "I'm sorry I don't please you."

"Oh, but you do!" she said.

They both fell silent for a moment: he was surprised at the remark, and she was surprised that it had slipped out, and equally surprised at how seriously she meant it. "I simply did not desire to be bound," she said. "I have been bound before. I killed my husbands."

He looked at her with even more surprise. "Not that way," she said, rather desperately. "It was the killing gift. You know—from the stories." She bowed her head. "I have it. No one survives the binding."

He gazed at her a long time, and finally she had to turn her head away.

"I think I would take the chance even if the choice were mine," he said, very slowly, as if just discovering this for himself.

T'Thelaih looked up in shock. "You must not!" she said. "You must flee! There's still time for you to get away!"

He shook his head. "You do not know my grandam," he said. "She would have me hunted down and brought back. And besides, why would I want to disgrace our house? She is our Eldest. It is my duty to obey her."

"She sent you here to kill you! She *knew!*"

He actually shrugged.

"You are an *idiot*," T'Thelaih said in wonder.

He shrugged again. "That's as may be. There's no escaping, in any case, so I shall not try."

The argument went on for nearly an hour. T'Thelaih wondered what the eavesdroppers must be thinking of it all . . . for certainly, there *were* eavesdroppers: she might be mindblind, but she was not so stupid as to think that every mind in the house was not bent in this direction at the moment. And once the thought crossed her mind, *Why am I trying to talk him out of it? No worse blame will fall on me this time than has before. My father has practically given me leave to kill him. Why am I arguing the point?*

She could think of no reason.

Finally the argument trailed off, and she found herself staring at her hands. "Come again tomorrow," she said.

"I will," he said. And he paused and colored again. "I hate to say this," he said. "They announced it when I came in, but I've forgotten your name."

"T'Thelaih."

"Mahak," he said, and got up and bowed her reverence and left.

She sat there shaking her head for a long time, and then went back to the accounts.

He came back the next day, and the next, and the day after that, and they argued. The arguments always started about the binding itself, but then they began to stray out into more interesting topics—the relationships and interrelationships in their families, the politics that went on, and the doings of the kingdoms and lordships of the world; and finally, about themselves, or rather, each other. The arguments started early and ended late: it was *almost* improper.

After about three days of this, T'Thelaih realized that she was going to *have* to be bound to this man, just to have the leisure to argue properly with him.

On the fourth day she realized, with a start, that she was in love with him, and he with her. He realized it, for his part, the next day. The argument that day was particularly noisy.

Two days later, T'Khut was full.

The public part of the binding was held with great splendor in the hall of the High House. Mahak had decided to take his grandam at her word: tables actually bent under the weight of the food, and drink ran more freely than water. Petty-kings and great lords and Eldest Mothers filled the galleries to look down on the formal touching, as the priest of the god of bindings took the hands of the two to be bound, put them each to the other's face, and saw that the minds were properly locked together. Not even he saw how each pair of eyes, resting in the other's gaze, told the other that the locking had already happened, perhaps a hand of days ago, while both parties were shouting at one another at the tops of their voices. Neither of them cared a whit for one of the things they had argued about, the exchange of mind-technicians taking place, just about then, elsewhere in the house. Neither of them paid the slightest mind to the cold, interested glance bent down on them from another of the high galleries, as Lady Suvin looked down satisfied on her handiwork. They completed the binding and spent the afternoon and the early part of the night celebrating it with the assembled dignitaries, not caring in the slightest who had just declared war on whom, or what border skirmish was taking place because of an insult or a strayed sehlat.

They lay together that night and found that there was at least one thing about which they had no argument whatsoever: though afterward, there was some sleepy discussion as to who had a right to the most of the sleeping silks.

T'Thelaih was the first to awaken. Without looking to the side where her husband lay, she reached over to the little table by the head of the couch and picked up the knife. It was as sharp as it had been when the moon was thin. She knew what she was going to see: she knew what she was going to do about it.

She turned over and saw him sleeping quietly and breathing. And quite alive.

The knife fell with a clatter to the floor and awoke him.

They began to quarrel. It did not last long. . . .

"I am with child," she said to him, quite shortly thereafter. He was so surprised that he forgot to start an argument about it.

"All the good Gods be praised," he said, taking her hands, "and bless the bad ones for staying out of it!"

"Sit down, beloved," she said, "and be calm a little. We need to think."

"About what?"

"The child, for one thing." T'Thelaih sat down on the couch in their chambers in the High House and looked at him keenly. "This child could be something that our houses have been waiting for for a long time."

"There are lots of children," Mahak said, somewhat confused.

"But none of both our houses. Mahak, listen to me. My father has as good as sold me to Suvin. I'm not bothered by that. Something like it was always bound to happen someday. But this child, depending on how and where it is raised, could be mistress of both my old House and my new one."

"Mistress—"

"A girl, yes."

"My grandam is not going to like that," Mahak said.

T'Thelaih was silent for a moment. "We are going to have to find some way to stop her not liking it," she said, "or to see to it that it does not matter. This child can be a bond, an end to the old warfare between our houses. Or the opportunity can die with us."

"Have you any idea how we are going to bring this to pass?" he said.

"Have you?"

He shook his head.

"Nor have I. But we must start thinking . . . whom we can cultivate, and how, to see that the child is brought up between the houses, not wholly of one or the other. Otherwise the child will be one more gaming piece, nothing more. . . ."

They sat quietly together for a moment.

"We must be very careful," Mahak said. "Otherwise this may be the death of us."

T'Thelaih nodded. "As you say."

He drew her close. "And in the meantime . . ."

And they discussed at some length the subject on which there were no arguments.

T'Thelaih woke up cold and alone. "Mahak?" she said, confused, and sat up on the couch, looking around for him. There was something wrong at the other end of their bond: he was upset—then she froze.

Sitting at the end of the couch was the Lady Suvin. She looked at T'Thelaih, and the look was cold and terribly pleased.

"You are a foolish child," Suvin said, "but it does not matter. I have what I want of you."

"Madam," T'Thelaih said, holding on to her manners, "what do you mean?"

"The child," said Suvin. "This will be your home now: you need fear no interference from your own house, poor thing though it be. I much regret that Mahak may not join you again until your confinement is done. But you will be given every care . . . so long as you take proper care of the child."

T'Thelaih felt her head beginning to pound. "What good can our child do you?" she said.

Suvin leaned closer, looking even more pleased. "Fool. You have the killing gift. Imperfect, at best: you did not kill my grandson, for some reason. I suspect it is the usual problem, that one must feel her life to somehow be threatened. But did you not know? His great-grandmother had it as well. When two with the gift in their blood, so close in degree, engender a child, it will have the gift as well."

T'Thelaih shook her head, numbed. "A weapon," she said at last.

"Such a weapon as none will be able to defend against," said Suvin. "Trained with the Last Thought technique, raised under my hand, obedient to me—those who resist me will simply die, and no one will know the cause. How much simpler life will become. I have much to thank you for."

She saw T'Thelaih's glance at the table. "Forget your little bodkin," she said. "You'll not lay hands on yourself: if you try, Mahak will suffer for it. I shall see to that. Resign yourself to your confinement. It need not be uncomfortable."

"Bring me my husband," T'Thelaih said. "Now."

Suvin's eyes glittered. "Do not presume to order me, my girl. You are too valuable to kill out of hand, but there are ways to punish you that will not harm the child."

The pounding was getting worse. "My husband," T'Thelaih said.

"Folly," said Suvin, and got up to go. "I will talk to you when you are in your right mind."

And from the courtyard below came the sound of swords, and the scream.

"T'Thelaih!!"

And nothing else . . . except, in T'Thelaih's mind, the feeling of the bond, the connection, as it snapped, and the other end went empty and cold.

"My husband," she said. Suvin turned in shock, realizing what had happened. An unfortunate accident—

She realized too late.

T'Thelaih was getting up from the bed. The pounding in her head she had felt before, at her first binding, and remotely, in the heat of *plak tow,* at the second. Now she knew it for what it was, and she encouraged it. *Yes. Oh, my husband, yes—*

"Old woman," she said to Suvin, getting out of the bed and advancing slowly on her, "beg me for your life." Suvin backed up, slowly, a step at a time, coming against the wall by the door.

"Beg me," T'Thelaih said, stepping slowly closer. "Bow yourself double, old *lematya*, let me see the back of your neck." Her teeth gleamed. Suvin trembled, and slowly, slowly, began to bow.

She didn't finish the gesture: she came up with the knife, poised, threw it. T'Thelaih sidestepped it neatly and replied with the weapon that could not miss: slid into the hateful mind, cold as stone, reached down all its pathways and set them on fire, reached down through every nerve and ran agony down it, reached down into the laboring heart and squeezed it until it burst itself, reached down into the throat and froze it so there should not even be the relief of a scream. From Suvin she turned, and her mind rode her gift down into the courtyard, and wrought death there, death—left minds screaming as a weight of rage like the whole universe collapsed onto them, in burning heat, pain, blood, the end of everything. Her mind fled through the house, finding life, ending it, without thought, everywhere.

Finally the rage left her, and she picked up the little knife that Suvin had taken, thought about it . . . then changed her mind. "No," she said aloud, very softly: "no, *he* is down there."

She went to the window. "Child," she said, "I am sorry."

The fall was too swift for there to be time to start an argument, even with a ghost.

The extermination of the High House set back the first manned landing on T'Khut by some fifty standard years. Much of the psi-communications technology had to be rediscovered, and the gift bred for again, in the centuries that followed: it is still the least developed of the Vulcan arts of the mind, though the most broadly disseminated.

T'Khut was mined later, of course, and colonized, and thereafter the Vulcans set off for the outer planets. Several small wars broke out on Vulcan at the first successful landing, in token of the shifting of balances, which are always feared. But other balances were shifting as well: love became increasingly less of a reason for a binding than eugenics. Lives were sacrificed, long wars begun, for the sake of some marriage which might or might not produce a talent of one sort or another. And the terrible example of the attempted union of the High House and the Old

House dissuaded many another house from trying such a solution to its problems. Houses grew away from one another, as nations did: grew in enmity and pride, forgot working together for the joys of conquering separately. *Fear the other,* was the message of that time: *keep to your own. Beware the different. Those too different should not seek union. Alone is best.*

Alone, T'Khut, her face now scarred with mines, took her way around the planet, and as the centuries passed, the fires that began to kindle on Vulcan's surface mirrored her own. She had no clouds so strangely shaped as Vulcan came to have in later years: but the fires burned on and on. . . .

ENTERPRISE: FIVE

───────────── ☆ ─────────────

"Most disturbing," Spock said. "It is indeed most disturbing."

He and Jim and McCoy were sitting in one corner of the rec room. They had beamed back up to the ship from Sarek's and Amanda's, after dinner with them, and none of them had felt able to go to bed, not yet.

"That's the understatement of the year," McCoy said. "Spock, I thought she was the great logical one, after all that business at the Place of Marriage and Challenge. She seems to have changed her mind."

"People change, Doctor," Spock said, "Vulcans no less than humans. But I will be very, very interested indeed to find out what the extent of her involvement with this business is, and what her motives might be."

"I have my suspicions," Jim said. "Revenge for being ditched."

Spock looked at him mildly. "If so, it will be an epic revenge," he said. "And I am curious, if she is indeed behind all this, how she has been managing it. She has held some minor government office for some time—that much I know—but nothing that would particularly assist her in *this*."

Jim nodded. "Uhura came back to me with the information about that clipping from the information service," he said. "It comes from one of the names on Bones' list. The writer, Selv, who seems to be doing so much of this work."

Spock frowned slightly. "Selv," he said. "I seem to remember that name from somewhere."

"And *you* can't remember who it is right away?"

"Doctor," Spock said gently, "not even all *full* Vulcans have eidetic memory. One must be trained to it, and I have not been so trained. I think I may be pardoned for knowing a lot of Vulcans, and not remembering all of them, any more than you remember all the people you have ever met on Earth."

McCoy nodded. "At any rate," Spock said, "we will soon enough find out who he is. As for T'Pring—" He looked indecisive, a rather surprising expression for him. "Generally when one has a query to make of a bonded Vulcan woman, at least a query that does not have to do with her work, one makes it through her bondmate. Doctor, is Stonn's name mentioned anywhere in your list?"

McCoy flipped through to the first group of S's—a considerable number, bearing in mind the traditions about Vulcan male names—and then to the rest. "I don't see it," he said, sounding cautious. "I'll run a check with the copy I have on solid."

"Do so. I would find it very interesting if Stonn's name were not somehow involved as well."

"Come to think of it," McCoy said, "so would I." He riffled through the list a little more, then chucked it aside.

Jim stretched. "Best I should turn in, I suppose: it's going to be a busy day."

"Captain," Spock said, "are you comfortable with the briefings you have had on the debate format?"

Jim nodded. "It's not as structured as I'm used to—the interruptions from the floor are going to get fairly interesting, I suppose. At any rate, I think Sarek has told us pretty much what we need to know."

"Correct me if I'm wrong," McCoy said, stretching as well, "but the debate format reminds me a lot of the format for the Romulan Right of Statement."

Spock nodded. "There are striking similarities, which have

been noticed before. There are of course differences—you are allowed to eat and sleep if you desire to, or to have a rest break—"

Bones grinned. "I think I'll do all right," he said. "The only question is whether the Vulcans have ever seen a good old-fashioned Southern-style filibuster."

Spock's eyebrows went up. "Don't get carried away, Doctor," he said. "If you tire out your audience with too many brilliant displays of illogic, you may force an early vote."

"I'll be careful," McCoy said, as he got up. "I dare say I can keep them interested . . . and I have a little logic of my own."

Spock nodded. "So I have seen . . . though I would never dare attempt to quantify it."

"I just bet you wouldn't," Bones said. " 'Night, Spock. Jim."

"Good night," they both said as McCoy ambled out.

When the door shut behind him, "Spock," Jim said, "are there any indications of the odds shifting at all?"

"They are getting worse," Spock said. "But I am becoming uncertain of the computer's ability to predict odds accurately when there are so many variables involved." He put one eyebrow up. "Such as the doctor."

"Well," Jim said, "we'll just do our best. It's all we can do." He sighed, then yawned. "I have to admit," he said, "I wish I could be a little fly on the wall when you have your talk with T'Pring."

Spock looked at him oddly. "Why," he said, "would you desire to be a fly? And specifically a small one?"

Jim laughed. "You know perfectly well what I mean."

Spock looked at Jim sidelong, and allowed himself the smallest smile. "More often than I used to," he said, "yes. Good night, Jim."

" 'Night, Spock."

They met in the transporter room, the next morning, about half an hour before the session in the Halls of the Voice was due to commence. Spock was setting the transporter controls himself, from memory apparently. "Are you ready, gentlemen?"

"Ready, willing, and able," Jim said.

"At least two out of three ain't bad," McCoy muttered.

They stepped up onto the pads and watched the room dissolve out around them. What they reappeared into was echoing dimness, and before they were even solid, Bones was complaining.

"You've done it again," he said. "Why do your people go for *size* all the time? Can't you do anything *small?*"

Spock looked resigned. The space in which they stood was, if anything, larger than the Hall of Pelasht had been, all made of a smooth, cool-colored, blue gray stone. The ceiling was as high as Pelasht's and shafts cut through it let in the sunlight in bright slanting columns. "Why do Vulcans like to conduct their business in railroad stations?" McCoy muttered. "Can you just tell me that?"

Spock let out a breath. "I believe that what you are complaining about," he said, "is pre-Reformation architecture. It did tend to the unnecessarily grand, at least according to present tastes. The room where the debates proper will be held is not this one, so you may relax, Doctor: you won't have to shout."

"Spock," said Sarek's voice from away off to one side. Regal in his dark ambassadorial robes, he came over to meet them.

"Father," Spock said. "I was not expecting to see you here today: your testimony does not begin until tomorrow."

"I had hoped to meet you before you went in, that is all." Sarek's eyes narrowed. "I have come across a piece of information that may or may not aid you in your assessments of matters: it is for you to judge."

Spock inclined his head.

"I was interested in your revelation about T'Pring, Doctor, and so I made a discreet inquiry or two," said Sarek. "It seems that Stonn is dead."

Jim glanced at Bones and at Spock. "How did he die, sir?"

"Privacy seal was invoked on the information," Sarek said.

"Which means," Spock said quietly, "that it is likely to involve *plak tow* in some manner. There is almost no other reason for which the seal is invoked, not in these times."

"Precisely," Sarek said. "At any rate, T'Pring is now a free agent, released from any obligations laid upon her as a bondmate. I thought you should know."

"Thank you, father," Spock said, and bowed slightly to him.

"I must go now: there are still things to be handled at the embassy and consulate. I hope you find the morning illuminating. Captain, Doctor." And he was off, all dignity, though it was amazing how fast dignity could move when it had appointments elsewhere.

"Well, well, well," Bones said softly.

"We should not begin discussing this here, Doctor," Spock said: "it would be in execrable taste. Let us go into the Hall of the Voice and let them know we are present."

They walked off toward one side of the great entry hall. "Where are we, physically?" McCoy said. "I must admit I didn't check the map."

"We are on the other side of shi'Kahr from Pelasht," Spock said, "and possibly this will surprise you, but we are several hundred feet underground. The shafts are at ground level. This complex—*va'ne'meLakht* it was originally called—"

" 'Hiding from the Rage,' " McCoy said.

"Yes. It was a refuge built for sunstorm weather—there was some of that just before Surak's time, though not since. It was meant to hold the whole population of shi'Kahr and the environs, hence the size. These days it has been taken by the Academy and is used for the biggest lectures and meetings and for some ceremonial occasions."

Spock led the way over to a group of doors, all of which stood open. There was a young woman standing there tapping away busily at a computer keyboard: as Spock approached she looked up and said, "Attendee or testifier?"

"Testifier. Spock."

She tapped at the keyboard. "And you, sir?"

"The same. McCoy, Leonard E."

"And you?"

"The same. Kirk, James T."

She hardly looked up. "Row eight, seats one through three. Someone will be around to you with your schedule, sirs, and a program."

"I want popcorn," McCoy said suddenly.

The young woman looked up at him from underneath very

pertly slanted brows and said calmly, "No eating in the auditorium, sir. Next?"

They headed into the auditorium. Spock was looking bemused: McCoy was grinning. "You cut it out," Jim said. "Just for that, you're not getting the aisle seat."

"Spoilsport."

The auditorium was indeed not as big as the hall they had beamed into, but it wasn't exactly snug, either. It was built in the round—or perhaps carved would have been a better word, for the stone showed no joins whatever. More of the big shafts were cut in the thick ceiling, a group of them directly over the round stage in the center, and the seats sloped up and away on all sides. It was a design that the Greeks and Romans had found successful to work in, acoustically satisfying, and Jim felt as if he would have no trouble speaking there. *Always assuming I can find the right things to say. . . .*

They found their seats, and the place filled up around them fairly quickly. There were a surprising number of non-Vulcans in attendance, but no more than about a thousand all told, in a place that could hold fifteen thousand easily. Vulcans filled the rest of those seats, silently, and Jim found himself suffering from the ridiculous feeling that he was being stared at. *Well, the Fleet uniform is plain enough to see. And I'm here to be seen. Let 'em stare.*

"Do they play the national anthem?" McCoy said, leaning over to whisper to Spock. He had gotten the aisle seat anyway.

"No," Spock said softly, "nor does the fat lady sing, I am afraid. The debates will merely be called to order, and begin."

"Who's on first?"

Jim looked quizzically at McCoy. "Maybe we should have gotten you that popcorn after all."

The audience started to become quiet, as if they saw or heard some signal that Jim had missed. He looked around him, but saw nothing but impassive Vulcans everywhere.

Then one walked out onto the stage, and Jim winced a little. It was Shath.

"On behalf of the government of All Vulcan," he said, "I declare these proceedings to be open. The debate will take the traditional form, and the proposal put is: That the planet Vulcan, and all its citizens, shall withdraw from the United Federation of Planets. Testifiers will please state their affiliation, their position on the proposal, and then make their statement. Proceedings may only be closed by the electorate, and the threshold number is one billion, eight hundred thousand. Opinion may be registered with the data and news networks carrying the proceedings.'' Shath consulted a datapad that he was carrying. ''Number one, please.''

There came a soft chiming sound from the far side of the audience, and Jim could see a lot of heads over there turn in curiosity. He smiled as a small, bright form like a giant twelve-legged glass spider clambered up onto the other side of the stage and spidered into the shafts of sunlight at the stage's center.

''My name is K's't'lk,'' she said, and her voice filled the place as the amp field found and focused on her. ''I hold the recallable rank of Commander in the Starfleet of the United Federation of Planets. As regards the proposal: I say nay.''

She shuffled and chimed a little. ''There is a traditional courtesy of this planet,'' she said, ''that in any gathering, the least hominid guest, to be made to feel most welcome, is asked to speak first: and I see you've done it to me again, since there are no Hortas, methane-breathers, or aphysical creatures here.'' There was a slight rustle of amusement in the crowd. ''Well,'' she said, ''at any rate, I thank you most kindly for the welcome, and with that formality out of the way, let me also say that I'm glad to be back here on the Academy grounds, here where I've read so many papers and been led to doubt my own sanity. Or to cause others to doubt theirs.''

She turned slightly to face another portion of the auditorium: or maybe this was simply a courtesy on her part to the hominids there, since K's't'lk's eyes were spaced evenly on the top and sides of her domelike body, and she could see equally well all around her without turning. A little storm of glitter shifted and moved with her as she turned in the brilliant sunlight. ''I want to talk to you about the pursuit of science in the universe,'' she said, ''and its pursuit on Vulcan, and some of the things that have happened in the sciences since Vulcan joined the Federation, a hundred eighty years ago now. I said 'nay' to you just then because I counterpropose that the Federation has done Vulcan more good in the sciences than another thousand or five thousand years of isolation would have done her. You will pardon me," she said, "if for the moment I stay out of the ethical mode. I have strong feelings about that as well, but today is for the sciences."

She turned again, chiming. "You will doubtless hear enough people willing to tell you about all the things that Vulcan has done for the Federation," she said. "And I will agree with all of them: the improvements in transtator technology, on which practically ninety percent of our present technology rests; the extraordinary advances in medicine, especially in genetic engineering, at which Vulcan is more expert than almost any planet in known space; the pure researches in astronomy and cosmology and cosmogony, which have opened up more and more of space to the Federation's starships; and so much more. Most of you have done your homework for this proceeding and know exactly what you've given us." Her voice got a happy sound to it. "My own research fellows here have given me many a gift, many an astonishing insight, and I treasure that.

"Let me add this, however. The affiliate species of Starfleet, and perhaps most specifically the humans of Earth, have a gift to give the Vulcan species that is surely a match for any you give us. Human beings are especially good at making a scientist ask questions that they might not have asked otherwise. Unexpected questions, bizarre questions, even illogical questions. I know," she said, at the rustle that went through the place then—a somewhat disgruntled sound. "Logic is important. But there are things in the world that logic is no good for."

"Humans, mostly," remarked someone somewhere in the audience. Jim was surprised. He was also surprised at the fact that the amp field seemed to focus instantly, as soon as one spoke above a certain voice level.

"That was an easy one," K's't'lk said, sounding slightly amused. "They have things to teach you about humor, too. Even Surak had that, and he never said anything about feeling that it needed to be gotten rid of. There is more confusion about what Surak said, and didn't say, and what it meant or didn't mean, than I've ever seen about anything else on the planet."

"You said you were going to stay in the scientific mode," said another voice from somewhere.

"I am," K's't'lk said. "I am talking about semantics. Surak

was many things, and one of them was a top-flight semanticist: doubtless there are none as good working here today, since there seems to be so much difficulty working out what he meant. Anyway," she said, "as I was saying, there are realms of the sciences where logic is useless, such as the so-called 'non-causal' sciences that are my primary study here. When cause does not necessarily follow effect, logic becomes a feeble reed to lean on. Yet put aside logic in dealing with these sciences, and suddenly great riches of results come pouring out of a universe that has been quite mulish and uncooperative while logic in the classic sense was being applied.

"I am saying," she said, turning again, "that as regards the sciences, Terrans have something you need. For one hundred and eighty years Vulcan researchers have been availing themselves of that resource, whatever you choose to call it—creative illogic, the skewed viewpoint, the 'aha' experience. Turn them away, and you may say and do what you like, but your sciences will never be as effective, as nourishing to the spirit, as dangerous again. The danger, perhaps, is the key. Without the unpredictable, the mysterious, there is no joy in science. And the mad suggestions of Terrans are definitely part of the unpredictable—since they are part of a universe that we are beginning to realize is more sentient than we ever dreamed. To turn your backs on the voice that speaks through Terrans is to reject part of the Universe, speaking for itself as all things do, and your data will be incomplete forever."

She paused, and laughed a little, a soft arpeggio of amusement that echoed from the walls. "I remember the last paper I wrote here," she said, "on what the press later called the Elective Inversion drive for starships. My colleagues at the Academy were uncertain about most of the equations. Well, actually they thought most of them were crazy. They were willing, though, to make allowances for the basically different world-view of Hamalki mathematics. They also had to admit," she said, with a smile in her voice, "that when we built our prototype drive apparatus, the equations worked. They were a little annoyed at first, if I remember right. So far, so good. But it took installing that apparatus in a human starship, and having it tinkered with by a human engineer with a genius for physical things, to make that drive come back from wherever it had gone when it went where no one had gone before."

"That mission was the one that practically destroyed the starship *Enterprise,* was it not?"

"I think quite a few of her missions may qualify for that description," K's't'lk said. "I think you are implying that the apparatus was useless and a failure. Well, it was one of the more glorious failures that science has had lately. During that 'failure' we found out more about the structure of neighboring alterdimensionate space than any *hundred* Vulcan hyperphysicists had told us for years. It needed the human variable to make it happen, and there is no better example of a wild success in my chosen field. I think that to purposely turn away from human influence, to purposely reject an approach which produces useful results, simply because you dislike the style of the approach, or it makes you nervous, is to purposely limit what your sciences can achieve. And since the purpose of the study of science is to know the universe as completely as possible, then you are sabotaging that purpose at its root, and you might as well stop studying science entirely. It is illogic of a particularly distasteful kind, and frankly, I expected better of you people."

There was a sort of cheerful scorn about the last statement, a sort of all-right-let's-fight! attitude, that produced an immediate response from the crowd. If it had been a group of humans, Jim wouldn't have been particularly concerned; but the spectacle of a big group of Vulcans, usually so protocol-conscious and restrained, now interrupting one another and speaking with that icy clarity that meant extreme anger—

"It's a regular free-for-all," McCoy said under his breath to Jim, astonished, after a few minutes of listening to angry responses, and K's't'lk's cheerful and somewhat angry responses to them. "This is what we're going to have to deal with, huh?"

Jim nodded, wondering, *Am I going to be able to keep my temper under control? There's a* lot *of anger out there. . . .* "Maybe you should slip me an Aerolev before I go on," he said, sotto voce.

McCoy snorted. "Drugs? You just do your deep breathing like the rest of us."

There was some sort of argument going on now about "the

active versus the passive mode" and "the life of physicality versus the life of the mind." A Vulcan, a tall, respectable-looking gentleman, was speaking at some length about how too much involvement with the active life and physical reality was an error in balance, since even K's't'lk as a physicist would have to admit that the universe was almost all empty space, and nothing was real—

"Tenured," McCoy whispered to Jim. Jim nodded.

"Ah," K's't'lk said, "the old dichotomy problem. Don't you think that one or the other of those 'lives,' physical reality or theoretical unreality, might sometimes be senior to the other? More valid, shall we say?"

"Indeed not," said the Vulcan. "It is a classic error in thinking, particularly, if I may say it, of the human sort. The illusory or internally subjective nature of physical existence is perhaps its most important and revealing characteristic. When one remembers that, on most levels of consideration, one does not exist, such matters as the question before us today assume their proper *aaaaaaaiigh!"*

The gentleman had been so busy expounding on the illusory nature of matter that he had never noticed K's't'lk come softly down from the stage and walk down the aisle next to which he was standing. As for the rest of it—even a Vulcan will react when a silicon-based life form bites him in the leg.

"Fascinating," K's't'lk said. "For someone whom on most levels of consideration doesn't exist, you scream with great enthusiasm. And I *heard* you, too. Better have that looked into."

Jim's eyes were wide as he glanced at Spock. "Is that kind of thing allowed?"

"In the more formal forms of the debate," Spock said, "everything is allowed up to ritual duels to the death."

"Remind me not to get into a fight with anybody here about science," McCoy muttered.

"Anything else?" K's't'lk said, as she resumed the stage. There was no response. "Now like the humans of Earth, I do come of a brash young race. We've only had space travel for, oh, about two thousand years. But speaking for myself, I throw in my lot with the Terrans. Their unpredictability and their ability to look 'sideways' and see through a problem makes them the

perfect partners in the sciences; and for those who would exclude
them because of youth or strangeness, I can only say that you
should enjoy your universe . . . because we and they will someday
be enjoying others, and we'll miss you. I thank you, one and all.''

There was some muted applause. K's't'lk got off the stage
and walked up the aisle past them. As she went by McCoy, Jim
could hear her chiming very softly, ''. . . showed *him*. Get all
Zen with *me* . . .''

Two more speakers followed—an elderly Vulcan woman and
a handsome young Tellarite—and their statements were dry and
calm, not interrupted as K's't'lk's had been. Jim wondered
whether this was because they were both supporting the secession, on the grounds of inequities of Federation funding to non-
Terran research projects on Vulcan and elsewhere. Then there
was a break for the noon heat: the debating would resume three
hours later.

''Is it all going to be this exciting, I wonder?'' McCoy said
as they headed out to see about some lunch.

''I suspect it'll heat up a little when we go on,'' Jim said.
''Spock, can you suggest somewhere around here?''

''Yes,'' he said; ''the *Nakh'lanta* in the Old City is very good
indeed. I will give you the coordinates. But I will not be with
you.''

McCoy looked at him with concern. ''Where are you going?''

Spock looked amused, but there was something a little
hollow about it. ''I think you would say,'' he said, '' 'I need to
talk to my ex.' ''

Finding her proved to be no particular problem, especially
when Spock checked the sign-in list at the Hall of Voices and
found that she was not there. Her commcode was a matter of
public record: it was listed to a semirural community nearly a
quarter of the way around the planet. He called the *Enterprise*
and had them beam him over.

The house was big, bigger than his father's. More than that:
it was ostentatious. It was built in one of the styles that had been
popular just before Vulcan joined the Federation—partly buried
underground, so that the landscape could be enjoyed with as little
hindrance as possible. The gardens around it were full of exotics,

many of them imports from other planets—tender plants that required an exorbitant amount of water to keep. Taken together as a whole, house and grounds said loudly to every passerby that the one who owned this place had all the money they needed, and few wants.

Spock walked to the front entrance and touched the annunciator. "Yes?" said a voice.

Very cool, that voice. Hers. He hesitated. "Spock," he said at last.

For nearly two minutes nothing happened: no reply, no movement inside that he could hear. He was about to turn away from the door—the "silent" response was a proper one to the privacy codes implicit in the Rules of Silence. But then the door opened.

It was a cliché, and he knew it; but T'Pring was almost exactly as he had last seen her—cool, slender, tall, extremely beautiful. He studied her face for any sign of the years since their ceremony at Marriage and Challenge. There was none. The beautifully tilted eyes examined him too.

"I did not think you would come," she said.

"Explain."

"I did not think you would have the courage," she said. "Come in, if you like."

He followed her into the entry hall, feeling intensely uncomfortable. "May I offer you refreshment?"

"Yes," he said, but only because it was incredibly rude to refuse. One thing, though, was certain: he was not going to ask for water.

T'Pring went off and brought two flasks of fruit juice. Spock saluted her with the glass, in the correct fashion, and drank it all off in a draft—a gesture that would be read as that of a person on business, or one who had no intention to spend a long time under the other's roof.

"Please sit down," she said to him, sitting down herself.

"Very well. I have come to ask you," he said, putting the glass down, "what your involvement is in the debates presently going on."

"I caused them," she said. "Surely your logic has led you that far, unless the humans have completely addled your wits."

"My logic led me that far," Spock said. He was not going to give her openings for baiting him or respond to hers.

"Stonn died," she said.

"I heard. I grieve with you." It was not quite a lie.

She sat quite still and erect on the bench across from him, her hands folded in her lap, meeting his gaze without flinching. "You will have gathered something of what was going on, then. When he took me after the Challenge, after you 'defeated' your Captain and released me, we lived well enough together for a time. But I was discontented. The matter had not gone as it should have, at the *Koon-ut-kalifi*. It did not go as I had planned." This was delivered in utter coolness of expression, but T'Pring's voice had something of the very small child about it: a balked child, angry because it did not get the sweet it wanted. "Stonn grew discontented himself, thinking that perhaps I desired you again, or some other. He attempted to induce *plak tow* in himself prematurely, to make me desire him." Spock nodded: there were drugs that could be used for this. They were risky, but some felt it worth the risk. There were some Vulcans who felt that no joining was real unless it happened in the blood-madness.

"He died of a hormonal imbalance, a form of 'endoadrenal storm,' " T'Pring said. "I was not entirely displeased. He had made me mistress of his estates, and though they were small, they satisfied my needs. But then as time passed, I came to realize that once again you had robbed me, you and your captain: it was fear of your desire that had made Stonn take the drugs. Once again I did not have my desire, and once again it was your fault."

Spock held quite still. *How shall I say what I am thinking? She cannot be entirely blameless in this*—but he held his peace.

"So I decided to take from you such things as you had taken from me," she said: "your future life, your captain, and anything else I could manage that would cause you such pain as you have caused me. It would be *ashv'cezh*, and my satisfaction would be great."

Spock nodded, numb. *Ashv'cezh* was literally revenge-worse-than-death: death would seem uncomplicated and pleasant next to the situation that this kind of revenge implied.

"I looked about me," she said, quite calmly, "and found

that there were many of our people, more than I had ever suspected, who feared the Federation, and especially against Earth. It seemed to me that my weapon lay ready to my hand. SoI began first to invest the proceeds of Stonn's estate with some care. I did very well, and made a great deal of money in the interstellar commodities markets.

"Then," she said, "I began making substantial donations to various small organizations and publications. You will have noticed them to have come to me so quickly. Through them, I found such other Vulcans as were willing to say the things about Earth people as make Vulcans angriest against them: appeals to logic, and to emotion as well, for some of us still have emotion." Hardly a muscle of her face moved as she said it. "I took my time: it was worth taking. Slowly a groundswell of opinion started to build up: it fed on itself—for people will say things that they hear others say, whether they truly believe them or not. And if they say them often enough, they will come to believe them anyway. I used other weapons, as well. I bribed some government officials, who had found their posts increasingly diminished by the influence of Terrans on Vulcan. I suborned various media and data network personnel to add emphases to certain stories and downplay others. And slowly the public came to perceive a problem with Terra, and slowly the government came to feel the public's unease, and they grew uneasy themselves, fearing for their positions. When it became plain that what the electorate wanted was a chance to secede from the Federation, the government complied quickly enough."

She smiled, just a little. It was a wintry look. "And so we find ourselves where we are today. If all goes well, the vote will be taken quite soon, and we will be out of the Federation: and it will be forever beyond your power to take anything from me again, for you will either stay here and lose your starship and your captain—without which you are nothing—or you will go into exile with him, and your father and mother will become exiles as well, and I shall be well avenged indeed."

It was almost a minute before he could speak. Then all he could say was what he had said before:

"Flawlessly logical."

"I thank you," she said. "Is there anything else I can tell you?"

Spock shook his head.

"Then I will ask you to leave," she said. "I have some calls to make. I think perhaps you will see me once more, before the end; I shall come to the Hall of Voices to watch you and your captain plead for leniency for Terra. I shall find it most amusing."

"I dare say you shall," Spock said, and got up.

She saw him to the door.

"Farewell, Spock," she said.

"Live long," he said—and the rest stuck in his throat.

He left the house, walked out to the quiet, dusty road, and called the *Enterprise:* and beamed up, feeling, for the first time in his adult life, faintly sick to his stomach, for a reason that had nothing to do with McCoy's potions.

VULCAN: FIVE

---------------- ☆ ----------------

Darkness, and stars. In the great silence, nothing moves: or at least nothing seems to, in this old emptiness, except the shadows of superstructures as the ship turns toward the distant Sun or away from it. Peacefully it slips through the long night, the slender dark hull, spinning as it goes; silently it drifts past, the picture of peace.

Fighting continued in ta'Valsh for the eighteenth day as the Mahn'heh Protectorate defied the claims of neighboring Lalirh for debated territory in the Tekeh area. An image, in her mind, of running figures, a bolt of blue fire being shot out of a smoke-stained window, the sound of glass shattering: and dirt stained green by the body that lay on it, one arm cauterized away, the head half-missing from someone's explosive charge. A whole street of what might once have been pleasant suburban houses, now burnt, their windows blown out, all the ground before them blasted and scorched, pavings upturned or cracked asunder. *Representatives for the Lords of Mahn'heh and the King of Lahirh said today in statements to the nets that there were no plans for talks at this time.* Images of well-fed men and women reading their statements in quiet rooms full of newspeople. *The Lords of Mahn'heh claim that the Tekeh area was settled in 164330 by people of their lordship and have been demanding the immediate cession of the territory and payment of reparations, including as an additional reparation the hostage-exchange of one of the sons of the Lahirhi King. The Lahirhi deny these charges and have stated in the past that any further movement against them by the Mahn'heh may cause a nuclear exchange like that with which they brought down the government of neighboring Ovek two decades ago.* An image of craters, nothing but craters—a stretch of land, perhaps farmed once to judge by the rural road running through it, now devastated by low-yield packed neutron charges.

The hostilities between Duveh and the Lassirihen provinces show some signs of settlement, but a minor terror and kidnapping guild has threatened to destroy both ruling houses if their demands for a part in the negotiations are not met within a tenday. Images of richly robed people coming with great gravity down the front stair of a shattered, bombed-out palace, much patched and repaired. *The Night Alliance, an offshoot of the old Mastercraft, now disbanded since the death of its leader T'Meheh in a hovercar accident, has demanded marriage into both the Duveh and the Lassiriheh royal houses, and bride- or groom-payments in excess of five million nakh—*

She sighed and let her mind drift away from the images. They bored her. It seemed there was nothing else on the news these days but all the fighting at home. At least there was peace here.

Alieth shut her eyes and saw the image again of the battered palace, while the inreader went on about divisions of lands and money. She sighed again and did the change in her mind that took her into one of the entertainment channels, changed again for first the hall, then the room she desired. Idly she scanned around for mind-IDs. No one she knew was around, not even Mishih, who was usually in the net whenever he was awake. Alieth supposed that it was night where he was, wherever that might be. She seemed to remember he was somewhere up near one of the poles—Retakh, that was it, a frightful place to live, out in the middle of nowhere.

Rather like here, actually: but at least here, no one was likely to drop a selective chemical bomb on you suddenly in aid of a herdbeast raid.

Alieth scanned around. Scanning was what one called it, though what it looked and felt like was an effortless drifting through a geometrical landscape, filled with vague solid-geometry shapes that contained messages. Their outsides were tagged with ID information, so that by brushing up against one, you could get a feel of the mode of the mind that had sent it: angry, affable, interested, informational. If you were interested, you reached in and grasped the message: perhaps added to it. She brushed a few as she passed them, found nothing that interested her. Increasingly she had no interest in touching the frozen messages, only the live minds. Hanesh complained about this, but then Hanesh complained about everything, and he hated the nets.

I might as well come out, she thought. There was no telling what was going on in the ship at this point; though it was true that Pekev was supposed to be coming back at this point, from that survey. But Alieth was sure that there would be nothing interesting. There had not been anything interesting for months.

That was the problem.

Ah, she thought, *why come out?* And she sank back into the net, changing rooms, and went looking for someone to talk to. Someone who breathed real air, who walked on the world, someone who might have a bomb dropped on them at any moment. Alieth drifted gently through the colored landscape, under a firefly sun, and wished there was some other state of mind than peace or war. . . .

Pekev swore softly in the spacesuit. There was a soft hiss inside it that was not the air processing system, and a whisper of outgoing breeze tickling his skin, low down, near the leg seam. It had to be leaking again. *I don't need this,* he thought, but there was nothing he could do at the moment. It would cost much more than a suit's worth of air to get back in the ship, repair the leak, and get back out again: and his father would not be pleased. There would be violence at mainmeal again.

Then again, he thought, *when was my father last pleased at anything?* He wobbled a little in the hard cold starlight as he

wrestled with the specific gravity apparatus he had attached to
the rock.

It was not a particularly large asteroid, but theoretically they
did not have to be large to be good, and this one had the right
look: that sootiness about the outer shell, or the hard glassy glint,
that spoke of a high carbon content. You learned to recognize it
after a while. It took time: the carbon-matrix asteroids were not
all that common—they comprised only about a tenth of a percent
of all asteroids—and the iron and nickel ones, so much commoner, were useless for the family's purposes.

The spec-grav apparatus was big and unwieldy. It had to be:
it carried its own small thrusterpack, suitable either for maneuvering an asteroid close to the ship—and even the smallest of
them were fairly massive—or for holding the rock stable while
the pack's core drill drove itself into the asteroid and took a
sample. It was all sampling today, for Pekev. Yesterday he had
spent some eighteen or twenty hours with the long-range pack
on, rounding up several promising-looking rocks: the usual routine—scan, lock on, spend an hour or two or three in transit, find
the rock and examine it; if it was any good, bring it home. Or
near home, at least—match its intrinsic velocity with the ship's
(often another two hours' brutal work with the thrusterpack),
make sure its course was stable, and then go out again after the
next one. Pekev could still feel the ache in his back from the
insistent push of the thruster against his mass, and his leg was
still bothering him where the first rock, the one that had since
turned out to be worthless, had pinned him briefly against the
thruster—a tiny miscalculation of thrust, but one that he was
lucky hadn't killed him. Probably that was where the seam leak
had come from.

But today was easier: the pack used for the core samples
was a little more tractable, not having as heavy a framework and
as much mass as the big long-range rock mover. All Pekev had to
do today was go from one rock to another, sample them all, and
take the samples back for analysis. That would take him another
few hours: if he was quick about it, he could get to sleep early.
Then tomorrow, back out with the long-range again. It was his
routine. Sometimes he thought it would drive him crazy: some-

times he thought it was the only thing that kept him sane. At least it was quiet, when he was out here and the family was back there.

Its self-diagnostics satisfied with its hold on the rock, the core drill started up: he could feel the vibration of it through the thrusterpack's framework. Pekev sighed a little, looked over his shoulder at *Rasha*. *She's getting old,* he thought. It was a sad sort of thing to say about a ship that you had loved from when you first moved into it as a child. But there it was: Pekev was almost fifty, now, and so was the ship, and she was near the end of her effective life. Unfortunately, the family didn't have the money to buy another one.

The drill whined through the framework. Pekev breathed out. There had been a time, long ago—he could barely remember it—when there had been enough of everything: when *Rasha* was only one of seven ships, a small but respectable fleet, and the family had been doing well. They had been numerous, then. The biggest of the clan ships, *Urekh* and *Gelevesh*, had held a hundred people each. He had some faint far memory of *Gelevesh* with its huge shining corridors. He could hardly have been more than a babe in arms then: now, from looking at the old specs, he knew that the ship had not been the vast cavernous thing he remembered. But nonetheless it was enough to keep a subclan of a hundred people comfortable and well for a year's mining in space.

But they were all gone, now: all of them but *Rasha*. *Urekh* had been caught on the ground and blown to dust in the five years' war between the Teleiw and the Nashih, and *Gelevesh* had been taken by the Nashih as a prize of war and recommissioned as a scoutship or somesuch. Pekev's father still muttered threats of disembowelment at the memory of the petty little voucher the Nashih had given him as they turned him and the family out: "payment," they said, "compensation"—but they sneered at him as they said it. No other ship of the clan was big enough to take them all: *Gelevesh*'s original complement, whole subfamilies, were forced to scatter across the planet and find work on the ground or in someone else's ship—a bitter thing. And the clan head, Pekev's father, was forced to move from ship to ship of the dwindling fleet—for one after one they had to be sold, to service the still huge debt owed for the building of *Gelevesh*. Finally there was nothing left but *Rasha,* meant for a long-range seven-person ship and now holding eleven.

The core drill stopped. Pekev checked the sensors to make sure the drill had completed its punch and not simply aborted—though sometimes an abort was good news: sometimes it meant diamond—and that was what the family had always mined for. Let others handle the large mining operations like nickel-iron. Indeed, they had to let others do it. Not even at its most successful had the family had capital enough to buy a ship of the size needed to handle the really big rocks, which you had to handle to make the enterprise pay off. But diamond, especially the industrial kind, was plentiful enough in asteroids to pull in a fairly respectable income . . . at least, plentiful enough to keep a small ship running. And sometimes, where there was industrial diamond, there was gemstone as well. Sometimes. But that was mostly a dream. . . .

He touched controls on the thrusterpack, and the core came back out of the drillhead. Pekev pocketed it and touched more controls: with small thunking vibrations that he felt through the framework, the pack turned itself loose of the rock and drifted gently toward him. In instant reaction he pushed it, shoving it and himself away at the same time—the thing had more inertia than he had, and could push fairly hard if you didn't take care. He had seen his father Nomikh pinned against the *Rasha*'s hull more than once by it: a mistake that could kill under the wrong circumstances. It was a shocking mistake for his father to make . . . but his father was not quite what he had been anymore.

The leak sighed away against his leg. There was only one more rock to do. Pekev maneuvered himself around the framework, hit the rear controls for the forward thrusters, checked his sensors for the radio beacon he had put on the last rock waiting for him, and programmed the pack for a three-second burst. Little pencils of blue chemical fire stood out from the edges of the framework in four places, then went out. Pekev hung on to the framework, and it and he began to drift away through the dark.

He never once looked at the stars.

* * *

The Vulcan historians' name for the period was always the Age of Expansion. Only much later did it begin to be referred to as "the pre-Reformation" period. It was the time in which many of the petty kingdoms of the old world had been unified—mostly against their will. This process had, of course, been going on for a long time. There are historians who will point out that from the time of Earth's Bronze Age, around 10,000 B.C., and the fall of the Spartans at Thermopylae, there was only one period of ten standard years during which as much as ten percent of Vulcan was *not* at some kind of war, economic or political. But in the so-called Age of Expansion, the process of "unification" sped up considerably.

It was actually consolidation, rather than unification: larger territories and tribes swallowing smaller ones, either by annexation or political blackmail. Vulcan technology, especially weapons technology, was becoming more and more advanced. Atomics had been achieved, were used a few times with results similar to those at Hiroshima and Nagasaki on Earth . . . but the result was not the eventual disarmaments that Earth achieved. Instead, the Vulcans retailored their atomic weapons to be less "dirty"—neutron bombs were an early "happy" solution to the problem—and there was also much research into chemicals, and artificial amplifications of such psi talents as the killing gift. The latter was refined until it could strike down thousands at a distance of thousands of miles. It usually also killed the adept, but since most of those with this talent were using it under threat of harm to their families, it did nothing to stop the gift, or the governments who bred for it.

Nor were conventional weapons abandoned: guns and bombs and particle weapons of all kinds continued to proliferate in endless variety. And more to the point, the angers of the annexed, and the outrage of the great nations that the annexed should attempt to resist their will, proliferated as well, until nearly the whole planet was a patchwork of ancient grudges, constantly being avenged on the "wrongdoers"—and countervengeances were taken, endlessly. It perhaps says more about the time than anything else that the Vulcan language included no less than several *thousand* words for terrorism and its applications, each precisely describing or defining a different kind of violence as to degree or type.

The terrorism spread into space, but not as quickly as it might have, since Vulcan merchant ships by tradition were never armed, and military ones, oddly enough, had not yet been conceived of. (Earth historians who find this astonishing should also remember that, until fairly late in its history, Vulcan did not have the concept of the standing army . . . simply because for thousands of years, there were not the resources to support such a thing. There was no way to feed such a monster, or give it water, and usually nowhere to keep it. Technology changed this, much later . . . but mercifully, it did so very late.) Space stayed peaceful for a while, and many people who were able to, chose to live there full time, rather than on the turbulent surface of the planet.

Their only mistake was in believing that they had left the warfare behind them.

When Pekev came in and unsuited, he found his father where he usually found him—sitting at the common-room table, his head in his hands, looking at a computerpad that lay before him, with the ship's accounts on it. There were times when Pekev wondered whether his father actually looked at the numbers there, or was merely trying to be awake, but at the same time trying not to think about anything, while seeming to. *If that's so, I wish he wouldn't,* he thought. *He ought to go hide in the nets like Arieth. At least we wouldn't have to stare at him all day.*

Nomikh raised his head and looked at Pekev when he heard the sounds of the spacesuit seals being undone. "How did it go?" he said. It was what he always said.

Pekev pulled the core samples out of his pocket and tossed them, one by one, to his father, who caught them out of the air expertly enough and peered at them. Even by naked eye, two of them had the faint dark sparkle that spoke of enough industrial diamond content to make them worthwhile. "Nothing big," he said softly. His voice was very deep.

"Nothing big, father," said Pekev, and breathed out. Sooner or later that question always came out. *Anything big?* His father had been looking for the big one, the rock of the gods, ever since Mother had died. Before that, he had not cared about such a thing . . . or if he had, he would have given it to his mother. But Mother was dead forty years, now. *It must be terrible. He thinks he should have been rich forty years ago. Instead, he's spent forty years breaking even, just barely. . . .*

"Going to get them in tonight?" his father said. It was just sunset, by ship's time.

Pekev didn't look at his father. "It's late," he said.

"Early yet," said his father. "You could get one of them in before you go to couch."

"Father," Pekev said, "I'm sehlat-weary, and my suit has a leak in it."

"Carelessness," his father said, and his voice began to scale up. "Carelessness! Do you think these things can be dug out of the sand? What do you take me for, a man with hundred-*nakh* pieces coming out of his pockets? I've told you again and again, you have to take better care of the equipment! We can't afford to waste—we don't have *anything* to waste! Not air, not water, not suits, not—"

Pekev shut him out as best he could and kept on unsuiting. There were few days when he did not hear a variant on this lecture. He was rather hoping he might have been spared it today, but apparently there was no chance of that. "And you're getting as lazy as your sister, you won't even go out for one more run before you eat your meal, not that you've earned it—"

Pekev was much tempted to take the leaky seal between his hands and pull it right apart, so that he would not be able to go out until the adhesive that would be needed to patch it had cured, and that would take a couple of days. But he resisted the temptation, though the flexfabric was smooth under his fingers and it would have been easy enough to do. "Not that you've earned your food for the last moonaround, let alone this week, the hours you've been working, or not working. When I was your age—"

Pekev went off down the cramped little corridor, into the workshop area, and slung his suit over the worktable, then spent a moment looking up at the hanging board for the electric sealing tool he needed. His father's voice was diminished, but there was no escaping it. That was always the problem: on a ship this small, there was no way for anyone to escape from anyone else—except perhaps in Alieth's manner, in the telepathic networks. Pekev was not sure he approved of that method at all: and Alieth's tightbeam charges were a constant drain on the ship's income. But at least it kept her out of the way when she had no rock to work on. . . .

Pekev found the sealer, thumbed it on, and rustled the suit around until the seal was properly exposed, then ran the sealer down it. His father was still going on about the hours he had worked when he was a boy. To hear him tell it, he had built *Gelevesh* with his own hands, in his spare time, after wrestling asteroids into the ship he was working with his bare hands, and nothing but a tank and a tube to breathe from. *I wonder if other people have this problem with their fathers,* he thought.

Along the bond in his mind, she said, I did with mine. But yours is worse, I think. I almost pushed him out the airlock in his singlet this morning.

Beloved, Pekev said, and looked over his shoulder, feeling the nearness of her. T'Vei came in from the coreside workshop, holding an assay dish in her hands. It was full of what remains after an asteroid has been crushed and the good parts extracted: in this case, nearly a threeweight of granular black diamond, the crystals very perfectly separated, and large.

"There's more where that came from," she said, and smiled at him. "Nearly three hundred times as much."

"From that wretched little rock this morning? You are a genius!"

She tilted her head at him. "Possibly. I suspected the presence of a couple more pockets than the ultrasound showed. I was right."

"That's our next week's fuel paid for, then. I was beginning to worry."

"With me around?" she said lightly, and went off to show the diamonds to their father.

Pekev shook his head and went back to the sealing. T'Vei was the one who handled the actual "dismantling" of an asteroid. It was delicate work, though one might not have thought so: many people thought that all you had to do was crush the thing and take the diamonds out. But crush it how? Do so incautiously, and if there were any gem-quality stones inside, they might be destroyed: even the value of the industrial diamonds could be destroyed if too many of them were fractured or powdered. There were machines of all sizes in the coreside lab for the handling of rocks—from huge magnetically driven hammers to tiny things that took off no more than a flake at a time—but it took a specialist's sense for how a stone would fracture, and what was inside it, to use the tools effectively. T'Vei was the specialist, though Pekev would never have suspected she would become so expert, when they were bonded. It was in fact something of a joke in the family—though not in her hearing—for T'Vei had been bonded into the house to pay off a debt that House Balev owed Pekev's father. Pekev didn't care. Their love was one of the only truly good things in his life, and that she was as good at processing as she was only made things easier.

He heard his father's tirade break off short for the moment, heard T'Vei's sweet voice murmuring to him about payload percentage and bulk discounts. "Well," his father said, "if your husband were as good at what he does as you are, we might become something again, this family might, but he won't even go out and bring in one more rock before he settles down to his evening of sloth—"

She came back in with the assay dish, and her eyes were annoyed, but there was also pity showing in them. *He's not well, my love*, she said along the bond. *You know how it is with him when these moods strike. He's been thinking about how much he misses Yiluv, that's all, and when he's like this, the sun would look black to him. I'm done up there: let me just get into my suit and I'll go in and fetch that last one into close orbit.*

"No," Pekev said, wearily, though he really didn't want to, "I'll do it."

No, truly, she said. *You're tired.*

"Not that tired," he said. He turned the sealer off, checked the seal to be sure it was tight, and started to put the suit on again. *One more won't kill me*, he said in the bond. *You be off. We'll bring it in ahead of the others and show it to him to make him happy. Maybe that'll buy us a night's peace.*

She smiled at him and went back to the corelab.

Pekev swore softly, trying to keep it out of the bond, and headed for the airlock again.

* * *

Exotic music fills her ears: the sound of deep trumpets and martial gongs. Their sound lures her along through the landscape to one of the "experience gates." She has not tried one of these for a long time. She allows herself to drift through it, borne along on the music.

Viewpoint dissolves into day under Vulcan's burning sky. Sand stretches out everywhere: and far in the distance a point of stone rears up, terrible, a dark shape in the bright day. Viewpoint pushes in on it. It is Mount Seleya, and the awful stair carved up it, ten thousand steps cut around and through the ancient weathered stone. Effortlessly she drifts with the viewpoint up those stairs, sees the great desert spreading out below her, the Forge, a place of old dread, where powers move that men do not understand, and there are hints of great incomprehensible voices speaking secrets in whispers under the sand. But no matter for that. She goes to her destiny at last, to find her fate.

They are there waiting for her, all of them, robed and solemn: the priests and priestesses of the secret arts of the mind. As she approaches she drifts no longer: she is a body, has a body, that of a young woman, armed and armored. But she has no sword, and a great anger burns in her heart.

I have come for what you owe me, she says. She has no idea from where the words come to her, but she speaks them as if they are her own, and the anger in them her own as well.

The chief priestess stands forth and raises her empty hands. *We have it not,* she says. *The evil one, the mind that resists, has taken it from us. You must win it yourself.*

This was not in the pact, she says, and steps forward wrathfully.

The chief priestess looks at her coolly and moves not an inch. *You speak true. And so we give you something that was not in the pact as well. Know then the name of the sword: that this is indeed Nak'meth the Great, forged of these sands by the Mastersmith, three thousand years agone, and with a virtue set on it that one who holds it shall achieve their dream and their right. And know too,* the priestess says, paying no attention to her gasp, *that your right is a mighty one, for you are no peasant's child, as you were told, but castoff child of the Lady of Yiliw, and heir to*

all the lands of Yiliw, which now lie under the evil one's domin-
ion. Go, then, and take the sword, and take back also what is
your own—

"Arieth," someone said in her ear, "we need you."

She opened her eyes. She hated opening her eyes.

Her room. Her tiny room, after all that space, after the fresh
hot smell of the sand, the scorch of the sun beating down. Her
bed, her chair, her clothes. A little box, a tomb such as one of
the ancient kings would have been embarrassed to use to bury
his pet *aalth* in.

She got up angrily, pulling the commlink away from the
neural contact at the back of her neck. It was T'Vei's voice, the
hateful thing. She had her Pekev; why couldn't she leave other
people alone? Hadn't Arieth been up all this morning doing assay
on cores while T'Vei was slugging abed? Useless, bought-in—

The door opened, and she began to shout "Go away!" but it
was Hanesh, and he had as much right to the room as she did.
Unfortunately. He was all over grease: he had been in the
mechanical grappling systems again, by the look of him. *He*
spends more time with the machinery than he needs to, said a
suspicion in her mind. *Or he seems to. I wonder*—

"Pekev's bringing in one last stone tonight, to see if it won't
calm Nomikh down a little," he said softly. "Come on up and do
the assay on it when he gets it in, so we can all have a little peace
from the old man."

"I did my work this morning," Alieth said, and started to lie
down on the couch again. "Let T'Aria or Tasav do it—they
haven't been doing much of anything lately." She sniffed. "I
should have trained to be a pilot. Three seconds of work in a
halfday and then eating and drinking and sleeping for a week
after. Besides, I'm having my rest now."

"You're not," Henesh said. "You're on the link. You're
always on the link."

"I do my share of work," she said. "Just because you don't
care for the link, don't dictate how I can spend my spare time."

He said nothing, but down the bond she could hear him
thinking. *I just wish you would spend a little more time with me.*

She ignored this. "Go on," she said. She lay down again and
waited for him to go away: but he would not. Finally, because it

was the only way to get rid of him, she said, "All right, then. I'll come, but only when the stone's up in the hold, and not a minute sooner."

He nodded and went out.

Alieth sighed and felt around for the neural connection, slipped it cool against her neck, lay back. The shadows swallowed her, and then the light turned to the wild heat of the sun again.

The high priestess lifts her hands and says, "Go with the blessing of our order on you. And that you may prosper, take these gifts—" More horns are blown, and the tiny bells are sounded, and jeweled treasures of antique make are borne forth on brocaded cushions. She accepts them, and the underpriests and priestesses cry her praise.

Their voices drown out the bond very satisfactorily.

"It's in range," Pekev said from outside the ship. "Got a lock on it, Hanesh?"

"Locked," Hanesh said, not needing to look up from the console to check the image on the screen. He was strapped in his seat, as was T'Vei beside him: there was no gravity in the core, which was just as well for handling asteroids anyway.

Hanesh put his arms into the control boxes and flexed his fingers as they fit into the gauntlets. Outside the ship, the grapples flexed too, mirroring his action, and reached out slowly and carefully for the asteroid. One had to be careful. The carbon-matrix asteroids were not nearly as solid as the nickel-iron ones, and could shatter . . . and when they did, you had wasted fuel and energy, and Nomikh would make your life miserable. Every now and then Hanesh wished the ship had a tractor beam, but such things were much too expensive when *Rasha* was built, and they certainly couldn't afford one now.

He reached out iron arms for the asteroid, watching his progress using the stereo cameras mounted on the outsides of the "fingers." The asteroid was a medium-sized one, perhaps as wide across as a man was tall, but easily within the hold's ability to handle. The outer part of the hold was already evacuated, waiting to have the asteroid placed in the handling cradle.

Hanesh reached out carefully. This maneuver was always the trickiest part of the business, because typically one did not stop the ship's spin unless the stone was of unusual size. His arms, therefore, were spinning on their vertical axis, just as the ship was. Pekev had done his part, carefully aligning the asteroid with the ship and putting the proper spin on it so that they seemed to be stationary relative to one another.

"Here we go," said Hanesh, reaching out close. The arms were within a height: a half-height: they closed.

And he felt the clutch, and the crunch, through the remotes, and swore.

"What?" T'Vei said.

"It shattered."

She peered at the screen. "Not very badly. Look at it. Just bring it in carefully: it's too big to waste the energy that throwing it away would take."

Hanesh considered this, then thought of the mood of the old man downstairs, and agreed. "Handling a cracked stone," he said, as he carefully pulled the arms in, "is not easy, you know."

"Yes," T'Vei said, and was silent: but she smiled at him.

Hanesh watched the view. The arms turned inward on themselves, rotating on universal gimbals so that the evacuated hold yawned before them, and the cradle came up on its tracks to meet them. Very carefully he snugged the asteroid down into the cradle, and its own servos came up with soft-tipped probes and secured the stone all around.

"Well done!" T'Vei said. "Let's get it in."

It took very little time to seal up the outer hold, repressive it, and open the secondary doors to bring the cradle down into the main lab area. "You might as well page Alieth now," T'Vei said, launching out into the middle space of the corelab and using handholds to pull herself over to the cradle.

"Must I?" Hanesh said. T'Vei flashed a smile at him and turned her attention to the stone. Carbon matrix of one of the harder sort: it had that heat-seared look about the outside of it. She floated around the circular crack, looking at the stone. "You did a nice job on this one," she said. "Very little fracturing from the remotes. A little bit of flaking here—"

"I'm not surprised," he said. He used the mechanical page to the comm network, rather than the voice comm, then grabbed

another set of handholds and launched himself down toward
T'Vei. "I squeezed it pretty hard. What are you looking at?"

She was gazing at the crack, which was about half an inch
wide. "Would you reach me one of the handtools?" she said.
"The sonic chisel, the little one."

He handed it to her: she thumbed it on and applied it to the
crack. A few flakes of stone sprang away.

Something translucent and white showed underneath them,
about an inch wide.

She used the chisel again. Another inch of translucence was
revealed, roughly paralleling the surface of the asteroid.

T'Vei looked at Hanesh with astonishment. "I don't think
we're going to need an assay on this one," she said. She chiseled
once more, and another flake of stone fell off: and inside the
crack, another inch of diamond showed.

"Get Father," she said.

His first response was to hang staring from a handhold,
without speaking, for nearly fifteen minutes, as T'Vei ran an
ultrasound scan on the asteroid. There were three diamonds
inside it, two in the upper half of the asteroid, undamaged, and
one that Hanesh had unfortunately squeezed and cracked with
the rest of the stone. The cracked one was the biggest: nearly a
hundredweight in mass, and roughly half a height in diameter.
The whole family came to see: the children, the pilots, everyone.
Even Alieth had stayed, even after finding that she wasn't needed.
Ten astonished faces stared at the diamond on top as T'Vei's
skilled hands freed more and more of it.

Finally Nomikh turned to Tasav, one of the pilots. "Set us a
course for Ashif Belt Station," he said, "and don't spare the
fuel."

Tasav nodded eagerly and went off to see to it.

"This is it," Nomikh said. "The stone, the stone of stones.
We are rich!"

"Let me get it out of the matrix safely first, Father," T'Vei
said, not looking up from her work. "I'd prefer not to crack any
more of these."

He nodded, and fell silent. T'Vei felt fairly sure she knew
what they were thinking about. Gemstones from space were

highly prized on Vulcan, and brought a great deal more at market than ones that originated onplanet. What diamonds of this size could bring—she hardly dared think. She suspected that Nomikh could buy a fleet twice as big as the one he'd had, and still have plenty left over afterward.

But what would he do?

Funds that came to the family in the course of work were used to fuel the ship and take care of its running expenses: after that, what was left over was usually divided evenly among the crew. Even the children got a share. The only problem was that there was usually nothing left after the ship was taken care of: a little extra for a few luxuries, some food other than the standard dried reconstitutable rations. T'Vei sighed, remembering a time on Ashif Station when she had had fresh meat for dinner. Well, perhaps it had been frozen. She hadn't minded.

But now—there would be no question of keeping the ship running anymore. There would be enough money, enough for everything. And would all the members of the family want to keep mining?

Why should they? We can all retire, wealthy.

But to where? And to whom? Will we never see one another again? For indeed there had been and were often times when T'Vei heartily wished one or another of the family dead, and doubtless they had had the same wish about her. It was hardly to be avoided, when people had been in such close quarters for so long. What was going to happen now?

She had a horrible feeling, as flake after flake of stone fell out, that she would find out soon enough.

Nomikh did not come to dinner that night. Many of the others didn't care: their spirits were too high as they discussed their plans. Some of them were extraordinary. Almost everyone wanted to buy a house on Vulcan, a *big* house. A couple of them were more interested in a "sealed cottage" on T'Khut, in one of the colonies, away from the trouble on the planet. But most seemed to be willing to take their chances with trouble, convinced that money—the kind of money they were dealing with now—would buy them plenty of protection. And then there would be luxuries. Fine clothes, personal vehicles, servants, ships of their own, trips to all the places they had wanted to see. It would be a wonderful life.

T'Vei was not so sure. Several times she looked with concern at Pekev, and once he said to her, down the bond, *I am beginning to wish that you had never made me go out and get that thing.*

She looked at him quizzically. *I didn't make you go,* she said, *and I would have gone out, if you hadn't. I think we had better take this as an intended thing.*

He shook his head, but inwardly agreed with her.

The discussion kept going long after the meal was done. T'Vei slipped away, after a while, and went down to Nomikh's cabin. She knocked, but there was no answer: she peered in.

She found him lying on the narrow bed, eyes open, staring at the ceiling, with the tears streaming down either side of his face.

"It doesn't work anymore," he was saying. "It doesn't work."

She slipped in softly and sat on the floor by the bed. "What doesn't work, Father?" she said.

"The bond," he said, and wept hard.

T'Vei bowed her head. There were mate-bonds that broke, at death, and ones that did not. There were always the tales of the ones that did not break, when one bondmate could still feel the other, regardless—even sometimes speak to them. There was no predicting it, and you never knew which kind you had until it happened.

"She never," Nomikh said. "So hard she worked, and she never had anything. I wanted everything for her. But all I had was this. Forty years, without her. And now this—!" He wept again. "She should have been here," he said; "this should have been forty years ago. Riches, leisure, everything she wanted. But it comes now. Why now? Why now?"

And then a long pause, and whispered, the worst, "This was not it. This wasn't what I wanted after all . . ."

There were no more words in him, only tears. T'Vei touched his brow gently, then went out to go upstairs and finish the assay, the weighing and measuring of the stones. She had no heart for the talk around the scruffy dinner table, all the ornate plans. She was afraid, to the core of her, but Nomikh would want a reckoning of the stones in the morning.

She climbed up to the core and tried to do her work without looking at them more than necessary. But they looked at her, the cold white eyes of the stone, the eyes. . . .

In the morning they met again around the table, after the mornmeal things had been cleared away, and T'Vei sat down with her pad. Nomikh was last at the table, and he sat down with an odd quelling expression on his face.

"Tasav?" he said first, to the pilot.

"We will be at Ashif Station in four hours," he said.

"Good. T'Vei?"

"Well." She looked at the pad with a great desire to say, *They are worthless.* "We have three stones, as you have all seen, and some fragments. They mass, all together, seventeen point six three hundredweight." Astonished glances went around the table. "At present market value—well, there would be some change in the value as the stones are cut. But I estimate the value of the stones at around two billion *nakh.*

Silence.

Nomikh breathed in, breathed out. "Very well," he said. "We will dispose of them to the gemological service group at Ashif. And then—" He cut in on the happy gabble that rose up around the table "—we will refuel and go out again."

Everyone looked at him in shock. Then the gabble started again, but loud and angry.

"—why—"

"—we can retire—"

"—don't want to work anymore—"

"—not fair—"

"Haven't I taught you anything about thrift?" he said. He did not shout in return at their anger. His eyes were strangely cool. "What happens when this money runs out?"

"Runs out??" said Tasav incredulously. "Even divided eleven ways, we could all be dead before that happens!"

"Divided?" The cool eyes looked at him. "There will be no divisions. The money stays with the ship. And we go out and earn our keep."

The silence that followed this statement had a terrible waiting quality.

"This is not the one," the old man said, looking at them one by one. "This is not the great stone, the stone of stones. This will keep us for a while, for as long as it takes us to find that other. We will keep looking until we find it. And then we can all retire. But for the time being we must be thrifty, we must be prudent, we must save our air and energy. Someday we will be rich. But we are not now. Not yet."

Eyes sought one another around the table, and what they mostly said was, *He's gone mad at last. We always saw it coming. Now here it is*

"You're just afraid we'll leave you all alone," Hanesh said, jumping up from his seat. "Don't you trust us? Can't we be trusted to keep working together—or living together, even if we don't have to work—aren't we still a family, even if we don't *have* to be? Won't we be a family still, even if we're not cooped up in this wretched metal can? Father!"

"Children must stay with the family," Nomikh said placidly, "until they are old enough to take care of themselves."

There seemed no answer to that.

"We will be at Ashif soon," Nomikh said. "Alieth, make a shopping list. We're getting low on dry stores." And he got up to leave.

"Getting low!" Alieth screamed. She had not been on the net for almost a day, to everyone's astonishment, and there was a greed in her eyes that was terrible to see. "We're getting *dead,* trapped in here, nothing but work, and want, scrimping oxygen and eating scraps, and hurting, and never having any of the good things— Let us out of here, let us free, give us what's our right, let us go home and never have to be out here again in the cold and the dark! *Let us away from you!*"

Nomikh looked at her gently. "Not until you're older," he said, and left the room.

"We could kill him."

The silence into which this suggestion fell was awful. More awful was the feeling that some of the people around the table agreed to the idea.

The mutiny had been going on for an hour and a half now. That was the only thing T'Vei could think of to call it. All the adults on the ship save for Nomikh were still around the table, where Nomikh had left them. They had risen, sometimes, several of them, to pace, to shout, to strike the walls in frustration: but they always sat down again, to mutter, to lay bitter plans. No one had mentioned *this* one before . . . but T'Vei had feared it. And now her fear was upon her.

She shook her head. "He is Head of House!" T'Vei said, looking around the table, trying to meet their eyes. They would not look at her. Not Hanesh: not Pekev, next to her, his heart oddly closed to her, purposely shutting down the bond: not Tasav, his fists clenching and unclenching: not T'Aria, his bond-mate, the other pilot. And not Alieth, who had made the suggestion, the terrible one, the one that everyone had thought of, and no one had dared utter, until now.

"He is Head of House!" she said again. "There is no relationship more sacred, none! Without him, who are we?"

"Free," Hanesh muttered. "Free to do what we want, for the first time in our lives."

"And defiled!" T'Vei said. "Just because we are angry at him, does not give us leave to kill him! To kill the Head of House is as good as to kill the House!"

"The House *is* dead!" Alieth shouted, and this time she looked up at T'Vei, and the expression in her eyes, of anguish, and horror, and anger, was terrible to see. "It has been dead since *Gelevesh* was taken from us, since the fleet was broken and nine-tenths of the House became groundlings, scratching at the hide of the world for a living, begging other houses for their sufferance! Now comes a chance to finally be something, to become something, and what does he do? He forbids it to us, and says he will doom us to the rest of our lives out in this cold waste—"

"Alieth," Pekev said, "give him a little time. The shock may have unsettled him, but he may yet come back to his senses. Give him a few—"

"What? A few moons? A few sunrounds? How many? Ten? Twenty? Fifty? How long are you willing to live this life, Pekev? It's all very well for some, who have the bond as you do—"

Hanesh flinched hard: Alieth never saw it. "But what about the rest of us, who are a little more interested in the rest of the world, who weary of living our lives like container cargo? Who would like a little more to drink than water, and a little more to eat than dry protein extender, and a little more to see than the dark, and the inside of a metal can? Who would like a *nakh* of our own to spend, and somewhere else to spend it than a filthy, smelly orbital station full of broken-down scrapings of the system—" She gasped for breath. "How long do you think it will take Nomikh to come back to his sanity? If he ever had it, these twenty years gone? There he lies in his cabin, blubbering and wishing he were dead, and I for one wouldn't mind seeing him get his wish!"

That stunned silence fell again.

"We could keep him in his cabin," Tasav said, very low, in his reasonable way. "There would be nothing wrong with that. When we get to Ashif, we can tell the port authority that he's lost his mind. They'll agree to that, certainly, once they see what's happened, and how he is. And then—"

"Then what, Tasav?" Pekev looked over at him. "Then we choose a new Head of House, right? The eldest?"

All were still for a moment. That would have been Pekev. He was closest by blood to Nomikh, and eldest of the close blood relatives.

Alieth stared at him. "And let *you* decide what happens to us all? You, the Good Son? You'd do as your father did. And hold to yourself the decision of what to do with the money—"

Everything got still again as this new thought went through all minds. What was to guarantee that a new Head of House would be any more sane, one way or another, than the old one? What was to keep a new Head of House from keeping everything for himself, or herself, and turning all the others out, or doling out pittances to them that would keep them working on the ship, as wage slaves, for the rest of their lives? Who could trust any agreement any one of them would make, with control of such massive amounts of money at stake? Heads turned, and T'Vei was horrified to see the family looking at one another with terrible suspicion and assessment. Who might be managed, if they became Head of House? Who could be bullied or swayed into managing the money the way each of *them* would prefer it?

Who would be permitted to live—?

"No," T'Vei whispered, horrified. "Listen, all of you, you will kill the House—"

"The House is dead," Alieth said, very low. "It died the moment Pekev brought that rock on board."

"It is not dead yet," T'Vei said. "It lives still. If you will all see reason!" She glanced at Pekev, more terrified for his life, now, then she had been for Nomikh's. "We can appeal to the port authority against Nomikh's decision, as soon as we dock there, and get a ruling dividing it equally—"

"After bribing the authority with how much?" Alieth said. "How much of what you bled and starved and sweated twenty years for? Why should they have so much as a copper cash *srikh* of it? What have they done to earn it? Oh, no, darling sister-in-House. Indeed not. Let us settle family matters in the family, as has been done among our people these many years—"

A chair scraped back. "Tasav—" T'Vei said, more horrified than ever, for he was making for the door, and in his hand was the pilot's sidearm that he never, never drew.

Tasav paused in the doorway. "We need not go straight to Ashif," he said. "There is time to work matters out beforehand, to everyone's satisfaction . . . and make sure all the stories match."

T'Vei's heart raced in her. "Tasav, this is madness," she cried. "*All* of it is madness. Nomikh has the computer keywords for navigation and helm! You cannot manage the ship without them . . . and the Head passes them to the computer through dermoneural link—"

"So he does," Tasav said softly. "I think he can be encouraged to pass them on."

And he went out into the corridor.

Alieth got up, knocking her seat over in her haste, and went after him.

T'Vei looked at Pekev in utter horror. *This is the end for us,* she said down the bond. *Did we think by coming out here into the dark that we were getting away from the madness of the world? We have brought the madness into the night with us—or else we pretend we have it not, like Alieth—but it is here. It is here—*

They heard the first shot, then. Everyone in the room scrambled to their feet. Some ran one way, some another: but the end was the same for all of them. For T'Vei and Pekev, trying to stop Tasav, the quick bolt through the body or the head that killed their bond in fire: for Tasav, the answering bolt from Nomikh's room that caught him, and several of the others, as they forced his door: for Nomikh himself, floundering in madness and old mourning grief, a last bolt that put out his pain forever: for the few remaining adult members of the family, and the children, crouching terrified in the living quarters, a long, long wait, while the ship went its way, the computer locked on course and unlockable save by passwords that no one alive now knew.

And in one small room, a drifting over a misty landscape, a passage through a door—and one stands again before a robed priestess who gestures forth the sub-priestesses carrying objects of ancient rarity and virtue. They give her the spear, and its point runs green with blood: she brandishes it in the dawn. They give her the horn, graven about with dire runes and prophecies of death to her enemies: she lifts it, and winds it, and the walls of the mountain give back the terrible sound as if it were the cry of an avenging army encamped below. And they give her the most terrible weapon, the helm that teaches one to read the dreams of men, for by learning their dreams and turning them against them may they most easily be crushed. She fits it on her head, and it fits perfectly, and she knows her foes vanquished already.

Take these, the priestess says, *and go forth to victory*. And all is swallowed up in a great burst of white fire as the Sun comes up, victorious and terrible, above Seleya—

The ship came into Ashif Station on the wrong vector, at the wrong angle. It answered no hails: its engines were running at full, so that it was accelerating at a deadly seven g's all the way in from the time it was first sensed. There was no way to catch it, no way to stop it. A particle beam targeted it at last, and blew the ship into pieces that rained down, around, and sometimes onto Ashif Station for hours. It had not been carrying any cargo that could be detected: its holds seem to have been empty. The asumption was that the ship had been pirated, or more likely taken by terrorists, and used in an attempt to destroy the station.

Mahn'heh Protectorate, which owned the station, accused Lalirh of having engineered the attack, and shortly thereafter destroyed one of Lalirh's orbital stations in the asteroids with something new: a weapon that seemed to involve the combination of matter and antimatter. There was general alarm about this, since it seemed likely that now someone with the proper technology, and the access to the necessary materials, could actually destroy Vulcan. But in the several wars that started as a result of Mahn'heh and Lalirh destroying one another's populations with neutron bombs, this possibility seemed a little too remote to waste much time considering.

Far out in the asteroid belt, the day the *Rasha* was blown up, a small storm of glitter rained past Ashif and off into the endless night: odd small micrometeorites, crystallized carbon of some sort, very hard, very tiny, and mixed up with other meteors. The station's defensive field vaporized them in a shower of little sparks as they hit it, and the tourists from Vulcan pointed up through the dome and talked about the beauties of the universe.

Far away, T'Khut looked over the edge of the world at the new fires burning on Vulcan . . . possibly some of the last ones.

ENTERPRISE: SIX

————————— ☆ —————————

FROM: Curious
DATE: 7466.31
SUBJECT: Oh really?

A lot of people have been making some pretty definite statements in here, the past couple of days, about the Vulcan
situation and what they think should be done about it. It's easy
to do. But none of us are actually sitting in the hot seat: or
none of us except the captain. A lot of people in here are acting
as if he's supposed to save this situation somehow. Well, how?
No one has made a single suggestion that could actually be
implemented. If you people are going to insist that the situation
can in some miraculous way be saved from disaster by one
man, the least you can do is share your wisdom with us as to
how. Otherwise, you might have the grace to keep your traps
shut.

I await with interest what will probably be an echoing silence.
best, C

"Now what do you make of that?" Jim said to McCoy. They
were in his quarters the next morning, ready to beam down to
the Hall of the Voice.

McCoy studied the screen. "Piquant," he said. "Very much to the point. A little rude. I wish I'd left it."

Jim looked at him sidewise. "I thought maybe you had."

McCoy laughed. "Not me. My spellling gives me away every time."

"Why don't you use the spelling checker? There's one built into the system."

"I don't like the way it punctuates."

Jim chuckled. "Well, look at the answers. You want rude—!" He leaned over the keyboard and started the replies scrolling down the screen.

"Goodness," McCoy said, staring at it, fascinated. "Temper, temper!" Once he laughed out loud: several times he frowned very severely. But mostly he shook his head. "Generally," he said, "they sound a little sheepish. 'Curious' caught them out."

"But look at this one, Bones." Jim scrolled ahead a few pages more. "Here we are."

> FROM: Llarian
> DATE: 7466.35
> SUBJECT: Re: Oh, really?
>
> Those who know others are intelligent:
> Those who know themselves have insight.
> Those who master others have force:
> Those who master themselves have strength.
>
> Through nonaction nothing is left undone.
>
> L.

Bones was nodding. "How about that," he said. "We have a Taoist on board."

"I was wondering why it sounded familiar. The *Tao Teh Ching?*"

"That's right." Bones looked at the message. "What do you think of the advice?"

"It sounds good." Jim smiled slightly. "It always sounds good. I remember thinking how sensible a book it was, the first time I read it at Academy. But it's always harder to practice the advice in the field."

"I guess you just have to keep practicing," McCoy said. He scrolled through the rest of the messages, then cleared the screen and straightened up. "I wonder who 'Llarian' is."

"That thought has crossed my mind as well." Jim shrugged. "I would love to know what he, she, it, means. But it's not something I can find out."

"Maybe someone else could. . . ."

Jim looked at McCoy in shock. "Bones! And you're usually so careful about confidentiality." He shook his head. "Let it be. Whoever Llarian is, I appreciate the advice. Meanwhile . . ." He glanced at his chrono. "Where's Spock?"

The door signal chimed right then. "Come in," Jim said.

Spock entered. "Captain," he said, "are you ready? The doctor will be needed in the Hall shortly."

"Just about. Off," Jim said to the computer. "You set, Bones?"

"Ouch," McCoy said. "I assume that pun was meant to make me feel better, or else accidental. I am *never* set to talk in front of large groups of people, especially not while sober." He made a rueful expression. "But I'm ready to go."

"Do your deep breathing," Spock suggested gently.

McCoy made a friendly suggestion to Spock that did not involve the Vulcan's respiratory apparatus.

They headed out into the hall together. "I must admit," McCoy said quietly as they went, "I still can't get over your little tête-à-tête with T'Pring yesterday. And the sheer coldness of the woman. I had trouble believing what you told me she said the last time, when she challenged . . . but this was a hundred times worse."

Spock nodded. "She is implacable, Doctor. Even if there were something that she could do to stop this situation, she would not do it. And truly," he added, "I much doubt that anything she might do would make any difference, at this point. This context of bigotry and exclusion is already finding too secure a foothold in too many Vulcans' minds: they would overrule any attempted suspension of the proceedings."

Jim thought back to that cold, lovely face and the words Spock had later reported: *You have become something of a legend among our people, Spock. . . . I became aware that I did not desire to be the consort of a legend.* And the word she and her family had given at the original binding, and any concern about Spock's feelings—not that a Vulcan would have admitted them, granted—went out the window at that point. All she needed was someone to challenge Spock when the time came: and Stonn, who had desired her then, had been willing.

If you lost, then Stonn would be mine. If you won, then you would release me because I had challenged, and still there would be Stonn. And if your captain won, then he would release me because he did not want me, and Stonn would still be there. . . .

The sheer coldness of it. And the logic. That so sharp a mind should also be so cruel. . . .

I think I would like a little talk with this lady myself.

But it would have to wait. They headed into the transporter room and climbed up onto the pads. "You have the coordinates?" Jim said to the transporter technician, Mr. Schneider. And then added to McCoy, "Why, Bones, you're sweating."

"Your turn will come," McCoy muttered.

"Number six," said Shath.

McCoy stepped up there with great calm. Considering that those who spoke before him had been vehemently anti-Federation, and the audience was (if Jim judged the mood correctly) in a very satisfied mood, Jim thought he was being even calmer than he needed to be. McCoy stood in the shafts of downpouring sunlight, glanced up at them for a moment, and then looked once right around the room, as if taking the measure of it. His stance was remarkably erect for a man who habitually slouched a bit. But Jim looked at this and wondered if he was not seeing Vulcan body language, rather than Terran. Bones was shrewder than people usually thought.

"My name is Leonard Edward McCoy," he said, and the focusing field caught his voice and threw it out to the back of the room, all around: but there was still something about the tenor of the voice itself that hinted that the focusing field might be doing slightly less work than usual. "I hold the rank of Commander in the Starfleet of the United Federation of Planets: my position is Chief Medical Officer of the Starship *Enterprise*. And as regards the question of the secession of Vulcan, my position is, hell no!"

There were chuckles from some of the humans present, a bemused stirring from some of the Vulcans. "I hope you will pardon me the momentary excursion into my mother idiom," McCoy said: "perhaps I should more correctly say, with Surak, *ekhwe'na meh kroykah tevesh.*" This time there were murmurs from the Vulcans, and they were of approval. The translator did not render the words—Jim assumed they were in classical or "Old" Vulcan, which the translator was not equipped to handle.

When the crowd settled a bit, McCoy went on in very precise Vulcan, and this caused a minor stir as well, which died down eventually. "I want to keep this on a friendly basis," he said, "despite the fact that some of you are feeling decidedly un-friendly toward Terrans. Nor am I here to lecture you. Others here have been doing that a lot better than I could." There was a dry sound to his voice for a moment. "I am here to ask you, as a planet, not to pull out of what has been a very old and successful affiliation for everyone involved."

He paused for a moment, looking around. "It's kind of sobering to be looked at by an entire planet," he said. "You people have hidden the cameras perfectly: I appreciate the effect. Anyway. Some people here have spoken about the mode of their comments—scientific or ethical or whatever. Well, for my own part I'm not sure there's a difference, or should be. Science is barren without ethics, and ethics has very little to use itself on without science. But I'll speak of what I know, if I may. The medical mode, I suppose we might as well call it. I understand that Surak valued the healer's art highly, so I suspect there's some precedent."

Bones walked around the stage for a moment, his hands clasped behind him. Jim had to smile: he had seen this particular pacing mannerism many times, while McCoy tried to figure out the best way to deliver some piece of good or bad news. "The first thing I would want to say to you," he said, "is that it is illogical to re-wound what is already healing. Or as my mother used to say, 'If you don't stop picking at it, it'll never get better.'" A soft sound of amusement ran around the hall.

"Most of the agreements going these days between Terrans, or the Federation, and Vulcan, are in the nature of band-aids. One of our species hurt the other, somewhere: the other said,

'Sorry,' and put a bandage on it. It's the usual thing you see when you see two children playing together. At first they hurt one another a lot—''

"Our species is hardly a child compared with yours," said someone in the audience, a sharp angry voice.

"Well," McCoy said, turning that way and searching the audience with his eyes, "that depends on how you reckon it. Certainly your species was making bombs and guns and missiles and such while ours was still mostly playing with sharpened sticks and stone knives, or in a few favored areas, bronze. But I'm not sure that any particular virtue accures to that distinction. And even if we *have* been kicking one another's shins for less time than you, it's still true that era for era, Terra's people have kicked a lot fewer shins *per capita* than Vulcan has. You have several times almost reduced your population to below the viability level: it took a miracle to save you. We may be a bloody, barbaric lot of savages, but we never went *that* far. Even when we first came up with atomics." He chuckled softly at the slight silence that fell. "Yes," he said, "you saw that article in the data nets last night, too, some of you. Where *is* Selv?" he said, peering amiably around the audience. "You in here?"

"Here," said the sharp voice.

"Aha," McCoy said, looking out in that direction and shading his eyes. "Long life and prosperity to you—though I doubt you'll attract much prosperity with that kind of world-view. Still, maybe wishes count. But it might help if you went to Earth some day and checked out what you talked about so blithely—"

"The data about Earth speaks for itself—" Selv's thin, angry voice came back.

"*No* data speaks for itself," McCoy said, forceful. "Data just lies there. *People* speak. The idiom 'speaks for itself' almost *always* translates as 'If I don't say something about this, no one will notice it.' Sloppy thinking, Selv! You are dealing with second- and third-hand data. You have never been to Earth, you don't understand our language—and this is made especially clear by some of the material you claim to be 'translating' from Earth publications: an Andorian spirit-dancer with a Ouija board and a Scrabble set could do a better job. Though I must admit I really liked the article on the evolution of the blood sacrifice in Terran culture. That is *not* what major-league football is for. . . .''

McCoy let the laugh die down, and then said, "Anyway, where was I? Agreements as bandages. *Every* species in this galaxy that bumps into another one, bruises it a little. Some of them back off in terror and never come out to play again. Some of them run home to their mommies and cry, and never come out again without someone else to protect them. That's their problem. I for one would like them to come out and play—''

"And be exploited? The Federation's record of violations of the Prime Directive has been well documented—''

"Selv, I love you. How many violations of the Prime Directive have there been?''

A brief, frantic silence. "Well documented," McCoy said, good-humored, "but not well enough for you to have seen it. Too busy reading about football? Anyway, don't bother looking it up," McCoy said, "I'll tell you myself. In the last one hundred and eighty years, there have been twenty-nine violations. It sounds like a lot . . . except when you consider that those took place during the exploration of twenty-three *thousand* planets by the various branches of Starfleet. And don't start with me about the *Enterprise,*" he added, "and her purported record. There have been five violations . . . out of six hundred thirty-three planets visited and physically surveyed over the last five years.''

"And all those violations have taken place under a Terran's captaincy—''

"Oh, my," McCoy said, and it came out almost in a purr, "can it be that Vulcan is leaving the Federation because someone here *doesn't like James T. Kirk*? What an amazing idea! Though it would go nicely with some rumors I've been hearing." Bones strolled calmly around the stage for a moment, while Jim and Spock looked at one another, slightly startled. "Well, no matter for that. Still, Selv, your contact with the facts about things seems to be sporadic at best. If I were the people who've been reading your material in the nets—and a busy little beaver you've been of late—I would start wondering about how much of what I was reading was for real. That is, if I were logical—'' McCoy lifted his head to look up over the audience's heads, and Spock glanced meaningfully at Jim. McCoy knew perfectly well where the cameras were.

"You may say what you like," Selv said, "but even five violations are too many! And your use of your data is subjective—"

"Of course they're too many!" McCoy said. "Do you think I would disagree on that? And as for my data, of course it's subjective! So is yours! We are each of us locked up in our own skull, or maybe skulls, if you're a Vulcan and lucky enough to be successfully bonded. If you start going on about objective reality, I swear *I'll* come down and bite you in the leg!" There was some chuckling at that.

"Though I hope you've had your shots," McCoy added. "If not, I can always give them to you afterward. I've become pretty fair at taking care of Vulcans over the past few years. At any rate, I was talking about bandages—"

"The doctor is tenacious," Spock said softly.

"The doctor is a damn good shrink," Jim whispered back, "and knows damn well when someone's trying to give him the runaround."

"—There's no arguing the fact that Vulcans and Terrans, or the Terran-influenced functions of the Federation, have had a lot of bumps into one another over the course of time," McCoy said. "There have been arguments about trade, and weapons policy, and exploration, and exploitation of natural resources, and the protocol of running a Vulcan space service, and everything else you can think of. And every one of those arguments is a bandage over one of the other species' hurts. Now," he said, "you would destroy all that hard-built cooperation at one blow: rip off all the bandages at once, yours and ours together—"

"We can bind up our own wounds," Selv said angrily. "And when two species are no longer going to be cooperating, what does it really matter about the other's?"

McCoy gazed up at him. " 'The spear in the other's heart is the spear in your own,' " he said: " 'you are he.' "

A great silence fell.

"So much for the man who claims, in the net media, to speak for a majority of all right-thinking Vulcans," McCoy said, glancing up over the audience's heads again. "You see that there is at least one Vulcan he does *not* speak for. Surak."

Jim and Spock looked at each other in utter satisfaction.

McCoy strolled about calmly on the stage for a moment, as if waiting to see whether Selv would come up with anything further. "Can't have Vulcan without Surak," he said: "most irregular. At least, that seems to be most people's attitude here. But a few of you seem quite ready to throw him out along with us." He kept strolling, his hands clasped behind him again, and he gazed absently at the floor as he walked. Then suddenly he looked up.

"*We* are what he was preparing you for," McCoy said. "Don't you see that? Along with everything else in the universe, of course. *Infinite diversity in infinite combinations!* That means people who breathe methane, and people who hang upside down from the ceiling, and people who look like pan pizzas, and people who speak no language we will ever understand and want only to be left alone. And it means *us!* A particularly hard case. An aggressive, nasty, brutish little species . . . one that nonetheless managed to get out into space and begin its first couple of friendships with other species without consulting *you* first for advice. A species that maybe reminds you a little too much of yourselves, awhile ago—confused and angry and afraid. A hard case. Probably the hardest case! . . . the challenge that you have been practicing on with other species for a while now! And you met us, and welcomed us, though you had understandable reservations. And since then there have been arguments, but generally things have been working out all right. We are proud to be in partnership with you.

"But now . . . now comes the inevitable reaction. There's always a reaction to daring to do the difficult thing, day after day. Every action has an equal and opposite reaction: this is it reaction. The temptation is arising to chicken out. It would be easier, some people are saying. Cleaner, nicer, tidier, without the messy Federation and the problems it raises just by being there. And you are backing off, you are panicking, you are saying, No, we can't cope, Surak can't have meant *everything* when he taught the philosophy of IDIC: he actually meant everything *but* the third planet out from Sol.

"COWARDS!!"

McCoy paced. The Hall of the Voice was utterly still.

"Pride," he said finally, more quietly. "I keep hearing about Vulcan pride. An emotion, of course. One you were supposed to have mastered, those of you who practice *cthia:* or something you were supposed to have gotten rid of, those of you who went in for Kolinahr. Well, I have news for you. The stuff I've been seeing in the nets lately, that is *pride*. Not to be confused with admiration, which is something else, or pleasure in integrity, which is something else entirely. This is good old-fashioned pride, and it goes with fear, fear of the Other: and pride and fear together have gone with all your falls before, and the one you're about to take now, if you're not very careful." McCoy's voice softened. "I would very much like to see you not take it. I am rather fond of you people. You scare the hell out of *me* sometimes, but it would be a poor universe without you. But unless you move through your fear, which is the emotion Surak was the most concerned about—and rightly—and come out the other side, the fall is waiting for you: and you will bring it about yourselves, without any help from our species or any other. This," he gestured around him, "all this concern about humans, and indirectly about the Federation—this is a symptom of something else, something deeper. Trust me. I'm good with symptoms."

He took one more silent turn around the stage. "If you throw us out—for what you're really doing here is throwing the Federation out of Vulcan, not the other way around—beware that you don't thereby take the first step in throwing out Surak as well. We are, after all, just a different kind of alien from the sort you are from one another: the first fear he taught you to move through was the fear of one another. Unlearn that lesson, and, well, the result is predictable. Ignore the past, and repeat your old mistakes in the future."

McCoy gazed up over the audience's heads one last time. "Surak would be *very* disappointed in you if you blew up the planet," he said. He bowed his head, then, regretfully.

"And so would we."

McCoy straightened after a moment and lifted the parted

hand. *"Mene sakkhet ur-seveh,"* he said, and walked off the stage.

There was a long pause, and then the applause. It was thunderous.

McCoy found his way back to his seat between Jim and Spock and wiped his forehead.

"I take it the deep breathing worked," Spock said quietly.

McCoy laughed out loud, then looked at Spock a little challengingly. "That," he said, "was just about every argument I've ever had with you, rolled into one package."

"Then I would say you won," said Spock.

McCoy shot a glance at him and grinned. "Thanks."

"Pity you weren't on last," Jim said softly. "You would have brought the house down."

"I would have preferred that placement," McCoy said, looking up.

"Number seven," Shath said from the stage.

Sarek stepped up.

"Sarek," he said. "I hold the rank of Ambassador Extraordinary and Plenipotentiary to Terra and to the United Federation of Planets from the planet Vulcan. And as regards the proposition: I say yea."

He stood there, immobile, in the shafts of sunlight, and they struck down on his darkness and could not lighten it. More than ever, to Jim, he looked like a carved statue of a Vulcan rather than a living man whom he had heard pleading against this eventuality the other night.

"This is a bitter duty for me," he said. "Yet it has not been my way, in my career, to fail to do as my government has asked me. It must be understood by all that the government of All Vulcan has asked only that I speak as I feel I must speak. Many will not believe this. I cannot, however, allow that fact to influence me, either.

"There are numerous considerations that make this duty even more distasteful for me personally. Some of you will know them." Sarek looked around the great room. "My personal affiliations with Terra are well known. There have been some who have said before that those affiliations have made me unfit for my duty. I will not deal with that now." He looked toward where Jim and Spock and McCoy sat, and Jim shivered at the pain in the regard. It was that look again, though it sealed over quickly.

"I rejoice to follow the doctor, an old acquaintance," Sarek said, bowing slightly in McCoy's direction, "and rather than rebutting his statements, I should like to note something very specific about them: the facility with which he quotes Surak, for instance. On Earth there is a saying that 'the Devil can quote scripture to his purpose.'

"We have never claimed that Surak's truths were meant for any species other than our own. He was Vulcan: perhaps quintessentially Vulcan, speaking to his own. We have never desired that other species should necessarily adopt his teachings. Nevertheless, especially on Earth, this seems to have happened."

"We know a good thing when we see it," McCoy remarked, meaning to be heard.

"Terrans," Sarek said reluctantly, "have seen many good things—or rather, things that they perhaps prematurely conceived of as good for them—and adopted them wholeheartedly. But at the same time they seem to throw away large parts of their own culture. For example, many ancient languages of Earth have been lost, stamped out over time by other languages that were somehow convinced they were better simply because they were new: people died, sometimes, for speaking their own ancient tongues.

"There are other examples of this kind of behavior, and enough to make us wonder whether it is wise for a culture such as ours to have much contact with Earth, when its people and institutions so easily throw away their own nature, to adopt that of another species. We are concerned that our culture may already have done Earth's culture irreparable harm and turned it away from courses which it was meant to follow, determined by its own structure. Whether it will ever find those courses, now, is difficult to tell, since Earth's cultural structure has been irreversibly altered by ours. If this sounds like an application of the Prime Directive, perhaps it should be considered as such. The government of Vulcan is not certain where the Prime Directive should stop—for the Federation, or for us. There is the possibility that *any* species, no matter its advancement, may easily and innocently damage another, no matter *its* advancement. There is enough Vulcan blood on our hands: we have no desire to add human blood to it, no matter how figuratively. This, most definitely, would be in contravention to Surak's teachings."

Sarek took a long breath and turned to face another part of the hall. "We are not sure that Earth people really benefit much from contact with Vulcans. Concern for the sciences is all very well, but scientific information has a way of being discovered in many places at almost the same time: it is unlikely that discontinuing our affiliation with the Federation would cripple its sciences. Ethics are another situation. We are not sure that Vulcan ethics work for humans. Despite their statements that they desire peace—and we do not discount the sincerity of these statements—many of us have noticed that the *result* of Terrans' involvement with almost anything is turbulence, difficulty, and strife. While not wishing to impugn the doctor's statements regarding the necessity of enjoying the infinite combinations of the species of this Galaxy in all their infinite diversity, still it is said, again by Surak, that one can best judge what a person *really* intended by the result they produce. Speaking simply, the turbulence which ensues from most dealings with Terra ought, for the good of our own people, to be avoided if possible—and it would often seem wiser to enjoy the Terrans' diversity from a distance.

"Which brings me to the main concern. I wonder often whether we are not in fact destroying the Terrans' diversity, and that of the Federation, by too close contact with our own. The Terran culture, the planetary culture as a whole, *has a right to be what it is without outside interference*—especially interferences and influences which it is not strong enough to resist, or against which it lacks the data or experience to have any resistance to, to begin with. Vulcan logic is of a different sort from Terran, for the most part: there are similarities, of course—the basic texture of logic remains the same regardless of the species mastering it—but *we are not the same species,* and nothing can, or should, make us so. Our mental contexts are, and need to be, vastly different. Our sociological and ethical structures are built on the science of the mind, rather than that of the hand: such structures go deep. To change them would be unwise, unless we could find something that we knew was better, to replace them. We know of no such substitute or compromise structure that would work.

"And there is an additional ethical concern. While not precisely in violation of the Prime Directive—which the Federation Council and other affiliated decision-making bodies in Starfleet formulated themselves, taking only minimal advices from other bodies—the Federation frequently, in our government's view, takes actions which can be read as attempting to influence other species for political means and advantage, rather than for the 'good' of the species in question. Not that *that* is an adequate reason at all. We hold that no species has the right to impose its ethics or beliefs on any other species, for *whatever* reason. And despite the fact that the Federation makes this same statement in its own founding Charter, under this fair appearance it becomes plain that the political decisions of many planets are decided in terms, not of what the electorates of those planets desire, but what the Federation wants—and how the decisions of a planet's people will affect its Federation grants. We deplore this; we have long deplored this and protested against it in the Federation Council, to no avail. And we are no longer desirous to remain in association with an organization that behaves in such a manner . . . thereby indicating our tacit support. We wish the Earth well, and all the peoples of the Federation. But we must quit their society. The Government does not specifically request such a vote of the electorate. It merely asks that you consider the topic well before you decide."

Sarek sagged a little. "With that said, I must add something personal. My loyalties as a servant of my government are clear-cut. But I now find that my loyalties to my family have entered into such conflict with them that I have been forced to choose between them. Therefore I must step down from my post, effective immediately: and I thank you and the government for your support of me in the past and wish that you may all prosper and live long."

The stir went right around the room and would not quiet. Sarek stood in the middle of it all and did not move. But then a voice was raised.

"Sir, before you go any further," McCoy said, "would you mind telling us one more of the government's opinions? What do they think of the scheme to sell off formerly Federation-owned property on Vulcan, after the secession, to secret buyers with strong anti-Federation leanings, who have already made substantial payoffs to Vulcan officials to ensure that the property will be sold to them at 'lowest bid,' before anyone else hears about it? . . . Just curious," McCoy added.

Spock stared at Jim, and Jim at Spock, and both of them at McCoy. He leaned back, looking casual.

Sarek looked stunned. "Doctor, I should want to see substantiation of such claims before I or my government could comment."

"Sir," McCoy said, "I await your convenience."

And the room went mad.

VULCAN:
SIX

———————— ☆ ————————

He was born the night the da'Nikhirch was born, the Eye of Fire: the sudden star that appeared in the Vulcan sky, blazing, looking over T'Khut's shoulder. T'Leia, his mother, did not notice the star. She had her work cut out for her, for her child was overdue, and very large. In fact, she quite *literally* had her work cut out for her: the child was delivered by the technique known on Earth as Caesarean section. The pun exists in Vulcan as well as in Anglish, and she was teased gently about it before the delivery, and afterward, when they placed the baby in her arms. . . . Also born that night were two bush wars and the final attack on one nation's central city by another. T'Leia paid little attention to those, either.

There was nothing whatsoever unusual about Surak as a child. He teethed at the usual time, ate normally, learned to speak and write and read at the normal rate: he clamored for toy swords and guns at the same time other children did (and as often happens, right after he saw a particularly nice one that another child had). His schooling was uneventful: he did well enough at all his subjects (though there are records that suggest he did not do as well at math, which must have been the despair of his mother, one of the most prominent chemists and mathematicians on the planet). He was popular, made friendships easily, and many of those friendships remained in force until the end of his life. His home life was apparently a model of normalcy: T'Leia his mother, and his father Stef, seem to have cherished him and one another with astonishing steadfastness. When Surak had completed his schooling, his father invited him into his business—a consultancy which served several of the large corporations in de'Khriv, which had become the chief city of the Lhai nation. Surak was glad to join his father, and for years, until he was forty-six, they worked together amicably and made the business a success.

And then something happened.

He was working late. It often happened, and Surak was not bothered by it: he considered late working hours one of the things that his people's stamina had been designed for. He was deep in a costing exercise for one of the psi-tech companies, which had found a way to produce mindchange adepts on the assembly line, by cloning brain and other neural tissue and administering various processed by-products of the cloned tissue to people who had not actually been bred to the trait. It was going to be very expensive—the recruitment of the sources of the clone material, particularly so—but Surak was working busily at it, certain that the company very much wanted the technique. Mindchange was popular—having your enemy, or your friend, suddenly change his mind about something important to you, was a great advantage. But it was very much a seller's market at the time: trained adepts were expensive to hire, and often too demanding. The company wanted to be able to put mindchangers on staff and wanted to be free to fire them without fuss if they got out of hand. Surak had wondered, at first, why the company didn't simply have one mindchanger change the mind of another one who had become a problem. But the mindchangers themselves were not vulnerable to the talent.

He sat there in the office, tapping at the computer as he wrung the cost analyses out of it, adding variables, removing the more unlikely ones, inserting market projections and probable effects on other affiliated firms of the company. Finally he kicked the computer into report mode and sat back, sighing, leaning back in his chair.

He was a striking figure, even then, so young: very much of the typical "Vulcan" somatype, tall and lean and dark haired, with an unusually delicate face for the raw-boned body, and deepset eyes. He looked around and saw that the office had darkened around him while he was busy: the big place, all done in charcoal and black, to his father's tastes, was shadowy, and outside the wall-to-ceiling glass windows, he could see T'Khut coming hugely up, her phase at the half, shedding ruddy light over the sand of the garden outside. It was a handsome office, and like the rest of the house, reflected the firm's success. Surak stretched, enjoying the sight of the place, the thought of himself inside it, working hard, helping make it work. Someday it would be his, of course, but he didn't think of that: he enjoyed working with his father, enjoyed the teamwork and the laughter, and even the occasional argument, that always bound them together more closely afterward.

The computer sat silently doing its thinking, and Surak reached out to a control for one of the wall screens, took it out of data display mode, and flicked it to the one of the information channels that showed nothing but news. They were in the middle of a general news roundup, the one that usually came before the update on the hour. He left the picture on and killed the sound and got up to open the window-doors to the warm wind off the sand, then watched the screen idly while walking around the room to work the kink out of his back.

The pictures were the usual: fighting, skirmishing, people marching on large buildings in this city or that one: shots in the streets, robberies, ceremonial murders, politicians waving their arms about this or that. A few smaller pieces about someone's public bonding, a feature about the old temple on Mount Seleya, then a prediction of the planet's weather for the next day. Cloud here and there, but no rain, naturally: it would not be time for that until nearly the end of the year. He planned to go take a trip to the North, to watch it rain. He had never seen it do that in person, only in pictures. Surak looked out at the garden and wondered what it would be like to see it rain there. *Water falling from the sky: how strange. . . .*

He glanced idly up at the screen, then froze at what he saw.

Desolation. There was a picture of land, or what might have been land once, but now was only a vast glassy crater. The scale of it was difficult to grasp at first, but then the camera taking the picture seemed to back away, and he realized that the scale was much larger than he had thought. The crater filled one third of the entire Yiwa peninsula, one of the largest markings on the near side of T'Khut. Hurriedly Surak gestured the sound back on, staring at that horrible hole, easily five hundred miles across and ten miles deep. The bottom of the hole had cracked, and was smoking gently as heat escaped from the planetary mantle below.

The reader talked calmly about a test of a new matter-antimatter technology by the Lhai nation, on some of its testing-ground property on T'Khut. And a few seconds later the picture shifted to something else, some story about an assassination in some government official's office on the other side of the planet. But Surak had no eyes for it. All he could see in his mind was that desolation, that utter blasting, the glassy ground, cracked, smoking, with further destruction waiting beneath it, and barely restrained from bursting through.

Antimatter, he thought. *A new technology, indeed—* Until now, the use of matter-antimatter weapons had been confined to the outer planets and the space colonies. There had always been concern about the superluminal effects of such explosions, and people were worried about possible effects on the Homestar, if they happened too close, or to the planet's electromagnetic communications media. But now— *And on T'Khut,* he thought in horror. *Not a test of someone's new technology. They never said what technology—not something for power stations, or space-ships, the way they keep saying, but a warning. To whom? Irik?* For Lhai's and Irik's areas of influence were contiguous, and the two nations continually rubbed and fretted against one another; their borders were never quiet anymore—always some argument about who had owned what territory how long, or which people had been removed from some one piece of land once, and now wanted it back. That huge, terrible crater—that was a warning. *This is next,* it said. And if *this* kind of weapon got out of hand—

But weapons never really got out of hand, on Vulcan. Look at atomics, how carefully they had been confined to such kinds as did not leave dirty radiation all over the place—

Such as will merely kill everything in a given area, and leave the resources undamaged. We cannot have the waste of resources, can we—

He sat down at his desk again, staring at the screen, oblivious to the computer telling him that it was finished with the report, and did he want it transferred? Surak stared at the screen, which was now showing some sumptuous room with well-dressed people talking earnestly, and only saw the devastation. It would have taken a fairly small device to produce such an effect. Someday such small devices would no longer seem so threatening. Someone would make a bigger one. And bigger. And then one that, quite accidentally, would crack straight down deep into the mantle, or perhaps, to the planet's core—

He looked out at the window-doors, and T'Khut looked back at him, looming, and both her dark face and her light were bright with troubled volcanoes, that had felt the sting in her side, and now roared.

Surak watched T'Khut, motionless, until she rose out of sight, and then got up and went out. The screen sat and babbled quietly to itself about war and business, crime and war and trivia, until the sun came up and Surak's father came in to look at the reports for the previous evening.

Surak had gone missing. His parents were alarmed: he had never done such a thing before. The authorities were alerted. It was feared he had been kidnapped, to put pressure on one or another of the firms for which their own small business did research: or perhaps another company had done the kidnapping, to acquire confidential information about one or another of them. There was little chance of that—Surak and his father had had their mindblocks installed by highly paid experts, and not even a mindchanger could do anything about them . . . or at least it would take several working in concert. But that fact made it that much more likely that Surak would be killed out of hand, and his body simply dumped somewhere. Such things had happened many, many times before. Surak's mother sat in her offices at the university in great pain, unable to take any refuge in the cool

bright corridors of mathematics; and Surak's father stormed and
threatened and bullied the local security forces, and pulled strings
and generally made prominent people all over Lhai hate the sight
of his face on a commscreen.

But Surak was not dead. Much later, he would say, "That
day was the day I came alive."

He went out into the darkness, took one of the family's
aircars, took it up, put it on auto, and told it, "Drive." He had
no idea where he was going and hardly cared. To him it seemed
as if the world had already ended, and such things didn't really
matter. All he could see was death, death everywhere, death
unregarded; death that had become a casual thing, that was
reported on the news without horror, that seemed to have been
accepted as part of the natural course of Vulcan life. What real
joy did one see, as a rule, on the information channels? If any
crept in, it was by accident. The information was all about death,
one way or another: either about the little deaths that people
inflicted on one another every day—lies, greed, crime, negli-
gence, cruelty, pain—or about the bigger ones, the more obvious
ones: the explosive bullet in the gut, the pumped laserbeam
through the eye, the bomb in the trashbin, the battlefield strategic
N-weapon glazing the ground, the trained adept wreaking destruction in the undefended mind. And now this last, most horrible sight. Death, it was all death, there was no escape from it.
Destruction was very near, the death to end all the deaths, unless
something was done.

But what?

He spent the day flying. The car had enough fuel, and
managed the business itself without consulting Surak: it con-
ferred as it needed to with the various air traffic control computers, each of which thought briefly about what to do with a pilot
who had given no concrete driving instruction, and then, with a
faint electronic sigh of relief, shunted him off to the farthest
possible fringe of its control area. So it went all that day, while
Surak sometimes wept, sometimes sat staring at the face of
desolation and despair: so it went till the evening came, and
T'Khut began to lean up over the edge of the world again.

The sight of her shocked Surak back into some sort of sanity. "Land when convenient," he said to the aircar.

It took him at his word, being then in conversation with yet another landing control computer, which headed him for the nearest landing area marked with a beacon that the aircar could find. In a storm of dust and sand it settled toward what was obviously a small provincial port on the edge of a desert. The port was on automatic: there were no lights in the tower. Everyone had apparently gone home for the night.

That was fine with Surak: the last thing he wanted to see, just then, was another Vulcan—the cause of all this trouble, and soon to be the end of it. He did not land, but overrode the controls and paused on hoverjets to look down at the little town by the port. It was the kind of desert settlement built by people who want to get away from it all with a vengeance. Everything was very plain and simple—small houses built of the usual heat-reflecting stucco or foamstone, small windows to let in light but not too much heat, thickly glazed in small panes, when they were glazed at all, to resist earthquake damage. Some of the houses had cracks in them, not yet replastered: there had been a quake here recently.

He did not want to be near houses, though. He guided the aircar on into the desert, a good ways on, and out into a great sea of sand without so much as a footprint. That suited him well. In a storm of dust and sand he landed and killed the engine: then got out wearily, scrubbed at his face, muttered a little at the stiffness of his joints. He looked around him.

He was distracted by a sudden jolt as the world shifted under his feet. Just a bump, repeated once, then all was quiet; but the shock was still enough to make him grab the aircar for support and gasp a little. It seemed no wonder, at that point, that not many people lived out here.

When things had settled again, Surak turned away from the car, toward the desert . . . and saw it, something he had been too busy to notice while landing. T'Khut was looming up behind it, as if to show him the way. Silhouetted against her, against the coppery light and the dark side with its uneasy volcanoes, was the peak: tall and slender in its top two-thirds, slumped down a bit toward the foot of the cone, as if from some old melting—

black, silent, huge enough even at this distance to block out a third of T'Khut's immense bulk. Mount Seleya stood there, precisely dividing T'Khut's brightness and darkness, one from the other. The image, or perhaps the mountain, seemed to say: *Here is your choice. The light, or the darkness with its fires. It has always been your choice. It is late. Choose now.*

Never had anything in the world, not even his parents, spoken so directly and imminently to *him*. Shocked, Surak simply sat down in the sand where he was and gazed at the mountain, while the moment seemed to stretch itself impossibly long around him. *Choose?*

Choose what?

The mountain said nothing, merely looked at him.

You mean, choose for everyone? his mind asked, whirling with confusion. *What right do I have? And choose what?*

The mountain said nothing, merely looked at him.

He looked back at it, looked at the bright side, the warm innocent light; looked at the darkness, and the fires. The fires had quieted somewhat since last night, but they could be awakened again easily enough. Such fires lay and broiled beneath the skin of Vulcan as well. They were usually quiet, but they too could be easily awakened by the desolation that Surak had seen the night before. He began to despair again. *Someone has to do something—*

Then do it.

He gazed at the mountain and breathed fast.

He saw his death, at that moment. Not the manner of it, merely the fact. He had seen it before, on occasion, but never had he realized that it was *his* and no one else's, to spend as he liked. Much could be done, with a death. He was going to have one anyway.

He might as well do something with it.

Yes, he said. *I choose.*

The moment broke. T'Khut seemed to hesitate, as if giving a sort of sigh, and then continued to slip upward in the sky, breaking the perfect positioning of the mountain between its two halves. Surely it had been an illusion, that hesitation, that seemingly endless moment in which everything hung poised and waited for him.

Surely.

But what do I do now? he thought.

He sat there all night, wondering that. Somehow he had to stop people from killing each other: that was plain. Or rather, had to stop them hating each other: the killing would take care of itself, after that. *Nothing really difficult,* he said to himself, finding it funny to be so earnest and dry, even sarcastic, over an impossibility . . . one which he was nonetheless committed to bring about. He had chosen, had chosen life, and he knew, somehow, that even the simple fact of the *choice* mattered; if he died right now, it would matter not a whit less. But it would matter much more if he found some way to *do* something about this problem. There were several small earthquakes, mutterings in the sand, while he sat through the night thinking about this: while T'Khut stood high, and the Red and White Eyes rose to look at him. The earthquakes were not frightening: in his weary state, they felt like a friendly hand trying to shake him awake when he nodded. He wished he *could* awake, could simply wake up from this wondering and find the answer, and start doing something about it.

And the earth quaked again, rather harder this time than before. "Ah, come on, now," he said, for he was becoming inured to this, "stop that."

The quake got worse. Surak became uneasy and started to scramble to his feet.

And subsided, as the earthquake rose up before him.

With frightened calm he watched the sand vibrate, heard it drum like a hundred ancient war-parties all around him. *Well,* he thought, as the bulge came up and up, *I chose, and I suppose that was enough. And now I die—*

The sand started to slip away from the great shape it covered, as the Underlier arched its back against the night, huge as a house, as a hundred houses. It blotted out Seleya, it blotted out T'Khut, and the sky. The low rumbling of its voice would have blotted out a real earthquake, had one had the temerity to take place right then. Terror was a poor word for what possessed Surak in that moment. His tongue clove to the roof of his mouth, and he shook all over. He had not thought that his death could be so *big*—that *anything* could be so big.

And then his death spoke to him . . . and he found that he was mistaken about it being his death.

The song was of incredible complexity and depth—the kind of melody you might expect a mountain, or perhaps a geological stratum, to sing. The thoughts that came with the song, that blasted into his head and crashed through him like a continent collapsing on him, were immense, wide, old—and so strange that he could not even begin to say what they were about. But he got a clear sense that this immensity, this ultimate power, was looking at his smallness, his delicacy, his tiny precision, with astonishment.

And with delight at his difference.

And suddenly everything shifted for Surak. The fear abruptly became awe, and the greatest possible pleasure to feel. How delightful to be so different from something: how wonderful that there should be creatures so huge in the world, so strange! No need to understand them, particularly: that might come with time, and would be an added delight. But it was enough to accept their difference, to celebrate just that, without anything added. Creation, in itself, was joy. The difference was joy, the celebration of it was joy. There was nothing that could stand against that joy: sooner or later it would triumph. All evil, all death, was a tiny, fretting, posturing thing that knew its own defeat was coming, and might rage and destroy as it liked. It was doomed. Celebration would win, was winning, had won *now*. Everything was one moment, and the moment was nothing but triumph and joy.

As best he could, Surak looked up at the Underlier and gave it to understand as much.

It roared. The sand shook, the earth trembled; the echo came back from Seleya until it seemed that a voice answered, many voices.

Joy! said the roar. And nothing else needed saying.

It fell silent, then, and slipped into the sand, silently, easily. The sand shook a little as it went, rippled, as water ripples when a fish slips into it. Surak watched it with calm delight, knowing that it was not going away, not really. Nothing could ever go away, not completely: not after what he knew now.

The sand grew still. It was as if nothing had ever been there.

Surak sat for a few breaths: then got up and brushed the sand off himself in a businesslike manner and headed back for the aircar. He had a lot to do. He knew now what needed doing. He knew what would finally kill fear: the wonder, the appreciation, the delight in the Other.

It would work. It might take a long time, but he knew it would work. He knew it.

And to his astonishment, he had the strangest feeling that the Other was looking over his shoulder, and knew as well.

"Here is the first part of the secret," Surak would write, much later, when people started to pay attention to him. "Cast out fear. There is no room for anything else until you cast out fear. . . . Now, do not mistake me when I speak of 'casting out.' Some people will immediately think this means rejection of fear, by pretending not to be afraid. They are not the same thing. Pretending there is not a *lematya* in your house will not make it go away if there *is* one. You must first admit to yourself the fact that there *is* a *lematya*—you must first accept its presence. Then you can call the animal control people and have them come and take it away. But until you first admit that it is there, you are going to have a *lematya* in your bed every night. It may save your pride not to admit it is there, but your bed will be increasingly crowded.

"So it is with fear as well. To cast it out, you must first accept it; you must admit it is there. Is there anything a person would rather do *less?* The last thing you want anyone to hear is your voice saying, 'I am afraid.' The last thing you want to hear your enemy say before you kill him is 'I am afraid,' because—in our culture—it means he has been reduced to total helplessness. What our culture must learn is that *that* point, total helplessness, is potentially the most powerful in our lives. Just past it is the great leap to true power: the move through the fear and the helplessness, accepted at last, to what lies beyond fear. So many things lie beyond it that pen and keyboard are helpless to write of them . . . but as more of us learn to move past that point, more will be written. Not that what is written matters so much as what one *does* with it.

"And the rest of the secret," he concluded, "is that all of us fear one another more than anything else in the world. The fear of the Other, of what the Other will do if he finds out we are afraid of *him*—that is what has brought us to this pass. We must turn and realize that the Other *is* afraid—and then say to him, 'You have nothing to fear from me,' in such a way that he knows it to be true. Another thing we have no desire to say! Each of us secretly desires to keep the Other in some slight fear of us, so that he will not harm us. But if we can only bring ourselves to say those terrible words, and have them be true, then the Other will become what he should have been from the earliest days— the constant companion, the source of delight in all his differences.''

They did not listen to him for a long time, of course. Nor did he begin speaking for some time after that night in the desert. Surak went home and quit his job, much to his parents' dismay. He asked for, and got, his share of the family properties and banked them safely, and then went off into the desert and was not seen or heard of again for several years, except remotely, through the communications nets.

He took with him nothing but a small portable terminal and an aircar, and spent much time alone. Some time he spent with various members of this or that holy sect. There were many on Vulcan, at that time, perhaps more than there ever had been. Vulcan had always been rather infested with religions, a fact that has surprised some species that never discovered Immanence. Vulcan was littered with it: as far as the Vulcan mind was concerned, gods, demigods, animae, noeses, golems, angels, devils, powers and principalities, and every other possible kind of hypersomatic being, were thick on the ground. Various specialists in comparative religion have pointed out that this proliferation made it seem as if perhaps the Vulcans were looking for something they had lost. Whatever the truth of this, there were religions aplenty, with priests and priestesses and holy people and hermits and votaries and nuns and eremites, and Surak went and talked to quite a few of them, over the five years of the Withdrawal, as it is called. There are not many records of what he said to them, or what they said to him: and the conversations often seem to have nothing whatever to do with *cthia*. One tape, lovingly preserved for centuries, is of a conversation with a hermit who lived near a lake by the Lesser Sea, and seems to be concerned entirely with the art of fishing with a rod.

At any rate, after five years Surak came out of the wilds, took a small apartment in the capital, near his parents' house, and began to write for the information networks. There was some interest, at first, in the strange writings from the man about whom there had been such a stir, those years back, when he was first not kidnapped, and then vanished. For a while it was a fad to read his work. Then the interest died out somewhat.

Surak was not concerned by this. He kept writing about this strange way of life that all Vulcan needed to live, to save itself from itself. The basics have been codified many times, in many translations of the *Guidelines*, but Surak's initial notes on the subject, still preserved, are perhaps the best summation of them.

"Ideally, do no harm. Harm speeds up the heat-death of the Universe, and indirectly, your own.

"More practically, do as little harm as possible. We are creatures of a Universe in which entropy exists, and therefore see no way of escape, but we do not need to help it.

"Harm no one's internal, invisible integrities. Leave others the privacies of their minds and lives. Intimacy remains precious only insofar as it is inviolate: invading it turns it to torment. Reach out to others courteously: accept their reaching in the same way, with careful hands.

"Do no murder. The spear in the other's heart is the spear in your own; you are he. All action has reaction: what force you inflict, inevitably returns. The murder of the other is the murder of your own joy, forever.

"As far as possible, do not kill. Can you give life again to what you kill? Then be slow to take life. Take only life that will not notice you taking it. To notice one's own death increases entropy. To die and not notice it increases it less, but still does so.

"Cast out fear. Cast out hate and rage. Cast out greed and envy. Cast out all emotion that speeds entropy, whether it be love or hate. Cast out these emotions by using reason to accept them, and then move past them. Use in moderation emotions that do not speed entropy, taking all care that they do not cause others pain, for that speeds entropy as well. Master your pas-

sions, so that they become a power for the slowing of the heat-death.

"Do no harm to those that harm you. Offer them peace, and offer them peace again, and do it until you die. In this manner you will have peace, one way or the other, even if they kill you. And you cannot give others what you have not experienced yourself.

"Learn reason above all. Learn clear thought: learn to know what is from what seems to be, and what you wish to be. This is the key to everything: the truth of reality, the reality of truth. What is will set you free."

There was of course more, much more. Surak wrote steadily for years, submitting his material to the nets, and more and more people began reading it. Eventually some of them began to seek him out: often angrily, demanding how he dared dictate such rubbish to the whole planet, which had been around for millennia and doing quite well without *him*. Surak welcomed these people into his house calmly, gave them food and shelter for as long as they felt they needed it, and let them watch him write.

After a while some of them went away and began writing themselves, about the astonishing philosopher living in the third-floor apartment: the man who, though seeming a perfectly normal person—a good listener with an unpredictable sense of humor—still conducted himself with such secret, joyful calm, as if he knew something that they didn't, a delightful secret. Some of them later wrote that there was often a feeling about Surak as if someone else was in the room with him, even when he seemed alone.

Surak did not react much to this: he kept writing, knowing that there would be a fair number who came to scoff and stayed to learn. But it was when one came to learn, and Surak realized that this was the one he was waiting for, that things got interesting, and the writing stopped for a while.

S'task records something of that first meeting in the memoirs he left before he went off-planet. Surak looked up from his writing, as the young man came in, and put down the fruit he was eating. "Who are you?" he said.

"S'task," he said.

"What can I do for you?"

"Teach me what you know."

S'task says that Surak put the fruit down and said to him most sincerely, "I thank you very much indeed. Please leave."

"But why? Have I done something wrong?"

"Of course you have," Surak said, "but that is not the point I am making. You are about to get in a great deal of trouble, and I would save you that if I could. Entropy will increase."

"It will increase anyway, whether I get in trouble or not," S'task said.

Apparently it was the right thing to say. "You are quite right," Surak said, nodding. "That is why you should leave."

"You are not making a lot of sense," S'task said, somewhat nettled.

"I know," Surak said. "Logic is a delight to me, but there are some things it is no good for." And he shook his head regretfully. "But I must cast out sorrow," he said. "And you too. Please leave."

S'task thought he would stand his ground, but a few seconds later, he says, "I found myself sitting on the pavement outside the front door, and he would not answer the signal. I never met anyone that strong, from that day to this. But I was determined to work with him, so I sat there. For four days I sat there—there wasn't a back door to his apartment—and I was determined to catch him as he went in or out. But he did not go in or out, and I became very angry and decided to leave. Then I thought, 'What am I doing sitting here, being angry at him, when I came all this way to learn how not to be?' So I sat there longer. I don't know how long it was: it might have been another seven or ten days. And finally someone came in from the street and stood over me, and said, 'What about windows?' It was he. He opened the door, and we went in, and I stayed and studied with him for the next three years."

They were busy years. Surak's message was being increasingly noticed. It was not, of course, immediately accepted: there were many false starts, renunciations, debunkings, persecutions, and attacks of what seemed massive inertia. But slowly, slowly, first as a sort of fad, then more seriously, the logical life began to spread. One of the chief councilors of Lhai called in Surak, as a last desperate measure, to talk to the emissaries of Irik, at a time

when it was feared that full-scale war was about to break out.
Surak went gladly, went among the emissaries, shut himself in
with them for a day and a night, and then sent them on their way.
Two days later they returned, to the utter astonishment of the
Lhai councilors, with the entire High Council of Irik. "Now
come," said Surak to the Lhai councilors, and they went up into
the council room and shut the doors and did not come out for a
week. When they did come out, a peace had been signed, each
nation had made major concessions to the other, and all involved
were slightly dazed, except for Surak. "It seemed like a good
idea at the time," said one of the Lhai; and one of the Irik said,
"We have been fools. He told us so often enough. But somehow
when *he* says it, it is as if he is doing you the greatest kindness,
and having a joke with you. Or someone." The peace held, and
held straight through to the unification of the planet, despite the
occasional efforts of the power-blocs of both nations to restart
the hostilities.

So it went. *Cthia* continued to spread, however slowly,
however much in fits and starts. And then came the signals from
space. Surak looked up on hearing the news, S'task said, and
smiled. "Now I know I have been doing rightly," he said, "for
now entropy will bite back. Here is the great test. Let us see how
we deal with it."

It did not go well, by his standards. Surak was scheduled to
be among the dignitaries welcoming the aliens to shi'Kahr, but
an aircar mishap at the port facility at ta'Valsh held him up.
While he was waiting calmly in the port for the problem to resolve
itself, the Duthuliv pirates fell on the Vulcans waiting to welcome
them, killed many, and took the rest as hostages against massive
payments by the various governments who had sent them. When
the news reached Surak, he immediately offered to go to the
aliens and "deal peace" with them. No government on the planet
was in a mood to listen to him, however, since half of them were
at that moment mourning their leaders, and the other half were
fuming over massive and extortionate ransom demands.

Thus war broke out: *'Ahkh,* "the" War, the Vulcans called
it, thereby demoting all other wars before it to the rank of mere
tribal feuds. No ransoms were paid—and indeed if they had been,
they would have beggared the planet. But the Vulcans knew from

their own bitter experience with one another that once one paid
Danegeld, one never got rid of the Dane. The Vulcans' trading
ships were still unarmed, but they did not stay so for long. The
chief psi-talents of the planet, great architects and builders, and
technicians who had long mastered the subleties of the under-
mind, went out in the ships and taught the Duthuliv pirates that
weapons weren't everything. Metal came unraveled in ships'
hulls; pilots calmly locked their ships into suicidal courses,
unheeding of the screams of the crews: and the Vulcans beamed
images of the destruction back to Duthul and Etosha, lest there
should be any confusion about the cause. The message was meant
to be plain: kill us and die.

Surak was greatly disturbed, no less by the fate of the aliens
than by the loss of his disciple. S'task was at the meeting at
shi'Kahr and was one of those taken hostage. This was the sowing
of the seed of a great trouble between him and Surak, for it was
S'task who organized the in-ship rebellion that cost so many of
the pirates their lives. He was the one who broke the back of the
torturer left alone with him, broke into and sabotaged the ship's
databanks, and then—after releasing the other hostages safely on
Vulcan—crashed the luckless vessel into the pirates' mothership
at the cost of thousands of pirates' lives, and almost his own.
Weeks later he was found drifting in a lifepod in L5 orbit, half
starved and almost dead of dehydration, but clinging to life
through sheer rage. They brought him home, and Surak hurried
to his couchside—to sorrowfully rebuke him. "I have lost my
best pupil to madness," Surak said.

Much else he said, but that is lost to us, along with S'task,
who spent the rest of his life on Vulcan fighting his old teacher
on the subject of the uses of violence, until with many Vulcans
he left the planet to peace. Perhaps the invasion of the Duthuliv
pirates, which continued over the next fifty years and was beaten
back every time, was a blessing in disguise for Surak; perhaps
nations threatened from without felt more like quickly resolving
their conflicts with one another, lest the aliens should find a
divided planet easier to conquer. Or perhaps the changes were
wrought entirely by Surak and the people who took up his way—
the people who increasingly said they felt another presence
encouraging them, or at least just *there*, whether it encouraged

them or not. But whatever the cause, slowly, *cthia* took the planet. Those who most resisted it—S'task and his followers, determined to keep at least some of the old ways, along with some logic—left the planet on the long journey that would take them at last to the worlds where they would become the Rihannsu, or as Federation usage has it, the Romulans.

Cthia eventually killed Surak, of course, as he had long before seen it would do. It was the Yhri faction who killed him, a Vulcan international terrorist group that saw its business being destroyed by nations that no longer desired to undermine one another's frontiers, or economies, or leaders. The other nations united so far—almost three-quarters of the nations on the planet—had asked Surak to deal peace with the Yhri on their behalf. They welcomed him graciously, for the cameras: and then they took him away and killed him. When this was discovered, the outrage was terrible at first: but then a strange sort of calm descended, and one by one emissaries from the major nations went to the Yhri and asked to deal peace with them on their own behalf. Many died: the emissaries mostly, at first. But eventually—after about a year during which several governments fell with the deaths of their leaders, gone dealing peace—the Yhri's heart simply seemed to go out of them. There has never been any satisfactory explanation of it, not even afterward, when some of the Yhri talked at length about Surak, before going into self-exile or ending themselves. They said they could never shake the feeling that no matter what they did, something associated with this man knew their deepest secrets, and all the evils they had ever done, and still forgave them.

And to this day much has been written about it—many commentaries on Surak's writings, many independent works. But then as now, there are some things that logic is not good for. People still go out to the sands of Vulcan's Forge and sit there, looking out and waiting. But the sands keep their own counsel, as T'Khut looks over the shoulder of Seleya, with only an occasional flicker of fire. . . .

ENTERPRISE: SEVEN

☆

"Doctor," Sarek had said, sounding quite severe, "I am ready to hear the substantiation of your claim." They were standing outside the Hall of the Voice, in the great entry hall. Vulcans were milling about everywhere, media people were running for the commlinks, and their little group was getting some very strange and hostile looks indeed from some of the Vulcans passing.

"I'm ready to give it to you," McCoy said, "but I don't have the hard copy with me. Also I need to satisfy you as to the *bona fides* of the source. For both purposes, we need to be up on the *Enterprise*." McCoy cocked an eye at Jim.

Slightly nettled, Jim flipped his communicator open. "Kirk to *Enterprise*," he said, "four to beam up."

"Make that five," Amanda's voice said from behind them. "I'm sorry I wasn't able to sit with you this morning. But at least I didn't miss any of the excitement."

"Five," Jim said, and shut his communicator again. "You know," he said to McCoy, "you might tell me that you have these things up your sleeve. It would make my life a little calmer."

257

"I didn't know until this morning," Bones said, "and I was wondering how and when to break the information. But that moment seemed perfect to me . . . so I *carpe'd* the *diem,* as we used to say in medical school."

The transporter effect set in, and the hall went away, to be replaced by the transporter room. They all got down off the pads and headed for the turbolift. "I must admit," Sarek said, "that I admire your timing . . . if this data is accurate."

"You'll judge for yourself. But I had to do something. You're so damned sincere, even when you hate what you're saying."

Sarek looked rueful. "Was it that obvious?"

"To a human?" Jim laughed. "It was rather noticeable."

"I have said distasteful things on behalf of my government before," Sarek said, "but never one quite so much so. Still, that is no excuse—"

"There's no excuse for not telling me what you were going to do, either," Amanda said, rather tartly.

"Peace, my wife. *I* did not know either, until I had finished the statement. *Cthia* rose up and demanded the truth, whatever else happened."

"If it was *cthia,*" Amanda said, "then I don't mind what you told me, or didn't. I ask forgiveness, my husband."

Sarek bowed his head to her and reached her two fingers as the group came to the turbolift. She touched his fingers with hers with a gentle look. "Forgiven," he said. "But I fear my reputation for professionalism in embassage is done."

"For acting, you mean," McCoy snorted. "Never mind. Rec One," he said to the lift, as its doors closed.

"Doctor," Spock said, "this is no time for a game of tennis."

"As for *you,*" McCoy said mildly, leaning against the wall of the lift with his arms folded, "you've been royally had, Spock old son. I will remember this day with delight every time you out-data me from now on."

" 'Had'?" Spock looked indignant, and one eyebrow attempted to ascend above his hairline.

"I want to thank you for taking the time last night to tell me about your conversation with T'Pring," McCoy said, "because something occurred to me about three in the morning." The lift slid to a stop: they got out and walked down the corridor.

"She talks a good game, does T'Pring," McCoy said as they went. "But not quite good enough. *Nobody* makes that much money, just like that. But at any rate, consider the *kind* of money T'Pring has needed to do the kinds of dirty deeds she was discussing with you yesterday. She couldn't have openly made that much without being noticed. No, indeed. So as regards her explanation, it is incomplete, to put it mildly. Though you bought it." McCoy looked at Spock with cheerful reproach. "I have a bridge on Earth I want to sell you. Very nice view of Brooklyn."

Spock looked both annoyed and sheepish, though he covered the expression over quickly enough. "I fear my logic is not clear where T'Pring is concerned."

"And why should it be, for pity's sake? You're angry at her! Or if you were in your right mind, you'd admit that you are. No harm in that. It's hiding the fact from yourself that makes trouble. But I'm not interested in psychoanalyzing you except in the line of duty. I'm more interested in getting to the bottom of all this. Come on."

The Rec Deck doors slid open for them. There was no one there, rather odd at that time of day. Harb Tanzer came out to meet them. "Doctor," he said, "I cleared the place, as you asked."

"Good. Let's use the little tank, the one with the printout."

Harb led them over to the smaller 3D tank. "You might as well sit," McCoy said as they came to it. "The printouts will probably take some time. Harb, now you're going to find out what I was up to last night."

"This should be interesting," Harb said, and sat down himself.

McCoy perched on the arm of Sarek's chair. "Moira!"

"Good afternoon, Doctor," said the Games computer's voice out of the middle of the air.

"Would you do me a favor and print me out the goodies you retrieved last night?"

"Code authorization, please."

"Oh, for pity's sake, girl, don't get started with me. Check my voiceprint."

"Code, or nothing."

McCoy sighed. " 'If blood be the price of Admiralty, / Lord God, we ha' paid it in full!' "

"Correct. You romantic." The printer began to silently spit out pages.

"When I realized that T'Pring had to be getting her money from somewhere else, and quite a lot of it," McCoy said, "I sat down and began to think about where she might lay hands on so much. Gifts seemed unlikely. She couldn't have multiplied the little amount she got from Stonn into so much. Where did it all come from? Or where *could* it all come from?

"Then something occurred to me. What happens when the Federation is kicked off Vulcan?"

His audience looked at him somewhat blankly. "Well, we all have to leave—" Amanda said.

"Ah, but private persons can take their property with them, or sell it. Property held by the Federation, though, is another matter. It was never sold to us, only leased for 'good and proper considerations'—usually trade agreements—and it reverts to the Vulcan government, which may then dispose of it however it pleases. They won't want to keep all of it: especially the quasi-defense installations—those would be dismantled, and the land used for other purposes. Yes?"

Sarek nodded. "It would be logical. And equally logical to suppose that it would be sold off, for the government will be looking to raise some money to replace the various lost revenues."

"That's right. Well, consider. Someone who wanted to make some money off the deal, and knew that the secession issue would come up, could easily go to various interests that have had an eye on that land, and offer to make sure it was offered to them before anyone else. For a consideration, that person would bribe a government official in a high place to see to it. The bribe would come from what that person was paid, of course: they would skim off the rest for themselves, as their 'finders' fee' for managing the business. The business of the bribery could be highly lucrative, for the Federation has a lot of property on Vulcan, all highly developed, all very useful for industrial exploitation."

Sarek's eyes were hooded: he was beginning to look angry.

McCoy said, "If the industrial contacts knew, as well, how their money was being used—to run 'advertising campaigns' and propaganda that would ensure the secession—it would likely make them donate a little extra to the cause. More than enough to keep it ticking along nicely. And so the racket would go, one side of it feeding the other. The person managing it from behind could stand to make a pretty packet. So could the government contact."

Sarek said, "Will you hand me some of that printout, Doctor?"

"My pleasure. You will note," McCoy said, "that the bank account numbers are all in place, and all the corporate and private transactions are cross-indexed by their Central Clearing Bank reference numbers.'

Sarek looked up in shock from the printouts. "Doctor, the "satchel" format for the access codes to the Central Clearing computers is printed here!" He went as close to ashen as a Vulcan can get. "And the trigger codes for the satcheling process!"

"Yes, I thought you would recognize them," McCoy said. "You designed them, didn't you?"

Sarek was shaking his head. "However useful this information is, Doctor, I want to know how you laid your hands on it! The confidentiality of this system should have been unbreachable! There should have been no way to break this pattern!"

"There isn't . . . not unless you have a friend in high places." McCoy gestured with one thumb at the middle of the air.

Harb stared at him. *"Moira??* You've got my Games machine hacking into strange computers and stealing data??"

"Harb, Harb! 'Borrowing.' "

"But you cannot do that, Doctor," Spock said, looking rather distressed. "I am not speaking in the ethical mode, but in terms of possibility. The Games computer does not have outside access, does not have any of the access or authorization codes you need, does not have—"

"Spock," McCoy said, "there's one thing this computer definitely *does* have. A personality. And you know who put it there."

Sarek looked at Spock, very surprised. "I did not know you were doing recreational programming, my son."

Harb looked from Spock to Sarek. "I asked him to, sir. It's easier for me to work with a machine that has some flexibility in its programming ability. The 'personality' overlays have that: they're effectively self-programming. I had a personality program in here before that was a great joy to work with—the For Argument's Sake personality generator—but it was a little limited. So I asked Spock if in his spare time, he would add some memory to it, and increase the number of associational connections."

Sarek looked at Spock. "You surpassed the critical number, did you not? And the machine—"

" 'Woke up' has always been an anthropomorphism," Spock said, a little defensively, "and at any rate there is no evidence that—"

"The point is that a computer that's had that done to it *acts* alive," Jim said, "and some of them have created problems. That way lies M5, for example."

"I would never do any such thing," Moira's voice said reproachfully, "and you know it. My ethical parameters are very stringent."

"Not stringent enough to keep you from calling a system that should be locked up tighter than the Bank of Switzerland," Jim said, "prying it open, and yanking out reams of confidential material that—"

"It was the right thing to do," Moira said. "Dr. McCoy explained the situation to me. And he *is* my superior officer, Captain, after Mr. Tanzer. Programming requires me to obey a commanding officer's orders. So I asked the bridge computers to handle the downlink, and as for the satchel codes, they appear in various altered forms in my own programming, because it was Spock who designed them—"

"From *my* algorithms," Sarek said, very quietly, paging through the printout.

"Yes, well, Father, they were the best and most complex available—" Spock looked nonplussed.

"Like father, like son," McCoy said. "And a starship's computers have more problem-solving power per gig than any other computer, groundbound or loose. They're built that way. The Clearing computers never had a chance, poor things. Sarek, does the data bear out my allegations?''

"It more than bears them out," Sarek said, "and it adds some most interesting data." He tapped one sheet. "The government connection."

"Shath," McCoy said. "Yes. And a few others on his payroll: and several people in the Expunging Group: and one of the High Councilors. It's a pretty can of worms, isn't it?"

"That does not begin to describe it," Sarek said, passing the sheets on to Amanda.

"So as usual," McCoy said, "*cthia* operates to take care of itself. Here is a very interesting weapon, put in your hands at a very interesting time. The only question becomes, are you going to use it? You don't want to create the effect of making it look like some Federation operation to sabotage the secession vote."

"Not that that's not what it *is*," Sarek said, bemused, going through another pile of printout.

McCoy shook his head. "No, it certainly was not, and is not. Just an old country doctor in search of the truth . . . which is what all this is about, supposedly." McCoy smiled. "I seem to have found more of it than usual, though."

Sarek looked up with something like hope in his eyes. "I must say," he said, "I am impressed. You are quite a detective, Doctor."

"*All* doctors are detectives. All the ones worth their salt, anyway. . . ."

"I will get you as much salt as you want, Doctor," Sarek said, piling all the printout together. "T'Pau must see these. After that—we shall see. I would recommend to her that we confidentially send copies to the guilty parties and then give them a chance to 'come clean' about the attempts to bribe them. As regards the government officials . . ." He shook his head. "Fortunately it is not many people. But corruption at these levels is a dreadful thing. I must see T'Pau." He stood up. "If I might use your transporter?"

"Of course." The others rose to see him out. Sarek paused in the Rec Room doors as they opened. "In the meantime,

Captain," he said, "you are speaking this afternoon, are you not?"

Jim nodded. "As well as Bones, I hope."

"I hope so too." Sarek hefted the papers. "You know, of course, there is a strong possibility that not even this will do us any good."

" 'Us'?" Amanda said, sounding innocent.

Sarek's eyes crinkled. "It is interesting to be a private person again, though I have no idea whether it will last. Come, my wife. We must not keep T'Pau waiting."

"Number eighteen," said the Vulcan who was doing the introductions. For some reason, it was not Shath.

"My name is James T. Kirk," he said, standing calmly under the great skylights. "I hold the permanent rank of Captain in the Starfleet of the United Federation of Planets. To the proposition, I say nay."

He was shaking all over inside—worse than he would have done on the bridge, where he knew which orders to shout, which way to turn, what to do. Fighting with words he understood as well, but fighting in this particular arena was still intimidating. There was so much to lose.

"I am not very sure which 'mode' to work in," he said. "There are several which appeal to me—the exploratory, the purely ethical. The emotional, certainly. For my people, that's considered a valid mode."

He walked around a bit, wanting to be as easy on the stage as McCoy had seemed. "Perhaps I should start with that," he said. "The first time I came to this planet, it was to attend a wedding . . . I thought. It was something of a shock to find that I was one of the intended, and those of you who know about the circumstances under which I left will suspect that I was glad to get away from the place again." There was a murmur of rather restrained amusement. Spock had warned him to tread lightly on this subject: it was delicate. But on the other hand, it could hardly be ignored.

"It was rather a shame," he said. "I had been looking forward to seeing Vulcan. This planet is one of the first places a schoolchild on Earth learns about that's not in Sol system: right after the Alphacent worlds. There is a perception on Earth of Vulcan as a neighbor—even more so, for some reason, than the Cetians. Maybe it's because they're more like us. Maybe the neighbor we finally notice is the one who's a little different." The thought amused him, and some of them as well. "But neighbors you are. In this big galaxy, what's twelve light-years among friends? . . ."

He paced a little more. "We would be sorry to lose you," he said. "I think that's one of the first things that needs to be said. Sorrow is certainly an emotion, and one that a person prefers to avoid if he can. But I think we are sufficiently alike to be familiar with it, nonetheless, and when one sees it coming, certainly there's some logic in trying to avert it. There's no way to explain, in logic, *precisely* what it is about you that we'd be sorry to lose. Some of the characteristics are ones, perhaps, that you don't like. But I'll try a little.

"You people have courage," Jim said. "Not so much an emotion as a virtue. It's certainly one we can admire. Something like forty percent of the mapping of this part of the Galaxy was done by Vulcan teams, at the beginning of your alliance with the Federation. People in little scoutships, going out into danger, or boredom, because exploration was the logical thing to do. And a delight—more knowledge of more diversity. But the courage was always there, and it has never stopped: the kind of thing that took the first *Intrepid* to its death, some years ago. I don't know if you people knew how much the other ships in Fleet mourned that vessel and her crew. She was special."

Jim paced a bit more, looked up at those cameras that he knew were up there somewhere. "You keep us honest," he said. "It may not be precisely true that it's impossible for a Vulcan to lie, but by and large, you do not . . . and that cannot be said, in the same sort of way, for any other hominid species in the Galaxy. I leave the nonhominids out of it for the moment: for many of them, their structure or their environment determines their ethics, and we are not competent to judge them. But we're closer, and I think it's all right for me to say that in our judgment you are an honorable people—you keep your commitments and your word. A Vulcan promise is one of the solidest things there is. It's a peculiar thing, but many Earth people will sooner trust a Vulcan, even if they don't know them, than an Earth person, sometimes whether they know them or not." He smiled a little ruefully. "It says something about us, too. I am not sure I agree with what I've heard others say, that you're not good for us. Certainly we have no desire to be made into Vulcans. Or to make you into us."

"Your government's policies," said a voice from the audience, "do not always seem to bear that out."

"Yes," Jim said, "that's right. Theoretically, our government is by the consent of the governed. The system is not a perfect one, and we know it: we're still feeling our way around, trying to find something that works perfectly. Though it may be that 'perfection' and 'government,' in this world at least, are mutually exclusive terms."

There was a little stir at that: apparently the news of McCoy's little bombshell had hit the Vulcan news services. "Sorry— perhaps I should have said 'this universe.' At any rate," Jim said, as he resumed his pacing, "it's hard to talk to a 'government' and find out why it's doing what it's doing, since it tends to consist of a large number of people, all pulling in what is supposed to be the same direction . . . but sometimes doesn't turn out to be. Ask one person in a government something, and you may get an answer that's a little different from that of the next person on the rope." He shrugged. "It's one of the occupational hazards. If you ask one of the governed, rather than the government, you may hear something very different. Though in service to the Federation, I'm one of the governed; and what *I* say is that I don't want Vulcans to be anything but Vulcan."

"That is what all this is about," said another voice from the audience.

Jim nodded. "I agree. But I have yet to see any evidence that we're stopping you from being Vulcan or interfering in the process." He looked a little indignant. "You people don't know your own power, I don't think. It's possible that those who are made uncomfortable by us find it a useful excuse, that we're somehow ruining your development. But is that really likely to be possible, in a civilization so old and stable? And on the other side of the argument, if you're concerned that Terra is too unstable and malleable to be able to bear contact with Vulcan,

I'm surprised we're having these discussions at all . . . and only now, a hundred and eighty years after our association began. Surely we should have all had our ears sharpened by now! Truly," Jim said, a little more loudly, running over the laughter that started, "we've been hearing both arguments at once, and I don't think you get to have it both ways."

The laughter peaked, then settled down. "I should be a fairly good example of the situation," Jim said. "For quite a while now I've been serving with a Vulcan first officer—"

"Half Vulcan," said a voice from the audience.

"I was wondering when that was going to come up," Jim said, smiling a bit. "What's it supposed to mean? It can't be a reference to his genetics. There's no logic in pointing it out on those grounds alone. Or do you mean to imply that as such, he's somehow less perfectly or properly Vulcan than a 'full-blooded' member of the species? That he's *really*—" Jim twirled a fake moustache and looked shiftily from side to side—"a fake Earth person?? Oh dear. Lock up your daughters."

Laughter welled up. Jim shook his head. "Well, if that's what you think, you people must not be very familiar with your own species' psychology, because my own observation of the result is that it tends to turn the person 'more Vulcan than the Vulcans.' Icy logic, utterly perfect; brilliant performance at anything attempted: no signs of emotion to be found anywhere: a tendency to go in for Kolinahr. Overreaction, perhaps one might call it," Jim said. "Precious few of you are *that* perfectly and properly Vulcan." Jim stalked the stage for a moment, then said, rather quietly, "My first officer has a right to be judged on his own recognizance—not by his genes, not by what you think his mother did to his Vulcanness, or to the inside of his head, when his father and his teachers and the rest of the planet weren't looking. If you doubt your own influence so thoroughly, if you're so sure that one woman can completely triumph over the culture and presence of an entire planet—goodness, she must be tough. And why did we waste her on *you?* Why didn't we just drop her over Klinzhai? Would have solved the Klingon problem." Laughter broke out. "But seriously, if that's what you think of her, then it's no wonder you're hosting this little gathering. I'm just amazed you invited *more* Earth people here to speak. Aren't you afraid you'll all suddenly rush out and get your ears bobbed?"

There was more laughter at that. "Now you've put me off what I was going to say," Jim said. "Maybe it's better that way. Look. I am living proof of the kind of friendship available for Vulcans among humans. I'm not claiming that the friendship is perfect, or ever was: there have been misunderstandings and incidents of pain, but they've been mercifully few. Mostly my experience of Vulcans, in the one I work with, has been of great courage, intelligence, an insatiable curiosity—the heritage of a proper descendant of all those people who went out in the little scoutships, both in company with Federation people, and for all the years before you ever met us. And wisdom, as well, and compassion, and a great openness of mind. I thought those were Vulcan traits. I would be sorry to be wrong."

"You are not wrong, I hope," someone said from the audience, "but we are not all of a piece."

"I know," Jim said. "Neither are we."

There was a little silence. "This I want to say, too," Jim said. "It's impossible for me to ignore the fact that, if Vulcan does secede from the Federation, numerous people with affiliations to both are going to get caught in the middle, and hurt—"

"The needs of the many—"

" 'Outweigh the needs of the few, or the one,' " Jim said. "Yes, I knew that was going to come up. I have arguments with that statement. I don't think you can count up lives, souls, and say, Here are twenty of them over here, and one of them over there: these twenty over here are more valuable than the one over there, because there are more of them. What if the soul in the other side of the balance is Surak's? What right have you to decide that one person's needs are less important that twenty people's? And you people are *telepaths!* You can get into other beings' brains and find out what their needs are—and how important they seem, or don't seem, from inside. Numbers are a poor excuse. Counting bodies is just a way to abrogate your responsibility for the situation."

Jim shook his head. *"I* say," he said, "I submit to you, that the many *are* the one. That every one of you-the-many is yourself a one, and without all the 'ones,' there would *be* no many. You

must each realize in your own self that it is *you* who will be
causing the suffering to the many who will be caught in the
middle—the Earth people who live here happily with their children, in peace with you, and will have to give up their homes: the
Vulcans, content in their career in Starfleet, or on Earth, who
will have to make the decision to come home and leave their
work, or else remain there, but exiled, never to see their homes
again. And of course my friends," he said, "who will have to
make that choice as well. *You* are forcing that on them," he said,
pointing up at the cameras, and turning to face, one part at a
time, the whole room. "The spear is in *your* hand. Not that of
some vague other person, not the 'government'—and what's the
government but a whole lot of people? *You* are holding it. *You*
will cause their pain.

"I hope," Jim said, "that people who so revere that man
who said 'Do not cause others pain,' will listen to what he says.
Even if he *was* only one."

There was a movement off to his side. He looked over,
surprised, as Sarek hastened up on the stage. Jim blinked: he had
never seen Sarek move so fast before.

"There is an emergency," Sarek said to the audience. "I
must ask the Captain to come with me immediately. I beg the
assembly's indulgence and ask that he be allowed to complete his
statement tomorrow."

And Sarek grabbed Jim's arm in a grip of steel and hustled
him off, leaving the audience murmuring. "What's the matter?"
Jim said to him, completely befuddled.

"Jim," Sarek said, "we must hurry. T'Pau is dying."

VULCAN:
SEVEN

—————————— ☆ ——————————

He was in his lab, in the middle of programming a computer, when the note arrived, utterly astonishing him. He was not used to getting hard messages from people; everyone with whom he had any business tended to get in touch with him on the computer, that being where he was almost always working. But there it was—a thin, fine piece of plastic bound down with a wafer of wax. He got up from the console, stretched a bit, and opened it. In a beautiful, clear calligraphy that spidered its way down the paper, it said:

Please come to my office at once. T'Pau

He almost sat down, such was his surprise. *What might she want with me?* he thought, wondering rather frantically what offense he had committed. She was the Eldest of House, and he was nearly the youngest: well, excepting young Silek, at least, who had just turned fifty. He scoured his memory and could find nothing to which to attribute this summons.

—and it occurred to him then that he was standing there being most dilatory, when his first duty was obedience to his Head of House. He looked around the workroom, again rather frantically, for something decent to throw on over his coverall. There was nothing: he had not done his laundry in two days. Shocking, but when one got working on a good bit of programming, and was not expecting any visitor, and had no social obligation—

Finally he simple brushed himself off as best he could and ran out. It was a fine, fair day, the sun bright over the Academy, people going to and fro about their business, as usual. He ran down one of the paths, then got hold of himself and schooled himself to a dignified walk. It was illogical to hurry: T'Pau would know how long it would take him to get to her offices from his lab. All the same—

He hurried a little. Some people looked after him, as he went: he ignored them, or tried to.

Her office was near the joint libraries, in a small, simple building by itself, a country-looking place of white stucco. He paused at the door, started to brush himself down again, and stopped as the door sensed the motion and entered.

Slowly he went into the outer office. Her assistant was there, tapping busily at a computer herself. "Sarek," he said to her as she glanced up.

"I know," she said. "Please go in: she is awaiting you."

Sarek bowed to her a little, went slowly toward the inner door. It opened for him.

He walked into T'Pau's office. It was spare and simple, the white stucco of the walls unbroken except in one place, where a tapestry of striking abstract weave hung down. The desk was clean, except for the computer pad she was working on and an old yellowed sheet of paper that lay by itself, as if it were something of importance. She was gazing at it. As he came in T'Pau looked up and rose to greet him.

It was a courtesy she hardly needed to show him, and Sarek bowed deeply to her. "Madam," he said.

"Sarek," she said. "You are welcome. I have not seen you since your trial," she said.

He nodded. It had astonished him then, as a child, when she showed up for his manhood trial—the morning he went out into the sands, faced the *lematya,* and came back to tell about it. That was many years ago, but to his eyes she was no less beautiful than she was now. Under the tightly coiled and braided hair, hers was a fierce face, like one of the flying predators of the lesser mountains, a *vakhen's* face. But at the same time cool and wise, as befitted an Eldest Mother. *How old* is *she?* he wondered, and then called back the unworthy thought. He could find out, if he wanted to. But for now those keen dark eyes were trained on him, and the consideration made him twitch. He sought down inside him for his calm. He had done nothing wrong, and T'Pau was no *lematya,* and unlikely to bite him.

"I hope you will pardon my calling you away from your work in the middle of the day," she said, "but I have a question for you. Please sit down."

Sarek sat down, bemused, as she too seated herself. "You have been here at the Academy for eight point six years," she said. "All your graduate and degree work is long since completed. I am not saying that your research work has not been invaluable. It has: computer structures on this planet have improved considerably since you turned your hand and mind to them. But now I would like to suggest something to you."

"Please do," Sarek said, completely mystified and concealing it, he hoped, splendidly.

"I have been in contact with the planetary High Council," she said. This was no news, for T'Pau as Head of House of Surak's line might be expected to have the council's ear: her opinion was eagerly sought, not only because of the lands and resources the house had come to control, but because she had acquired a reputation for a sharp mind that missed very little. "They have asked me to suggest the names of some people that we might send along with the embassy to Earth."

Sarek held on to his control with all his mind.

"I had thought to ask you whether you would be interested," she said. "I do not think your parents would protest too much. You are well of age to go off-planet: in fact, you are overdue for it. Someone of your intelligence should not be content to sit here, as so many of our people are, while the Universe passes them by." She paused, looking at him carefully. "Would you be interested?"

"In what capacity would I be required?" he said, and hoped desperately that she had not noticed the squeak in his voice.

"Computers, naturally," she said. "The new embassy will need someone to see to it that communications and data storage and transfer are properly handled. You have a gift for such. You would be a technical attaché, paid as such, and with the appropriate leave and benefit package. Some of your duties would require contact with the Terrans: we will be exchanging various technical information with them. It would be part of your business to discover just where their computer technology stands, so that we may work out what best to offer them, and what to ask for from them in return. Do you think you would be capable of such?"

"Yes," he said, "I would."

"Will you do this?"

"Yes."

"Then you should prepare yourself to leave within the ten-day. The Federation has sent a ship, and it will take about four days in transit to Earth, we are told."

"That is very swift," he said, surprised.

"It is indeed. Their technology is surprisingly advanced in some regards, though surprisingly delayed in others." She tilted her head, watching him. "I should like you to examine as much Earth technology as you can, without prying," she said, "and send me reports on what you find of interest, as soon as your communications are sufficiently secure to satisfy you. I desire privacy, and general information, no more: I desire to know a little more about our new allies. You need not limit yourself to technology, either. As far as your duties make it possible, get out and see the planet . . . talk to the people you meet." She had a considering look. "I suspect that this will be a fascinating diversity to study up close."

"I will do that, gladly," he said.

"One word of warning," she said. "I have met some of them. They are very charming people, but the charm is as that of children: their emotions are uncontrolled by our standards. Do not judge them harshly—beware of that: there is no logic in it—but also beware of their influence on you. You will be a long way from home, and their psyches will have yours outnumbered."

"I will be careful," he said.

She lifted the parted hand to him. "Then long life and

prosperity to you, in that other place. Come back to us as your duties make it possible: and may you find satisfaction in your posting.''

He bowed to her and hurried out.

A tenday later, he was already homesick, and had not even left yet. On his last day on Vulcan, with all his effects already packed—a great pile of reference data solids and tapes, mostly—Sarek stood at the edge of the Academy grounds, outside the walls, and looked across past Pelasht to the immensity of the desert. It was that time of month when T'Khut came up during the daytime, and she was even now easing her bulk up over the horizon, looking somewhat transparent in the daylight, somewhat ephemeral, as she always did. But this time the transparency seemed a sort of omen: a sign that Sarek was losing the real things, that the real world would shortly be fading away from him, to be replaced by—what? A cold place, by all reports—he had packed enough warm clothes to stock a small arctic expedition—and a strange one: a little planet, light in gravity, with no decent sun to speak of, just a small yellow dwarf star that sounded very pallid and unwelcoming. He was aching with immunizations that no one was sure he, or anyone else, needed: it was unknown as yet whether Vulcans—oh, the odd name, would he ever get used to it?—whether Vulcans could give Earth-humans their diseases, or get theirs from them in return. Theory said not, but Sarek and many others had preferred certainty to theory.

He dealt with the aches and pains as best he could, while wondering at the oddness of it all. That he should be the alien to another species: that someone else should translate the name of their planet as "the world," "the earth," and call themselves human beings—and then give *his* planet and his people names of which he didn't know the meaning or derivation. . . . It was all very strange. But he must do something about that, must find out what the name meant, when he got to Terra. *Earth, rather*, he thought. If he was to be a diplomat, however junior, he must begin acting and thinking diplomatically. And as T'Pau had said, it would be a fascinating diversity to study. He must do it properly, must miss nothing. As one of Surak's line, it was his business to follow the Guidelines as closely as he could, and be, as it were, his ancestor's eyes and hands in that time and place.

He gazed at T'Khut. She was a wonderful color on a morning like this, when the sky was clear: her ruddiness took on the blue of the bright air she shone through, and went a rich violet, shading to lavender in her maria and scarred places. She was gibbous: on her dark side a few volcanoes could be seen, erupting desultorily in the palest gold tinged with blue. Sarek's heart turned in his side, and he breathed out in pain. Had he been far enough away from anyone, he would have said aloud, *When will I see you again? I do not want to leave!*

But he was within eyeshot of the walls, and the thought of his own self-pity abashed him. He turned around and headed back into town to catch the transport for the ship.

It was more than fifty years before he came back.

In the fifty years, many memories did not so much precisely fade as have to be filed far back, out of the way. His landing on Earth, for example: stepping out of the shuttlecraft into what had to be the coldest morning he had ever experienced, surely no more than (in the strange new system of temperatures he had been learning) sixty degrees Fahrenheit. He had stood and looked about him there, for a moment, on the alien concrete: at ships standing berthed, and small vehicles driving and flying every-where, and the smell of burning internal-combustion chemicals in the air—*T'Pau was quite right,* he remembered thinking, in total amazement. And then looking up to the sky—it was night—and seeing the stars, and being amazed even more to find them so much the same: their patterns a little bent out of shape, but otherwise little different than at home. And high up, small and silvery, a moon. A tiny thing, but bright, bright, like a beacon. That finally convinced him that he was on an alien world. Until he saw it, he had wondered, in a moment's bemusement, whether some with a tricksterish turn of mind might not change Vulcan's climate, take away the familiar technology and substitute some-thing else, intricate and bizarre, like the technology here. But the stars, and that burning silver disk, *those* told him that this was indeed another world, full of people who did not think like him, and doubtless thought a tiny, rather pitiful silver moon was part of the proper order of things. . . .

That memory had been filed away over years, along with many others, to make room for business. He could of course still look at them, when he chose to. A spring morning in Paris, one of his first holidays, when it rained softly, actual rain out of the sky, as he strolled the Rive Gauche. Standing on the lip of the Grand Canyon, nearly drowning in the beautiful, sandy, stony immensity of it, and thinking that this piece of Earth was actually rather like Vulcan, only (treason!) even better. An evening in Reykjavik, spent sitting on a boggy hillcrest, watching the volcanoes bubble and mutter a quarter mile away, and watching the sluggish lava meander like snakes of hissing fire down the cracking hillsides. . . .

And the people. T'Pau had been right: they were astonishing and uncontrolled: noisy, irrepressible, difficult, devious, untruthful, hyperactive, shallow, dissembling, incautious, maddening, and most of all, wildly illogical. But he would not have missed them for anything, for they were also cheerful, often wise, courteous, welcoming, eager to learn and understand, gallant, surprisingly prudent, clever—

It had taken him a while to find all this out. Sarek was about ten years in the embassy as technical attaché. He spent his time in consultation with Terran computer people, mostly, talking code and software, getting into the guts of their hardware and being continually amazed by the elegance of parts of it and the crudeness of others. He was delighted to discover how very much like him they were: they would find nothing odd about being awake for three days at a time, hammering away at a recalcitrant piece of code, though their frail constitutions were hardly up to such abuse. All they cared about was the art of their work, and doing it right. It was hard not to admire such dedication and love of computing for its own sake. The programmers were the first Earth people he came to understand as being really human.

He sent reports home to T'Pau on a regular basis, and as she encouraged him, he widened the focus of the reports and made them about anything he saw and enjoyed. (He was careful to moderate his use of the word, lest she suspect he was going native on her: but 'enjoyed' was the truth, however straight he kept his face while "researching" them, and however he rewrote his reports.) One of them dealt almost entirely with the World Series race in the fall of 2180, the year the Mets and the Giants spent the late season struggling to the tops of their respective leagues, and then savaged one another with such memorable elegance, in a series every game of which went into extra innings. Another had to do with littoral biology of the Mediterranean, and (marginally) with bouillabaisse, and a small fish called *racasse,* and the people who fished for it, and the old-fashioned way they made their livings in a world where ion-drivers came to pick up their catch. Another report was about the restoration of St. Basil's in Moskva: another about research into whale language. Late and happily Sarek came to realize the truth that T'Pau had somehow seen in him—that he was a tourist at heart, and as such a potentially sympathetic eye on the planet, though wholly Vulcan: an eye which might see things that the more diplomatically inclined would miss. When he came to realize that she had sent him more for this purpose than for his computer skills—though those were certainly useful—he was annoyed for a day, then put it aside and never gave it a thought again. There was too much to see and do here, and too many people to meet, and too much to tell about.

It was not too long before Sarek's keenness for and with Earth people began to be noticed at the embassy. The staff there, despite all their specializations, began to realize that if there was some aspect of Earth culture that puzzled them, Sarek was the one to call: if he couldn't explain it immediately in terms that made sense to a Vulcan, he would simply nod and go away, and a day or so later he *would* be able to explain it. About ten years into his posting—he never really seemed to have time to go home to Vulcan—the senior ambassador, Sasav, called him in and promoted him to cultural attaché. Sarek protested gently, but Sasav told him that there was no logic in it; the computers needed almost no maintenance in terms of their programming—or any that they did could be handled by the young Vulcan assistant Sarek had trained—and hardware support could be handled locally. It was time he used his talent with Earth people to help the many who came to the embassy seeking advice about tourism or immigration.

Sarek did as he was bid, of course, though he found it a little strange at first to do some other work on a computer besides writing programs on it, or the daily letter to his parents. He found himself handling paperwork, visas, and advice, which he was able to give with extreme efficiency, having gotten an idea over his travels of the kinds of things Earth people could deal with. As more years passed, and the embassy grew, he found himself with a growing staff, people whom he taught to handle the details of trade delegations and package tours and cultural exchange programs. He became a familiar face around the planet, not least because of his fluency in the various languages. To Sarek, who had been master of at least twenty different programming languages, the spoken kind were a hobby he had studied happily, especially since they had early proved to be the best way to find out the truth about bouillabaisse, or the people who ate it. His grasp of dialect and idiom was amazing for anybody, off-planet or on. He once reduced the President of the United States—then a ceremonial post, but one much loved by people who lived within the old borders—to tears of laughter at a state dinner, by delivering a learned dissertation on computer data storage technology in a flawless Texan accent. The lady was later heard to propose an amendment to the Constitution to allow off-worlders to hold high public office, so that she could have him for her running mate in the next election.

It was just as well he was as good at languages as he was, for this was before the universal translator was perfected, and misunderstandings were, if not rife, at least commonplace. People began to notice that the one office in the embassy that *never* had context problems was Sarek's, and he was moved from cultural to diplomatic, around twenty-five years into his posting. There he spent the rest of the time until his return to Vulcan: for there he found his great love, and the art for which all the rest of his life had been practice.

It was no simple art. Diplomacy on Vulcan (since *cthia,* at any rate) mostly consisted of telling the other person what you wanted, and hearing what they wanted, and then working out some solution that would work for everyone. But on his entrance into the diplomatic service proper, Sarek found that he had been thrown into a sort of timewarp, back to the kind of diplomacy that must have taken place in the old turbulent days before Surak—and complicated by the fact that there were few mind-readers on this planet to assist one in finding out what the other *really* wanted. The base cause of the problem was that these people were not committed *not* to lie to one another . . . or to him. This added a dimension to diplomacy that he was not entirely sure he liked.

It helped a little that Sarek was surprisingly high-psi, even for his training—there had, in fact, been some disappointment in his youth that he had not gone to Seleya to take the training for full-adept status. But Sarek was too much in love with the active life at that point. He did the usual training in psi, when young, that any Vulcan did—how to handle the mindtouch; bonding technique, for when he should need it; bearing the Sense of the Other (for even now, all these years after Surak, there were still people who found the Sense, and its implications, difficult to handle); and of course *na'Tha'thhya*, the Passing-On, the investiture of one's self-that-has-been in *katra* mode, so that it might not be lost to the Other. When he had completed his psi training—for that was always the last thing one learned—Sarek had gone away unconcerned about the end of his days. Now, under this little yellow sun, he sometimes wondered what would happen to him if he died outside the embassy—what he would do with his *katra*. He had finally sighed to himself and made a resolve to be careful crossing the street.

But his other psi training held him in good stead, here. Business executives and various Earth officials might come to him and lie, but there was no point in it: Sarek could hear a lie coming a week off, and he learned to ask the gentle questions that would shame the truth out of hiding sooner or later. In the course of his diplomatic work he ran into much greed, some cruelty, much dishonesty, but it did not disillusion him. He knew that Surak would have been as right about the Terrans as he had about Vulcans: they were simply afraid, afraid of one another, and more so of him, because of his strangeness; but assist them in casting out fear, and truth and agreement would always slip in to fill the gap. He eventually heard about the stories that grew up around him, that it was not so much that a Vulcan could not lie, but that he could not be lied *to*. Sarek would smile, privately, when he heard as much. He did not mind the legend, if it kept the people who came to him from wasting their and his time with lies. Life was too short, and there were agreements to be made, and the prevarication only slowed them up.

He made a name for himself as a negotiator. The Vulcan-Terran Interstellar Comprehensive Trade Act of 2192 had Sasav's name signed to it, but it was Sarek's handiwork, and various members of the Federation Council noticed it—a tightly woven document, scrupulously fair to everyone concerned, and as closely reasoned as a computer program. There was no surprise in this: after many years of studying Earth with a student's delight, from up close, Sarek knew what the industries and the industry executives wanted, almost better than they did. Various people in the Federation government began to notice Sarek.

He was interested by the notice, but not flattered: there was too much to do. He still wrote to his parents daily; he still sent T'Pau reports, though these days they were more often about the fine details of moving and shaking the diplomatic world than about fish soup. Not that Sarek was usually seen to move or shake anything. His style was more subtle: situations seemed to calm themselves on the sight of him, or arrange themselves tidily in the shape he wanted them before he got within arms' length. It was an art much envied by his fellow diplomats, both on the Federation side and among the Vulcans.

It was summer of 2212 when he returned to Vulcan. It was not a recall. Sasav was retiring, and he asked Sarek to come back with him and assist him with the debriefing to the Council, and assist him and them in the choice of a replacement.

Sarek's feelings when he stepped out into the port facility were mixed. Everything looked strange, everything had been changed since he left. The sight of so many Vulcans all around seemed odd, suddenly, and the fact of the oddness struck him to the heart. But this far on in his life he was beyond showing such a reaction openly. He went on his way with Sasav's party, not noticing the heads that turned as he went by, as people looked with interest at the ambassador, whom everyone knew, followed by the tall, broad-shouldered presence, dark and intent, the personification of a brooding, keen-eyed calm. People wondered who he was.

They found out soon enough. The debriefing with the council was long and boring, though Sarek never showed it, and his mind was often on Earth during the proceedings. The dry realities and recitations of pacts and relationships were shouldered aside in his mind by the memory of the events that accompanied their forging—some abortive shouting match with a union leader, or a dinner at which wine and some delicate mindprobing unlocked some of his erstwhile adversaries' desires to him and made a solution possible that he might not otherwise have found. He did not speak of such things, naturally: it would have violated the humans' privacies, as well as his own.

Sasav's retirement was a sorrow to him, though he concealed that as well. Over the fifty years, the relationship had gone from a distant sort of superior-worship to a warm and cordial working relationship with a man both wise and clever. But Sasav was almost a hundred and eighty, and was certainly entitled to spend the last third of his life in comfort at home after his long service. Still, Sarek found it difficult to conceive of an Ambassador to Earth who was someone other than Sasav.

So his surprise was forgivable when the council chose him as Sasav's successor.

He was tempted to argue the point with them, pleading excessive youth, but he knew there would be no point in it. They would have their reasons in logic marshaled, and those reasons would be correct. His long experience there from a young age, his fluency in Earth languages, the relationships he had built up with officials there, the results he had produced in negotiations—All he could do, with Sasav's eyes on him, and T'Pau's, was bow slightly, and accept the posting.

He made a resolve to see T'Pau again, before he left. The diplomatic briefings that followed, with Sasav and the High Council, made it plain to Sarek that there was much more to keeping a relationship with Earth in place than he had thought. The government's *cthia* was mostly in place, but there were slippages: they were afraid of the Terrans, of their strangeness, their expansionist policies, their energy, their capacity for violence. To many Vulcans they seemed very young children, running around the Galaxy with dangerous weapons. By comparing what he was hearing now from the government with what he had heard Sasav say in the embassy, Sarek now discovered the careful and sympathetic way in which his superior had been portraying the Terrans to the council, to avoid panicking them where no panic was necessary. Many other situations, viewed in this light, now made it apparent to him what a fine line Sasav had been riding, keeping the two governments in communication, preventing misunderstandings, avoiding anything that might inflame the Vulcans' xenophobia. For such it was. More than ever Sarek doubted his ability to do this job this well . . . but his determination increased to *attempt* to do it this well.

That night he saw T'Pau for dinner. She was older. *Illogical,* he thought to himself. *Did you expect her to go into stasis when you left?* But that fierce face was calming a little. The fierceness was very much there, but the wisdom that had always been there was beginning to make itself more obvious. He had some things for her—some data solids from Earth, literature mostly, and music and film, including those World Series games, about which T'Pau was highly curious.

They talked about a great number of things, and when they were at the end of the meal Sarek was surprised to hear her say in the formal mode—actually the mode of the Eldest to one of the family—"There is one thing I must discuss with thee. Thou wast never bonded as a child, as the bonding on our family has been elective by tradition. Thee is now well of age to be bonded. What are thee doing about this?"

It was a topic that had been in his thoughts oftener than he liked, over fifty years, with some slight sorrow. But the sorrow was long behind him. "I have put that option aside, T'Pau. I have no close relationship with any Vulcan woman: and if I did, I am not sure I would ask her to accompany me to Earth. It can be hard, being a Vulcan there. They are not far along in their version of *cthia* as yet, and their attitudes toward strangers are sometimes imperfect. . . ."

"Thy logic is in abeyance," she said, which was about as severe a reprimand as anyone had given him these fifty years. "I know thy reasons. Nonetheless, thee should keep thy options open. Cast out fear."

He nodded, and thought no more of it. They finished the meal and said their farewells.

Sarek completed his business with the council, collected the necessary documentation, went to visit his parents for a moon-round, and then at the end of the month, took ship for Earth again. Two days later he was presenting his credentials to the United Federation of Planets as the Ambassador Extraordinary and Plenipotentiary from Vulcan. He did not feel particularly extraordinary, but there was something exhilarating about walking into the upstairs office in the embassy, afterward, and sitting down in the chair behind the desk, and knowing that he spoke for his people here. He would do it well.

Quite shortly thereafter, he met Amanda Greyson.

It was, of course, in the line of business. She was involved with a Federation program intended to develop a universal translator, and Sarek was happy to have his linguistics department assist her: such an instrument could only be a tremendous breakthrough, in a world where until now wars might be caused or averted by the mistranslation of a term. She did not make any particular impression on him when he saw her first—a handsome woman, tall for her people, with wise eyes. Later, he found that she reminded him of T'Pau, in some odd fashion, though he had trouble identifying exactly what the likeness was.

His people down in Linguistics kept him apprised of their work with her (she had begun to help some of them with their English), and the reports began to be very glowing indeed. Sarek began to take some interest in the woman. She had, it seemed, traveled to Vulcan and lived there for several years while studying language, semiotics, and kinesics at the Science Academy. He made it a point to drop down to Linguistics, once or twice, when his people had told him she was expected there. Their meetings were cordial: more than cordial, when she found how fluent and idiomatic his Vulcan was . . . and how fond he was of Szechuan food. That was what brought them together the first time. She had found a Hunan place in the city that she wanted him to try— that was when the embassy was still in London—and they sat down over homestyle fried noodles and a word list and spent the whole meal conversing in Vulcan.

It was refreshing in a way he found difficult to understand to hear his own language coming so easily from the lips of an alien.

Perhaps easily was not the right word. There were problems with her pronunciation—she had picked up a very peculiar Lesser-sea accent somehow, which amused him, since in the old days the Lesser accent had a country-bumpkin connotation to it, and to hear it coming from this polished young woman was droll, to put it mildly. But her vocabulary was strong in the sciences, and her translations were surprisingly accurate for the most part. Most to his surprise, she had studied *cthia*.

"It seems to make such sense," Amanda said to him over the green tea. "But that kind of thing always does, when enlightenment comes suddenly out of nowhere, and you look at it and wonder what took it so long. . . . I suppose our obtuseness is so much greater than we think, that it always seems surprising . . . when in fact the Universe has been hammering at our heads, trying to get the answers in, forever and ever. . . ."

He nodded. "I think you may be right. Your planet's various enlightenments have the same effect on me."

"I wonder what we would have done with Surak?" she said softly. And then she laughed, a rueful sound. "Now that I think of it, probably what we have done with various other of the great enlighteners. Nailed them up to crosses, or chased them across deserts, or shot them. We are not a very enlightenable people, I'm afraid. But sometimes the light breaks through. . . ." She tapped the word list with one chopstick. "That's what this is for," she said.

"To the light," he said, and raised his cup of tea to her.

They met fairly often after that. Sarek's Anglish was more flexible and idiomatic than any of his staff's: that was the excuse. But increasingly he found himself delighting in having a friend. He had had few, on Vulcan: from a very young age, his work had possessed him. During his earlier posting here, he had been on the move all the time, even when working—gathering data, rarely staying mentally in the same place for very long. But now, in his early maturity, he felt a little more settled, and that settlement found great satisfaction in the expression of friendship.

They frequently quarreled. The quarrels were genteel—he kept them that way, since mostly he was right—but when Amanda became annoyed over what she perceived as his smugness about being right, her eyes would flash and she would become splendidly insulting, usually in bizarre Anglish idiom that Sarek found as refreshing as it was annoying. She caused him to laugh out loud for the first time in many years when she told him, after a disagreement over the translation of a word for war, that he should only grow headfirst in the ground like a turnip. Later that month, when he was right about something again and made the mistake of not immediately down-playing it, she issued him with a formal malediction, wishing that the curse of Mary Malone and her nine blind orphan children might pursue him so far over the hills and the seas that God Almighty couldn't find him with a radio telescope. Sarek laughed so hard at that that he entirely lost his breath, and Amanda panicked and started to give him cardiopulmonary resuscitation, which was useless, because his heart was somewhere other than the spot on which she was pounding. It took him nearly an hour to recover: he kept laughing. He had never been cursed like that before, not even by union leaders, and it was very refreshing.

There came a time when the day seemed somehow incomplete if she had not called him and asked him about something, or told him what she was doing. There came a time when it seemed odd not to have dinner together at least one day of the weekend, if not both. There came a time when it seemed quite normal that he should visit her at her house, and have dinner with her, and stay late, talking about everything in the world. The worlds. Now there were truly more than one, and he felt as if he was living both of them. The word lists had started the process: it was the word lists that finally put the finishing touch to it.

"You have mistranslated this," he said, sitting on her couch and tapping the printout. "I thought we had discussed this. Do you mean to tell me that this revision of the list went to the committee?"

She frowned at him. "I told you it was going to. What's the problem?"

"This word." He pointed at *arie'mnu*. "It does *not* mean elimination of emotion. That is not what we do, by and large."

"But all the earlier—"

"If you will pay attention to all the earlier translations, you will perpetuate their mistakes! Nor, what is this, down here, nor is it 'suppression.' *Control* is wrong as well. Mastery, it is mastery. There is a difference!"

She shrugged and sighed. "It's going to be hard to get it changed now. It's just one word, we can catch it in the next translation—"

"And leave everyone who hears the word for the next ten years thinking that we *have* no emotions? Do *you* think we have no emotions?"

"*Do* you have emotions?" she said, arching her eyebrows at him. He was being teased, and he knew it.

And instantly he knew something else, as well.

"You will have to judge," he said . . . and drew her close.

And showed her that he did.

And found that she did, too.

Some time later, a small, soft, lazy voice spoke. It was astonishing how her voice could change, sometimes.

"You know, it's funny. . . ."

"What is?"

"Well, everybody wants to know if Vulcans are . . ."

"I do not think I shall ask you to complete that. Well? And are we?"

She laughed. "Let them catch their own Vulcans and find out."

"Catch? That implies that I ran away. . . ."

More laughter. "At least you did it slowly."

He smiled. "Was that a pun?"

"No." She giggled. "Goodness, though . . . how this is going to look in the papers. *I Married An Alien!*"

"So will I have," he said wryly, "and I suspect the response may be similar, at first."

"Has it ever been done?"

"Not to my knowledge."

A thinking silence. "And shall we have a child?"

"Can you?"

"Yes. Can *you*?"

"I suspect so."

She thought a moment. "The question is . . . can *we*?"

He thought too. "All we can do," he said, "is find out."

The marriage was a quiet one, but the news was still greeted with astonishment on Earth. Sarek took it calmly. One particularly annoying newspaper, which published a slight alteration on Amanda's headline—"*I Married A Little Green Man!*"—received an interesting riposte from Amanda, when she was interviewed on one of the broadcast news services shortly thereafter: "There is nothing little," she said with great dignity, "about my husband." Sarek did not at first understand the amused ripple that went through the crowd of reporters standing around. Certainly he was tall by Earth standards. He had to have it explained to him, and afterward laughed harder than after the radio-telescope incident.

Things quieted down eventually. After a few peaceful years on Earth, Sarek requested a sabbatical on Vulcan, which was granted him without question. He and Amanda were granted a ride on a starship—their first one—and were on Vulcan the next day. The day after that they had their first of many appointments at the Vulcan Science Academy.

There are of course people who will claim that "crossbreeds" between species are impossible. In nature, they are. But the Vulcans were at that time the best geneticists in the Galaxy, having been practicing the art, one way or another, almost since before their history began. It had never been done: but there was no reason why it should not be done, for both parents were hominids, in their right mind, and of sufficiently similar physiology that a compromise could be designed.

"Designed" was the most accurate word. The process started with extensive genetic mapping of both of them. The geneticists at the Academy took their time—there was no room for mistakes. After a year, every gene on Amanda's and Sarek's chromosomes had been typed and identified and assessed for viability.

Then the design began—working out how the body should work physically, for Vulcans and humans each had organs that the other did not, and all the necessary vital functions needed to be covered. Differing chemistries had to be reconciled, differing means of ATP and ADP synthesis and interaction: the basic bodily cell structure had to be redesigned from the mitochondria up. Differences in metabolism had to be handled. Neural chemistries had to be carefully juggled. There were thousands of similar details. And then every change had to be "programmed" into the template chromosomes, by computer-controlled or manual microsurgery.

It took four years.

Finally the technicians were ready. They called Amanda in and borrowed an ovum from her, to use for its membrane. The other genetic tissue they needed, they already had. With great care, in an operation taking three days, they scooped the original genetic material out of the ovum, replaced it with the material they had tailored from Amanda, introduced the equivalent material from Sarek, closed the little cell up . . . and waited.

It sat thinking for about half an hour, and then divided.

And divided again.

And again.

They did not cheer: they were Vulcans. But there was an insufferable air of satisfaction about the Parturitic Genetics lab for days. About a week later, Amanda went in and officially got pregnant. It was an office procedure, and took about five minutes.

Then began the long wait to see whether the embryo would implant properly, whether the placenta would hold.

It did. Amanda showed no ill effects, except that in her second month she lost her appetite for everything but sour foods, and found herself (to her utter disgust) wanting to eat nothing but pickles. She complained bitterly that she felt like a cliché. Sarek laughed, and got her pickles, regardless of the expense.

The child came to term after nine and a half months, and was born in an easy delivery, without incident. Amanda had been instructed in Vulcan pain-control techniques well before the delivery and was awake and lively all through it. At the end she was tired, but she breathed a sigh of relief as they brought her the child, and Sarek stood by her, looking down at him.

Their son looked like most Vulcan babies: rather green, very bald, his head a little pushed out of shape from the stress of delivery misshaping the soft fontanelles at the top of the skull. That would straighten itself out after a day or so. "He's gorgeous," Amanda said happily.

"I should think he would be," Sarek said mildly. "The

designers would hardly have ignored the outside, after working so hard on the inside. But I think you are biased, my wife."

"You are right as usual, my husband. What are we going to call him? An S-name?"

"It would seem appropriate," Sarek said. "So many others have done it to honor Surak: it would be looked at askance if we did not. We will think of something."

"And then he'll go to the Academy, like his daddy," Amanda said, a little sleepily. "And then . . ."

"There is time to plan that yet," Sarek said, and put a gentle finger down to the little fist that grasped and held it, hard. "My son."

They took Amanda out, and Sarek followed, glancing through a window as he went. It was near dawn, and T'Khut was setting. He had never seen her look quite so real, so fierce, before: and behind her, the stars glittered fiercely too, as if in rivalry.

We shall see, he said silently, and went after his wife and his son.

ENTERPRISE: EIGHT

———————— ☆ ————————

Jim beamed out with Sarek from outside the hall. When the glitter died down, they were in a large room done in warm colors and filled with unobtrusive machinery. Several parts of the room were concealed by the soft opaque glow of postionable, non-sound-permeable forcefields, and quietly dressed Vulcans passed through the room checking the various pieces of the machinery or looking into one or another of the field-shielded cubicles.

McCoy put his head out through one of them, as if looking around for something—a bizarre effect, as if he had put the front half of him through a wall—and seeing Jim and Sarek, beckoned urgently to them. They stepped through the field after him.

T'Pau lay there unconscious in a Vulcan-style diagnostic bed, with Amanda and Spock on either side of her. Next to Amanda, a woman in a soft brown tunic, with long dark hair, was looking at the diagnostic panel: her face suggested nothing about what she thought she saw. "How is she, Doctor T'Shevat?" Sarek said.

"She has been slipping in and out," said the doctor. "This is normal for her condition, but it is not a good sign."

McCoy nodded, and looked over at Jim. "Liver failure," he said. "She's past the point where even the healing trance would do her any good."

"She has forbidden it to be initiated," T'Shevat said, looking around at them all. "Her declaration of refusal of 'heroic measures' has been on file with us for ten years. She has specified the medications she will allow herself to be given, and the procedures she will allow us to perform. But beyond those, we are helpless to take action."

She looked at McCoy, and he nodded in agreement. "It would need more than heroic measures," he said to Jim. "She would need a liver transplant, and her immune system isn't up to it, even with retroviral immunosupport."

"I will be within call if I'm needed," T'Shevat said, and she slipped out through the field.

Jim looked down at T'Pau sadly. She looked extremely thin and worn, the skin tight against the bones of her face, the eyes sunken: even the piled-up hair seemed to have lost its gloss. "They could at least have given her a private room," he said softly.

"That kind of privacy—has never been my concern," said the tired, cracked voice. T'Pau's eyes opened, and she looked up at him. "So," she said.

She looked around at the others: the motion made it plain that even that little movement cost her. Her eyes came to rest on Sarek. "I regret—my lapse in timing . . ." she said. "I was attempting to forestall this collapse as long as possible. It seems—there are things—"

Her breath gave out: she lay there a moment, getting it back. "You are not to think of that," Sarek said to her. "Matters are going as well as they can be expected to."

"They are not," she said. "There is this small matter of T'Pring."

"Do not think of that now—"

"If I do not do my thinking now, it will do you little good later," T'Pau said, and there was a touch of the old snap in her voice. Then she lost her breath again. McCoy looked concerned: Jim noticed that her color was changing slightly, shading into a darker green. It made him nervous.

"Now," she said. "Sarek, you have asked my counsel about what should be done with this material. Your plan is subtle." She breathed hard. "It is too subtle. Subtlety and acts hidden in the dark were the root of this plan. If you feed it on more darkness, it will only prosper. You must tell the truth about it, and at once."

"Simply give the information to the media?" Sarek said.

"Sometimes simplicity—is best," T'Pau said. "Do as I bid!" Sarek bowed to her.

"The truth—is able to care for itself," she said, and ran out of breath again. "But it must be set free. Release the information immediately."

"I will do so."

But Sarek did not move. T'Pau was looking at Spock and Kirk, standing together by the side of her bed. Jim looked at her and had one of those sudden odd visions that one sometimes has of another human being. Sometimes one looks at a friend and sees them as they will be when they are old. But Jim gazed at her and saw her when she was young . . . and breathed out, slightly glad he had not met her. They might have killed each other, or been the best of friends: there was no telling.

"Yes," she said. And she smiled a little: an astonishing look on that face, that usually seemed if a smile might crack it. "When first I saw thee two together, I thought that I should see one or the other of thee die. Now see how incorrect thought traps us in the end; for I little thought that I should see thee two together again, but that the death should be mine."

Jim wanted to say something like "You're not going to die," except that it would have been so patently absurd, and besides, it seemed like an insult to refuse to acknowledge what was going on. "I would have liked to know you better," he said. "I'm sorry I haven't had the chance."

"I too," Spock said: and then reached out and took her hand.

She nodded. "Yes," she said. And she looked around at them all, and said, "I shall go now. There is no use waiting to see when it will happen."

Sarek took a slow step forward. "No," T'Pau said. "You do not need this gift, son of my house. You will be Head of House now, and you would have difficulty dealing with my *katra*, I think. No." She turned her head, looked up at Amanda. "I think we will do well together, my daughter. You have the necessary training from Seleya to manage the Gift once I have left it to you: and it will qualify you as Eldest Mother of the house, whatever others may say. Best to so manage matters. If you consent—"

Amanda's eyes were full of tears. "Of course I do," she said, her voice quite steady. "Let it be done so." And she leaned close.

T'Pau reached up one shaking, wrinkled hand to Amanda, who took it and pressed it gently to her face. For a moment, both their eyes closed. The withered lips whispered something inaudible. Amanda nodded.

Then there was no movement, but they knew she was gone.

Slowly her breathing stopped.

Amanda let go the hand, laid it on the coverlet, straightened up slowly. "It's done," she said.

The doctor looked in, looked at them.

"She is with the Other," Sarek said.

T'Shevat nodded. "I grieve with you," she said. "All Vulcan will grieve with you."

"Did she leave instructions with you?" Sarek said.

The doctor nodded. "She is to be cremated and the ashes scattered on the sands of the Forge," she said.

"We will see to it, then."

The doctor bowed and left. One by one, they all stepped through the field and stood outside it a moment. "Now what?" McCoy said.

"Now we carry out her instructions," Sarek said. "But first . . . we tell her world that she is gone."

"No, my husband," Amanda said, very firm. There was an odd note in her voice, and everyone looked at her.

"What?" Sarek said, surprised out of politeness.

"No. You must tell them about T'Pring's plotting first . . . and you must tell them who has been notified. *Then* tell them about T'Pau. She would not want—would not have wanted it otherwise: she would not like it, to have her personal life take precedence over the proper running of the government."

Sarek looked at Amanda as if he had never seen her before
. . . then nodded. "Very well," he said. "Let us be about it."

They left the clinic, Jim and Spock last of all . . . and Jim
was wondering a great deal about the small, odd smile on Amanda's face.

The first piece of news threw the planet into an uproar. There
were accusations, counteraccusations, denials, carefully worded
protestations of innocence, and much dust thrown up to confuse
the issue by people who wished to seem as if they knew nothing
about it. The debates went on. Jim declined a second session of
testimony, feeling he had already said what he needed to.

The second piece of news brought the planet to a standstill.
The streets grew silent, and mostly empty of people; the news
services did little but talk, in a muted way, about her life: some
shut down entirely. Her will was read later that day, including
the request for cremation.

Jim went with the family, that night, to the Forge. The
cremation had been handled earlier in the day, and when they
beamed out, Sarek was carrying a small, pale green porcelain
container, exquisitely made, which Jim had seen in the house and
not recognized.

What none of them were expecting, when they arrived, were
the three million Vulcans gathered around the edges of the Forge.
They went on around the miles-wide curve of the desert seemingly forever, the largest single gathering of people in the history
of the Federation, all silent, all waiting. Jim was staggered. He
looked over at Spock, who shook his head, wordless, and at
Amanda, who smiled, slightly and gently, and shook her head
too.

Sarek stood there awhile, in the silence, listening to the wind
blow: and finally came the sign he was waiting for. There was a
bulge of light against the horizon, a curve, a dome, growing,
ruddy, shining.

Sarek stepped forward. "Here is what is left of her," he said
to the night. He did not raise his voice, but all the hairs stood up
on Jim's neck as he had a sudden sense of the sound of that voice
being passed from mind to mind, at faster than lightspeed, right
around that great desert, held in every mind at once, and echoed

so that he heard Sarek's words in millions of individual voices, but all silent. It was overwhelming: he found it hard to bear. He glanced at his fellow humans. Amanda seemed untroubled, and McCoy was standing there with his eyes closed, perhaps in prayer.

"We give her remains to the night from which we arose," Sarek said, opening the porcelain container to the light wind that had sprung up. "Surely we know that this is not she; she and the Other know it well. And we wish her well in whatever may befall, till the Moon is no longer, and the Stars are no more."

The wind carried the dust away into the silence. T'Khut slipped upward in silence, flooding the ocean of sand with light.

"Light with her always," he said, "and with us."

And he turned away.

They all went home.

"Number twenty-three," said the voice. Again, it was not Shath.

"I am Spock," he said, standing still and erect in the middle of the stage. "I hold the rank of Commander in the Starfleet of the United Federation of Planets; I serve as First Officer of the Starship *Enterprise*. And as regards the proposition, I say: nay."

The room was quite still. Spock said, "My family are in mourning today, and we are grateful for the many expressions of support which have come to us. But meanwhile, the one whom we mourn would desire that we do the business which has brought us here, and so I have come to see it done."

He turned a little, to favor another part of the auditorium. "I am in a peculiar position, for many of you will know that I am a son of the tradition that now debates casting Earth out, and also a son of Earth itself. Many voices have been raised against Earth here. I could not allow that to influence me. What matters is doing right, not merely blindly defending what is attacked. That is *cthia* in its true form: and whatever my heritage, I was trained in *cthia*, and hold it dear."

He looked around the auditorium. "Much has been said," he said slowly, "about the tendency of humans to emotion, or our own mastery of it. Little has been said about the *purposes* of emotion. It has many—primarily to guide one toward one kind of behavior or away from another. Doing good, brings joy: doing evil, sorrow; and all these emotions we possess, and master, so as not to contaminate others' mastery with them."

Spock took a long breath. "We are much concerned," he said, "with the damage our emotions may do one another. We are right to be concerned, perhaps. There have been many millions of people killed on this planet, over the millennia, due to the lack of management of emotion. But it is possible to overdo this concern: to be overly concerned over what damage our emotions (or management of them) may do others: sometimes even over what damage others' emotions may do us.

"I am a Vulcan, bred to peace," Spock said. "Many of us have said that, after S'task, who said it first, even though he was of the first generation of that breeding. I think that breeding was more robust than most of us allow ourselves to believe. It seems too much like ego, like self-aggrandizement, to say openly, 'We are strong'; and so we pretend not to be, and do ourselves, perhaps, more harm than if we simply admitted our strength and moved on.

"But that pretense betrays our great secret to those who can see: and the secret is that, *cthia* or not, we are still uncertain about our mastery. We are still, as Surak said, afraid of one another, and of ourselves: afraid that the emotion we so carefully manage will somehow break loose and doom us again.

"The trouble is, it is doing so now. It is doing so, most perniciously, disguised as *cthia*, as concern for the other's well-being." Spock lifted his head. "For some years now I have been privileged to serve with some of the finest beings that any Vulcan could imagine. I came among them most concerned for my *cthia*, and their safety, due to what seemed like rampant emotion: I saw them as unstable, illogical, potentially dangerous. It took time to find out otherwise. I spent years watching humans wrestle with their emotions: and from their wins and losses alike, I discovered something—that those who wrestle with emotions, learn far more about mastering them than those who seek to hide their emotions, or suppress them. The humans never stop this wrestling, and as such they have mastered emotions for which we may as yet not be prepared.

"We therefore have a great deal to learn from them. But it is entropy's way to push us away from what will benefit us, and the fear that we should have cast out is once again attempting to betray us. That fear makes us look so hard at the entropic nature of emotion, its power to drive us apart, that we ignore its ability to *resist* entropy, its power to draw us together. As we were drawn together last night."

Everything was silence. "It is illogical to ignore such a power," Spock said. "It is illogical to turn away from another species which has taught us so much about our own fears, and our own hopes, and has shared so many of its fears and hopes with us. I shall not turn my back on such a species. I may not: I am of them. My choice is made." He looked around the auditorium again. "For you, perhaps, there remain only decisions. I would remind you, though, that the word for 'decide' is descended from older words meaning to kill; options and opportunities die when decisions are made. Be careful what you kill."

And he stepped down from the stage, to silence.

An official stepped up right after him, a slender little woman with the first curly hair Jim had seen on a Vulcan. "I must inform you now, you here and the audiences on the various nets," she said, "that the threshold number of notifications to stop debate has now been received. Voting on the motion will begin immediately, and conclude in one solar day, or twenty-two point one Federation standard hours. Thank you all for your attention."

Jim got up from his seat as many other people did. Beside him, McCoy stretched lazily, and stood up too. "Now what?" Bones said, as Spock came up to them.

"Now," Jim said, "we wait."

They spent the night at Sarek and Amanda's, eating and drinking and talking, and occasionally bringing up the news on the computer to look at it. There was nothing about the vote: there were no "returns" as such. All the information was correlated in one central computer at shi'Kahr, and would be released only when the vote was complete, late the next afternoon.

But there was quite a lot of other news, mostly relating to T'Pring's undercover smear campaigns. "I see that she and Shath are 'assisting the authorities with their inquiries,' " Jim said, sounding faintly satisfied.

"You mean she's in the clink," McCoy said. "Serves her right."

"Doctor," Spock said, sounding faintly offended, "it has been a long time since any form of custody here has gone 'clink.' "

Bones laughed. "I still can't bring myself to be particularly upset," he said. "The poisonous little creature. I hope she doesn't bite anyone while she's there. They'd probably have to have something amputated."

"Doctor . . ."

"All right, all right."

Amanda and Sarek were out sitting in the garden together, talking in low voices; Spock was toying with the computer keyboard. "You look nervous, Spock," Jim said.

Spock looked at him sidelong. "Emotion again. . . ."

"And after your wonderful defense of it today."

"I was not defending it," Spock said. "What *is*, and is valid, does not need defense."

Jim chuckled. "All right. Listen, can you get me an uplink to the ship from there? I want a look at the BBS."

Spock thought a moment. "That should be no problem. Wait a moment." His fingers danced over the keys.

McCoy was looking at a watercolor hanging on one blackstone wall, a beautiful semi-abstract of spring flowers native to Earth. "Sweet peas," he said. "How long has it been since I saw real sweet peas?"

"Talk to Bio," Jim said. "They have some seeds, I think."

"No . . . I mean a whole field of them. Waving in the breeze and smelling wonderful. That beautiful sweet scent."

"Talk to Harb Tanzer. He may have something on file."

McCoy rolled his eyes.

"Ready, Captain," Spock said. "It will be wanting your password."

Jim sat down and tapped at the keyboard for a moment, giving the command to find out whether he had any messages waiting.

The computer screen said:

(1) COMMON ROOM

Jim changed areas. He typed: *Read message.*

FROM: Llarion
TO: Jas. T. Kirk
DATE: 7468.55
SUBJECT: Further Advice

Those bold in daring, will die:
   Those bold in not daring will survive.
      Of those two, either may benefit or harm.

Nature decides which is evil,
   But who can know why?
      Even the enlightened find this difficult.

The Tao in Nature
   Does not contend,
      yet skillfully triumphs,
   Does not speak,
      yet skillfully responds,
   Does not summon,
      and yet attracts,
   Does not hasten,
      yet skillfully designs.

Nature's network is vast, so vast.
Its mesh is coarse, yet nothing slips through. . . .

"Now what the devil do you make of that," Bones said from behind him.

"Do I read *your* mail over your shoulder?" Jim said, amused. He sat back in the chair. "I'll tell you what I think of it. I think someone's telling me to have a quiet night, because everything's going to be fine."

"Hmf," Bones said, and wandered off. But Jim rocked a little, there in the chair, and smiled.

The next afternoon found them all in the living room together again, waiting for the announcement about the vote. The news was practically blathering, in the meantime, full of the details on the corruption investigation and revelations of the briberies; but none of them had any ears for it. They waited.

Finally, at exactly one Vulcan day after Spock had stepped down from the stage, the image in the tank flickered, and they found themselves looking at a simple 3D display of letters and numbers. Jim couldn't read them, since the translator worked only on the spoken word. But McCoy read it out loud.

"For secession: five billion, four hundred million, three hundred eighty thousand, six hundred five.

"Against secession: nine billion—"

Jim whooped. Sarek leaned back in his chair. Amanda grinned, and McCoy grinned too, and squeezed her hand.

Spock looked over at Jim and put up one eyebrow. "I seem to have won my side bet," he said.

And he turned to McCoy. "I believe the correct phrase is, 'Ante up.'"

EPILOGUE

───────── ☆ ─────────

"T'Pring has asked to see you," Sarek said to Jim.

Jim was on board the *Enterprise,* in Sickbay as it happened, sitting and talking to McCoy—his usual off-the-record debrief with the Chief of Medicine, after a particularly trying time. He looked over at the screen, now, and said:

"What brought this on?"

"I have no idea," Sarek said. *"You are certainly not required to see her if you do not desire to."*

I don't, said Jim's look aside to McCoy; *most emphatically I don't!* To Sarek, though, he said, "Was it me specifically she wanted to see?"

"Spock and McCoy as well."

Jim tilted his head toward McCoy. Bones nodded slowly, though he had a dubious look on his face. "We'll be there," Jim said then.

"So Spock said," said Sarek. *"I have left the coordinates with your communications officer, Captain."*

"Then we'll be down shortly. We'll see you tonight, sir?"

"You will indeed, Captain. Out."

Jim sat back in his chair. " 'So Spock said'?"

"He knows you too well," said McCoy. "Correction: he knows *us* too well."

"Logic?"

"I doubt it," Bones said.

Jim reached out for the communicator button again, punched it. "This is the Captain. Mr. Spock to the Transporter Room, please." He punched the button again, and stood. "Let's go."

The room they beamed into was possibly the most pleasant one Jim could remember having seen while on Vulcan: it was practically a jungle of native Vulcan plants, all spiny or leathery, but all in flower, and some very sweetly so. McCoy wandered around poking and sniffing the various specimens while Jim explained to the handsome young woman sitting behind a desk what they had come for.

He was astonished when she actually made a small curl of smile at him: a reserved look, but a charming one. "A pleasure to meet you," she said. "May one thank you for saving us from some of ourselves?"

Jim was so astonished that he could do nothing but bow slightly, in a manner he had seen Sarek use to his advantage at times. The young woman bowed back, then said, "I will ask T'Pring if she will join you," and with great suddenness she beamed out.

Jim blinked.

McCoy came back to him and Spock, and said, in a very pleased tone of voice, "If this is a jail, there should be more like them."

"Vulcans do not believe in punishing prisoners," Spock said mildly. "The act is usually its own punishment . . . for a Vulcan, at least. But even when it is not, neither are malefactors allowed to suffer a confinement that makes the problem worse than it was to begin with. They are treated, you will pardon the expression, like human beings . . . and they stay here until our best mind-technicians can guarantee that they will behave that way, permanently."

McCoy looked momentarily dubious. "We've been to other planets where they made similar claims. . . ."

Spock looked at McCoy and refused to rise to the bait. "We would as soon mindwipe or 'adjust' a mind out of health, for the sake of docility or obedience, as *you* would, Doctor. It would be a direct violation of the IDIC principle, and several of the Guidelines. If a person does not himself or herself come to regret their actions, and change their patterns of behavior away from such, then here they stay . . . until they die, if necessary. But there is always hope that they will not have to. . . ."

The Transporter effect hummed again. All three turned. It was not the young attendant: it was T'Pring.

She stood there and looked at the three of them, cool and beautiful. Jim found the regard a little difficult to bear, at first, but then he thought of T'Pau's old, prickly, fierce aura, and had no further trouble with this cool remoteness.

T'Pring sat down on a cushioned bench near a particularly prickly tree with huge pink flowers. Jim and Bones and Spock remained standing. "You wanted to see us," Jim said finally.

"Yes," she said. "I wanted to see you before you went off to your lives again. These great lives, spent flaunting about the Galaxy and saving worlds."

Jim found nothing to say to this. T'Pring eyed Spock. "You are strangely silent," she said. "What is your thought?"

He lifted his head and looked back at her with an expression as cool as hers. "It is that mockery is illogical . . . but . . . ."

"But my logic is obviously suffering, and you have no desire to mock me in turn."

"If that was my thought," Spock said, "there is nothing in it to do me ill credit."

She looked away from him, and for the first time, anger showed in her eyes. Jim thought again that it was just as well that most Vulcans were in mastery of their anger . . . or at least, control of it: this was not a planet he would ever want angry at him. *And perhaps it is a little angry, still. But at least the anger has been mastered by their own methods . . . for the time being. . . .*

"Your good name," T'Pring said, "that is all you are ever concerned with, ambassador's son, officer in Starfleet. The Other forfend that you should ever be seen doing ill. *That* it was that made you release me to Stonn: not desire for me, or lack of desire, but that others saw you kill your Captain. You feared that they would count the bond of loyalty broken worse than the conquest made and kept, and think the worse of you."

Spock took a step forward and stopped. "You may find this difficult to believe," he said, "but even after the events and revelations of the past tenday, I have no need or desire to lie to you: so I will hope to be heard when I say to you that our binding was not my idea. I was seven years old when our parents' families bound us. I thought you beautiful beyond belief, and far above me. Then later, when grown, and dedicated to Starfleet, even then I desired nothing from you that you did not desire to give. And after our binding was broken, I wished you well, however strange that may seem to you. It seems my binding is to another, finally, neither man nor woman, neither human nor Vulcan: an odd fate, perhaps. But one that is shared, and somewhat understood." Spock glanced at Jim, and McCoy, and then away. "And I would still be in your thought, as an acquaintance," he said, "if not in your mind, in the bond, as was so once long ago . . . and ceased."

T'Pring sat still, looking at him: then her eyes shifted to Kirk and McCoy. "And you . . . you have once again stolen from me what should have been mine. . . ."

Jim could find nothing to say to this. But McCoy moved up to stand beside Spock, and said, once more in that perfect Vulcan, "We have never taken from you anything that was in your right to possess." She looked surprised—*possibly at his accent,* Jim thought. But McCoy kept going. "Not even *here* does a bonding imply possession . . . except when one challenges and loses. You *won* . . . or so it seemed. Spock warned you that winning was not everything. Now you see that the truth was on his side. But for the meantime," and though the language might be Vulcan, the expression on his face was very much human compassion, "we look forward to seeing you out of here some time very soon."

"I have no time for your pity," T'Pring said, but there was a little uncertainty about her arrogance.

"I have no time to give any, young lady," McCoy said, actively annoyed: and the sound of annoyance, and the Vulcan language together, made her eyes go wide. "You pull yourself together and start acting like a Vulcan, hear me, and get out there again where you can do somebody some good."

T'Pring blinked at that, and then looked at Kirk. "And you," she said, "will doubtless be noble like these others, and wish me well."

"I don't need to," Jim said, shaking his head. "You'll do all right whether I wish you well or not. Meanwhile—" He put his eyebrows up, amused by the thought as it occurred to him, and determined not to give her anything with which to bait him. "May you complicate my life again someday. Preferably in a more productive manner."

T'Pring simply looked at them for a moment, and then lifted the parted hand. "Live long and prosper," she said, and touched a bracelet she was wearing: and was gone, dissolved in the golden light of the Transporter effect.

The three of them looked at one another. "Well?" Jim said.

Spock shook his head. "She is a woman of powerful personality, Captain," he said. "There is no telling what she might or might not do, should she give up her anger and move on to other things."

" 'Confusion,' " McCoy said, in suddenly blatantly Southern-accented Vulcan, " 'is a great weapon toward redemption.' "

Spock glanced at him. "Surak, Doctor?"

McCoy grinned a little as they turned away to prepare to beam up. "Yes. But also someone else. 'Either leave 'em laughing . . . or leave 'em wondering what the hell you meant.' "

"Let's go home," Jim said.

The next night they sat in the Rec Deck again, in the middle of a large impromptu party that was going on around them by way of celebration. The sense of relief in the ship was palpable. A group of about a hundred crewfolk, mostly human, had surrounded Spock earlier in the evening and sung "For He's A Jolly Good Fellow," accompanied by twenty crewmen on kazoos. Sarek had been given champagne. The two of them had taken it all in good stead, but Sarek had privately gone off to McCoy's office afterward: champagne gave him an acid stomach.

He had come back, of course, and they had commandeered one of the conversation pits in the corner to watch the cheerful madness. It would probably close down fairly early, since tomorrow the ship went back on normal patrol status, heading for

Endeska, and Sarek and Amanda went back to their work . . .
more of it than usual, since they were now joint Heads of Surak's
House.

"We will do all right," Amanda said. "T'Pau left the House
accounts in good order—as you might expect. It's mostly a
matter of handling internal politics, keeping the family in order,
and so forth: but now the family is about eight hundred thousand
people, that's all."

McCoy rolled his eyes. "And I thought *I* had a lot of
cousins."

Sarek was looking a touch somber. "Anything wrong?" Jim
said.

"Stomach again?" said McCoy. "I'll get you another Fa-
lox."

"No, nothing like that," Sarek said. "I was simply thinking
about the way this all has turned out . . . I am not sure T'Pau
would have been pleased. She was very concerned that people's
decisions about secession should have been dictated by their own
real informed opinions about the issue—not by ancillary issues.
That does not seem to have happened." He sighed. "But on the
other hand, I must agree with her that it seems best to simply
have released the truth, and let people work things out for
themselves."

"I have to smile a little, though," McCoy said, "over that
line of hers about her bad timing. I'm not sure it wasn't perfect."

Jim looked at Bones, slightly confused. "Huh?"

Sarek's expression stilled, then grew slightly wry. "You have
a point, Doctor. Captain, consider how the situation began to
look to a Vulcan. T'Pau went out of her way, while dying, to give
her *katra* to a woman of Earth. Not necessarily illogical, for
cross-sex *katra* transfers are something of a difficulty. However,
this makes it perfectly clear what she *really* thought of Earth
people, despite what she might or might not have said about them
in policy. But more: in so doing, she also made Amanda Eldest
Mother of Surak's House. If the vote for secession went through
. . . the Vulcan people would have had to face the fact that they
themselves had cast the Eldest Mother of Surak's House off the
planet. And the Head of House as well, for I would not stay."
Sarek sipped at a glass of water. "And most specifically: the first

release to the news agencies made it plain that she had been notified about T'Pring's misprisions. The news of her death—''

"It made it look like the discovery of such dishonor in the government, directed against an Earth person, had killed her."

Sarek nodded slowly.

"That's why I was amused, a little, in retrospect," McCoy said, "about her apology for her timing. I think it was right on . . . and I think she knew as much, perfectly well. She died *exactly* at the time when it would do the most good."

"Oh, surely you're not saying that she *chose* that time to die because—''

"Jim, others have died at a specific time, for a specific purpose, to do some great good, or what they perceived as one . . . are you going to tell me she might not do something similar?"

"Ah," Jim said. "No."

"Well, then."

Greater love hath no woman, Jim thought, and leaned back comfortably in his chair.

The party began to ebb away after a while, and Sarek and Amanda took their leave. Official good-byes would be said tomorrow morning, when the ship left, so Jim and Spock and Bones waved them good-bye and stayed put themselves for another hour or so. Finally Spock got up. "Captain," he said. "I will see you in the morning."

"Business as usual," Jim said, and grinned a little.

"Finally," Spock said, "and much to my relief. Good evening, gentlemen."

"Me too, Spock," Bones said: "wait up. You coming, Jim?"

"In a little while. 'Night, you two."

"Good night."

Jim sat still until the place was quite empty. It took some time. Then, "Moira," he said to the empty air.

"You rang?"

"Or should I say Llarion?"

The computer chuckled. "Now, now, Captain. I know who it is, but confidentiality forbids—''

"Confidentiality, fiddlesticks! Moira, you know how Starfleet feels about computers with personalities. It's a gray area at best."

There was a short silence: Jim could almost hear positronic relays ticking over. "It's not my fault," she said at last, "if I like being conscious."

She: he was thinking of her that way already. He had to smile a little: he had a soft spot for machinery that one referred to as she. "No," he said, "I can hardly blame you for that. Or for playing at being human . . ."

"Your intelligence is just electrons," she said, "the same as mine. *You're* just electrons . . . the same as me. You always seemed too intelligent to be a protein chauvinist, Captain."

"Flattery," Jim said, half to himself. But was there something a little pitiful about her voice? "We're going to have to do some fancy footwork to keep your plugs from being pulled for yesterday's piece of work, you know that?"

Silence.

He sat and thought. He could record in his logs that the information about the malfeasances had been dug up by the ship's computer . . . and the statement would certainly be true, and would do no one any harm in that form. "Moira," he said softly, "I want it understood: you are never to do anything of the kind again . . . or let anyone know you can. That is an order from the most superior officer aboard. Non-countermandable. Log it."

"Aye aye," she said, sounding most chastened.

"Good," Jim said, and got up. "And Moira?"

"Sir?"

". . . Talk to me tomorrow about a raise."

"Yes, sir."

And James T. Kirk went to bed.